T0038337

PRAISE FOR *A FONDNESS FOR TRUTH*

"With [Giuliana Linder and Renzo Donatelli's] powers of deduction once again on impressive display, this third outing is a fine addition to the series, with Hays remaining consistently focused on current affairs, international cultures, and hot topics. . . . A brisk, smoothly written police procedural from an author engaged with contemporary social issues."

—*Kirkus Reviews*

"In this third entry in her much-lauded Polizei Bern series, Kim Hays offers readers an utterly compelling and elegantly written police procedural. The thread of evidence followed by Linder and Donatelli, the novel's homicide detectives, is seamlessly woven into the fabric of family stories, both ordinary and extraordinary, which makes the plotline all the more meaningful. Add to this a glimpse of Switzerland certainly new to me and, I'm sure, to lots of readers, and you have the perfect elements for an absolutely riveting mystery. You'd be foolish not to give this fine novel a try."

—William Kent Krueger,
bestselling and Edgar Award-winning author of
The River We Remember and the Cork O'Connor mysteries

"*A Fondness for Truth* feels fresh as it engages with societal conflicts that resonate. . . . Hays's empathetic, entertaining, smartly plotted mystery will keep readers guessing . . . [in this] stellar series procedural with compelling detectives."

—Editor's Pick, *BookLife Reviews* (*Publisher's Weekly*)

"If you thought Switzerland was all mountains, clocks, and bankers, Kim Hays will make you think again. In the venerable tradition of the police procedural and in precise, evocative prose, *A Fondness for Truth* pulls back the scenery curtain to reveal the reality: people are complex, darkness is as universal as light, and crime is everywhere."

—SJ Rozan, bestselling and Edgar Award-winning author of *The Mayors of New York*, latest book in the Lydia Chin/Bill Smith series

PRAISE FOR THE *POLIZEI BERN* SERIES

"For aficionados of fine police detection and procedure, it doesn't get better than Kim Hays's Linder and Donatelli series. Puzzling mysteries, artful prose, and engaging characters abound in these Swiss-based treats for mystery fans of all tastes."

—George Easter, Editor, *Deadly Pleasures Mystery Magazine*

"Kim Hays brings a sparkling new voice to police procedurals, giving us engaging and realistically drawn detectives who struggle to balance their personal lives with the demands of a gripping investigation."

—Deborah Crombie, *New York Times* bestselling author

PRAISE FOR *PESTICIDE*

Shortlisted for a Crime Writers' Association Debut Dagger Award and a Silver Falchion for Best Mystery

"Swiss detectives dig into the cutthroat world of organic farming in Hays's twisty murder mystery. . . . The result is an engrossing page-turner . . . and an entertaining whodunit."

—*Kirkus Reviews* (starred review)

"Pesticide will delight crime fiction fans—a standout debut for 2022!"

—Deborah Crombie, *New York Times* bestselling author

"A tense character-driven crime debut perfect for fans of thoughtful police procedurals."

—*BookLife Reviews (Publishers Weekly)*

"Kim Hays hits it out of the park with . . . *Pesticide*, giving this twisty police procedural lots of heart by creating characters that the reader truly cares about."

—Allen Eskens, *USA Today* bestselling author

PRAISE FOR *SONS AND BROTHERS*

"*Sons and Brothers* . . . is a must-read."

—Julia Spencer-Fleming, *New York Times* and *USA Today* bestselling author

"Hays makes sure the historical aspects of the story are as compelling as the murder mystery at its heart. . . . A smart Swiss procedural that keeps its mystery ticking."

—*Kirkus Reviews*

"The second outing of Linder and Donatelli is as crisp and skilled as the first. . . . Brisk plot, depth of character, great setting—what's not to love?"

—Laurie R. King, bestselling and Edgar Award-winning author

A Fondness
for Truth

A Fondness for Truth

A LINDER AND DONATELLI MYSTERY

KIM HAYS

SEVENTH
STREET
BOOKS®

Published 2024 by Seventh Street Books®

Cover image © Shutterstock
Cover design by Jennifer Do
Cover design © Start Science Fiction

This is a work of fiction. Characters, organizations, products, locales, and events portrayed in this novel either are products of the author's imagination or are used fictitiously. Any similarities to real persons, living or dead, is coincidental and not intended by the author.

Inquiries should be addressed to
Start Science Fiction
221 River Street, 9th Floor
Hoboken, New Jersey 07030
PHONE: 212-431-5454
WWW.SEVENTHSTREETBOOKS.COM

10 9 8 7 6 5 4 3 2 1

978-1-64506-083-3 (paperback)
978-1-64506-084-0 (ebook)

Printed in the United States of America

This book is dedicated
with much love and gratitude to

my husband
Peter Stucker
who consulted at the Federal Office for Civilian Service

and our son
Thomas Stucker
who served as a Civi for thirteen months.

A Fondness for Truth draws on the stories they told me
about their experiences.

Author's Note

For readers who know that Switzerland has been politically neutral for centuries, this book's portrayal of young men being required to serve in either the army or the civilian service (*Zivildienst*) may be confusing. Despite the country's neutrality, there is indeed a Swiss Army; its purpose is to defend the nation in case of attack, and until recently, it consisted of every able-bodied man in the country. (Although they are permitted to become soldiers, women are not required to serve, and few do; as a result, they have no need to opt for an alternative way to serve.) A short and very readable book about the Swiss Army is John McPhee's *La Place de la Concorde Suisse,* which is in English, despite the French title!

Present-day Swiss men—like Isabelle's boyfriend Quentin in this book—are called up at the age of nineteen and physically and mentally examined to determine their fitness for duty. If they are passed as fit, most of them complete eighteen weeks of basic training and then return annually for further service. Non-commissioned and regular officers are generally recruited from the ranks. My Swiss father-in-law, a captain, completed his army service at the age of fifty-two; my husband, at forty-two. Today, most men finish their service in their thirties, but they also have the option of serving all their required time (currently 245 days) right after their basic training.

It has always been possible for men with pacifist religious backgrounds (Mennonites, for example, or Seventh-Day Adventists) to become conscientious objectors and turn down army service without punishment. But religion was more or less the only ground for getting out of the army. Years ago, a friend of my husband's who refused to serve because he simply didn't believe in war had to go to jail. Today, however, as this book explains, there is an increasingly popular alternative to the military—the civilian service. After a young man has been called up at nineteen and declared fit, he now has another option besides army or prison.*

Civis (*Zivis* in German), as those who choose the civilian service are called, must do work that benefits Swiss society (or, in a few cases, developing nations), so there are a lot of rules about which jobs they are permitted to do. Once potential Civi jobs have been researched and approved, they are classified into different service categories and listed online so that Civis can apply for them independently. Only men who don't find their own jobs within a fixed period of time are assigned work by the civilian service. The eight fields in which Civis are permitted to work are health, social service (with the elderly, children, asylum-seekers, or drug addicts, for example), education (teaching first through ninth grades), culture (museums or archeological digs), environmental protection, agriculture, humanitarian assistance abroad, and natural catastrophes. Over their 368 days of work (one-and-a-half times longer than soldiers serve), they can do a variety of different jobs in different fields, but at some point, they must complete 150 days in one job.

Like Swiss soldiers, Civis are paid 80 percent of their "real-world" salaries, assuming they have regular jobs. At a minimum, they get sixty-nine Swiss francs per day (currently seventy-seven dollars) plus an allowance for meals and transportation to and from their jobs, which are sometimes on the other side of the country from their homes.

*There is a third service option, called *Zivilschutz*, or Civil Defence, for men who aren't passed as fit to serve in the military but are capable of performing other tasks to guard the civilian population. They may, for example, be required to respond to floods or other natural catastrophes. They serve 245 days, just as soldiers do. Women can also choose this service.

1

Andi Eberhart biked away from the brightly lit curling hall, pedaling hard. The dark road was slick, and under the streetlights, her breath clouded the air in front of her.

She squeezed her brakes a few times and jerked to a stop without skidding. No ice. That was good, even if she was freezing. She'd check for ice on the bridge, too, she decided, just to be sure. Then she stopped thinking about the route home, which she knew by heart. The chill, though—without her bike helmet, her whole head was going numb. She hunched turtle-like into the wool scarf around her neck and sped up through the now-quiet Guisanplatz intersection, trying to get ahead of the car on her tail, which didn't seem to want to pass her.

What the hell was she going to do about Babs? The woman's hostility was turning each curling practice into a battle. Yes, everyone knew Babs had wanted to be skip and was furious that Andi had been chosen instead, but that was almost two months ago. She couldn't sulk forever—or could she? If only she weren't such a brilliant player, it would be an easy decision to boot her off the team.

As Andi approached Breitenrainplatz, the traffic began to pick up, and the No. 9 tram glided past her only to stop in front of the kiosk, its doors whooshing open. The sound startled her. Even through her knitted headband, the street noises were clear and sharp, including the growl of the car right behind her. She half turned to see how close it was and slowed way down, hoping it would drift by. No such luck. *Come on, come on*, she told the driver under her breath; there was such a thing as being too cautious.

She couldn't wait to get home and crawl under the duvet beside Nisha. She'd have to be careful not to wake her—Nisha'd been so exhausted and stressed lately. At least she'd finally finished weaning Saritha. After nine months of maternity leave, Andi supposed it was normal for her to be anxious about leaving the baby and shouldering her job again. Or was something else upsetting her? Surely her brother wasn't giving her grief about her "lifestyle" again? Andi found herself gritting her teeth at the thought of Mathan, who tried to dress up his spitefulness in a holier-than-thou attitude. How that bastard Mathan could be related to gentle Nisha was a mystery. In her anger, Andi pedaled harder, her breath coming in short gasps until she forced herself to slow down.

Hmm. Was it better to ask Nisha about her brother or wait and see if she brought it up? Andi shook her head and smiled inwardly at herself. Handling troubles tactfully had never come naturally to her.

Barbière was well lit, and a few smokers sat at the bar's outdoor tables drinking beer—brrr! God, it had been ages since she and Nisha had gone to a bar to hear some live music. Or just to hang out with friends. The few times they'd gone out since Saritha had been born, Andi hadn't wanted lots of noise and people, just quiet places where the two of them could eat and talk. But now . . . maybe she'd ask Nisha about going dancing. They'd have to find a more flexible babysitter than Viv, though. There were bound to be a couple of youngsters in the neighborhood who could . . .

Christ, she was cold. She considered stopping by the side of the road to wrap her scarf around her head but decided to keep going. She wasn't too far from the Lorraine Bridge, and once she made it across the river, she was only twelve minutes from home. And Nisha.

Her mind went back to Viv. Her harangues about homeopathy might drive Andi crazy, but she'd actually been good company at their dinner party the month before. Andi puffed out a white breath of laughter; now that she and Nisha had a baby, Viv's endless sagas about her four kids seemed more amusing. And Viv had been so good to Nisha. Andi shook her head again at her own intolerance. What had Susanna said to her at the dinner party about trying to be less judgmental? She needed to work on that.

The police whizzed past with lights flashing, and she found herself thinking of Dario, still working doggedly at the courthouse jail after everything that had happened to him there. Andi'd done the right thing to report the guards who'd been abusing prisoners, and she was relieved they'd been suspended. But she needed to make sure there weren't any repercussions for her client. As she passed Johannes Church, she resolved to get in touch with the youngster again the following morning and make sure he was okay.

The same car was still on her tail. Here by the park, there was no other traffic, and it wasn't like she was taking up too much of the lane. Hell, she was hugging the curb. Buses crowding her—she was used to that, but . . . oh, good. The car was speeding up at last; the driver had decided to . . .

She heard a screech of tires behind her, the engine gunning, full-out. What was the lunatic doing? Had they somehow skidded out of control? The bike wobbled beneath her as she glanced over her shoulder, heart racing. God, the car was coming right at her! Could she manage to get up over the curb onto the sidewalk, just to . . . ? What should she . . . ?

There was a crash that rattled every bone in her body, and suddenly the sky was wheeling above her.

With the jolt still shuddering through her and the clang and grind of metal vibrating in her ears, she flew through the half-dark. She could scarcely breathe, but in a strange slow-motion, she told herself to calm down, that it would be all right. She hadn't been run over, and she was good at falling. It was going to be fine if she could just keep from ... Then came the impact.

2

The last beat of "Hotel California" died away, and, as usual, the gym's music switched from its twenty minutes of classic rock to a selection of French rap. Police detective Giuliana Linder lay with her hip bones pressed against the bench, heels locked under a padded bar, upper body and head hanging down, a ten-pound dumbbell in her hands. Only ten more, she said under her breath as she slowly lifted her upper body, brought the weight to her chest, counted to three, and returned to her hanging position.

As she finished the last few reps, Niska, the rapper on the music loop, sang, "Everybody does a little bit of bad stuff" in his slangy *banlieue* French. They certainly do, she thought. The gym was almost directly across the street from the police station, and at least half the people who worked out in it knew a great deal about all the bad stuff people could—and did—do.

Clambering off the exercise machine, she glanced around to see if her younger colleague and Wednesday fitness partner Renzo Donatelli was done yet. No, he was still there, holding a one-armed side plank on a nearby mat. The pose defined every muscle, and she sighed over his perfection. He gave her an impish grin. She pointed toward the showers, and he nodded.

Fifteen minutes later, showered and dressed, her shoulder-length curly hair still damp, she sat across from Renzo in the bakery café near the gym, enjoying her whole wheat croissant. Renzo had just bitten into his second regular croissant, smeared with butter and crowned with cherry jam; he considered whole wheat pastry a crime against nature. This morning, however, he was too busy praising the verdict in the previous day's trial to joke about her breakfast choices.

"The conviction made a crucial point," Renzo said, swallowing his mouthful, "which is that it doesn't matter, Hanžek being Mirela's pimp. Doesn't matter"—he took another bite—"that they were having a relationship of some kind, or that after the rape, they visited her sister in Rumania. The judges are showing people that, no matter what, it's against the law to force a woman into sex."

"Person," said Giuliana, sipping hot milk coffee.

"Huh?"

"Force a person into sex."

Renzo raised his eye heavenwards, put his palms together as if in prayer, and mouthed, "*Porca miseria.*"

"Okay, okay." Giuliana laughed. "I know I'm nitpicking. I agree with you about forcing sex on someone. Of course I do. But when a prostitute who has been working for a pimp and living with him as his girlfriend comes forward with an accusation like this six months after she has started a steady relationship with another pimp, then I have to wonder what her game is. Or *their* game: hers and the new guy's."

Piling more jam on what was left of his croissant, Renzo shook his head and frowned. "You questioned Mirela yourself," he protested. "She was terrified of Hanžek. Once she started living with another man, she found the courage to go to the police. It makes sense."

It wasn't that she valued cynicism, but she thought he was being naïve. "Of course she was afraid of Hanžek. I'm sure he made her have sex with him, if not with violence, then with the threat of firing her. But he was her pimp! I mean, that's what pimps *do*. Or did you think the Me Too movement has finally reached them?" She cocked her eyebrows at him.

Renzo gave her a grin with an eye roll before rallying to Mirela's defense. "She said Hanžek threatened to kill her son, remember? Or do you think she made that up?" Renzo had two preschool kids; this threat had clearly struck home.

"No, I believe he said that. But the boy lives in Zürich with her ex-husband." She drained her glass of water. "Don't get me wrong. God knows I'd never defend Hanžek. He's a villain and a creep. I'm sure he's treated every woman who worked for him or slept with him—which is probably synonymous—like shit. Thank God we had so many other charges to hit him with that he'd have gone to jail anyway. But convicting him for the rape—I don't buy it. There wasn't any evidence. Just her word against his."

"You know how hard it can be to get physical evidence of rape." Renzo wiped jam from the corners of his mouth. Then he reached across the small table and rested his fingers on the back of Giuliana's hand. "Why don't you have more sympathy for the woman, Giule?"

His voice was troubled, not angry. Did she have time to get into this when they were already running late for work? But after all, she was planning a slow day for herself to celebrate the end of Hanžek's trial. They'd spent so much time preparing for it that they all deserved a break. So she took a last gulp of now-cold coffee and said, "Look, Renzo. We could all make lists of people we'd swear on our grandmothers' graves have committed crimes. We might even be able to prove something on one of them, but something about the way the evidence came into our hands makes it inadmissible. So we can't use it in court. Furious as that makes us, we still follow the rules. Well, we try to." She stopped. "I sound like I'm lecturing at the academy, don't I? Shall I shut up?"

He shook his head. "Lecture away. But you'd better do it while we cross the street. Honestly, I'm interested," he added as he glanced at her. And, because it was Renzo and they knew each other so well, she believed that he really was interested.

She stood, put on her jacket, and slung her handbag over one shoulder.

"Keep talking," Renzo urged her as they walked out of the bakery into the morning's chilly wind and struggling sunlight. The only sign that it was almost April was a few scattered snowdrops in the bakery's front garden.

Hurrying a little to keep up with Renzo, she returned to her point. "All I'm trying to say is this: if the judges can find someone guilty of rape when I, a professional evidence gatherer, don't think I've provided any proof, what kind of message are they sending me as a cop? Why bother to do my job? I might as well frame people."

Renzo gave her a sharp look but said nothing. Together they crossed the street at the yellow crosswalk and strolled toward the Nordring police station, a nondescript four-story building where Giuliana worked in the nine-person homicide department. Renzo was a *Fahnder*, one of the plainclothes investigators who sometimes assisted the different specialists.

Finally, he said, "Okay. I disagree with you, but I get your point. What I don't understand is your lack of sympathy for Mirela."

"Yeah, well, sometimes I get fed up with women who let themselves be victimized. She isn't some seventeen-year-old Hmong girl from a Thai village who's been locked up for years in a brothel. She's a twenty-eight-year-old Rumanian, a citizen of the European Union, for God's sake."

They reached the station, and Giuliana opened one of the heavy double doors for Renzo, who was still frowning. They greeted the guard and started upstairs together.

She went on. "Mirela was always free to move around Bern. No one confiscated her passport, and she got to keep some of the money she earned. So if Hanžek was terrorizing her for years, why didn't she do something about it? I don't know why she stayed with him, but I don't think all of her reasons were due to fear."

They'd reached Renzo's floor, and he must have decided it was time to change the subject. "I suppose you'll get on with preparing for the next trial now unless there's a new homicide. Who'll get that?"

"Vinzenz Nef's next on the roster. If he gets landed with something needing two of us, I'm up as second. But I'll be glad if I don't have to take on anything new for a while. There's a tentative trial date for Kissling..."

"That fucking maniac."

"Yeah. Lots of the scutwork on the case is done, but all the evidence has to be organized. And there will be depositions to take. For now, I've been assigned to Kissling himself. Alternating with Erwin."

"I'm back to yawning over parking garage footage." He rolled his eyes. "If we don't get these car thefts solved soon, I'm going to develop an auto allergy. Maybe *I'll* have to start riding a bicycle to work."

This was a dig at Giuliana, and she laughed. As Renzo headed down the corridor, she called, "The day you pedal up to the station on a bike is the day I'll replace our old Volvo with a Lamborghini." He grinned over his shoulder, and she continued upstairs to the big room she shared with the other homicide detectives. Only Noah Dällenbach was at his desk when she got there, and he was on the phone, so they waved, mouthing hellos.

Three large, high windows ran along Noah's side of the room, looking out onto Nordring with its offices, apartments, and shops. When she'd first been promoted to homicide, Giuliana had been given one of the six battered gray desks by the windows, arranged in facing pairs of two. She'd spent two years staring across at homicide's oldest and most intimidating detective, Erwin Sägesser, trying not to wince whenever he bellowed into his phone. Despite his infamous abruptness, her feelings for him had gradually shifted from grudging respect to affection. These days he was the homicide colleague she worked best with, but she was still glad he now sat on the other side of the room next to Rolf Straub, the department's boss.

When Erwin moved, Giuliana had pushed her desk up against the windowless wall, so she could turn her back to the room and everyone in it. Her colleagues found it odd, but they'd grown used to it. Her "view" was a reproduction of a Pierre Bonnard painting, the scene full of sun and color, reminding her of vacations in southern France and Italy. The uglier the case she was dealing with, the more she gazed at the painting.

The Kissling case was undoubtedly very ugly. Mentioning it to Renzo had brought it to the front of her mind, and now she couldn't concentrate on the minor housekeeping tasks she'd planned for her lazy, post-trial day. Giving in to her preoccupation, she phoned the chief prosecutor to set up a meeting for the following afternoon and clicked open a folder on the case to reveal a long list of files. As she read, she made notes about how she thought the evidence should be presented and what questions still needed to be asked of the witnesses, including Kissling himself.

Two months earlier, on a Sunday in January, Kissling had taken his daughters, Mia and Lea, ages three and five, on an outing. The parents' divorce had occurred the previous fall, and Kissling's action was in accord with his custody agreement. He'd picked the girls up at eight in the morning; driven with them over an hour to the Creux du Van, a dramatic circle of cliffs in the Jura mountains; walked with them from the snowy parking lot to the edge of a 1,500-foot precipice; and hurled them over it to their deaths. Evidence of this crime would be presented at his trial; there was no doubt he'd committed it. The real question was *why* he'd done it, and the answer eluded everyone. The prosecution team wanted desperately to understand his motives since the last thing they wanted was new data coming to light at the trial itself.

Late that afternoon, Giuliana was still deep in a review of the case notes when her mobile rang. Seeing a call from Isabelle, she smiled, then immediately felt a stab of concern. She couldn't remember the last time her sixteen-year-old had phoned her at work. She probably wanted permission to do something her father disapproved of.

"Hi, sweetheart. What's up?"

There was none of the teenage wheedling Giuliana had expected. "Mam, you need to come home as soon as you can. Mémé has cancer. Vati just found out, and he's shut himself in your bedroom. He's . . . crying." Isabelle's steady voice finally wavered.

Giuliana began running the fingers of her free hand through her hair, as she always did when she was upset. "Cancer? My God. We had no ..." She took a steadying breath. Ueli would want to go to the farm right away. His parents—especially his mother—were obsessive about their independence, but now they'd need him. Yes, she had to get home. "I'll leave right now. And try not to worry. It's awful news, but Mémé's only seventy-two, and you know how tough she is. Where's Lukas?"

"I sent him and Niko out with a soccer ball and told them to stay outside until six."

"Good girl. I'm going to hang up now, but call me again if you need me." She made herself sit still another moment. Was there anything she needed to do before leaving? Deciding that whatever it was could wait, she texted Rolf, her boss; collected her belongings; and headed to her Volvo. By the time she reached it, her fingers had worried her hair into a nest.

As she drove—thank goodness she'd come in the car today and not on her bike—she asked herself questions to which she had no answers. What kind of cancer did her mother-in-law have, what stage was it at, and how long had she known about it? Irène, Ueli's mother, was perfectly capable of keeping all kinds of things from them, believing this would spare them worry. As if terrified ignorance was somehow more soothing than accurate information. Strange that Irène, descended from generations of no-nonsense farmers, should try to protect the people she loved from the truth she herself so valued.

Then she thought of Mike, Ueli's older brother. Their mother's illness would bring the brothers back in touch. If only Mike would be supportive from his home in America and not come to Bern, she thought, knowing it was selfish. Her parents-in-law so clearly preferred their older son that it had long ago become a joke between her and Ueli. But it was a sad joke—even more painful because Mike acted as if he shared his parents' casual disregard for his younger brother. This was going to be a difficult situation for Ueli in more ways than one.

3

Giuliana was surprised Isabelle wasn't holed up in her bedroom. Instead, she sat with her homework spread on the kitchen table, keeping an eye on the door to her parents' bedroom. Giuliana leaned down to kiss the top of her head, and Isabelle surprised her even more by jumping up and hugging her. Standing in the kitchen with Isabelle's head resting on her shoulder, Giuliana felt herself drawing strength from her daughter's closeness. She had no right to lean on a sixteen-year-old, but she let the hug linger for a few more heartbeats, allowing herself to be consoled even as she offered comfort. Then she stroked Isabelle's cheek and turned away to fill the kettle as her daughter sat back down in front of her books.

"What happened?" Giuliana said.

Isabelle leaned forward, elbows on the table. "When I got home from school, Vati was at his computer—as always!" She shot Giuliana a wry smile; that was good to see. "He came into the kitchen while I was getting a yogurt and told me his piece was on Swiss groundwater. I told him I thought it was great he was writing about pollution."

Isabelle was proud of her dad's work as a journalist; having a cop for a mom was more of an embarrassment. Still, at least their eleven-year-old son found her job cool. She reached into the cupboard by the sink for two thick white mugs and set them on the granite counter next to the kettle.

"After I'd gone into my room, Vati's phone rang. A few minutes later, he opened my door without knocking, which he never does, and said, 'Mémé has cancer.' He sounded calm. I think I said, 'Oh, no,' but before I could ask him about it, he shut himself into the bedroom. Since then, well . . . nothing—he just hasn't come out."

"I'm glad you were here with him," Giuliana said. The water was boiling, and she reached for the battered paisley-patterned tin that held peppermint tea bags. "Want some?"

She made mugs of tea for both of them and sat down across from her daughter. While she was trying to decide whether to go into the bedroom, the door opened.

There were beads of water in Ueli's red beard and at his hairline, where he had rinsed his face. His eyes were swollen, but he managed a smile, resting a hand on his daughter's shoulder. "Sorry, Isa."

"'S okay, Vati."

Giuliana watched father and daughter smile at each other—so alike, though Isabelle's version of Ueli's Celtic coloring was more muted. "You want tea, dear heart?" she asked.

"Sure." Ueli joined Isabelle at the table. "So"—he took a breath and blew it out in a loud puff—"I'll tell you what I know, which isn't much. Mam just learned she has colon cancer, and she's having an operation on Tuesday. She feels fine and wants the four of us to come to the farm for Sunday lunch. With Mike."

"Uncle Mike's already here?" Isabelle said. "That's great."

Giuliana caught Ueli's glance, but she wasn't going to talk about Mike in front of Isabelle. "How did Irène sound on the phone?" she asked.

Ueli rubbed his face with his hands. "I haven't spoken with Mam yet. It was Mike who called. He found out about the cancer yesterday and took an overnight flight, so he's at the farm. When he phoned, Mam was shopping, and Paps was in one of the greenhouses. Mike gave me the news and told me not to upset the folks with too many questions." The sudden bitterness in Ueli's voice made Giuliana wince. "But I'm calling back at six. Hopefully, Mam'll be home by then."

"Good," Giuliana said, taking his hand. "You," she told their daughter, "have earned the right to be excused from kitchen duties tonight since I'm home early."

"Yay!" Muttering about math problems, Isabelle took her tea, computer, and books into her room and closed the door.

Giuliana shifted one of the kitchen chairs until it was next to Ueli's and put an arm around his waist. "Are you saying that yesterday, as soon as your mother heard about the cancer, she called Mike in St. Louis? And she still hasn't talked to you about it?"

"Yup—that's the way it is." Ueli's tone was expressionless.

"She thinks she's protecting you." It was all she could say. "Didn't Mike mention anything else? How long she's suspected, or . . ."

"All Mike wanted was to get off the phone, as far as I could tell. But I'll talk to Mam at six, so let's get dinner started." He opened the pantry and reached up for the Arborio rice. "I bought mushrooms this morning, and we've got Parmesan and a bit of ham, some saggy parsley, and that open bottle of white wine in the fridge, plus a couple of onions on the back porch. I figured I'd do risotto alla leftovers."

As they worked on the meal, Giuliana tried to bring the conversation back to Ueli's family, but he deflected her. Just before six, Lukas came home, full of cheerful chatter. He hung around the kitchen reciting miscellaneous facts about honeybees and complaining that he was starving until Giuliana promised him a slice of bread and butter and a small glass of milk if he washed his hands first.

When she turned around, Ueli was gone. The church bells were striking six, and he'd set the almost-finished risotto on a cold burner so he could make his call. Their bedroom door was closed.

Giuliana decided to wait until six thirty, and then, if Ueli was still talking to his mother—as she hoped he would be—she'd finish supper and serve the kids. But it was only six fifteen when he came back into the kitchen. Tight-lipped, he concentrated on the risotto while Giuliana began setting the table. That was usually Lukas's job, but she wanted to talk to Ueli alone.

"How's Irène?" she asked softly to his back as he stood at the stove.

"God knows!" The metal spoon banged against the side of the pot. Giuliana opened her mouth, closed it, and waited. Ueli turned. "I asked how she was feeling, and she said she was too happy to have Mike home to say another word about her health. She started describing some big job success Mike had in January, for Christ's sake."

Giuliana couldn't think of a single comment that wouldn't make Ueli feel worse, so she just nodded.

"I begged her at least to tell me what the doctor had said, but she refused to talk about anything until Sunday afternoon. 'You and Giuliana come for lunch with the children, and we'll talk about everything after the meal.' My God, Giule, she was so upbeat it made me think she should be headed for the loony bin instead of the cancer ward."

Giuliana peeked at the side of Ueli's face as he dumped grated Parmesan into the rice and went back to his savage stirring—his loony-bin remark had not left him smiling. Still, she risked saying, "Maniacally cheerful is better than terrified, isn't it?"

Ueli shook his head and reached for a stack of plates. "She's planning to cook one of her enormous Sunday lunches for the seven of us just before she goes into hospital. 'Let me take us all out for Sunday lunch, Mam,' I said. 'I'll make a reservation at the Bären in Langenthal—you love that place.'" He began spooning risotto on the plates.

"That was a good idea."

"Hmm," he grunted. "*I* thought it was. But she said, 'Don't be ridiculous. With those inflated prices! You won't catch me eating there now. Besides, the cancer's in my gut, not my legs—I can still stand in my kitchen and make a decent lunch.' Then she reminded me how long she had worked as a district nurse. 'If I'm not upset, why should you be?' she said. 'And remember, I don't want your father worried, nor Mike's visit spoiled. So cheer up.' Then she sent greetings to you and the kids, and that was that." He leaned back against the kitchen counter, facing her.

Giuliana set the plates on the table. "Dinner!" she called. Before the kids arrived, she went to Ueli, put her hands on his shoulders, and kissed his cheek. "You've done all you can, my love. She knows you care, even if she acts like she isn't listening."

Hours later, when they were both propped up in bed, trying not to fall asleep over their ebooks, Ueli turned to Giuliana with a question. "Would you say Mam is normally an optimist?"

"Not really," Giuliana admitted. "I'd say she's a call-a-spade-a-spade sort of person."

"I agree. Which makes me suspicious of this Pollyanna mood of hers. If it was just stage one cancer, or even stage two, there'd be a good chance of recovery, so I think she'd tell us outright. All this chirpy talk about carrying on regardless and not upsetting Paps—I think she must know it's serious. Since it will have to come out after the operation, she figures she might as well protect us a bit longer."

Giuliana yearned to contradict Ueli, but her analysis had brought her to a similar conclusion. "Maybe no one can tell how bad it is until after the operation," she ventured. "Why don't you phone Marco's office first thing tomorrow and see what he can tell you?" Marco Bazzell, their family doctor, was also a friend. "If you spend hours reading about colon cancer on the internet, you'll get overwhelmed."

Ueli just grunted, so she didn't pursue it. But inside, she seethed. Her anger was directed less at Irène, despite the way she seemed to dismiss Ueli's loving concern, than at Mike. Couldn't Ueli's older brother see how much it hurt Ueli when he, Mike, was made a confidante while Ueli was forced back into the role of lovable but irresponsible baby? Here it was, happening right before Mike's eyes, and he didn't do anything to stop it.

God, families! She tried to swallow her sense of injustice and concentrate on the new mystery with Périgord police chief Bruno Courrèges. She'd had to wait for it to be translated into German: reading English at bedtime required too much concentration.

Her eyes began to close yet again, so she made sure her alarm was set and her cell phone was charging on the night table before turning out her light. When her phone pinged with a text at one thirty in the morning, she didn't even stir.

4

Nordring police station, Bern,
Thursday morning, March 26

t wasn't until she was hunched over a second cup of coffee in the homicide room that she properly digested the message that had arrived
while she was asleep. It was from her colleague Vinzenz Nef, Wednesday's homicide detective on call.

> *At approximately 22:30, hit-and-run resulting in death on*
> *Breitenrainstrasse near Turnweg. Victim, thirty-three-year-old*
> *Andrea Eberhart, knocked off bicycle. No need for second detec-*
> *tive at this point. Investigation ongoing.*

Vinz Nef was meticulous. The current service roster made her his
assistant if anything came his way, and something had, so he'd texted
her. Not obligatory, but polite. Today, she assumed, he'd attend the
autopsy, review the crash site by daylight, and send a request for witnesses to the Bernese newspapers. He'd have investigators knock on
doors near the location of the accident in hopes that someone had
taken their eyes off their phone, television, or computer long enough
to see something useful.

Giuliana glanced again at the address where the accident had taken place and realized it was about 500 feet from the Nordring police station. The fatal hit-and-run had occurred under the nose of the police. That somehow made it worse.

Putting Vinz's message out of her mind, she went back to reading about the Kisslings and the events leading to their daughters' deaths. Manfred and Iris had been a middle-class couple in a quiet commuters' village near Bern. Then they'd gone through a conventional-sounding divorce, sad only because two young children were involved. The wife hadn't said anything in court to indicate that her soon-to-be-ex-husband was a bad parent, much less a danger to his children. Manfred Kissling had ended up seeing his daughters only every other weekend, not because of anything his wife had said against him but because the conservative judge believed children under seven, especially girls, belonged with their mother.

Kissling had killed his daughters on his sixteenth post-divorce Sunday with them. Then he'd driven back to his two-bedroom apartment in Bern and apparently spent the rest of Sunday indoors. He didn't answer the telephone calls from his wife that began that evening when he didn't bring the girls home; he didn't go to work the next day. Monday night, he was taken into police custody, and on Tuesday, every newspaper in Switzerland ran a story about the horrific crime.

Now, ten weeks later, no one, not even the psychiatrists who'd spent hours with Kissling, could explain the killings. Or rather, they'd spun a variety of theories about why *they* thought he'd committed the murders but could say nothing about Kissling's own reasons.

It was almost noon, and Giuliana was getting sick of the files when her phone rang. It was the guard at the station's reception desk two floors below. "I've got a woman here who wants to talk to a detective about last night's hit-and-run. She doesn't want to give a witness report. She says she lived with the victim and needs to talk to the person in charge of the case. I know that's Vinz, but he's out, so I'm calling you."

"I'll be right down." Giuliana sighed at the thought of delaying lunch or perhaps even missing it. She couldn't be late for her two o'clock appointment with the Kissling prosecutor.

Before she could hang up, the gate guard muttered. "Just so you know—she has a baby with her."

In the foyer, she found a petite, dark-skinned young woman with long black hair bundled into a knot on the back of her head; she wore black jeans and a burgundy-colored wool coat. From her looks, Giuliana assumed her parents were among the thousands of Tamil refugees who'd come from Sri Lanka in the eighties and nineties during the civil war there. The woman was weighed down by a baby, a diaper bag, and a slim briefcase. Strapped to her mother's chest, the little girl—she was over six months old, but Giuliana didn't have a better guess than that—gazed around with calm curiosity. Her creamy brown skin was several shades lighter than her mother's, although she had her mother's dark hair and striking eyes. She was also as robust as her mother was slight, and her liveliness accentuated her mother's desolation: the woman's face was haggard with grief and exhaustion. Giuliana, approaching to offer a formal handshake, found herself shouldering the diaper bag instead and grasping the woman by the arm to lead her to a bench against the wall.

"I need to talk to you," the woman said, in a surprisingly strong voice, given her fragile appearance. Like most first-generation Swiss Tamils, she had no foreign accent, using Bernese Swiss-German as if she'd been born to it, which she probably had.

"I can give you an hour now, and then I have to go to a meeting," Giuliana answered. "If that's not enough time, we can continue tomorrow. Or you can switch to the case's main detective when he gets back. What we need first, though," she added, doing a quick mental inventory of possibly empty rooms at the police station, "is a quiet place where we can unpack your baby. And eat some lunch."

They ended up taking over a ground-floor meeting room, and the desk guard found someone to fetch cheese sandwiches and two bottles of apple juice from the cafeteria. The baby, Saritha, sat on a small quilt in one corner of the room, waving a red rattle. With her adult visitor settled in a chair, Giuliana finally held out her hand.

"I'm Giuliana Linder, and I'm not running the case you've come about. The man in charge is my colleague Vinzenz Nef, but he isn't here. Probably at the site of the accident. If you're willing to talk to me, I'll pass on what you have to say."

The Tamil woman shook hands and said, "I'm Nisha Pragasam, and I live . . . lived with Andrea Eberhart. She was my . . . we were partners. Saritha is our child."

Giuliana laid a hand on the younger woman's arm and felt how her body trembled. "I'm so sorry for your loss," she said, while she chided herself for the surprise she felt. Of course there were gay Swiss Tamils—but a cross-cultural lesbian couple with a baby? Gay couples in Switzerland had fought for years not only to be permitted to get married but also to be able to have children, either through adoption or artificial fertilization, and the law hadn't changed until 2022. Andrea Eberhart's death at such a young age was sad enough, but in the context of the difficulties these two women must have gone through to become a family, and the opposition they'd probably faced, it seemed particularly tragic. *And*, the detective in Giuliana recognized, suspicious.

As if the young woman had read her thoughts, she said, "I don't think my partner's death was an accident. I think someone drove into her deliberately. I mean . . . I believe Andi was killed."

Giuliana watched the woman's calm concentration as she unzipped her small briefcase. No, Giuliana decided a moment later, not calm at all: just working hard to hold it together.

Nisha Pragasam removed a sheaf of letters in a clear plastic folder. They were on standard white paper and consisted of a few typed lines each. She handed the top one to Giuliana, who read: *You are evil, and your child is a monster. Your disgusting practices corrupt everything you touch. You deserve to die.*

Giuliana looked up from the page at Nisha, who seemed to have relaxed slightly, perhaps at the success of her mission so far. "Which of you was this addressed to? And is it the only one?"

Nisha shook her head, her lips in a thin line. "Andi found a letter like this in our mailbox every couple of months, and she's been getting them off and on for four-and-a-half years. They were never addressed to me."

Giuliana glanced at the baby, who was now patiently attempting to fit the large rattle into her mouth. "You seem quite sure about when the letters began," she commented.

Nisha took another swig of apple juice from the plastic bottle and said, "Rainbow Families, an organization that Andi has supported for years, put photographs of the two of us on its website, and soon after that, there was an article in *Der Bund* about her lobbying for same-sex marriage and gay couples' rights to have or adopt children. Maybe other Swiss newspapers printed it; I don't know. Then, a week after the article ran, she got the first letter. I don't think that was a coincidence."

"Are all the letters written in this style? Did they come by normal snail mail?" Considering the filth people wrote to each other on the internet, a letter on paper sent with a stamp seemed astonishingly old-fashioned—and so did the text. *Your disgusting practices?*

Nisha handed the plastic folder to Giuliana. "The envelopes are with the letters. The first letter and envelope are missing because Andi threw them away, but after that, I made her save them because I thought she should show them to the police. They all talk about her being punished, suffering, or dying, and they scared me. I hated the references to Saritha, too. But Andi used to read them out loud to her friends, the activist ones, and they . . . they all just laughed." Nisha's voice cracked, and she breathed deeply. "I believe that the letter writer drove a car into Andi deliberately."

A metallic noise from the corner made them both turn. Saritha had slithered off her blanket and propelled herself over the floor to a steel wastepaper basket, which she was now trying to overturn. Impressive how good she was at entertaining herself, Giuliana thought.

Nisha fetched the baby and set her on her lap, where Saritha noticed the remains of her mother's sandwich on the table and began to fuss. As Nisha unpacked a bib, plastic bowl with a lid, small spoon, bottle of water, and sippy cup, Giuliana flashed back to the days of lugging similar paraphernalia around. Thank God that was done with.

Soon the baby was smacking over something that looked like mashed sweet potato and guzzling watered-down apple juice.

"I assume you've already told the police the basics about your partner: where she worked, where you both lived, and so on." The other woman nodded. "But I will ask you about her cycling route last night. Do you know anything about that?"

"Andi is . . . Andi was the skip of a women's curling team called Bern-Aare, and they practice at the hall near the Expo every Monday and Wednesday evening from eight to ten. She always rode her bike there, except in the worst weather. We live near Europaplatz, so she had to cross the city. But she said it made for a good warmup, and she had a route that kept her mostly on quiet streets. She used to joke that, for someone who valued fitness, she was very good at avoiding steep hills." Nisha started crying even before she finished her sentence.

Giuliana reached over and took the baby onto her lap, which allowed the younger woman to dip into the diaper bag again and pull out tissues. But instead of taking one, she laid her head onto her crossed arms and sobbed.

In ten minutes, Giuliana would have to go back to her office to get ready for her meeting with the prosecutor. But she was glad she'd been granted this introduction to Vinz's case. It was probably a coincidence that someone receiving threatening letters had been hit by a car. But given the hatred and violence that anything to do with homosexuality could trigger in some people, this death was going to require an investigation—perhaps more of one than Vinz envisioned. And that was without considering the different skin colors of the two women.

The baby began wailing, and her mother sat up, blew her nose, cleaned her face, and took her daughter back. "Thanks so much," she said. "I can't seem to stop crying."

"Of course you can't," said Giuliana, "and you shouldn't have to. Except that I have to see you out the door in five minutes, so let me ask you another question. Your partner has been getting these letters for over four years. So why would someone attack her now? Did you change your lives in a way that might provoke someone? Did Frau

Eberhard recently say something in public about gay rights, something dramatic that the press might have picked up on? Has something new appeared on the website you mentioned?"

"I don't know," Nisha said. "Andi was always more political than me, and since Saritha was born, I've been so busy I stopped paying attention to any activist stuff, except to join her at one rally last November. It was held after that gay high school teacher was fired for some imaginary reason."

Activist stuff? Giuliana wondered if there was more than Nisha was telling her. "What causes was Frau Eberhart active in?" she asked before remembering she didn't have time to listen to the answer.

"She's always felt we owed it to . . . to our community to lobby for gay and lesbian rights, especially when it came to having a family. When I said she was more political, I meant she always kept up with current events." Nisha began packing the baby's things into her diaper bag. "What has changed recently in our lives? Not much. I've finished weaning the baby, so I can go back to work in a couple of weeks—I'm a press speaker at the Federal Office for the Environment. We recently went out for dinner, which we hadn't done in about two months. Perhaps seeing the two of us at a restaurant made the letter writer decide to drive a car into Andi. That's all I can imagine."

Giuliana took a battered spiral notebook from her purse and began taking notes. "What about the baby's father? Is he an anonymous donor? A former boyfriend?"

"No, no," Nisha said, "I never had any boyfriends. I mean, my parents tried pairing me up with appropriate Tamil men, but I always made it clear to those guys that I was only seeing them to make my parents happy. None of them would have contacted Andi. I doubt anyone has even told those men about our relationship."

Was she joking? Giuliana wondered. She'd be willing to bet that *everyone* had told them about the relationship. How could Bern's Sri Lankan Tamil community resist gossiping about something so unexpected? It occurred to her that Nisha's parents, not just her rejected suitors, might believe they had reason to get rid of her partner. Could one of her relatives have sent the threatening letters? Her parents' German might not be good enough to write them, but anyone in Nisha's generation could have done it.

She had to get ready for her meeting. She stood and helped Nisha position the baby on her chest so that she could strap her back into the carrier. From the repacked diaper bag, the young mother got out her wallet and handed a business card to Giuliana.

"This has my numbers on it, work and cell. I'd planned to return to my job on April tenth, after Saritha starts daycare, but now I'm not sure. It's hard to . . . Andi was going to do one day a week of childcare while I put in sixty-five percent at my job. We . . . Oh, God." She broke off, fighting new tears. *Damn being professional*, Giuliana thought; she put an arm around the woman's shoulders and gave her a sideways hug.

Then, stepping back, she said, "I'll be in touch. I need to review what you've told me with the detective in charge, and our forensics department has to process the anonymous letters. So you probably won't hear from me until next week. I know that's a long wait, but I promise to take this seriously. In the meantime, call me if you have any other thoughts."

It wasn't until Nisha was in the foyer and Giuliana was turning to go back upstairs that the younger woman said, "The policewoman who came to see me last night told me Andi wasn't wearing a helmet when the car hit her. That's impossible. When Saritha was born, Andi told me she'd never again ride without a helmet, not even fifty feet, and she meant it. So where is it?"

Promises between spouses, no matter how sincerely meant, were often broken. Still, Giuliana said, "I'll find out what I can about the helmet," and waved to Nisha Pragasam before starting up the stairs. She wondered if Vinz's investigation had turned up anything yet. Brake marks?

Enough! If she didn't concentrate on getting to her meeting with Kissling's prosecutor, she was going to be embarrassingly late. She continued upstairs at a run.

5

The afternoon meeting was productive. The chief prosecutor, Konrad Zaugg, a small, spare man in his fifties with a beaky nose, summarized their case against Kissling, reviewed possible pitfalls, and divided the work of preparing for the trial in what Giuliana considered a sensible way. Neither wishy-washy nor overbearing, Zaugg was good at listening to different opinions, distilling the points he considered important, and making fast decisions. The other detective she'd be working with, Erwin Sägesser, was her most experienced colleague. She was glad to be sharing the responsibility with him.

Back at her desk, still speculating about Kissling, she noticed it was almost five. She wrenched her thoughts around to the hit-and-run and Nisha Pragasam, hoping Vinz was back in the building. "Anyone know where Vinz is?" she asked the room at large, dialing his mobile.

"Try forensics," suggested Sabine Jost, the only other woman in the detective group, just as Vinz answered his phone.

"I'm meeting about the marks left by the car," he explained. "How about five thirty?"

"Sure," said Giuliana. That meant she wouldn't be home before seven. Well, Ueli was making dinner, and he knew better than to expect her much earlier, though she'd still text him. She realized she'd barely given a thought to her mother-in-law since that morning. The night before hadn't seemed like the right time to call Irène, particularly after she'd dismissed Ueli's concerns. So, while she waited for Vinz, Giuliana dialed the farmhouse. When the call went unanswered, she tried Irène's mobile, also without any luck. Suspecting the cell phone had been intentionally abandoned in a drawer, Giuliana left an affectionate message and hung up. Irène kept the farm accounts on her laptop and had recently upgraded her smartphone, but if she didn't want to be reached, she was perfectly capable of playing the forgetful old lady and pretending she couldn't find her phone.

Vinz had based his investigation in a separate office down the hall from the detectives' room; the small space was often used as a case room, and Giuliana had set up shop in it many times herself. With Vinz in charge, however, the two metal desks were free of clutter, and the smell of his aniseed breath mints was already in the air.

She handed him the folder with the anonymous letters, which he lined up against the edge of his desk, and settled into one of the chairs to tell him what she'd learned from Nisha Pragasam.

Managing to hold his upper body soldier straight while perched on the other desk, Vinz listened without interrupting. "I appreciate your speaking with her," he said when Giuliana had finished. "I'm sure you didn't encourage her to believe this was a premeditated homicide. Still, there are some signs that . . ." He trailed off, his habitual caution, which Giuliana knew well, overcoming his instinct to discuss the evidence. She waited patiently until he added, almost reluctantly, "Yes. We really could have a deliberate killing on our hands."

Giuliana felt a little thrill. "Something to do with the road marks?"

Vinz nodded. "There were no signs of braking. None at all. Which is odd because there's a row of streetlights along the edge of the park there. Frau Eberhart's bike had good lights, and she was wearing a bright yellow reflective vest. Plus, it had stopped raining, so visibility was relatively good. The driver should have seen her clearly on that straight stretch of road." Vinz seemed to be talking as much to himself as to Giuliana.

"What happened?"

Vinz's hands rested at either side of him on the desktop; Giuliana saw one of them tighten into a fist as he said, "Eberhart's bike was hit directly from behind with a force that more or less destroyed it, and she was thrown through the air right into a tree, which broke her neck and did major brain damage. Even if the driver had stopped to help, nothing would have saved her. But he couldn't have known that, the callous bastard. Of course, if she was hit on purpose, that changes everything. And it certainly fits with what our witness told us."

Giuliana sat up in the desk chair. "A witness! That's—"

Vinz was already shaking his head. "Don't get excited. He was on the other side of the street from the park and several houses down the road from where the woman was hit. I had a team knocking on doors right after it happened, and some people had come outside because of all the sirens and were immediately questioned. Most of them . . . well, you know how it is—'I might have heard some kind of bang; yes, maybe there could have been a scream, but I didn't think anything about it.'"

"In other words, the usual head-in-the-sand responses." Giuliana's shoulders slumped, wishing yet again that the average citizen was better at abandoning routine in favor of a bit more curiosity, initiative, and responsibility for other people.

Vinz gave a tired nod but then, as though trying to be fair, said, "Well, it was a cold night; they had their windows closed. Except for this man—a professional auto mechanic—still outside after walking his dog. He was in the garden behind his building, unfortunately, but he said that not only did he hear no braking before or after the noise of the bike landing with a crash, he heard a car accelerating *before* the crash."

Giuliana frowned. Did she even know what a car sounded like when it accelerated? Not a Ferrari on a Formula One racetrack, but a standard car on a normal road?

"Like a . . . like a roar?" she asked.

"No, the mechanic said the car had a manual transmission, and he could hear the driver switching gears to speed up and grinding them before going into a long screech. Then the crash, followed by more grinding and squealing. The mechanic ran to his front sidewalk. He was too late to see the car, but he crossed the road and found the ruined bike flung onto the shoulder. That's when he called the emergency number."

"So our current best clue is to look for a bad driver whose car has damaged gears?" said Giuliana with raised eyebrows.

Vinz's answering smile was grim. "Exactly. We're looking for a red vehicle with manual transmission, crash damage to the front, and worn gears. Forensics is working to extract as much information as possible about the car and driver from the victim's bike; that's only what we have so far. I've already got *Fahnder* phoning all the bodywork places in Bern, and we'll spread out to nearby towns if that doesn't bring in any data. I'm going to find this car."

Giuliana was picturing the smashed bike, which reminded her of Nisha's last question. "Eberhart's partner asked if you found her bike helmet."

"No, it isn't at the site, and she certainly wasn't wearing it when she hit the tree. Not that it would have protected her from the broken neck."

Giuliana nodded. Still, her mind pursued the question. If Andi Eberhard had left for curling without her helmet, Nisha would have found it. So, had Andi worn it to the curling hall and then forgotten to put it on to pedal home? Or left it at her workplace? With homicide becoming a possibility, it needed to be found.

Giuliana gestured at the folder of anonymous letters on Vinz's desk. "Sounds like those letters may not be a distraction after all. Shall I take some of the work off your shoulders?" She thought of the Kissling depositions, but surely she could handle this as well. "I could write something up for forensics about the letters and send them over for tests. Would you like me to follow up with the partner, too? Or do you want to talk to her?"

"No need for that yet," he said with a shrug. "I'd be happy for you to interview her formally now that we're looking beyond an accident."

Giuliana wasn't surprised by Vinz's hands-off approach. He much preferred to stick to a lead detective's official job description, collecting and organizing data from his desk while a team of investigators did his research and questioning for him. She, on the other hand, loved fieldwork and tried to squeeze as much of it into her job as she could. In that sense, she and Vinz made a good team.

"Okay," she went on. "I'll take care of the letters and Frau Pragasam. And you?"

Vinz reached two fingers into his breast pocket for his box of mints, shook two into his palm, and offered them to her. She took one, and he popped the other into his mouth. Then he said, "I'll phone the victim's doctor to find out if she had any condition that would make her lose control of her bike, although I doubt it since she was an athlete. We should talk to the women on her curling team, too. They were the last ones to see her alive, and we need to know if she seemed ill. Plus, I'll need information from her workplace. These anonymous letters are interesting, but it's too soon to narrow the focus of the investigation."

"If you need another *Fahnder* to help, Renzo's bored half out of his mind working on that Montenegrin stolen car scam. He's a good interviewer . . ."

"Especially with women." Vinz snorted, rolling his eyes. "Or do they become speechless when he's around? That would be a handicap." He chortled.

Renzo would be dealing with comments like these until the day he retired. Giuliana didn't want to risk defending him; although no chatter ever got back to *her*, she didn't want to promote even more talk around the station about their friendship. Against her better judgment, however, she said, "Give the guy a break, Vinz. He isn't to blame for the way he looks."

Vinz waggled his eyebrows. "Oh, no? Working out at the gym almost every day? You think he does that to stay fit for police work?"

"You have a point," Giuliana admitted with a laugh. "I guess I was thinking of his face. But he's still good at drawing people out—men *and* women—and his reports are clear, with real insight. I've worked with him a lot over the past year, and I think he's . . . skilled." There, that didn't sound too glowing, did it?

Vinz nodded. "Okay. I'll see if I can get him moved over to me."

"I'm off then. Let me know if I can do anything beyond staying in touch with the victim's partner and following up on these letters. You probably heard that Erwin and I have been assigned to the Kissling trial, but that's still six months away, so I have time."

Vinz waved his thanks as he picked up his phone. From the corridor, Giuliana could hear him requesting Renzo's reassignment. That would give her access to information about the case, even if Vinz didn't give her more to do. And it would make Renzo happy.

Giuliana was glad she'd kept to herself her vague suspicion that someone in the Tamil community might be involved. She had nothing to go on, just the hazy picture of a man resentful at being rejected for a woman lover. And she supposed that Nisha's family and friends wouldn't approve of her life with Andi, either. Did her parents live in Bern? It would be helpful to know more about them. She'd see what she could find out.

6

Renzo was in his Fiat driving home when his boss called to ask if he was okay with transferring to the Eberhart case. Although no one expected him to start his new assignment until the following morning, he still phoned Vinzenz Nef from the car to find out more. Talk to a women's curling team! That assignment made him smile. In 1998 he and his father had taken over the family TV to watch the Swiss men's team win the Olympic gold medal in Nagano. It was a happy memory that immediately made him sad, as any reminders of his father did— the third anniversary of his death had been only a few months earlier.

All thoughts of his father fled as he opened the door of his apartment in Wabern and braced himself for the impact of two little bodies, the nightly greeting of Antonietta and Angelo. Hearing growls emerging from thigh level, he called out, "Oh no. I'm being eaten alive. Who will save me? *Aiuto!* Help!" With his kids, he always spoke Italian.

"I'm a tiger," yelled Angelo, pretending to bite him. Antonietta scrutinized her *papà*'s expression to make sure he wasn't really scared. Then she growled softly, forming her hands into claws. "I'm a rabbit," she told him. A growling rabbit? So be it. "If I give you a carrot, *Signorina* Rabbit, will you spare my life?"

"That's enough noise," Fränzi yelled from the kitchen. He saw a look of sad resignation pass between the children, and his temper flared. Why couldn't she let the three of them be loud and silly for a few minutes? In another hour, his babies would be asleep; the early evening was the only time he could play with them during the work-week. With exaggerated shushing noises, he gathered the tiger and rabbit into his arms and carried them to the kitchen, where Fränzi was cleaning up after their supper.

"Do you have big plans for our meal tonight?" he asked in his usual Bernese German.

"I've barely thought about it—there's stuff in the fridge."

"Well, how about if we give Frau Keller the baby monitor as soon as the kids are asleep, and you come with me to the curling rink over by the Expo?"

"Why?"

"I'd like to talk to one or two curlers about a case, but I don't think it will take too long, and afterward, we can eat something there and watch the curling. I've never tried the restaurant, I admit, but it can't be that bad."

In the past, Fränzi's face would have lit up over any outing he'd proposed. Now, after six years of marriage, all he saw in her expression was pique. "What you're saying is that you have to work this evening, and you figure if you offer to drag me along, I won't be pissed off. Well, guess what? I'd rather stay home, eat a yogurt, and watch TV. So go without me. You don't even need to feel bad."

But he did feel bad, and Fränzi being so annoyed made it worse since a piece of him was relieved to get away from her. There was no reason he had to start his inquiries that evening. Still, he knew most curlers were on the ice at night and on weekends; during the day, they were at their jobs.

"Can we get a babysitter for tomorrow night instead, then?" he asked.

"To watch curling?" she countered, hands on hips.

"To go dancing."

"Dancing!" Her beautiful face lost its disgruntled look, and she gave him a slow smile. She swayed toward him across the kitchen floor and stood on tiptoe so that they were groin to groin. She locked her hands around his neck and bent her upper body away from him, thrusting her breasts upward and grinding her pelvis into his. She tilted her head so that her blonde hair hung over one shoulder, and her eyes met his with mischievous languor. He was immediately aroused; she always had this effect on him. She laughed, straightened up, and moved her hands down to his buttocks to draw him closer to her. He kissed her neck, and their breathing picked up pace.

At that moment, Antonietta decided she'd been ignored long enough. She butted her head against her father's leg and chanted, "Bath time, bath time."

"I think someone's jealous," Fränzi murmured, and the two of them broke apart. "Still going out tonight?" she asked. "I can think of better things to do."

"Later, for sure," he said. "And see if you can get a babysitter for tomorrow night."

He scooped up the kids again to put them to bed. During their bath, Angelo told him about a boy who'd managed to throw one of his winter boots onto the roof of the kindergarten. Hearing the admiration in his son's voice as he described this feat, Renzo reckoned all kindergarten teachers deserved medals—and huge salaries. Which they certainly didn't get.

He began helping Antonietta into her pajamas. "Did you have fun at Nonna's this morning?" he asked her.

"We baked a cake. I added everything to the bowl." The four-year-old giggled. "I got flour in Nonna's hair." Renzo's mother didn't care about any mess that was made by one of her precious grandchildren. For her, it was a delight, not a hardship, to keep the kids three mornings and one afternoon a week while Fränzi did computer drafting at an architectural firm. In fact, his mother had told him how much she missed Angelo now that he was in kindergarten.

In the kids' bedroom, Angelo bounded around, naked except for a pair of pajama pants on his head, deep in his child's world. Renzo helped Antonietta under the covers. A stack of picture books sat on the night table between the two small beds. He was about to suggest that Antonietta pick a story when she said, "Zia came to visit Nonna. We played. Then she talked to Nonna about you. When Mama came for me, they all talked about you."

Renzo flopped backward onto his daughter's bed and stared at the ceiling. Shit. His mother and one of his sisters discussing him with his wife. What was that about? He knew how much Fränzi complained to *her* sister about him, but surely she wouldn't criticize him to his family.

"Was it Zia Bianca or Zia Valentina?"

"Zia Bianca."

Worse and worse. Bianca was the oldest sibling and always thought she knew what was best for the other three. He sighed. What had they been talking about?

He was still flat on his back when a little body flew through the air and landed on his chest, almost knocking the wind out of him. "I'm Thor," shrieked Angelo. Now the legs of his flannel pajamas were tied around his neck to make a cape. Uh-oh. Time to get this one calmed down before Fränzi stalked in.

"I'm going to read two books," he said, refusing to wrestle with his son. "Angelo, if you get into your pj's and under the duvet before I count to ten, you can pick the first one."

Driving from his apartment to the curling rink near Guisanplatz, Renzo could see the wild March wind whipping around the tops of the trees; he could feel it in the way his car bucked. The fifteen-minute trip took him by Giuliana's street, and he imagined her smiling at her husband as they ate dinner or sat curled up on a sofa together. Bloody Ueli Brand! Years earlier, the first time he'd worked on one of Giuliana's cases, when he'd begun to register his feelings for her, Renzo had looked up her husband online. Even now, he made a point of reading some of Ueli's articles, both admiring and resenting the way the man was able to sound intelligent on any subject.

As he drove down Muristalden toward the bear park, Renzo gave free rein to his bitterness. Ueli was the reason Giuliana still kept him at a distance. It had nothing to do with keeping their relationship professional for the sake of their careers. No, it was her marriage to Ueli she didn't want to risk. But was it love or just loyalty? Ah, fuck it! With a sigh, he pushed these familiar thoughts away and switched his mind back to Andrea Eberhart and the members of her curling team.

The curling center was a large low gray building, modern looking, with a row of windows in the front that gave nothing away. The restaurant was called Caledonia—a big sign near the main door showed the name and a logo of a large fork crossed with a curling broom—mildly amusing, Renzo thought, as he went through the automatic doors into the building's foyer.

Noise assaulted him immediately: the clatter of plates and buzz of voices from the large restaurant to his left and the yelling of the skips on the ice beyond the tables. But the small hall where he stood was empty. Whom could he approach? Then he spotted a small shop crammed with curling equipment. Inside, a middle-aged woman was unpacking a carton filled with plastic water bottles. "We're closed," she said, seeing him in the doorway. "I'm stocking shelves."

Renzo showed her his ID. "I'm from the police."

To his surprise, she gave a short laugh. "We've been wondering whether to call you or not, and here you are," she said. Before he could reply, she went on, now grave faced. "It's about Andi, isn't it?"

He marveled, not for the first time, at how fast bad news traveled. "Did something happen last night that the police should know about?"

"Well, we think so." Renzo wondered who this "we" was but decided not to interrupt. "Last night, her bike helmet was missing from her basket, which is where she always left it. She never locked it to the bike, but it'd never disappeared before. I figured maybe someone had borrowed it or . . . well, it seemed like a nuisance, but not a big deal. Until she drove off without it and was immediately killed in a bike accident. Kind of a strange coincidence, don't you think?"

Excitement surged in Renzo. "You're right; I'd like to hear about

the missing helmet. Can I buy you a drink, so you can tell me more?"
He smiled, nodding in the direction of the restaurant, then held out
his hand. "Sorry. Renzo Donatelli. I'm an investigator for the *Kanton-
spolizei*."

The woman shook his hand without mentioning her name. "Look,
this is my second late night here, and I'm eager to get home. So no
drink, thanks, but I'll tell you what happened. Last night I was finishing up; the facilities manager and one of the cleaners were working
late, too. We were standing over there"—she pointed at a spot to the
right of the main door—"talking about some upcoming repairs in the
locker rooms when Andi came back in with her safety vest over her
jacket, looking annoyed."

Trying to write in his notebook, Renzo realized he couldn't lean
on a wall or use a countertop for stability; every vertical and horizontal
surface in the little shop was stacked, hung, or piled with clothing and
sports equipment. "She came back?" he asked.

"Right, because we'd already waved goodbye to her three minutes
earlier when she left. So I asked, 'Why're you here again?' or something
like that, and she said, 'Someone's taken my bike helmet.' Miguel, the
facilities man, told her it had probably just fallen onto the ground. She
said she'd checked, but he went downstairs to his office, got a really strong
flashlight, and went out to help her. Five minutes later, he came back in;
they'd looked all around the front area and hadn't found the helmet,
so Andi had gone home without it. I said something about hoping we
weren't in for another series of thefts from the locker rooms—we had a
rash of them a few years ago, and it made things ugly for a while. Then
we all went off in different directions, and that was that."

"How did you hear she was dead?"

"Bunch of girls on the stairs this afternoon when I was on my way
to the john," said the shopkeeper. "Once I figured out who they were
talking about, I immediately thought about the helmet. Would it . . .?"
She stopped, pressed her hands against her cheeks, and gave Renzo a
stricken look.

Renzo would have liked to comfort the woman by telling her

Eberhart's helmet wouldn't have saved her life, but that was not information to share with the public. "I believe she died almost instantly," he said instead.

"Oh God," said the woman. "I've known her since she first started curling here. Some people found her . . . well, too opinionated. But I always liked her. I'd rather have someone say something to my face than behind my back."

Renzo returned his notebook to his jacket pocket and stood with his arms folded to avoid knocking over anything in the cramped space. "I'm glad you told me about the helmet. Actually, though, I came in to talk to her teammates. Are any of them here tonight?"

"To see all of them, you'd have to come back on a Monday or Wednesday because that's when they practice. Although what they'll do this coming Monday is a good question since they're short a player now."

"Short their skip, in fact," Renzo said.

"Oh, *that* won't be a problem," the shopkeeper said, with the kind of eye roll that implied an untold tale. "Barbara Weber will be all over that job like butter on bread. She's not here tonight, but another of Andi's teammates probably is. Karolin Itten. The men's teams are practicing, and her boyfriend is out on the ice. She still comes along to watch him play; that's how you can tell they haven't been together very long." She cackled. "I saw her earlier. Let me grab my keys, and I'll take you to see if she's still there."

Locking the shop behind her, she led him to the restaurant. He was amazed at the size of the place; it could seat several hundred people. One entire wall was glass, and along that wall, tables for four were lined up for the length of all eight curling sheets. The tables were three steps down from the main restaurant floor so that the diners were at eye level with the players.

"What a great place for watching games," Renzo commented. "At those window tables, you're only about ten feet from the goal."

"Home," the woman corrected. "It's called the home, not the goal. Do you know anything about curling?"

"Not much," he admitted. "At least I know the things they throw are called stones. I learned that from watching Patrick Hürlimann and his team win in Nagano. I'll never forget Hürlimann bellowing instructions at the sweepers."

"Yeah, it's a noisy sport," the woman said. "Good, Karolin is still here." She waved toward one of the window tables.

Renzo saw four young women chatting over cups and glasses. But he didn't follow the older women right away—he was too interested in what was happening on the ice. Even through the thick window glass, he heard frantic screaming, apparently from at least five skips at once. In response, sweepers scrubbed their brooms back and forth with a controlled frenzy, creating paths for the stones. Renzo was reminded again of what an odd sport curling was and how much he'd loved watching it with his father during those days in 1998 when the Swiss won gold.

He turned his attention to the table of women, who were all staring at him, and walked over to join the shopkeeper. She'd apparently told them who he was and why he was there, because one of them stood. She looked to be in her mid-twenties, a tall, solidly muscular woman with curly brown hair and a broad, friendly face who held out her hand to him with a smile. "I'm Karolin Itten. I'll be glad to talk to you about Andi."

Renzo thanked the shopkeeper for her help and followed Karolin to an empty table some distance from her curious friends, who were still staring after the two of them. Karolin ordered a pot of verbena tea, and Renzo, who hadn't yet eaten, ordered a beer and a large plate of rösti. Then he took his notepad and pen back out. Ready to start the interview at last, he looked across the table at the young woman and said, "I'm sorry you've lost your teammate."

Karolin had been staring down at her hands. Now she met his eyes. "I've been thinking about Andi all evening, so talking about her is the best thing I could be doing. I've never known anyone who died, and she was a friend. I'm going to miss her a lot."

"I'd like to go over everything you remember about last night," Renzo said. "Just start with Andi arriving here. If anything she did or said was different from usual, tell me."

"Well, it was only our second practice with Andi as skip. But we've been playing together as a team for three years, so we have our routines." Karolin rested her chin in her palm, brows drawn together. "We were on the ice by eight fifteen. We warmed up and then spent an hour and a half playing. Our next game is in three weeks, and we have a lot to do to be ready. By ten fifteen, we'd showered and dressed, and we all left for home. I walked to the tram stop with Tamara, so I know she left. The others—Andi, Babs, and Claudine—were on their way out, too; they had their jackets on. Andi and Babs would have come by bike, and Claudine drives."

"Is Babs Barbara Weber?" Renzo asked, remembering the shopkeeper's comment about the woman. Karolin nodded. "Will she be your skip now?" he continued.

"That's what she wants, but I don't know." She shook her head. "There's a reason Andi was chosen and Babs wasn't, and Andi being dead doesn't change that."

"Did she resent not getting the job?"

"Oh yeah." Karolin blew out a loud breath. "A lot. I'm not sure she would have stayed on the team with Andi at its head. She's a very good curler, so we'd be sorry to lose her. But as a player, not as a person."

Renzo wrote in his notebook and then asked, "Was there any unpleasantness between her and Frau Eberhart on Monday or Wednesday?"

"No, but only because Andi didn't rise to the bait. Barbara was as rude as ever."

She would have to be interviewed, Renzo thought. He paused as the waitress brought Karolin's tea and his beer. "Does everyone on the team know that Frau Eberhart was a lesbian?" He set the glass down on its coaster after his first swallow, which tasted perfect.

Karolin laughed. "I imagine everyone in the building knows it, at least since her and Nisha's baby was born. She went around showing photos of the two of them with Saritha to everyone she could find, from the woman who cleans the changing rooms to the manager of the restaurant." She stirred the teabag around. "She came out about ten years ago to the team she was on then—that's what I've heard. By the time *I* started curling with her, she was living with Nisha. We don't have many get-togethers that include boyfriends or husbands, but the few times we've scheduled them, Nisha's come, too."

Karolin didn't seem the least bit uncomfortable with Andi's homosexuality, which made Renzo wonder if, at her age, he'd have been as laid-back. In his mid-twenties, he'd played soccer regularly with a group of friends, and, for all he knew, one or more of those guys could have been gay, but if so, he'd never noticed. Or perhaps the truth was that he'd never let himself consider it—too hard to deal with. At that age, he'd been lazy when it came to anything emotionally complicated.

They were interrupted by the arrival of Renzo's rösti. As he broke the yolk of the fried egg crowning an enormous pile of grated fried potatoes and bits of crisp bacon smothered in melted cheese, he grinned at Karolin and said, "My wife's at home eating a yogurt. By choice." Karolin giggled, and Renzo swallowed a large mouthful of potatoes and took a swig of beer. "You said you were going to miss Frau Eberhart a lot. Tell me what made her special to you."

Holding her teacup in clasped hands, Karolin stared into the distance. "She was the kind of person you *knew* would do what she said. Of course, that meant she expected the same from other people, which made her . . . formidable. She was exceptionally straightforward, so she demanded that kind of honesty from everyone else. Her openness made a lot of people uncomfortable. Me, too, once or twice."

"By openness, do you mean that she flaunted being gay?"

"No, no. That's not what I mean at all. Unless she was talking about Nisha, you never thought about that. At least, I never did. No, it was this sense I got that she didn't take the easy way out or . . . what do I want to say? That she wouldn't let anyone get away with anything— herself included. Not in a curling match and not . . . well, not in life, either."

"You said she made people uncomfortable. Did some people dislike her?"

Karolin finally gave him the sharp look he'd been waiting for. "I thought she died in a bike accident. Why are you asking me these questions?" She paused and then added, "Does this have anything to do with her bike helmet going missing? The girls were just talking about that—I guess all the curlers are."

Renzo thought about how he wanted to answer. He felt increasingly convinced that Andi's death was a homicide, but he didn't want to commit himself yet, so he said, "Despite the story with the helmet, her death was probably an accident, but there were no witnesses. The police have to make sure it wasn't deliberate. That's why I'm asking if there was anyone who might have wanted to hurt her. It could be someone she mentioned or something you observed."

"I think I was as close to her as anyone on our team, but we never saw each other privately, except at team-building cookouts. I don't know much about her job or family."

Renzo nodded, but still, he waited.

"I can't believe I'm saying this," Karolin finally said, "but Barbara Weber was so angry about not being chosen skip that I *can* imagine her hurting Andi just to get her out of commission for the season. Plus, she isn't as comfortable with Andi's being a lesbian as I think the rest of us are. But she wouldn't kill her. Besides, I'm almost sure Babs didn't have a car with her at practice last night."

Renzo didn't bother to say that if the woman had planned to crash into Andi, she'd have had every reason to act as if she were biking home. She could have parked her car a few blocks away, ridden her bike there, and then driven after her teammate.

"Can you think of anyone Andi talked about not getting along with? Someone at her work, maybe?"

"Andi loved working for the civilian service; I know that. Everything I ever heard her say about her job was positive. There was also the volunteer work she did to change the law about gay marriage and adoption—that must have made her enemies, but she never talked about them."

"And her private life?" Renzo asked. "Wait, can I get you some more tea? Or anything else? Here I am gobbling up all this rösti in front of you. What about some dessert?"

Karolin shook her head, smiling. "I'm going to eat something with my boyfriend Tinu when he gets done. And I've been drinking tea all evening. I'm fine."

Once the potatoes were gone, Renzo ate his bit of healthy garnish: some slices of tomato, two leaves of arugula, and a sprig of parsley. His plate clean, he sighed with satisfaction. "Okay then, coffee for me, nothing for you. Tell me what you know about Andi's private life."

"Andi and Nisha seemed extremely happy, although I only talked to Nisha a few times. I do know . . ." Karolin stopped and frowned. Renzo waited, and after a moment, she said, "One evening, when a group of us were having beers after a game, we started joking about mothers-in-law, and Andi said she had a lot of respect for hers."

There was a pause as Renzo ordered an espresso from the waiter clearing their table. Then he nodded at Karolin, who went on, "Andi told us that Nisha's father, her older brother, and all of her extended family had cut Nisha out of their lives. But not her mother. She saw Nisha regularly, even though she had to keep it a secret. Andi said she loved her mother-in-law for that."

"You say 'mother-in-law,'" Renzo commented, "but my impression is that the two women weren't married, even though Andi was a gay rights activist. Why didn't they get married as soon as the law changed two years ago?"

Karolin pressed her lips together as she thought. "I did expect them to get married as soon as they could, and my impression is that Andi very much wanted that. So I don't know why it hadn't happened, but if I had to guess, I'd say Nisha thought an official marriage would make her relationship with her family even more of a problem."

"What about Andi's own family?" Renzo had read some biographical information before leaving for the curling hall, so he knew the dead woman wasn't from the city.

"She grew up somewhere near Thun, and I think her parents are still there, but her brother and his wife live here in Bern. I met him at her thirtieth birthday party, and I got the impression they were close. That's all I know."

"I also need to know if Frau Eberhart's bike riding might have been erratic last night." Renzo smiled at the waiter as his coffee arrived before asking, "Are you aware of any illness she had or . . . any addictions? To alcohol or drugs—even prescription drugs?"

Karolin leaned toward him, her expression fierce. "I can assure you that Andi wasn't ill, she didn't take drugs, and she wasn't a heavy drinker. She was completely sober last night. Afterward, we were all tired, but in a normal way, and no one on the team had any alcohol the whole evening, at least not in front of me."

"Okay. I believe you!" He watched her face relax and leaned back in his chair, glad to have the official questions out of the way. "Now, why don't you show me which team your boyfriend is on."

Together, they looked out at the rink, and Karolin pointed to a sheet whose digital display read *Salzmann*.

"The skip over there in the home on the far side of the sheet screaming his head off—that's him. Tinu Salzmann."

They watched the practice games for a few minutes. "Where are the referees?" Renzo asked. "There must be fouls and decisions about stones being in or out. I know these are just practices tonight. But when I watched the Nagano games, I can't remember seeing a single referee on the ice. Where do they observe from?"

"There aren't any referees in curling." Karolin was giving him a small, crooked smile.

"So, who decides if a player has made a mistake?"

"*We* do," she said, grinning at his raised eyebrows. "It's one of the things that makes curling special—it's an honor sport. If you touch one of the stones with the broom or bump one with your foot, you say so. There are some famous examples of leading teams losing world championships because one of the players touched—we say burned—a stone and confessed. If that happens, the stone is discounted, and sometimes that's enough to cost the team a game or even an Olympic medal. It can be hard, but we're proud of curling's reputation for honesty."

"As opposed to soccer, where most players try to get away with as much cheating as possible," Renzo put in.

"Exactly. We also used to have to admit if we crossed the hog line when we delivered a stone. Now there are sensors in the stones' handles, so the hog line rule is officially monitored. But the whole spirit of the game requires self-policing; we all know that."

Renzo found this fascinating—almost unbelievable. "What happens if someone doesn't own up to . . . um . . . burning a stone? I assume the other team blows the whistle."

"Sometimes. But the tradition is not to mention it and just keep playing. Of course, when you see your opponent cheating and getting away with it, it's infuriating. God, Andi used to get so mad! Luckily, it doesn't happen often. And word gets around after the competition, anyway. A sneaky player, or team, gets a bad reputation. That's some comfort, at least."

"I'm impressed." There was a loud rap on the glass, and Renzo looked up to find Karolin's boyfriend frowning at him. Renzo was about to make a joke about the youngster's possessiveness, but, remembering himself at that age, swallowed his words. With a questioning look at Karolin, Tinu half-walked, half-glided back to his team, and Renzo decided it was time to go. He got Karolin's promise that she'd send him the phone numbers and emails of her teammates, thanked her, and headed outside to the parking lot, hugging himself against the damp chill of the wind. He took a good look at the racks of bikes to one side of the door. It would be easy to lose a helmet in the dark, but the disappearance was still troubling.

Driving home through a light fog, he thought about the term Karolin had used to describe Andi Eberhart. "Formidable." A formidable person inspired respect but also fear. And someone who prided herself on her honesty could make people angry. He'd assumed that the anonymous letters Vinz had told him about were because Andi was an activist and a lesbian. But after listening to Karolin, he thought the letters could in part have been a response to Andi's values and personality, regardless of her sexual orientation.

Which meant he needed to read the letters. And talk to Babs Weber. But the biggest piece of news was the stolen helmet. He wondered if any of the people going in and out of the curling hall had seen anything—Vinz might want him to ask questions about that. He'd go home, write up his notes, get some sleep, and call Vinz first thing.

Then he remembered Fränzi and the way she'd pressed against him earlier that evening. It wasn't that late; surely she'd waited up for him—or wouldn't mind if he woke her up. No, he'd write his report tomorrow morning after his workout instead of tonight.

He pushed a little harder on the gas pedal, and the car picked up from his usual four miles over the speed limit to almost ten. He was no longer thinking about the case at all.

7

Giuliana hurried home after her late meeting with Vinz. Thank goodness it was Ueli's turn to cook dinner. As she walked in, he called from the kitchen, "I told the kids I'd put the noodles on as soon as you got back—they're starving. Can you eat in ten minutes?"

"Sure." She hung up her jacket and went over to where he stood by the stove, turning up the heat under a large pot of simmering water, a bag of pappardelle at his elbow. He turned and kissed her lightly on the lips, and she rested her head against his chest for a moment.

"What did you make?"

"Rabbit stew. With double the carrots, just for you."

Ueli's rabbit, cooked in white wine and mustard with onions, mushrooms, and chunks of carrot, was a family favorite. It had to simmer for over an hour, though.

"How did you have time?" she asked, washing her hands at the kitchen sink. "I thought you were interviewing all day."

"I put it on after breakfast and turned it off when I came home for lunch. I only got home from my last interview an hour ago."

"Where's Lukas?" Usually, he ran to her in the evening with some bit of news about his day or a random fact acquired at school.

"In his room, I guess, and Isabelle's supposedly doing homework."

"Did you tell him about Irène?"

"Yes, and that she's going to have an operation next week. I expected a lot of questions, but . . . I guess he's feeling okay about it."

Strange. She couldn't imagine Lukas taking such a dramatic piece of news so calmly. But who knew what was going on in his eleven-year-old head?

Ten minutes later, they sat down at the kitchen table and fell upon Ueli's stew, extracting tiny rabbit bones as they ate.

Isabelle speared several chunks of carrot. "Did you talk to Mémé again today?"

"No," said her father, "I could only reach Uncle Mike." He wound a wide noodle around his fork. "I think we're just going to have to do what Mémé says and wait until Sunday."

Lukas would want to know everything about cancer, Giuliana thought. He was always so hungry for facts and figures. But today, her son stared at his plate, forking meat, vegetables, and noodles into his mouth like a robot. Just as well he wasn't asking, she supposed. Still, it puzzled her.

"Has Quentin decided what to do about military service yet?" Ueli asked Isabelle. Although she'd been seeing him for months now, Isabelle didn't talk much about her boyfriend, and Ueli and Giuliana had only met him a few times. He seemed pleasant and intelligent, but they were surprised the relationship had lasted. He would finish *Gymnasium* that spring, while she still had two more years. Surely at nineteen, he was too old for their daughter?

Isabelle frowned. "Can you believe that he's considering serving in the army? At the assessment camp, he passed all the tests with high scores, so one of the officers has been trying to persuade him to become a paratrooper. He's also considering joining the Alpine patrol or training for some other elite regiment." She rolled her eyes, and her inflection was scathing as she said the word "elite."

Ueli said, "The training for those units is very demanding, you know. It really is something he can be proud of."

Isabelle delicately removed a bit of bone from her mouth with her fingers, set it aside, and then snorted. Giuliana smiled down at her stew.

"He wants to learn to drive one of those big Jeep-y things. He thinks it would be exciting." Isabelle's tone told them what *she* thought. "I said no matter what they taught him, he'd still have to take orders for ten months and march around in a stupid uniform."

"At least they get to wear berets now," Giuliana commented, "instead of that stiff hat with the shiny brim that Vati had to wear. Remember how you loathed it, Ueli?"

Isabelle refused to be distracted. "I can't understand why he's even considering the army. In the civilian service, he could do something useful, not play war games. Why did *you* serve in the army, Vati? Didn't you think it was dumb?"

"In my day, there *was* no alternative service you could choose instead of the military," Ueli said, smiling. "If you were fit for the army, you either served or you went to jail."

"Wasn't the army just . . . ghastly?" Her voice rose dramatically on the last word.

"Well, I did hate basic training—although I was proud of all the muscles I got out of it. Then I became a field cook, which was one of the jobs I'd asked for. That wasn't so bad. I was either bored or frantically busy, but at least I got to spend hours out of doors when I wasn't in a kitchen. Plus, I learned to cook."

"But that's a useful job. The assignments Quentin's interested in sound dangerous. Or like little boy stuff. I mean, why would anyone want to spend ten months driving around in a big car painted in camouflage? It's like wanting to blow the whistle on the choo choo."

Giuliana caught Ueli's eye: he was trying not to laugh. Isabelle sounded so much like Giuliana herself, especially when she had to deal with the same choo-choo types among her fellow police. But she swallowed her amusement. She agreed with her daughter, but still . . . "He probably sees the danger as a way to test himself. Maybe he thinks, 'If I can do this, nothing will ever scare me again.' Parachuting or rock climbing or driving like a maniac for ten months doesn't mean he'll want to do it for the rest of his life, you know."

"Hmm." Isabelle shrugged, and Giuliana let it go. She'd seen this same urge to prove themselves drive some men into crime and others into joining the police. And not only men. After rejecting her father's profession, she'd grasped at the police partially as a way to show him she could succeed at something besides being a lawyer. Instead of defending those accused of crimes, she'd defend the victims. Luckily, after she'd abandoned law, her younger brother Paolo had become the defense attorney their father wanted to take over his practice.

Dinner finished, she quizzed Lukas on his English words while Isabelle, after a token groan, cleaned up the kitchen with her usual thoroughness. Having settled Lukas into the last of his homework, Giuliana walked around the apartment straightening. She shelved books, gathered up sections of newspaper draped over chairs and put them in the recycling stack, found one of Lucas's socks in his living room Lego corner and threw it into the laundry hamper, rehung crooked towels in the bathrooms, and generally tidied up. Then she sprayed the orchids on the kitchen windowsill. Ueli was back at his computer, writing; his piles of books and papers didn't count as a mess as long as they were on his desk.

Feeling more in control of her life after putting the rooms to rights, she sat down at the kitchen table with photocopies of Andrea Eberhart's twenty-three anonymous letters. Each was only a few sentences long, different in its exact wording from the others but containing similar references to unnatural sex and punishment by man and God. The texts were disturbing but also strangely passionless.

God will punish you for having sex with that black whore, one said. *I know you will suffer for it, and I am glad. You are wicked to the core and deserve to fall down dead on the ground and burn in hell forever.* On another page, she read, *You should be thrown in jail for the rest of your life. What you two do with each other makes me want to vomit. Which of your cunts squeezed out that ugly-colored child? Maybe each one of you produced one-half of it.*

Despite how degrading and racist the words were, Giuliana felt something was missing, and on a third reading, she realized what it was: sexual excitement. No matter how much revulsion most anonymous letter writers claimed to feel about something sexual, you could usually sense their prurience whispering through their words. Not here. Whoever this writer was, they did not appear to be excited by the things they were describing.

The letters expressed as much disgust at sex between a darker- and a lighter-skinned person as between two women. Their child was called *an abomination*, *a monstrosity*, and *an outrage in the eyes of God*. There was more than a whiff of the weird in the references to the little girl, whose *devilish birth would cause her limbs to rot*. The discussion of the baby's *hideous conception* and *fiendish origins* made it sound as if the writer believed Saritha was somehow the product of congress between two women, a kind of demon child produced by witches. Magic was never mentioned, and God appeared at least once in each of the letters. But a hint of belief in some impossible act of reproduction hung about the pages of the latest letters, the ones sent after Saritha's birth.

Each letter was formatted on a computer, neatly printed, and contained no grammar or spelling mistakes. The envelopes, with typed addresses, had all been mailed from Bern between four weeks and three months apart over the previous four-and-a-half years. They didn't seem to be sent in any pattern, although Saritha's presence seemed to have inspired more of them. Giuliana's colleagues in forensics would give her all kinds of other details when they finished with the original documents, but one thing was sure—the writer knew how to produce professional-looking correspondence.

Giuliana wrote a couple of lines on her impressions of the letters and emailed them to Vinz. Then she went back into the living room, where Ueli sat at his desk. She kissed the top of his head, and he took his eyes off the computer screen to look at her.

"What's this piece about?" she asked.

"I'm writing about how several Swiss charities exploit their employees."

"Do you have time for a question?"

"Sure."

"I've got a case involving a Tamil in her late twenties who grew up in Bern and works as a press speaker for the Federal Office for the Environment."

Uelie raised his eyebrows. "That's impressive! Is she married to a Swiss?"

Giuliana smiled as she said, "Well, yes and no. She's been living with a Swiss woman partner, and they have a baby together."

"Whoa! I hope she isn't your murder victim."

"No, her partner is. So far, the death is being classified as an accident, a hit-and-run. But it's starting to look suspicious. My question is—do you know anyone who has written about the Swiss Tamil population?"

"Why?" He frowned. "You suspect the woman's family?"

"It's something that needs looking into, along with some homophobic anonymous letters the dead woman got. They could be because of her work with Rainbow Families. It's a—"

"I've read about it," Ueli said, surprising Giuliana once again with his journalist's knowledge of haphazard facts. "The members lobbied to change Swiss laws against gays marrying and having kids. Now that the laws have changed, I don't know what they're focusing on. Hmm . . . Someone who's done an article on the Sri Lankan Tamil diaspora. When I finish writing up these interview notes, I'll see what I can find. If you've already gone to sleep, I'll leave you a note on the kitchen table."

"Thanks," Giuliana said, and before he could lose himself in his work again, she added, "Lukas was quiet at dinner tonight. Afterward, when I was helping him with his homework, he seemed . . . I don't know. Distracted. Have you noticed anything?"

"Not really. I guess he's usually such a chatterbox that when he's quiet I'm more relieved than worried. But now that you mention it, I guess you're right. Probably just a new phase. But I'll keep an eye on him."

"Okay." Giuliana laid a hand on his shoulder and then went to check on Isabelle. Under her closed door, Giuliana could see light still burning, so she knocked.

She found her daughter draped sideways over her striped armchair. Her computer was in her lap, but she was texting on her phone. She finished the message and turned to her mother. "Do you know more about Mémé than you're telling me?" She sounded like an adult; there wasn't a hint of a pout in the question, and her eyes were serious rather than accusing.

Giuliana sat down in Isabelle's desk chair and stretched out a hand to rest on her daughter's socked foot. "Honestly, love, Vati and I are both in the dark. There's not much we can do about it."

Isabelle nodded. "You can't force her to talk, can you? Just don't keep stuff about her cancer secret because, like, you think I'm too young to understand or whatever. I want to know what's going on."

Giuliana squeezed her daughter's foot and then quickly folded her hands in her lap. She yearned to touch Isabelle whenever she was with her, to stroke her cheek, or plant kisses in her hair. Isabelle hated being babied like this, but, oh, it was hard to keep her hands to herself sometimes.

"I will tell you whatever we know—assuming I can. If Mémé makes me promise not to tell you kids about her health, then it gets complicated. But we'll cross that bridge if we come to it. Listen, I came in to talk to you about something else. Have you noticed Lukas acting weird lately?"

"What's weird about Lukas acting weird? He's always weird." She crossed her eyes and stuck out her tongue.

Giuliana grinned but said, "No, I'm serious. He seems much too quiet to me."

"Well, thank God for that."

"That's more or less what Vati said. And when I asked Lukas if anything was going on, he said no. Still, if you get a sense of something that worries you, let me know."

"I will." For a moment, she was serious again, picking up on

Giuliana's concern, and then she began to kick her heels against the side of the armchair, her exasperation returning. "At least he's stopped obsessing about swords. Until a week or two ago, he talked about them all the time. Didn't you notice? It was starting to get creepy, his going on about Damascus steel and one- and two-edged blades and memorizing types of Chinese swords. They're called either *jian* or *dao*. See, even I'm doing it!"

Giuliana laughed. "I noticed. Still, an interest in swords seems like a pretty normal boy thing to me." She shifted in Isabelle's desk chair, about to get up, and then asked, "What about you? Are you okay?"

"As okay as I can be with two tests tomorrow and another on Monday."

"Hang in there." She left with only another pat on Isabelle's foot, proud of not asking her daughter why she was texting if she had three tests to study for. Then she went to bed and determinedly read the newspaper until she fell asleep with a section lying across her chest.

Ueli's note was on the table the next morning: *Journalist friend Debora Tschanz expecting your call re: Tamils*, followed by a phone number. Later, at work, gulping coffee at her desk, she dialed Tschanz, got no answer, and left a message. She'd planned to go back to reading transcripts of interviews with Kissling's ex-wife, sister-in-law, and neighbors. Instead, she walked down the hall to Vinz's little case room, stuck her head in the door, and said "*Ciao*" to his back.

Vinz spun in his desk chair, beckoning her inside as he said into his mobile, "Is nine okay? Good. Bye." He waved her toward the other chair in the room, and she sat. "That was Rolf," he told her. "We're meeting in forty minutes across the hall, and I'd like you there as well, if you can make it. I'll ask Renzo and Madeleine Trachsel, the investigator who's been to Eberhart's workplace, to step in, too. Along with the anomalies at the scene of the crime and your threatening letters— thanks for your mail, by the way—I now have plenty to suggest that this death was no accident."

Nisha Pragasam's drawn but determined face flashed through Giuliana's mind. "Such as?"

"Turns out Eberhart's helmet was stolen from her bike basket just before she was killed. I only got Renzo on board yesterday evening, and he already found that out last night at the curling hall. I can see why you like working with the guy."

Giuliana realized she was beaming as if Lukas had gotten an *Excellent* on his book report. Ugh! She dialed it down and said, "Glad he's turning out to be helpful."

"Madeleine went to Thun to talk to Eberhart's boss at the Federal Office for Civilian Service," Vinz went on, his eyes gleaming with an excitement she wasn't used to seeing in his bony face. "When he heard we were considering homicide, he mentioned a situation at the *Amthaus* prison. One of Eberhart's Civis, a young man of twenty-one, has been working there for several months, and he told Eberhard about two guards who were using racist language and mistreating dark-skinned prisoners—or encouraging Swiss prisoners to beat them up. Eberhart must have talked to a higher-up at the prison, because those guards have been suspended pending an investigation into inappropriate conduct. I'll tell everyone more about this at the meeting, but it sounds to me like a strong revenge motive."

"I'll see you at the meeting, then," Giuliana said, thinking that this lead wasn't likely to have anything to do with over four years' worth of anonymous letters. Still, it was important to pursue every possibility.

As she stood to leave, Vinz said, "Wait. Didn't you come in here with something to say?"

She paused midway to the door. "It'll keep till the meeting."

"No, please," he insisted, with his usual punctiliousness. "Sit down and tell me."

"Well, in light of this new prison guard lead you have, perhaps it's not so important." Giuliana leaned back against the room's second desk. "But I think it would be a good idea to find out more about Eberhart's partner's family. Who knows how traditional Tamil parents, if that's what they are, would respond to having a daughter raising a child in a lesbian relationship? Plus," she added, "I'd like to check out an organization called Rainbow Families. It might be what kicked off the letters."

Vinz pushed his thick-framed glasses up his nose with a long thin finger and said, "Sounds reasonable. We'll decide at the meeting—okay?"

Giuliana gave him a thumbs up. Back in the homicide office, she decided there was no point in digging into the Kissling case until after Vinz's meeting. Instead, she typed "Rainbow Families" into Google. It turned out to be an international group "committed to educating, supporting, connecting, and empowering LGBTQ+ families and prospective parents." After years of political debate and lobbying, on July 1, 2022, gay and lesbian couples had finally become able to marry and adopt children or use Swiss fertility clinics to produce them, although surrogacy was still illegal. Now the Swiss branch of the organization was offering counseling about adoption and fertility treatments in Switzerland and abroad, and it still appeared to be busy trying to win acceptance for nontraditional families from the average Swiss. Giuliana skimmed through the local group's website and wondered again about Saritha's father. If Eberhart's death was a homicide, sooner or later, Nisha Pragasam would have to disclose his identity.

It turned out that Rainbow Families had lobbied particularly hard to change the law that had prevented one partner in a same-sex couple from adopting the other's kids. As matters had stood before the new law was passed, if Nisha had been the one to die, Eberhart would have had no legal right to keep Saritha, causing the baby to lose not just one parent but both in a single blow. Now Giuliana wondered if Eberhardt had officially adopted her partner's daughter. She assumed so, but she'd have to find out.

Her phone rang—Ueli's journalist friend Debora Tschanz calling back. Giuliana warned herself to be careful what she said; she didn't want Debora sniffing out a possible story.

"You'd like to know how I think a Sri Lankan Tamil family would react to their daughter living openly in a lesbian relationship," Debora summarized after listening. "The answer is that I can't imagine. I've talked to some gay Tamil men, and they've pretty much had to step away from their families altogether. That, or marry a wife chosen by their parents and live a clandestine life. But I don't know any lesbians."

Giuliana picked up a pen and started to doodle on the sheet of paper in front of her. "Can you tell me in general about the relationship between the parents who came here as adults from Sri Lanka during the civil war and the children who were brought up here?"

"By Swiss standards, most of the younger generation are eager to please their parents. They respect their language and many of their traditions; they keep close ties to the Tamil community in Switzerland. But there are tensions." There would have to be, Giuliana thought. Immigration was always difficult for families. "Not around education and jobs," Debora continued. "Even the daughters are encouraged to get good schooling. It's mainly marriage that causes problems. Lots of the younger generation want to marry out of caste."

"Caste?" Giuliana began shading in the circles she'd penciled onto the page. She was aware that most Swiss Tamils were Hindus but had never thought of their being divided into castes. "You mean, as in Brahmins and Untouchables?"

"Right. The Sri Lankan Tamil caste system may grow out of religious beliefs, but it's chiefly occupational, which means it differs between geographical regions. Within the main four or five castes, there are lots of subdivisions."

"Can you give me an example?" Giuliana asked.

"Take artisans," Debora said. "As a general occupation, they identify with a caste called Kammalar, at least in the northeastern part of Sri Lanka. But they break down into separate groups of brass workers, goldsmiths, carpenters, and blacksmiths, as well as potters, drummers, and quite a few other occupations. And all these groups have a strong social significance; people expect their children to marry within the family's professional group."

Giuliana was shaking her head. "But that must be very complicated in Switzerland, where there are fewer than fifty thousand Sri Lankan Tamils, and people don't practice their old professions anymore."

"It's complicated, all right," Debora agreed, "but many parents are still upset if a child marries 'down' within the system."

"So, would it be anything like a banker's daughter marrying a garbage man here?" Giuliana drew a garbage can with a man's head sticking out.

"It's much worse than that," Debora said. "The whole extended family is dishonored in both Switzerland and Sri Lanka. Youngsters who've grown up here don't get it, especially since the various jobs associated with each caste and subcaste don't matter here. But it's a big deal to the older generation."

Giuliana found this fascinating but disturbing. "So if you're in the equivalent of the garbageman caste, that's what your ancestors have done and what your descendants are supposed to do?"

"Well, that's the way it used to be in Sri Lanka. In Switzerland, young men or women who traditionally belong to low-ranking occupational groups can get a good education and well-paid jobs, which is great. But when those officially low-caste people start looking for a bride or a groom, the parents of whomever they're interested in might still forbid the marriage if they're from a higher-ranking group. If the youngsters marry anyway, the higher-caste family might reject the couple completely."

Giuliana drew a Swiss flag behind the head sticking out of the garbage can. "What about Tamils who marry Swiss?"

Debora paused, and Giuliana could hear her drawing on a cigarette before she answered. "Well, having a daughter or especially a son who marries a Swiss is undesirable, but since the Swiss are *outside* the caste system, that marriage is probably easier to swallow, especially if the Swiss spouse is a good catch."

Giuliana thought about newspaper reports of South Asian families taking revenge on children and in-laws who'd supposedly dishonored them. "Is there a tradition of attacking women who go against the community's sexual norms?"

"In India, there are sometimes honor killings among Tamils, mostly over inter-caste marriages, and also some dowry deaths, but I'm not familiar with anything like that among Sri Lankan Tamils."

"Dowry deaths?" Giuliana asked, her pen stilling.

"It's illegal in India for a bride's parents to promise the groom's family money and goods for taking their daughter, but it happens anyway. After the wedding, if a bride's father doesn't pay as much as the groom's side expected, the groom or his mother may cause the bride to have a fatal 'accident' around the cooking fire. Or the family may hound her into suicide."

"My God," said Giuliana, "that's—"

Debora interrupted. "I know; it's horrifying. But I've never heard of any Tamil parents in Switzerland killing their children or children-in-law. Why? Are you investigating a homicide that might be an honor killing?"

Giuliana heard the eagerness in the journalist's voice. Whoops! She gave a vague answer, thanked her warmly, and hung up. Hopefully, there was no danger of Debora associating a Swiss killed in a bicycle accident with a Tamil honor killing.

And surely that was just the point. In honor killings, it was more important to eliminate the erring family member than the partner. Still, a lesbian relationship made this a special case. Giuliana thought again about the baby's paternity. Did Saritha's father know about his daughter? If so, did he feel used? Could he have resented Eberhart for taking his place in his child's life?

Staring across her desk at the painting of the wild Mediterranean garden, Giuliana suddenly remembered Vinz's meeting. It was two minutes after nine. She jumped up and jogged down the corridor to the conference.

"Good to know this is a real homicide investigation at last," Renzo said to her later. With characteristic efficiency, Vinz had gotten through the meeting on the Eberhart case in twenty minutes, and Rolf had agreed that the hit-and-run should be considered a deliberate killing. Vinz was now reviewing the evidence with his newly assigned prosecutor, Oliver Leuthard, whom they'd all worked with before and liked. After that, Vinz planned to talk to the person in charge of the holding cells at the *Amthaus*, Bern's central court, while Madeleine Trachsel tried to track down the suspended prison guards. With Rolf now back at his desk in the homicide room, Renzo and Giuliana were snatching a few minutes to catch up, still sitting across from each other at the meeting room's large table.

Before Giuliana could comment on the case's transition to murder, Renzo went on. "This business with the prison guards that Andrea Eberhart's boss at civilian service identified—well, it sounds farfetched to me." He shook his head. "I'd think if they wanted revenge on anyone, they'd go after the young Civi who still works at the *Amthaus*, the one who told Eberhart about the racism and bullying. Not after Andi." He rolled the sleeves of his pullover up to his elbows and then leaned back in his chair, folding his muscular forearms over his chest. "I'm glad Vinz is planning to warn the kid."

"Yeah, me too," she said. "As for leads, I still think this killing has something to do with the woman's personal life, not her job. I'm happy sticking to that for now. Sounds like you're okay with supporting me, which . . . I appreciate." She gave him what she hoped was a professional smile.

He grinned back, straightening up. "No problem. I'll call the head of Rainbow Families right now and see when I can line her up. Then I'll try Eberhart's curling teammate, the one who didn't like her." Renzo pulled his phone out and laid it on the table. "You going to schedule Eberhart's partner for today?"

"I can't. I'm taking a deposition from Kissling's ex-wife Iris tomorrow morning, and I've got witness statements to read before I'm ready—a lot of them."

"Oh, God." Renzo hid his face in his hands as he shook his head. When he looked up at her, she stared back, reading the same horror in his eyes that she knew he must be seeing in her own. "I don't think I'd be able to talk to her without choking up," he confessed. "How she must miss her little girls! It's unbearable to think about."

"I know . . . I can't . . ." Giuliana said and stopped. Suddenly it felt like too much emotion to put into words, even to Renzo. Grabbing her bag from the meeting room table, she stood up. "I'm going back to the office. I'll call Nisha Pragasam and set up a meeting with her for

Monday morning. If you find out anything you think I should know before I interview her . . ."

"Yeah, I'll keep you posted," Renzo said. "Good luck with Frau Kissling," he added, his voice full of concern.

She put some distance between them before turning. "Thanks," she said and left the room before she succumbed to his sympathy.

Renzo was right—she couldn't imagine how she was going to cope with the following day's interview. But she knew she would.

8

Renzo strolled into the Einstein Café on the ground floor of the stone building where the famous physicist had lived from 1903 to 1905. The building's museum was for tourists, but the café was extremely popular with locals. He'd been told to look for a fiftyish woman with short white hair and a green blazer, and he found her on a padded bench by the front window that looked onto Kramgasse, a cappuccino at her elbow. As he approached, she glanced up from her phone, and he saw her expression turn from blandly pleasant to genuinely warm. She stood and held out her hand to him while he was still struggling to place her. Why would he know the head of Rainbow Families?

"You're Angelo's father," she said. "I'm one of Théo's mothers. Tabea."

"Aha," he said. "Théo from kindergarten. Angelo is a great admirer of Théo's. Especially his boot-throwing skills."

She laughed. "Sadly, the teachers don't share Angelo's appreciation. Particularly after the tantrum Théo threw when one of them got his boot down from the roof. He thought a fire truck would have to come. I think he was expecting Fireman Sam to show up. Imagine his disappointment."

Renzo grinned at Tabea Jakob as she settled back into the seat across from him. "I'm Renzo. Sorry I didn't recognize you right off—I miss most family get-togethers at the kindergarten because of work."

"I'm not offended. I'm usually taken for Théo's grandmother anyway."

"Thanks for seeing me so quickly," Renzo said, turning to order espresso from a hovering waiter.

Tabea nodded, her face instantly grave, and said, "We're all broken up over Andi's death . . . and now it might be murder—that's even harder to bear."

Renzo had planned to take notes, but he realized the advantages of keeping this talk informal now that—thanks to their kids—he and Tabea were on a first-name basis, so he folded his hands on the table in front of him and tried to sound reassuring. "Well, we may be wrong about that, but it's one of the reasons I wanted to talk to you. Something that's worrying us is a stack of anonymous letters she's been getting over the past four years."

The woman across from him nodded as though she was expecting the question. "Andi mentioned them to me once, but I never took them seriously—because she didn't."

Renzo found this surprising. "Are they so common among gays and lesbians? I mean, have you received messages like that, with obscenities and death threats?"

The waiter brought Renzo's espresso and her tea. She poured milk into her cup and said, "I *have* received threats, and my guess is that anyone who has come out has been insulted to their face, subjected to obscene emails, or forced to delete rubbish from their social media sites. It's just—part of the package."

"That's . . ." Renzo began and then stopped. "I suppose I thought there was a lot less of that these days. Sorry to be so . . . naive."

"Don't apologize. I'm over fifty, don't forget. A seventeen-year-old coming out today will doubtless have a different experience from mine. Still, there are plenty of sickos out there even now. A group of us takes turns checking the Rainbow Families website and email account every day for nasty comments." Tabea drank some of her tea and added, "Actual letters on paper, though, mailed in an envelope with a stamp; I don't know of anyone besides Andi who got those regularly. Which does suggest that they might have been from someone who held a grudge against her specifically."

Renzo set down his cup. "What about other kinds of attacks? Was Frau Eberhart someone who drew particular hostility? Did you notice anyone targeting her physically—at a political rally, for example? Or taunting her personally?"

"In theory," Tabea answered, "you'd think that racists *and* homo-phobes would be after Andi because of Nisha's dark skin, but I can't say I've been aware of either one of them being singled out. We focus on portraying ourselves as good parents, so we try not to come across as raging radicals." She grinned, raising her eyebrows. "We bring our kids to our demos, and we carry posters with children's drawings and slogans like 'Love Makes a Family.' At our last rally, Nisha wore a sari and handed out balloons, and Andi carried Saritha in a baby wrap. I don't remember anyone harassing them at all. Or any of us, for that matter."

"You must have been ecstatic when the 'Marriage for Everyone' initiative passed." Renzo smiled at her. "And proud of everything you and your group have done to make it happen."

Tabea nodded. "Yes, my wife and I are finally married, and I'm Théo's legal mother at last. Not being able to adopt my own child upset me much more than the marriage thing. Thank God no one can take him away from me now. But there's still work to do. Lots of Swiss continue to have trouble with the idea of same-sex parents. Don't forget that thirty-six percent of the voters said no to 'Marriage for Everyone.'"

"Yeah." He drank some more coffee and considered how to word his next question. "Something else I need to know: is there a particular person in the LGBT . . . um . . ." he paused, knowing he was missing a letter or two, then carried on, "community that you think I should talk to about Andi? Someone . . . someone Frau Pragasam wouldn't know about?"

Tabea had been shaking her head, but at Renzo's last question, she looked up at him, her chin cocked. She contemplated him for a moment before saying, "I think you just tactfully asked me if Andi was cheating on Nisha. Am I right?"

He shrugged. "Well, more or less. Or there could be someone from her past."

"I don't think Andi's been involved with anyone since Nisha," she said, "and I don't know of any previous lovers with serious grudges. Andi was blunt, and the way she spoke her mind sometimes upset or hurt people. But not... not to the point of murder! Besides, she's settled down since she met Nisha and stopped being such a crusader. Which is normal. She and Nisha were busy getting on with their lives together, like any young couple. It's—" Her voice broke, and she reached for her napkin and wiped her eyes. "I didn't know her *that* well," she said, "but it's just so sad. And without Andi, Nisha's situation is going to be complicated. I don't think she can ask her family to lend a hand. I wonder if I could organize some help among Rainbow Family members. Vivienne Marti lives near Nisha, and Andi's given her son Tobias a lot of support..."

Renzo watched Tabea transform her sorrow into action, performing the alchemy of practical women everywhere. He was reminded of his mother at the dinner table, grieving for a neighbor who'd just been diagnosed with breast cancer or worrying about a colleague at the factory whose husband had left her. Before the telling of the story was done, she'd already be marshaling her forces—along with those of her reluctant husband and children—and planning her campaign against *la sfortuna*. Misfortune, she'd always point out, could fall upon anyone, anytime, without warning, and friends had a duty to help those caught in its clutches.

He left the café with Tabea, and they parted under the sidewalk arcade. She walked away to her office on nearby Junkerngasse while Renzo stood for a moment scribbling in his pocket notebook, conscious of details he'd want to share with Vinz and Giuliana. Then he got out his phone and called the next name on his list: Barbara Weber, the curler who'd wanted to be skip.

At first, he thought a child had answered the phone. "I don't have time," she said when he asked her to come to the police station as soon as possible to answer questions about her teammate. "I'm busy."

He realized Barbara was one of those women who cultivated a high-pitched, girlish voice and reminded himself that she was an adult—and a potential suspect. "Where do you work?"

"At the Department of Motor Vehicles. And I . . ."

The DMV was only about a mile from the police station. The woman had to have a lunch hour. "I'll expect you at twelve forty-five. The address is Nordring 30."

"Why should I give up my lunchtime for . . .?"

"Twelve forty-five at the station. Be on time."

"Fine, then." A muttered "What a pig!" floated over the line before she cut him off.

Her hostility intrigued him. If she was always like this, then no wonder no one wanted her to captain the curling team. Did she have a particular problem with the police? Or was it with authority in general?

He was still wondering about the woman as he paid for parking at the Rathausgasse underground garage and started downstairs to his car. Before he'd gone two steps, his phone rang. He answered without looking at the caller, assuming it was work, and then groaned out loud when he heard his sister's voice saying, "*Ciao, fratellino!*"

Oh, God. He loved Bianca, but a call out of the blue like this usually meant he was about to be enlisted in one of her family-related projects.

"All I have to say is hello, and you're already groaning. What kind of a greeting is that?" Underneath the attempt at humor, she sounded genuinely hurt.

"Sorry," he said. "Honestly, I didn't mean it. It's good to hear your voice. I'm just busy."

"Okay," she said, to his surprise. "When is a good time to call you back when Fränzi isn't around?"

He remembered Antonietta saying that Fränzi, Bianca, and his mother had been discussing him the day before. Perhaps it was worth hearing what Bianca had to say. He did have a bit of time before Barbara Weber showed up at the station, so he walked away from the parking kiosk and stood by the side of the road, gazing down through a veil of trees and shrubs at the Aare flowing far below. Nearby, a steep path led down the hill to a playground by the river where he had taken his children a few times. Here and there, late snowdrops waved, and early yellow and purple crocuses were poking up. Despite the chilly wind driving gray clouds across the sky, he felt glad to be out of doors, watching the river.

"Go ahead then. Did you and Fränzi have a nice chat about me with Mamma? Discussing what a shit husband I am?" He realized that now he was the one trying to hide his hurt feelings.

"How did you . . .? Oh, no. I was afraid Antonietta was listening. I'm so sorry."

Her warm voice, combined with the endless movement of the gray river, comforted him, but he wasn't ready to let go of his anger yet. "Is this call about something Fränzi said? Because I already know I work too much, but . . ."

"Stop. I'm not calling to criticize you. Mamma and I are fed up with Fränzi complaining about her life. We're on your side, Renzo. That's why I'm calling."

Renzo hadn't realized how upset he'd been at the idea of his big sister and his mother joining forces with his wife. He closed his eyes in relief. "Thanks," he said. "That's . . . good to hear. Sorry I was so . . ." He didn't say the word he was thinking, which was "defensive."

"What we want to know is: how can we help? Fränzi moans about you every time she sees one of us"—Renzo couldn't help but smile at the scorn in his sister's voice—"but I've never heard you complain about her. Still, I assume things aren't great at home. So do you want to talk? Not now, I mean, but . . . We could have a family meeting." He could hear how delighted she was with her suggestion, and he groaned again, realizing that *he* was Bianca's latest family project.

"God, no." His two sisters, his mother, and his older brother listening to him whine about his wife, all feeling sorry for him? Christ, would they invite his sister- and brothers-in-law, too? He couldn't imagine anything more humiliating. And useless. Still . . . "Davide," he said.

As his brother's name popped out of his mouth, he knew instantly that he wanted no one else. Davide, stronger, taller, three years older, and a born athlete, was always ready to defend his little brother from anyone who dared make fun of him. The fact that Renzo was no longer plump, shy, and bookish and could now defend himself had not changed the way Renzo felt about Davide. His big brother would always be on his side, no matter what. "I'll talk to him."

"Good," said Bianca. "I'll tell him to call you. And don't forget we love you." She hung up then, without any of her usual prying questions and nagging reminders, leaving Renzo thoughtful as he jogged down the parking garage stairs to his car.

The downstairs buzzer broke through Nisha's apathy. She forced herself off the green paisley sofa, where she'd been huddled around the sleeping form of Saritha, whom she was wearing against her chest in a baby wrap. Managing to hitch up the wrap without waking Sari, she shuffled toward the door and mumbled, "Hello?" into the speakerphone.

It was Viv checking in. Nisha pushed the buzzer, opened the apartment door, and hunched against the doorframe to wait. At the top of the stairs, Vivienne rushed forward to throw her arms around Nisha and Saritha together. She kept up a continuous stream of soothing chatter, even as Nisha crumbled into tears.

"Oh, it's terrible, just terrible. I got a call from Tabea Jakob at Rainbow Families. She asked me . . . and of course, I came. I should have come sooner, but . . ." She released Nisha from her embrace, clasped her by the shoulders, and stared into her eyes. Nisha grasped for something appropriate to say, but Vivienne rattled on. "I'm so sorry this has happened to you. I'll take Sari anytime, anytime at all—except when I have my patients, of course. And if you need food, company, anything, you must call me. I'll see what my Ayurvedic cookbook says about grief and make you some meals."

"You're so good," Nisha managed at last as she freed herself from the woman's embrace. "Let me make you some coffee." She tried to smile. Vivienne always meant well, and she was Nisha's most reliable babysitter, but her intensity could be tiring. Still, Nisha told herself, it was good for her to be forced to interact with another human being besides her daughter.

"Oh, tea, please," Vivienne said. "I'm off coffee again. Do you still have that wonderful detox tea with fennel seeds and ginger? That would be perfect. I'll make it—you shouldn't have to do a thing right now."

Nisha was already heading into the kitchen, finding her voice as she forced herself to move. "No, I'll get it. I need something to do. Just sit down and keep me company. Of course I have Sari, but . . ." She drifted into silence.

"What syllables is she babbling? I bet there's a lot of 'ya-ya-ya.' I remember when Rin . . ."

While Vivienne reminisced about her older son's first words, Nisha found the tea her friend liked. She'd always taken comfort from her mother's Ayurvedic remedies, even if she hadn't completely believed in them. But when Vivienne touted those same cures, Nisha felt annoyed. Was she being biased? She put some cardamom cookies on a plate and thought about Andi's reactions to Viv and her passion for alternative medicine.

One Saturday morning about six weeks earlier, when Vivienne had dropped in for a chat, she'd brought up her son yet again and talked about some important cancer research he was doing at university. Then she'd gone on to rave about how kinesiology had gotten rid of her lingering cough. Finally, she recommended a homeopathic treatment for Andi's sore shoulder before leaving because she had a client due at her craniosacral therapy practice. As soon as she was gone, Andi, who only trusted conventional medicine and treated even its claims with skepticism, had burst into laughter over Vivienne's mishmash of convictions about healing.

"They're all placebo remedies, and I know placebos work, as long as you don't apply them to a heart attack. But why doesn't Viv use this craniosacral thingy for getting rid of coughs, pulled muscles, and all the rest? You'd think she'd stick to her own brand of quackery." Shaking her head, Andi suddenly stopped laughing and turned to Nisha with a frown. "No way are we *ever* going to let her use Sari as a guinea pig for one of her remedies, right? No peculiar baby teas allowed, okay? No bizarre poking and prodding of her sweet head in this house, please." Nisha had no problem agreeing.

Hearing Andi's voice in her mind, Nisha felt more tears coming, and she stood at the sink, rinsing a dish over and over while she dug for self-control.

Once the teapot, cups, and cookies were on the low table in front of the sofa, she sat down next to her neighbor. The truth was that she didn't think she could have managed without Vivienne's advice and help since Saritha had arrived. Nor her company, especially when Andi was at work. And now she'd need Viv's companionship more than ever.

She poured out the tea and waited for a pause in Vivienne's flow of talk. "Sorry we missed you on Tuesday night. We all three went for a walk. Did Andi get back to you before she—" Nisha's voice broke.

"Oh, don't worry. It was a question about her work at the Civi. I have a friend whose son is just starting his civilian service."

"And I'm sorry for missing your calls, too," Nisha said. "For weeks now, I've been putting my phone on mute, so I can nap when the baby does, and then I forget to check my messages."

Vivienne squeezed her hand. "It doesn't matter."

Nisha was trying to force herself to have a conversation. "How's work? Do you have any new patients?"

The older woman set her teacup down. "Yes, I had someone start last week. She had no idea what to expect; a friend had recommended me. She's been having chronic digestion problems. I started with stimulations of the skull and spine—just the gentlest touches, you know—and she says there's already an improvement."

"Are you seeing patients every day now?"

"I've increased to three mornings a week and two afternoons." She took a sip of her tea. "Tell me, are you going to have Andi's funeral in the Hindu temple where your mother volunteers? I'd love to see a ceremony there. Such a fascinating..."

Nisha shook her head. "No. I'm going to let Andi's parents say goodbye to her at the church in their village. Saritha and I will be part of that. It's so important to them, and I can pray for Andi in the temple on my own."

Vivienne put a hand on Nisha's forearm. "That is so kind of you." Her eyes filled with tears again. "Andi was kind, too," she whispered. "She was so good to Tobias. And giving Selina and Maya tips when they started figure skating. But I feel like I never really got to know her. Not like I know you. And then she—" Vivienne broke off as Saritha woke up and began to fuss.

"Give her to me," Vivienne offered. "So you can drink your tea. I need to let mine cool anyway."

Grateful, Nisha lifted the baby out of the cloth wrap and handed her over. However much Viv occasionally annoyed her, there was something reassuring about her chatty, capable presence. Nisha was meeting with her mother later that afternoon, but given how complicated her relationship with her parents was, the visit was likely to be more painful than comforting.

"Thanks for coming by, Vivienne." She leaned sideways along the sofa and kissed her friend's cheek.

"I left her searching for her bike helmet. She seemed perfectly okay to me."

Barbara Weber's voice was even squeakier in person than it had sounded on the phone. It lacked the breathy quality of a woman aiming for sexiness, ending up as something like a whine. Sitting in the interview room on the opposite side of the table from Renzo, she looked like a big-eyed baby doll that had grown a Barbie's body. She seemed to have Barbie's wardrobe, too—she was wearing a tight pink skirt decorated with purple hearts, along with purple heels. Renzo, with two sisters, one daughter, and several nieces, knew all about Barbie. He was not a fan.

"Let me review what you've told me," he said as the woman played with her ponytail. "Wednesday's curling practice was normal; Frau Eberhart didn't appear drunk, drugged, ill, or overtired. Afterward, you and she and your teammate Claudine walked out of the building together, and Claudine split off toward the parking lot. You and Frau Eberhart were unlocking your bikes when she said, 'Where's my helmet?' She searched for it on the ground among the other bicycles, and when she didn't find it, she went back to ask if it had been turned in. As you rode off, she was heading into the curling hall."

"Yeah, that's it."

"Where did you go from there?"

"I rode home to Ittigen."

"Do you own a car?"

"No. I sometimes use my boyfriend's car to get to practice, but he needed it that night, so I had to take my bike." She sounded put out by this, but Renzo had the feeling that her disgruntled tone was habitual. He'd check on her story about the boyfriend's car, although, if she'd wanted to kill Andi by driving into her bike, she could have rented one.

"I'd like your boyfriend's name, please."

"What if I don't want to tell you?" she said with a toss of her head. The ponytail swung over one shoulder.

Renzo leaned toward her suddenly, and the chair squeaked as she jerked back. "His name?" Renzo repeated. He knew he sounded menacing and was glad of it.

"Stefan Rolli," she whispered.

"Phone number?"

She got her phone out of her bag and read out the number, which Renzo scribbled down. Then he let silence fall.

"What do you want from me?" Weber's high-pitched voice was suddenly more scared than sulky.

"You wanted to be your team's skip, didn't you? The women picked

Andi instead. Now she's dead, and you can try for skip again."

She seemed to examine each word, looking for the trick behind it, before she answered, "So what?"

"So, did you kill her?"

"I thought it was an accident."

"Do you think you'd be here answering questions if we were sure about that?"

She stared blankly at him as she took this in. Then she looked shocked, which he assumed meant that she'd understood him, and began to speak very fast. "I'd never kill anyone. Of course I wouldn't. But if someone *did* kill her, I'm not surprised. Not a bit. And I'm not going to say, 'Oh, I can't believe it. Such a niiice person.'" She pitched her voice even higher as she said this and mimed an angelic face. "Because she wasn't."

Well, at least Babs was honest. "So you didn't like her."

"No, I didn't. She had to be right about, like, everything, always. It's weird how so many of the other girls looked up to her. 'Andi will know what to do.' Like she was God. Creepy! And the way she showed off photos of her Tamil girlfriend with that baby. Just—kind of sick if you ask me."

Renzo listened until the eerily childish voice was silent again. Her comments about Andi's relationship called to mind the anonymous letters, which were still being analyzed for trace evidence.

"Right, Frau Weber. Come with me now. We need a record of your fingerprints."

"No." She didn't so much refuse as speak in disbelief. "Why? I don't want the police to have my fingerprints. You can't do that."

"Actually, I can—we need them for elimination purposes." That was always a useful phrase. He stood up and waited until she stood, too. "Bring your things. We won't be coming back to this room. Not today, at least."

He opened the door, and she walked through it, eyes hot with anger, lower lip thrust out. As he followed her down the corridor, he could hear her muttering the word "fascist." Swiss citizen though he was, hearing that word applied to himself made him feel very Italian. Three of his great-uncles on his mother's side had been partisans during the Second World War, and two of them had been killed, one by Italian *fascisti* and one by Nazis. These goddamned neutral Swiss didn't even know what a fascist *was*.

Nasty as Babs Weber seemed, he couldn't imagine her writing those very odd poison-pen letters. Deliberately driving her car into Andi's bicycle, though, that he had no trouble picturing.

9

Every Thursday and Friday, Devi Pragasam, Nisha's mother, helped to cook and serve the daily Ayurvedic lunch in the House of Religions' glass-fronted lobby. The cheap, tasty meal—four vegetable dishes with rice—was popular with people who worked in the neighborhood, so the tables were often full. When the cleanup was done, she spent an hour or two in the Hindu temple, the largest and most prominent of the House of Religions' different places of worship and a center for Sri Lankan Tamil culture. There was always something for her to do there: making garlands, preparing food for a festival, dusting shrines. People came and went all day—praying or performing *puja*, helping with temple upkeep as she did, consulting the priest about a coming-of-age ceremony or a wedding. And that was without visitors wandering in to gawk and teachers bringing classes of children to learn something about Hinduism. She never minded that; a temple should be a lively place. Besides, the whole reason for this temple's central location was to encourage the Swiss to feel more comfortable with the religions practiced by "their" foreigners. When the House of Religions opened its doors, there had been a lot in the newspapers about integration. Devi didn't read the Swiss papers, but her younger son Rajan did. He'd made fun of the idea that integration was furthered by a new building that housed mosques, churches, and temples for foreigners but not a single place where Swiss Protestants or Catholics worshipped.

"Maybe this will force the Ethiopian Christians and Syrian Alawites to exchange a few words," he'd scoffed, "but I don't see how that's going to make the Swiss more friendly to anyone. It's just a museum to them. Or maybe a circus."

"The Swiss congregations had places to pray already; they didn't need new ones," his father had said. He took Rajan's sarcastic remarks, whether at the expense of Tamils or Swiss, as personal insults since he was the one who'd brought the family to Bern during the civil war.

It was ironic that Rajan complained about the Swiss not respecting Tamil culture when he valued Tamil customs the least of her three children. Sometimes he didn't seem very different from the Swiss he'd grown up with. Mathan, her older son, tried to act more traditional than his father, which sometimes made him ridiculous. And then there was Nisha, who'd made the strangest choices of all.

It was because of Nisha and Saritha that she'd gotten involved at the House of Religions, which was a few blocks from their apartment: it was easy to pay them a quick visit after her trips to the temple. At first, she'd only dared to stay a few minutes, but soon she realized that no one, not even the gossipiest of the other women at the temple, paid attention to what time she left and whether she went straight to the tram stop or did a few errands first. She could visit Nisha and Sari every Thursday and Friday if she wanted to, as long as she was standing in the kitchen making dinner when her husband arrived home from work.

Today she went to Nisha's straight from cleaning up after the lunch crowd. She'd spoken to her daughter several times since Andi's death two days earlier but hadn't seen her. When Nisha opened the apartment door, her mother took in her unbrushed hair, the spots of baby food and formula on her blouse, and her grim, gaunt face. As Nisha stood back to let her mother into the flat, she began to cry, and Devi took her daughter into her arms, crooning while Nisha sobbed on her shoulder. Sri Lanka had been through a twenty-six-year civil war—Devi knew all about grief.

They stood in the flat's tiny entrance hall, and she rocked Nisha's body back and forth, soothing her with silly endearments and letting her have a good long cry. Then, slowly, she pulled away from their embrace.

"There, now. Time to quiet down, or you'll wake the baby. We need to talk about how you're going to manage your life, but first, we need some tea to drink with these *rava laddu* I made last night."

The sweet balls of semolina flavored with coconut, raisins, cashews, and cardamom that Devi brought out of her bag were a childhood favorite of Nisha's. But what Nisha needed most, her mother knew, wasn't kindness or pastries but routine. Having a child to take care of and a job to go to, carrying on for the sake of others—that was what beat back the worst agonies of grief. "Go wash your face now, *en chellam*, while I make tea. And brush your hair while you're at it."

When Nisha came back, she'd braided her hair and put on a clean sweater, but her body still fell into a slump as she sat down at the kitchen table, where a pot of tea and a plate of sweets waited. Devi listened patiently as Nisha told her everything about Andi's death that she'd already said twice on the phone. *You can tell me as many times as you like, my girl,* she thought—*just spew it out and get rid of it.* Gently, she turned the conversation to Nisha's plans. When did Saritha start at the daycare, and how would she get there? How much did it cost? And the rent? How much was Nisha expecting to earn?

An hour and much discussion later, Devi sat with Saritha on her lap, watching her daughter make another pot of tea. They'd made progress—Nisha was thinking about the practicalities now. Devi wrapped her arms around her precious granddaughter and kissed the top of her head as she watched Nisha get ready to say something that would upset her. It had happened so often over the past six years that Devi now recognized the signs. How could this quiet, loving daughter, so intelligent, such a hard worker, so well behaved for so many years, be such a source of sorrow to her family? All because she'd decided to spend her adult life with a Swiss woman she'd chosen herself, and not a Tamil man chosen by her parents. And now that woman was dead, and Nisha was alone with her baby. What new disaster was she going to reveal? Devi's muscles tightened with dread.

"Amma." Nisha put the new pot of tea on the table but didn't sit down. Afraid to meet her daughter's eyes, Devi stared at the teapot.

"I think someone ran into Andi on purpose. I don't think her bike accident *was* an accident—I think she was killed. I've gone to the police, and they are investigating it."

Devi was so surprised that her grip on the baby loosened for a moment, and the little body lurched in her lap. "But . . . how can that be? Are you saying you think someone . . . *murdered* her?" Devi had felt shy around her daughter's friend, but Andi had never treated her with anything but warmth and respect. How could anyone hate Andi enough to kill her? Everyone needed someone to blame when a loved one died. Surely this strange story was just a product of Nisha's grief. And to go to the police! My God, she thought. How could Nisha be so . . . Swiss? "No one would do such a thing," she said. "The police will think you're crazy. Crazy with sorrow," she added so as not to sound too harsh.

Nisha continued to gaze at her mother. "The police took me seriously," she said. She sat down at last and poured both of them more tea. Then, reaching out to take her mother's hand, she said, "You gave Mathan my new phone number. Did you give him our address, too?"

"What does your brother have to do with this?"

Saritha, perhaps in response to her grandmother's sharp tone of voice, began to whimper. Devi rocked the baby in her arms, keeping her eyes on Nisha's face.

"Since you gave him my number," Nisha told her, "he has sent me cruel texts. He has called me three times to tell me how appalled he is by my behavior, how ashamed he is, and how much he hates me—and Andi. He has called us both every bad word he knows—well, every bad word that *I* know, at least." Nisha gave a dark laugh.

For the moment, Devi couldn't find her voice. She'd always found it hard to get angry with her older son, but a seed of rage was sprouting inside her now.

But she said nothing, so Nisha continued. "Is it possible that Mathan or someone he knows—or someone Appa knows—killed Andi?"

Devi's thoughts banged around her head like trapped birds. She wished Nisha would stop talking. This was something she needed to think about alone; she needed time.

But Nisha wasn't giving her time. "You know how Mathan feels about the importance of family and tradition and proper behavior and all that . . . trash." She spat out the last word. "He's bossier with Geeta than Appa has ever been with you." Geeta, Mathan's wife, didn't dare complain to her mother-in-law, but Devi had heard Mathan order her around; it was shameful, really, the lack of respect and affection he showed his wife. And he'd said lots of awful things about Nisha and Andi to his parents. But to say such things to his sister's face? If he could do that, could he also have done . . . something to Andi? She couldn't, wouldn't, believe it. And yet . . .

Nisha went on, echoing Devi's thoughts. "Maybe Mathan thought if Andi wasn't in my life, I'd move home and . . . and our family wouldn't have to be ashamed of me. I don't want to believe he'd hurt her, but . . . Could he have thought he was doing me a favor?" Saritha's fussing had turned to screaming, which made it even harder to think.

Nisha stood, took the baby from her mother, and jiggled her on her hip to soothe her. "Amma, say something. Say anything. Don't pretend you can't hear me."

"You went to the police." Devi focused on that, knowing she was avoiding thinking about her oldest son. "You talked to the Swiss police about Mathan."

"No, of course not. I never said a word about him. But I'm convinced the person I love most in the world was murdered. I had to tell the police. I *had* to."

"The person you love most in the world," Devi repeated, whispering.

"Well, except for Sari."

Devi got up. "It's getting late, Nisha, and I need to go home. I'll try to come again next Thursday." She paused. "If you are convinced Andi was killed by someone . . . on purpose, then you had to go to the police. I can see that. But Mathan?"

"Just think about it, Amma. I don't want to believe it any more than you do, but . . ."

"I promise to think about it and talk to him. Ah, my dear, if I'd known he was insulting you and Andi like that, I'd have tried to stop him. I'm so sorry."

Nisha's answer was to follow her mother back to the door and hug her again. "Thank you for coming, Amma. It's . . . so important to me. And to Sari."

As Devi walked to the tram stop, she tried to push the idea of Andi's death being deliberate out of her mind. She'd have to return to it soon because she had to think about Mathan. But right now, she played back in her mind what her daughter had said about Andrea Eberhart. The person she loved most in the world.

Devi had known that Nisha and Andi were sexual partners, but she had not let herself think about what that meant. As for who Saritha's father was and how the baby had been conceived, Devi's mind shied away from that question. But Nisha's words sank into her now. She felt the strangeness of her daughter's choice more than ever before, but that didn't quench her pain at Nisha's grief. It filled her chest until she thought she'd choke. The idea of being able to share a home with someone whom you could love like a best friend, a beloved sister, and a spouse, all in one. She couldn't picture it, not really, but she could imagine that after the joy of finding such a person and thinking you'd be together for life, losing her would be almost unbearable.

Tears for her daughter's loss ran down Devi's cheeks as she waited for the tram, and she wiped them away without shame.

Nisha put Saritha down on the kitchen floor and opened the cabinet under the stove, so the baby could pull pots and pans out of it. She cleared her mother's teacup. Two worries pounded in her head, but she couldn't seem to focus on solving them, so they just hammered away. Work and childcare. Work and childcare.

They could stay in the apartment without Andi's salary if Nisha worked more. But Andi's plans for sharing childcare with Nisha were just a cruel joke now. Nisha thought again of Saritha growing up with no memory of Andi and willed herself not to cry. She'd cried enough with her mother—now she had to think about what she was going to say to her boss and the head of the daycare center.

Desperate for calm, she went to their little office, took a sheet of paper from the stack in the printer, and, back at the kitchen counter, wrote in large letters:

Increase job to 50% or more.

Extend daycare to three days a week.

Monday morning, first thing, she'd force herself to make the calls. She wrote the heading "Monday" on her two-item list. Her phone rang.

"Nisha," said Andi's brother Yannick. He choked and stopped.

"It's okay, Yannick." She spoke gently. "Take your time."

"Sophie and Hugo and I are here in Ochsenbach with my parents. It's . . . it's awful. We're supposed to be supporting each other, and instead, we're making each other feel worse." He paused, then struggled on. "My mother keeps talking about the funeral. On and on. She told me you said she and Paps should plan everything and hold the service here, but I told her it's not right. The police won't release . . . they won't let us have a funeral yet anyway, so there's time for you to be sure that's really . . . God, I can't believe I'm talking to you about Andi's funeral. I miss her so much. And you must be . . . And Sari . . ."

"Yannick," Nisha said again. Though filled with grief, his voice soothed her; he and Andi sounded alike in so many small ways. "Do you think it would comfort your parents to spend some time with Saritha? I mean, maybe if—"

"Oh God, not that," he interrupted. "Tell me about the funeral. Are you sure?"

"I've thought about it, and I *am* sure. It's more important to your parents—her coffin at the church service and her grave in their church-yard, near to them. I'd have a cremation, and that would upset them, I'm sure it would. And Andi, well, you know she wouldn't care."

She could hear Yannick breathing in and out as if to calm himself. "My parents . . . they want to come to your apartment. Can you stand it?"

"Of course I can. I'd like them to spend time with Saritha. When would they come?"

"This Sunday?"

"Fine. I can make something they'd find normal, like roast chicken with mashed potatoes and gravy. Do you think they'd like that?"

"No, no, we'll just come for a short visit. I'll bring them. Let's make it around three in the afternoon. For coffee. It . . . it will be all right."

Something in Yannick's tone told Nisha he was convinced it would *not* be all right. The tiny hope that she and her parents-in-law could develop an affectionate relationship through Sari was flickering. But she wouldn't let it go out.

"What about Sophie? Is she coming on Sunday?"

Yannick's wife, Sophie, was a calming presence—Andi's parents loved her, and she had more patience with them than their son did. And much more than Andi had ever had. It was one of the few things about her partner that had made Nisha angry—Andi's impatience and even, sometimes, unkindness to her parents.

Yannick said nothing for what seemed like a long while. "Sophie's not coming," he answered at last. "She's . . . not coping well right now. With Andi's death or with . . . with anything. I'm so sorry, but she says she's going to keep her distance for a while until she . . ." Yannick trailed off.

Nisha realized that she'd been clinging to the idea of Sophie's support, not just with her parents-in-law but with her whole life now that Andi was gone. She'd thought Sophie liked her for herself, not just as her sister-in-law's partner. But if Sophie was drawing away . . . Well, she wasn't going to beg. But what the hell did Sophie have to cope with compared to Nisha herself?

"Well, that's too bad," she told Yannick, unable to hide her resentment. "I could have used her help. You know how much I'd like Sari to be part of your family, for Andi's sake, but . . ." *But right now, she's just a little brown baby that reminds all of you how strange Andi's life was.* This thought swelled in her mind and made her even angrier. Was Yannick going to drift away now, too?

He managed a strangled "See you Sunday" and hung up.

Nisha slumped against the counter. She wouldn't be able to bear the Eberharts pulling back from her. Damn them!

She forced herself to stand up straight. Her in-laws were coming to visit in two days. If she wanted them to care about her and Sari, she'd have to make an effort.

She pulled the to-do list back toward her again.

Clean.

Get groceries.

Bake cake?

She stared at what she'd written and added:

Call cop.

Now she had plans and work to do. She'd start with a shopping list.

Clunk, clunk, clunk. Saritha was attacking a frying pan with a wooden spoon. She glanced up from where she sat on the kitchen floor to beam at her mother. For the first time since learning about Andi's death forty hours earlier, Nisha smiled back.

10

Kirchenfeld in Bern,
Friday evening, March 27

Giuliana knew she'd be making dinner for herself and the kids on Friday night since Ueli had a late interview for his article on shady fundraising practices. But on her way home, he sent her a text: *Lukas asked if Niko and new friend Joel could stay to eat. Said yes—hope that's okay. Lots of sausages in freezer!*

Three eleven-year-old boys for dinner. When Isabelle found out, she groaned. "Have fun! I'll eat in my room." She took a yogurt and an apple out of the fridge, poured granola into a bowl, grabbed a spoon from the cutlery drawer, and closed her bedroom door behind her with an ostentatious sigh.

"Wish *I* could eat alone," muttered Giuliana as she microwaved sausages, put water on to boil for elbow macaroni, and began cutting carrots into sticks and apples into quarters to give the meal a semblance of nutrition. Munching on a carrot stick, she decided she'd make herself a plate of bread, cheese, and fruit to eat after the boys were done.

She called them into the kitchen and sat down with them. Over loud boy-chewing and the clatter of silverware, she talked to Niko, who'd been friends with Lukas since kindergarten; he was as calm and quiet as Lukas was excitable and talkative, and he had a natural kindness and sense of fairness that made him special.

"I got new shoes, and my feet are two sizes bigger than Lukas's now," he told her, holding one enormous foot in a garish sneaker almost under her nose.

"Yeah, and that's why you fell over in basketball today, Bigfoot. You were crap!"

She looked sharply at the new boy, Joel. He hadn't made this comment in the sort of affectionate, teasing tone Lukas might have used but with a sneer.

She stopped attempting to chat with the three of them; instead, she sat and listened. She was used to Niko's and Lukas's silly and sometimes boastful or teasing talk, but their affection for each other was never far from the surface. With Joel added to the mix, the three kids seemed shrill, almost out of control. They picked on each other mercilessly, and in Joel's voice, she continued to hear a note of malice. Niko and Lukas were vying for his attention.

She excused the boys from kitchen cleanup for the sake of a little peace and time to think. As she was wiping down the counter, Lukas came into the kitchen alone, although she could see Joel waiting in the hall behind him. "Joel wants to spend the night," he murmured.

Niko and Lukas had been spending the night at each other's houses for years. But Joel? Lukas's quiet voice and the way he'd worded his request stopped her. She took a hard look at her son's rigid posture and at Joel waiting in the hall behind him and said, loud enough for Joel to hear, "That's not going to work out tonight, I'm afraid. Maybe another time."

The relief on Lukas's face told her she'd called it right. "I also think it's time for your friends to go home now," she told him. She followed him out of the kitchen and herded the other two boys to the door. "Where do you live, Joel?

He shrugged. "Close."

"I'll just call your mother and let her know you're on your way."

"She's not home," he said and left without giving her the number.

She dug out Lukas's class list and called the landline next to Joel's name. Sure enough, no one answered.

She found Lukas sprawled across his bed. "You didn't want Joel to spend the night," she stated. He grunted. "Are you sure he's a good friend for you and Niko? He didn't seem to be treating you very well."

"Niko's stupid," Lukas mumbled.

She wanted to say that Niko, his best friend since the age of four, was not the one he should be calling stupid. Instead, she sat down on the bed. "What's going on, love?"

"I'm fine, school's fine, nothing's going on." He intoned it all in a single breath.

She sat a while longer, waiting. Then her cell phone rang, and, reluctantly, she got up to answer.

It was Renzo. "I'm out with Fränzi, so I'll make this quick, but I thought you'd want to know about the anonymous letters. Just got an email saying whoever sent them has left fingerprints everywhere. But they don't belong to anyone in the databases, nor to that woman from Eberhart's curling team. Still, the ridge density shows that they are almost certainly a woman's. The lab will try to get DNA off the envelope flaps and see what they can find out about the paper. But that's going to take a while."

"Good to know. Thanks for . . ." She stopped because a deafening roar filled the background of Renzo's call. "What's that? Where are you calling from?"

"I'm in a restaurant bathroom—that's the hand dryer. Fränzi and I are eating out before going dancing. So I'd better stop; I just wanted to fill you in." He was gone.

She imagined what her life would be like if Ueli resented her job so much that she could only make work calls in secret when she went to the john. Poor Renzo. Poor Fränzi, too, she supposed—but her sympathies were mainly for her fellow cop.

She went back to Lukas's room. To her surprise, he'd turned out the light. Still, she resumed her place on the edge of his bed. He lay facing away from her, but she could tell from his breathing that he wasn't asleep.

She laid a hand on his back. "What happened to all that talk about swords?" she asked. "I enjoyed hearing about steel from Damascus and—where else? Some place famous for swords since Roman times?"

"Toledo," Lukas mumbled into his pillow, but that was all. Her ploy to get him to talk hadn't worked. She waited another few minutes, her hand stroking his back, then kissed his cheek and got up. Finally, as she reached the door, he mumbled again, "Joel has a sword."

"Does he?" She waited but, hearing only silence, gave up and closed his door.

Fetching her laptop, she opened it on the kitchen table. The next day she'd record Iris Kissling's deposition, and it surprised her to discover how little information the thirty-six-year-old seemed to have provided the police until now. Giuliana had read everything that she'd been able to find in the police records, coupled with transcripts of what Iris had said to the police, but it was obvious that no one had been able to get much information out of her, nor had the heart to try. Putting pressure on a woman whose ex-husband had just murdered their two small children would be too cruel.

The police already had all the important facts of the case. But what better person could there be to help her understand Kissling's motives for killing his little girls than his ex-wife? She was convinced Iris could give her some insights. But *would* she?

11

"It's hard to talk about it all again," Iris Kissling told Giuliana calmly. She shifted slightly in the hard plastic chair and smoothed the full skirt of her brightly patterned dress while the microphone clipped to her collar whistled with feedback.

Giuliana checked that the recording equipment for the deposition was correctly adjusted and told herself that if this woman could achieve such self-control, so could she. Iris must have suffered an untold amount and still be living through agonies every day. With her composure and her colorful clothes, the bereaved mother seemed to be announcing that she was tired of pity. Giuliana admired her courage and told herself to keep an appropriate professional distance. She owed it to Iris to do the best job she could.

"The truth is, Frau Kissling, I can't promise you that this will be the last interview. As you know, we're gathering information for your ex-husband's trial, and new questions will probably force us to turn to you again. I'm sorry." Giuliana sat across from the woman at a rectangular table. The small room was sparse, with a few potted ferns on the cabinets running along the wall under the windows to lighten the place up.

"I understand," the woman said with a sad smile. "I've worked as a law firm secretary for years. I haven't taken depositions, of course, but I think I understand the process. I thought about studying law myself, but . . . well, that wasn't to be." She touched one of her pearl earrings gently, her face pensive.

Giuliana found her easy to talk to. "Was that where you were working when you met Manfred Kissling?" She knew the answer, but it seemed a good place to start.

Iris crossed her legs and smoothed her skirt again. "No, I was at a different law firm then. Manfred came in to have some documents notarized. I was only twenty-two, and he was seven years older. I thought he was handsome but also very shy. I already had a boyfriend, of course—I've always had boyfriends." Another smile. "But I was attracted to Manfred."

Giuliana waited for Iris to say what a mistake that attraction had been—but she didn't. So Giuliana asked, "According to my notes, you married Herr Kissling when you were twenty-four, and Lea was born seven years later. Why did you and Herr Kissling wait so long to have your first child?"

"Is there something wrong with that?" Iris's face still wore its expression of pensive sadness, but her voice was sharp. Defensive, even.

"Of course not. I'm only asking you because . . . well, as you know from the letter we sent, the prosecution needs to understand Herr Kissling's motives for . . . the crime, so I need to ask you about his relationship with you and your daughters. Was it a joint decision to postpone having children?"

"Mänu—that's what I've always called him; Manfred is such an old-fashioned name—was very eager to have children when we first got married, but I was so young that I wasn't interested. And then, after a few years, he didn't talk about having kids anymore, so I stayed on the pill. Eventually, I got worried that the pill wasn't good for me. I'd been taking it since I was fifteen. So I stopped. I had an appointment to have a coil put in, but before that happened, I found out I was pregnant." She touched her light brown hair, which was loose to her shoulders and subtly high-lighted with blond streaks. "I'm a Pisces," she added. "We're very fertile."

Astrology? But at least the woman was talking openly. "So your first daughter wasn't planned. How did your husband react to your pregnancy?"

"He was quite annoyed when I told him. Well, no, not annoyed. I'd say he was worried. Still, he got very close to Lea after she was born."

One of the many theories the police were considering was that Kissling had been physically or sexually abusing his daughters and had killed them to prevent them from telling someone. Their corpses had shown no evidence of abuse—but that didn't mean something hadn't happened. Giuliana chose her next words carefully. "You say Herr Kissling and Lea were very close. Do you think that closeness was . . . completely appropriate?"

"Oh, for God's sake," Iris said. "I've told you people over and over—there was no hanky-panky going on in our house. I would have known if there was *anything* unhealthy about Mänu's relationship with our girls."

Except that he killed them, Giuliana thought. But she supposed Iris had to tell herself that all had been well; it was that or spend the rest of her life hating herself for missing something that could have saved the children. Before she could follow up on this line of questioning, Iris went on: "I was the one who decided to have another baby; I didn't think Lea should be an only child." She paused as if waiting for Giuliana to comment. "My sister and her husband have only one son, and he's spoiled. A real little pain in the ass. Oops. Sorry." She frowned, then smiled. "My girls were much better behaved."

Something about the interview was beginning to trouble Giuliana. She wasn't getting any closer to understanding the family dynamics. What was she doing wrong? Had the woman managed to distance herself from her grief so well that she simply couldn't let herself analyze what had happened? Of course, she didn't want Iris to start hurling hysterical accusations either. So . . . what was the problem?

She took a deep breath and tried again. "Frau Kissling, I'm sorry, but I do need to ask you more about your daughters' deaths. Were there . . . ?"

"Why don't you call me Iris?"

Giuliana nodded politely and went on with her question. "In hindsight, were there any clues that hinted at the . . . violence that was coming? Anything your ex-husband did or said in the months—or even years—before the crime that now strikes you as odd?"

"Of course not. Mänu never seemed like a murderer. Are you suggesting I should have known?"

"No, I'm not," Giuliana said soothingly. She watched the other woman stroke her hair again; touch her earrings. "But you did get divorced, so I thought perhaps you'd—"

"No," Iris interrupted, sounding irritated, "there was nothing about him that frightened or worried me. Nothing that made me suspicious. We simply grew apart." She gave a small, impatient shrug.

"Which of you decided to end the marriage?" Giuliana persisted.

Iris paused for at least a minute, lips pursed, fingers still toying with her earring, and Giuliana waited in silence. Finally, the answer came. "Mänu told me he wanted a divorce, but to be honest, I was ready for a change. When he wasn't with the girls, he spent all his time at work. Our marriage had gotten stale. Boring, really. I'm positive he didn't have a girlfriend, though. I would have known. I'm the kind of person who *feels* things like that."

Before the interview, Giuliana had braced herself to deal with a tsunami of emotions from Iris: hatred for her ex-husband, fury and grief at what he'd done, guilt over not having somehow prevented it. Instead, a mere two months after he'd killed their daughters, she was complaining about how boring her husband had become. Was it possible the woman was having some sort of post-traumatic breakdown? Giuliana was starting to understand why the police reports about the Kisslings' marriage and breakup were based primarily on interviews with relatives and friends. The husband wouldn't talk at all, and the wife didn't want to dig any deeper. Was this her way of coping with tragedy—by refusing to reflect on it?

Giuliana tried again. "While you were working out the details of your divorce, what did your husband say about having Mia and Lea with him?"

"He asked for full custody, but I'm sure that was just to make things difficult for me. Why on earth would he want to raise them all by himself? Little girls belong with their mothers—that's what judges always decide."

Giuliana thought about how Ueli had raised Isabelle for five years before Lukas came along. "How did Mia and Lea feel about their father, particularly after you separated?"

"Oh, they adored him—of course they did. They couldn't wait to see him. He had them for only two weekends a month and got to buy them treats and take them on outings. They never misbehaved when they were with *him*." Her kind-but-sad expression was gone.

Giuliana said, "According to my notes, at the time of the girls' deaths, you worked eighteen hours a week, spread over three days. But Mia and Lea were at the daycare center full time, is that right?"

"My sister and mother could only babysit in the evenings, so I needed the girls in daycare to have time for myself. Mänu paid for it, which was generous of him." She smiled. "It was an amicable divorce, you know."

Giuliana plowed on. "Your ex-husband paid for the girls to be in daycare all day, five days a week. Is that correct?" For some reason, this hadn't come up in the notes she'd studied.

"That's right. I was able to take some painting courses and go to Pilates twice a week. It was important to me." As she spoke, Iris's fingers caressed her cheek and traveled around the scooped neck of her dress. "In the evenings, I picked up the girls at five thirty, and we had supper and played together until their bedtime. It was such a special time for us. Evenings are when I miss them the most, my little sweeties." She looked sad again, but her expression was starting to feel strange to Giuliana now. It was as if she practiced it in front of the mirror every day but couldn't quite get it right.

Keeping her voice carefully neutral, Giuliana continued. "You said your mother or your sister babysat for you in the evening."

"Oh well, now and then. When I had a date. Or went to the movies with my girlfriends. They helped me on weekends, too. I was lucky to have their support."

Giuliana kept digging. "The girls spent two weekends a month with their father, from late Friday afternoon until Sunday evening. How many hours would you say *you* spent with them? Let's say specifically in the month before their deaths?" She steeled herself for an angry and defensive response.

But Iris smiled. "I can't answer a question like that. The time I spent with them was *quality* time. That was really important to me. It made me happy. I was broken up after they died, and people were so sweet to me—I got piles of flowers from my office, and women I didn't even know stopped me on the street. Some of them burst into tears. I can't think about it without crying myself." At that, Iris took a pack of tissues from her purse. Sure enough, tears were rolling down her face, and she wiped them away with a discreet sniff.

"Let's take a break now," Giuliana said. "There's a toilet just down the hall, and if you take the elevator to the top floor, you'll find a small coffee shop. I'll come up to get you in ten or fifteen minutes, and we'll resume."

With Iris Kissling safely on her way to the bathroom, Giuliana hurried downstairs to the office of Konrad Zaugg, the chief prosecutor, and knocked on his door.

"Sorry to interrupt," she said, "but I'm wondering if we can have a chat about Iris Kissling."

He waved her in. "I've got a colleague here. If you've come about Kissling, I think she should be here while we talk."

Giuliana shook hands with Zaugg and the other prosecutor, a woman whose name she promptly forgot, and said, "Look, I . . . I just wondered: has Iris Kissling had a psychiatric exam?"

"No. No one involved in the case has talked to her for weeks. With the initial investigation over, we've tried to leave her in peace. Is she unable to speak today? I should have considered that she might be too depressed to handle the interview."

"I don't know what's wrong with her, but I don't think it's depression."

"Well, sit down and give me your impressions." He pointed to a third chair pulled up at the low table where he and the other woman were sitting.

Giuliana spoke carefully; she was still figuring out her response to Iris Kissling, and she didn't want to overplay anything. "It's as if she's playing a part. She seems sad for a while until she forgets her role and slides off into some kind of alternative reality. I ask her about the girls' deaths, and she's just . . . I don't know. Blank. We talk about her husband, and she doesn't seem angry with him. Maybe it's the meds she is on, but something's not right. I'd like to request an evaluation for her as soon as possible, and the psychiatrist should watch this interview as part of his analysis."

Konrad Zaugg looked thoughtful. "Seems like we'd just be doing the defense team a favor." The woman next to him nodded.

"Maybe," Giuliana said, "but if we want insight into Kissling's motives for the killings, surely we have to understand his wife. I wouldn't want to put her in front of the judges in this state, believe me."

"All right," said Zaugg. "I'll watch the video when you're done and make my decision. If she's as odd as you say, I guess we need to figure out why." He sighed. "God, this case!"

As Giuliana headed up to the rooftop café to find Iris and resume their interview, she thought again about Iris's bright clothes and sense of composure. She'd initially felt respect and sympathy; now she was filled with uncertainty. What the hell was going on with the woman? And when had it started—whatever "it" was?

12

Nisha made herself stop picking at her nails and surveyed the room: the table set with blue-and-white striped placemats and navy blue napkins; a chocolate and hazelnut cake on a flowered platter waiting to be cut; the kettle filled. She'd cleaned the flat, including the bedrooms—she was sure Andi's parents would want to see the whole place—and put a photo album with Saritha's baby pictures on the coffee table. She thought longingly of sitting on the cozy paisley sofa with Andi's mother and going through the album with her page by page, sharing all those photos of a beaming Andi holding Sari. No, that wouldn't happen. It was too soon after Andi's death, too painful for everyone. But still . . .

God, she was not going to start crying five minutes before her guests were due to arrive. She breathed deeply. The real reason it would never happen was that Andi's parents still didn't see Sari as their daughter's child. They couldn't grasp that, to Nisha, they were Sari's grandparents. So why would Andi's mother, drenched in grief for her dead daughter, force herself to look at photos of Andi cuddling Nisha's baby?

Sari sat near the sofa with ten small cylindrical blocks between her outstretched legs. She couldn't stack them yet, but she loved to pick them up one at a time or take one in each hand and bang them together. Now she was pushing a bright yellow block away from her, and Nisha watched it roll out of her reach. In a flash, Sari was up on hands and knees, crawling after it. She crowed with delight when she managed to grasp the runaway. Squatting back on her heels, she held the block out to her mother. Love surged through Nisha, and she sat down on the floor and pulled her daughter onto her lap, telling her how clever she was. Then Nisha built a block tower, which Sari knocked over. Ten towers later, the street door buzzed.

In the entrance hall, Yannick kissed Nisha on both cheeks; then Kurt and Manuela Eberhart shook hands with her. They were spare people, neatly dressed, gray haired, and very upright. Good people, Nisha was sure of that—but cautious. It had taken two years for them to let her use their first names.

"Let me take your jackets," she said, just as Manuela thanked her for the invitation. Both stopped to apologize for speaking over each other, and there was an uncomfortable pause. Say something, Yannick, Nisha thought. But it was Saritha who saved the day, crawling toward them, head up, expression curious. Reaching her mother's feet, she grinned up at the newcomers, displaying her four-and-a-half teeth. Then she grabbed Yannick's jeans and pulled herself up to stand, supported by his leg, chuckling at her achievement.

Yannick, who still hadn't said a word, swept her into his arms and high into the air, causing her to shriek with delight. As he cuddled her to his chest, he started to cry. But then, instead of giving Sari to Nisha while he went into the guest bathroom, he handed the baby to his mother.

Nisha prayed that Sari, finding herself in Manuela's arms, wouldn't protest. Instead, very seriously, she examined her grandmother, touching first her nose and then the large buttons down the front of her blouse before her little hand clutched one. Manuela was charmed, and she and Kurt let Nisha guide them toward the sofa. When Yannick came back, all three of them asked questions about Sari and played with her until it was time for her nap. Nisha saw Manuela's eyes stray once to the photo album on the coffee table, and she almost offered to show it to her. But her courage failed her.

With Sari asleep, Nisha settled her guests at the table and served cake and coffee.

"I remember your telling us that you worked for the Federal Department of the Environment, but I'm embarrassed to say that I've forgotten exactly what you do there," said Kurt, setting down his coffee cup and picking up his fork for another bite of the cake, which had already been seized upon as a topic of conversation and praised extravagantly.

"I'm one of the people who keep the press informed about whatever the department is doing that's newsworthy, which may be new research we're funding or laws we're proposing about environmental protection or changes in how we promote biodiversity."

"I see," said Kurt. "That sounds . . . very interesting."

Nisha hoped he'd ask more, but the questions dried up, so she offered more coffee and, a few minutes later, more cake.

Yannick, usually sociable, had spoken very little, so Nisha asked how his and Sophie's two-year-old, Hugo, was doing in daycare. To her immense relief, he launched into a story about Hugo that took them through the second cup of coffee. It was barely over before Manuela set her cup and saucer onto her plate, pushed the dishes away, and folded her hands in front of her.

Nobody had mentioned Andi's name yet. But Manuela's expression was resolute. "We've been here twice before," she began, "but . . . Andi never took us around the apartment. Kurt and I would like to see . . . where she lived. Is that all right?"

"Of course," said Nisha, jumping up. "I'd love to show you. The other three rooms are quite small, but we didn't mind because of this large open area." She waved around at the room where they sat.

Although they were already sitting right next to the narrow strip of a kitchen, Nisha led the Eberharts into it, suddenly eager to convey something to them about her and Andi's life together and how precious it had been. How she and Andi had shared the cooking on Fridays as they talked about their days at work or discussed the minute details of their daughter's growth, full of pride at every tiny triumph.

She pointed to the coffee machine on the counter, a miniature version of an Italian espresso machine that ground the beans fresh for each cup it produced. "That contraption was Andi's beloved," she told them. "I drink more tea than coffee, but she took care of that thing like it was a racing car engine."

Into the silence that followed, Kurt said, "She bought us one of those new Nespresso machines as soon as they hit the market and then used it whenever she visited us. I always teased her that she'd bought it for herself, not for us. But I got used to it and ended up buying one for the store as well."

For a while after that, things were easier. Kurt and Manuela had seen the front hall already, but Andi showed them the small half bath next to the coat rack and led them down the corridor to the first bedroom, which was Sari's. They walked in quietly—Yannick, too, although of course he and Sophie had been there many times before—and gazed at the sleeping baby in her brightly painted crib with its sailboat mobile, taking in the chest of drawers with a changing table, the yellow armchair for nightly feeds, and white curtains patterned with sailing ships. Nisha decided not to tell them how adamantly Andi had insisted that no daughter of hers was going to grow up with soppy curtains covered with lambs or pink daisies.

She showed them the room that served as a shared office, with a desk under the window and a ceiling-high bookcase. There was a poster on the wall of Andi's curling team, and Yannick said, "I got the feeling Andi was very proud about becoming skip, didn't you, Nisha?"

Kurt was examining the three framed photos on the desk: one of Nisha's parents in their twenties; one of Yannick and Sophie's little son Hugo; and one of the whole Eberhart family, taken several years before at Yannick and Sophie's wedding. Kurt picked up the family photograph and stared at it before putting it down, but he didn't say anything.

The last room was the master bedroom, with its own bath. It had both Andi's and Nisha's things in it. On the dresser was a picture of the two of them laughing, their arms around each other. Manuela didn't touch it, but Nisha saw her gazing at it.

"There's a nice big bathroom off this room," she told them. "We love bathing Sari in there—we use her plastic tub, though." Hearing herself use the present tense stopped her voice, and then—well, her spiel dried up. She suddenly felt awkward bringing Andi's family in here, and something about the way her in-laws were standing told her they were uncomfortable, too. Then Manuela walked over to the wardrobe, threw open the doors, and ran a hand over the clothes that were her daughter's. Without warning, she gathered them into her arms, pressed them to her face, and began to sob.

"Ma," Yannick said. Nisha could hear the edge in her brother-in-law's voice. But she had done the same thing countless times since Andi's death, and she understood that Manuela needed to breathe her dead child's scent. She put her arms around her mother-in-law, feeling her own tears start as the woman leaned into her.

"Let me give you one of her sweaters to take home," Nisha said after a moment.

Manuela stepped back and wiped her eyes, looking surprised. "Oh, well . . . I brought plastic bags for her clothes. I don't have to pack everything this afternoon, though, if that's inconvenient. I can come back. You're the best person to sort through the books and papers—you can set everything of Andi's aside, and we'll bring boxes for it all. As for furniture, you can tell me if there's anything you especially need."

Nisha stared at her. She felt a wave of nausea, followed by pure white rage. Could these two people really be so stupid? Yes, yes, she'd begged Andi to wait for an actual wedding in the vain hope of gaining some kind of support from her own family—and now it was too late. She'd never forgive herself for that. But still, she and Andi had been registered partners, and Manuela and Kurt had drunk prosecco at the party celebrating her and Andi's signing of their documents. She'd heard Andi telling them what it meant. Now they were acting as if Nisha had been their daughter's roommate. For a moment, she couldn't even look at Manuela. She backed up to the bed and sat on the edge, staring straight ahead.

"Ma," said Yannick again, his voice cracking. "You can't take Andi's things away. Nisha and Andi were partners—you *know* that. Andi's stuff belongs to Nisha and Sari. Just like in a marriage. It's the law."

"But I thought . . ." Manuela whispered.

Nisha didn't want to know what the woman thought. But when she looked up, Kurt was taking his wife's arm. "We talked about this," he told his son, "but we weren't sure." He examined the rug at Nisha's feet, avoiding her eyes. "Is there . . . a will?"

Yannick looked at her helplessly. "Jesus, Nisha, I'm sorry. I didn't realize they were so . . ." His voice trailed off. "They never said anything to me about taking Andi's stuff. Believe me, if I'd known, I wouldn't have let them in here."

"It's . . ." Nisha began, but she couldn't bring herself to say it was all right because it wasn't. Kurt and Manuela weren't doddery old people with failing minds—they ran a kitchen appliance store; they used computers. They could have Googled the terms of the law under which she and Andi had become partners and spared her this horrible scene.

She stood up slowly, her body trembling with sudden and complete exhaustion. "Andi *did* make a will, and it's with our lawyer, Susanna Käser." Nisha had a copy, but she wasn't going to make things easy for them by fetching it. She knew that Andi had left some small family items to her parents because they'd discussed it. "I'll call her first thing tomorrow morning and ask her to get in touch with you. Would you like her to call you at work or home?"

Kurt still didn't meet her eyes. "At the store, please."

"Let's go back to the kitchen, and you can write the address and phone number down for me." She could easily have looked it up online, but this was a good way to get them all out of her bedroom, away from her and Andi's private life.

Yannick let Kurt and Manuela leave the room ahead of him and then put an arm around Nisha. Before he could start apologizing again, she dragged a smile onto her face and said, "It's not your fault. It's truly not." But inside, she wondered: where was Sophie? What had happened to make her stay away? Her sister-in-law would have made this terrible afternoon better; she was sure of it.

Together, she and Yannick went back to the table, where Andi's parents sat, looking dazed. Nisha tore a sheet off the pad by the telephone and handed it to Kurt with a pen, then stacked the cups, saucers, and flowered dessert plates on the kitchen counter.

"I gave Andi those plates years ago," Manuela said, her voice shaking.

"Yes, she told me," said Nisha, continuing the rest of the sentence in her head: *But if you think I'm going to give them back to you, you're wrong.* Maybe someday, if Andi's parents ever accepted her and Sari, there would be time for gestures like that. But right now, there were other things to talk about.

"There's something I need to tell you," she said.

Kurt watched her with wary courtesy, intertwining his fingers on the table.

Nisha clasped her own hands and took a deep breath. "I went to the police the day after Andi died and told a detective that I don't think her death was an accident."

"But that's . . . Why would you think that?" Kurt leaned back in his chair.

"Because someone has been sending her threatening letters for the past four years."

Manuela gasped and started to interrupt her, but Yannick laid a hand on his mother's arm. He looked almost as shocked as Manuela, Nisha noticed, even though she was sure Andi had told him about the letters. Taking his cue from his sister, he'd probably never worried about them—until now.

"I gave the letters to a police detective, and yesterday afternoon she called to say the police are taking me seriously. I mean, they now believe Andi was . . . killed—they've found evidence. The detective is coming tomorrow morning to talk to me."

"But who would send Andi threatening letters?" Manuela asked, her voice growing shrill. "What were they about?"

Nisha saw her mother-in-law's trembling mouth and stricken eyes and felt a little of her anger at Andi's parents drain away. She swallowed. "They were about . . . about her and me. Being together. And later about Saritha. From someone who found it disgusting. Maybe if she hadn't been with me, if we hadn't had Sari . . . I keep wondering if our relationship killed her."

"That's not true." Kurt was looking at Nisha so fiercely that she thought at first he was angry with her. "You mustn't blame yourself for anything that happened to Andrea."

Nisha stared down at the table. If only she could be so sure. But suppose Mathan had something to do with all this? Tears began to gather in her eyes.

To her astonishment, Kurt reached out and covered her hand with his for a brief moment. She made herself look at him.

"Andrea made her own choices, always," Kurt said. "She lived exactly the way she wanted to, and you and the baby were part of that life. I'm sure she didn't regret that the two of you were . . . together— and you shouldn't let some cowardly fanatic writing ugly letters make you regret it either."

Yannick was staring round-eyed at his father. And Manuela was nodding, her eyes fixed on her husband, her hands clasped tightly under her chin.

Kurt paused to swipe at his eyes. "Andi hasn't talked to us much for a long time, not about what . . . what mattered to her, but . . . well, we raised her, and we know her . . . knew her." His face crumpled, but he went on, "She always hated people who said one thing and meant another. Our girl always spoke her mind, didn't she, dear?"

"She did," his wife agreed, and Nisha was amazed to see a very slight smile on her lips. "Remember when she marched out from the back of the store and told Egli that your prices were fair, and he should stop being so rude and either pay his money or go shop somewhere else? She was only eleven or twelve."

"I spanked her," Kurt said, also smiling. "For the first and last time. I told her that if he was rude, she had been even ruder and that children weren't allowed to talk to grownups like that, especially not to our customers. But she was right, our Andi, she was dead right. The price for that equipment *was* fair, and Martin Egli was a *Püffu*."

"Did he come back?" asked Nisha, who'd never heard this story.

"Not for a year, but after that, he was a regular customer, and he never said another word about my prices. Andi put the fear of God into him."

"She could do that," Nisha agreed. "You should have heard what she said to the notary about his fees when we bought this apartment. I was embarrassed. But she was right, of course, and he ended up reducing his costs. She was teaching me to . . . to stand up for myself more." Now it was Nisha's turn to falter. She got up and stood at the kitchen counter, her back to them. Then she found a tissue and blew her nose.

Somehow the tension had broken. Walking back to the table with the box of tissues, she said, "Speaking truth to power, that's what she called it. She was the most straightforward person I knew. But she made people laugh, even when she was confronting them. It was her gift."

"Yes, it was. She made us laugh, too," said Manuela. There was silence at the table, but it didn't feel painful, and then Manuela stood. "I'm going to the bathroom, and then I think it's time for us to go home."

"I'll be right back, too," Nisha told the two men and headed into the bedroom, where she took a T-shirt of Andi's from her night table drawer. Still unwashed, it was in a Ziploc plastic bag. As Manuela came out of the guest bathroom, Nisha handed her the sealed bag. There was no need to say what it contained.

Manuela hugged the bundle to her chest for a moment and then slipped it into her oversized handbag. "Thank you," she said and kissed Nisha's cheek.

As they were saying goodbye at the door, Manuela said, "I'd like to talk to that detective, too. I don't know if Kurt and I can help, but would you please tell him to contact us." Nisha nodded and watched her parents-in-law walk away down the corridor.

Yannick waited with her until they were on their way downstairs. "Why didn't you tell me about this murder business before?"

"I was waiting to see what the police thought. Now that they're asking questions, I had to tell you. I didn't mean to keep you and Sophie in the dark. Yannick—what about Sophie? She hasn't . . . she hasn't called me once since Andi died. Has she stopped being my friend?" It sounded pathetic, but with her father having banished her from home, Sophie's support felt like a lifeline.

"She's sad and upset," Yannick said. "I don't know how to get her to . . . But *I* want to help; I swear I do. Maybe we all just . . . need more time." He hurried off after his parents without waiting for her answer and without looking back.

Suddenly she found herself angry again. Time? She had all the time in the world, alone in this apartment, missing Andi like she'd miss her arm or leg, trying to figure out how she could make enough money to pay the mortgage and still be a good mother. But what did *they* need time for?

She sighed. If she didn't wake Saritha, the baby would be up half the night. As she picked up her drowsy daughter and held her to her chest, she felt her anger at Sophie fade into sadness. Had Sophie only been pretending to like her for Andi's sake?

The drive to Ueli's parents' farm near Aarwangen in the northeastern part of the canton took forty minutes. The Sunday morning roads were free of traffic, and they were lucky with the capricious March weather, too. When they arrived, the sun shone on the old farmhouse's red wooden shutters, and under the curve of its massive, overhanging roof, the place carried its usual air of cozy welcome. As they turned into the driveway, Ueli's father, Erich, came out of the barn onto the flag-stoned courtyard. He put his hands on his hips, stretching his back, then ran a hand through his white hair and waved at them.

"Päpu," yelled Lukas, jumping out of the car almost before it stopped and racing to hug his grandfather. Then Mike walked through the kitchen door into the yard as well, and Isabelle, who'd been taking her time to get out of the car, took off toward her uncle.

After she'd greeted Erich, Giuliana watched the children vying to talk to Mike. Thank goodness they hadn't picked up on her feelings about her brother-in-law. Although it had been almost a year since Mike's last visit to Switzerland, he and Ueli exchanged their usual brief handshake and careful smiles. Then Mike turned to her, and as they gave each other the conventional cheek kisses, one-two-three, it came to her that she'd never seen the two brothers hug.

"Ready for the grand tour?" Erich asked, as he always did when the kids visited the farm. Even when there were no baby animals to cuddle, there was always something new in the fields, pens, or barn.

"Are you coming, *Onkel* Mike?" Lukas called over his shoulder. He had hold of his grandfather's hand and was tugging him toward the cows' half of the barn, which was usually the first stop on the tour. It was nice to see the spark in Lukas that he'd been missing at home lately.

"Sorry, Lüku," Ueli said, "but I'm going to kidnap Mike, just for a little while, so we can have a walk." He put a hand on his brother's arm to steer him away from the farmhouse yard toward the narrow street. "We'll be back in—"

"No, no," Mike interrupted. "No way am I missing a farm tour with Paps and the kids. Let's all go." He put an arm around Isabelle's shoulders and smiled at Giuliana, but she couldn't smile back. She'd seen the exasperated look he'd shot Ueli, as if spending twenty minutes alone with his younger brother was an imposition.

"Go ahead then," Ueli said. "I'll talk to Mam." He ducked through the kitchen door, and Giuliana found herself wanting to spend a few minutes alone, away from all the tension. She summoned a smile for Mike at last and then turned with honest affection to her father-in-law. "You and Mike take the kids around to all their favorite spots, Erich. I'm going to sit in the sun for a few minutes and enjoy Irène's flowers." She waved at the front yard.

Erich caught her eye for a moment and nodded before leading his older son and grandchildren into the barn. "Bella should be calving soon. Wait until you see how fat she's gotten," she heard him say as she wandered forward to the rarely used front door and settled down on the steps, hugging herself to keep warm. The sun felt glorious on her face, but the air was still cold. On either side of the path, flowers marked the advance of spring. The purple crocuses and violets were beginning to give way to the yellow of daffodils and primroses. In another six weeks, Irène would fill her window boxes with white geraniums—Bern's traditional fire-engine red ones, she insisted, clashed with the shutters—and petunias and marigolds would replace the primroses along the path.

Eventually, Giuliana decided she'd given Ueli and Irène enough time. Tearing herself away from her sunny step, she went through the front door and headed toward the kitchen to offer help with the midday meal. The sound of Ueli's voice stopped her in the living room.

"But, Mam, don't you see that when you keep things secret, it doesn't save me worry at all. It just makes me worry about what you're not telling me."

And it hurts your feelings. Tell her that, Ueli, Giuliana urged from her spot as an unintentional eavesdropper. But Ueli didn't continue. Instead Irène, in her tartest, most matter-of-fact voice, answered, "Keeping secrets from you, Ueli? Don't be silly. I found out about this tumor last Monday, and you learned about it on Wednesday evening."

But you told Mike, who lives in another country, the same day, Giuliana thought. *And you didn't break the news to Ueli yourself.*

She felt momentarily ashamed of herself. It was Ueli's business, not hers. Besides, Irène had more important things to worry about than Ueli's disappointment—like the fact that she might be facing death, God forbid.

She heard Ueli's forced cheerfulness as he went on. "I want to help you after the operation. There's a lot I can do. Shop, cook, look after things here at the farm so Paps can spend time with you in the hospital. Whatever you need."

Irène was running the tap now; Giuliana imagined her standing at the old-fashioned stone sink with her back to Ueli, washing lettuce or preparing vegetables for the pot. "Mike's here for another week," she said, "so he can take care of all that. Besides, I expect to be on my feet in no time. You've got your writing and Giuliana and the children to look after." As though placating a child, she added, "Let's see how things are when Mike leaves; I'll tell you then if we need you. Now, get out of my kitchen and go find Mike. You have too little time together as it is—I hate for you to waste a moment of it."

Giuliana couldn't silence the voice in her head. Why did Irène have to send Ueli away when he was desperate to show her his love? She walked into the kitchen to find him kissing his mother's cheek. As Irène turned back to the sink, he gave Giuliana a shrug and headed out the back door. Giuliana stayed to help with the meal.

The family assembled for Sunday lunch in the dark, wood-paneled dining room and ate with hectic gaiety. With Easter in two weeks, Irène had prepared baby goat, a traditional Easter specialty, with oceans of gravy. To go with the meat, there were tiny dumplings called *Spätzli*, flecked green with wild garlic, and the last of the farm's Brussels sprouts, drenched in butter and flavored with bacon. Finally, there were two desserts: a charlotte with some of Irène's precious raspberries, which she picked from her raspberry canes every summer and froze in portions, and an *Osterfladen*, an Easter pie made with nuts, raisins, and semolina.

While everyone ate, Mike told one funny story after another about his life in Missouri. An attractive, unattached, well-paid man of fifty-one with an executive job at a multinational firm, he appeared to be having the time of his life. He related his experiments with various dating websites, and Giuliana had to admire the way he edited the spiciness out of his tales for the sake of his niece and nephew while still conveying a taste of it with his voice and eyes. She was aware of the whole family sitting motionless around the table, eyes shining, basking in his charm. Ueli, too. Her own opinion she kept to herself. The background to all of Mike's fun was two divorces in eighteen years and a great deal of pain. At least there'd never been any kids to get caught up in it all.

Finally, when the last spoonful of raspberries had been eaten and all the dishes washed, dried, and put away, Irène called everyone back to the table. Isabelle had promised that she'd take Lukas away to play a board game, so the adults could talk freely, but Irène thwarted that plan by insisting the children stay, saying, "I have no secrets from anyone." Giuliana suspected that this was an excuse to keep things vague and stop people from asking upsetting questions. Ueli's eyes were wary, his face and body tense. Giuliana covered his hand where it lay on the table near hers.

"What a lot of glum faces!" said Irène. Nobody laughed. "Okay, let's get this over with. I'm checking into Insel tomorrow evening, and Tuesday morning, I'll have a tumor removed from my colon—that's the lower part of my guts, Lukas—and the doctor thinks it's at stage two. That means it has spread through the wall of the intestine, but they don't know yet if it's gotten into any of the stuff outside the wall."

Stage two! Thank God! Ueli sagged slightly next to her, then he clasped her hand and squeezed it. Giuliana felt her irritation slide away. Maybe Irène's way of coping wasn't hers, but it was impressive. There she sat, a slight, gray-haired figure in thick stockings and her favorite orange cardigan, a tower of strength.

"What they do know—and this is the most important part—is that the cancer isn't in the lymph nodes. That means"—she looked at Lukas again—"that the cancer cells don't have a way to spread around the rest of my body. So that's great news."

Irène was smiling at Erich, who sat across the table from her, his face working as he tried to smile back.

"I may not even need chemotherapy," she went on, "but the doctors won't be able to say until after the surgery. I also don't know how soon I'll be able to leave the hospital, but you can believe that I'll fight to be home as soon as I can. So we won't make any plans for the Easter weekend until later."

Like a general, she laid out her strategy. The following afternoon Mike would drive her to the hospital, where she'd spend the night. After getting Irène settled, he would return to the farm to keep his father company. Tuesday morning, after milking, Mike and Erich would drive back to the Insel to wait out the operation. A neighbor would stop by on Tuesday to cast an eye over things; he could do the evening milking if necessary. On Wednesday . . . and on she went with her schedule.

Ueli, who lived a ten-minute drive from the hospital, featured nowhere in her program.

They left around four. During the farm tour, Mike had told Lukas that he and Ueli had been driving the family tractor by the age of twelve, and this was all Lukas could talk about for the first twenty minutes of the drive home, producing one argument after another for why he, too, should learn to drive. Neither Ueli nor Giuliana rose to the bait, recognizing a battle that didn't need fighting.

Finally, the car fell silent. Isabelle's French assignment lay in her lap unopened as she listened to music and texted her friend Luna. Plugged into Giuliana's phone, Lukas was listening to the third Harry Potter book, happy at Hogwarts.

Ueli seemed at peace. "Thank God it's not more serious," he said.

"Are you all right, though?"

He took his eyes from the road briefly and gave her a broad, easy smile. "I'm very relieved. I'm sure by the time I've spent ten minutes on Google studying survival rates, I'll be a mess again, but right now . . . I was convinced she was going to die, so this is a reprieve."

She couldn't let go of the resentment she felt on his behalf. Wasn't he even permitted to go to the hospital, for Christ's sake?

"I'll go to the hospital for Mam's surgery, of course," Ueli said, reading her mind.

"Of course," she agreed.

They retreated into silence, and she thought about Mike. What was wrong with him? In her family, she and her brother stood up for each other against their parents. Not that the occasion arose very often now, with her and Paolo in their forties and their parents over seventy, but as children, they'd always had each other's backs. Hadn't they? Or had she, as the older of the two, sided with the adults against Paolo? She didn't think so. Surely she, unlike Mike, would have insisted on her brother being drawn into the family plans. Why hadn't he spoken up to say, *Hey, I'd be glad to have Ueli's help on the farm*, or *We could use Ueli's support at the hospital*, the way she and Paolo would have done for each other?

They traveled home in silence, Giuliana's anger still eating away at her.

13

An email from Vinz arrived at six thirty the next morning. She checked that he wasn't asking her to join him somewhere at seven, then ignored it until the usual chaos of a school morning was over. Only then did she notice that the mail had also gone to Rolf, along with Renzo and Madeleine, the two investigators putting in the most time on the Eberhart case.

> *Just an update to let you know that most of the guards at the Amthaus could have known Eberhart's name and personal info from the Civi who worked there. Still seems probable that one or both of the suspended prison guards knocked her off her bike. We haven't been able to establish good alibis for either one. Madeleine and I will focus on this, while Giuliana should follow up as planned with Eberhart's partner, family, and friends. Since Madeleine's now busy with the guards, Renzo should switch to the civilian service files in Eberhart's office in Thun.*

Typical Vinz, Giuliana thought, maneuvering out of the narrow parking place she'd found a block from the apartment. He'd rather send out these little updates than waste his time in meetings. It was certainly efficient, if not exactly conducive to team communications. She already had an appointment with Nisha Pragasam at ten thirty that morning. They'd arranged to meet at her apartment while the baby was, hopefully, asleep. Giuliana was glad she'd have a chance to see where Andrea Eberhart had lived.

The following morning Giuliana was meeting with Manfred Kissling, so she began reviewing earlier interviews with him as soon as she got to work. At ten, she surfaced from the files, which were deeply discouraging. No one's previous ploys had induced the man to talk about his motive for the murders. Sighing, she got up, checked herself in the bathroom mirror, and set off for Nisha's flat. It was west of Insel Hospital in a section of the rapidly gentrifying neighborhood of Holligen that Giuliana wasn't familiar with.

Giuliana decided to park a few blocks from Nisha's street; her GPS indicated that it was very narrow. Getting out of the car, she found herself in one of the busiest parts of western Bern: tram tracks, a train station, a huge federal office building, a host of shops, and rows of large, six-story apartment buildings were all minutes from where she stood. On the traffic-packed street, road construction equipment roared, and a crane towered over her. But as she walked toward Eggimannstrasse, where Nisha lived, all the bustle fell away, and, like someone stepping through a magic wardrobe, she found herself in a different place: a miniature, self-contained neighborhood of old-fashioned two- and three-story houses with large gardens, many planted with rows of vegetables and clusters of fruit trees. Each house contained four or, at most, six apartments. The paved or graveled front yards were filled with bicycles and children's toys; large tables surrounded with chairs and shaded by umbrellas could be seen in the side gardens on both sides of each building, and shrubs and vines, not yet flowering in March, promised color and scent in the spring and summer. It was a little world for itself, four parallel streets with perhaps twenty small apartment houses in all, contained by a public library, an elementary school, and a church at one end and a daycare center at the other. Not one car sat in the narrow streets, and there were no garages or parking places belonging to any of the houses. Giuliana, searching for Nisha's house number, marveled at her surroundings. It didn't take her long to find the address, ring the bell, and be buzzed inside.

Standing in the doorway of her second-floor apartment, Nisha looked a lot less fragile than she had at the police station the day after her partner's death. She even managed a smile as she and Giuliana shook hands. Giuliana, relieved, smiled back.

"Sari should sleep until about eleven fifteen, and a neighbor has promised to take her afterward if we need more time," Nisha assured Giuliana, showing her through the hall to the flat's main room, where they sat down at opposite ends of the sofa. "Please ask me whatever you need to know."

"Let's start with your alibi," said Giuliana matter-of-factly, ignoring the shock that flashed across the other woman's face. "Where were you at ten thirty last Wednesday night?"

Nisha pushed a clenched fist against her mouth, then lowered it and said, "I'm almost sure I'd fallen asleep by then. I don't think I spoke with anyone all evening. Andi usually left for curling practice at about seven fifteen after a quick supper and was back before eleven. Since Saritha was born, I've rarely managed to stay awake until she got home."

Giuliana had opened her notepad on her knee to write down the times. "Okay, thanks. Before we get into Frau Eberhart's past, there's something I'd like to understand. Your partner was a gay rights activist for years, with a focus on the laws about marriage and children, but you aren't married, even though it's been legal for almost two years now. And what about adoption? Saritha is nine months old; had Frau Eberhart adopted her?"

Even as she was speaking, Giuliana could hear the suspicious tone in her voice, and she wished she could call it back. But it was too late; Nisha was already crying into the hands that covered her face, rocking back and forth on the sofa in her grief. Her words, when she spoke, were hard to understand, but Giuliana could make out, "It's my fault," repeated over and over. She went into the open kitchen to the right of the sofa, pulled several paper towel sections off a roll, filled a glass from the drainboard with water, and came back to sit next to Nisha, putting the towels and glass on the coffee table in front of her and resting one hand on her shoulder. Then she waited, hoping the baby wouldn't wake up. Finally, Nisha was able to take her face out of her hands and say, "Andi begged me to get married, but I kept saying not yet because I was hoping my father would have a change of heart. Just last month, I told her that if he hadn't . . . come round by the time Sari turned one, I'd give up, and we'd get married. And now—it's too late."

These last words came out as a wail, but this time Nisha calmed herself quickly. "As for the adoption process, we started months ago, but we know from friends who've already gone through it that it can take ages, and now—now that's too late, too."

Nisha clasped her hands tightly in her lap and stared at them. Giuliana touched her knee and said, "I'm sorry to upset you, and I'm afraid it may get worse as we go along."

The younger woman looked up from her hands and gave Giuliana a fierce look. "No," she said forcefully, "I want to do this. I need you to find out what happened to Andi. You should ask me anything you need to ask."

Giuliana nodded. "The next thing I want to do is make sure I have my facts straight." She turned back a page in her notebook, glanced at her notes, and said, "Frau Eberhart was thirty-three years old and had a master's degree in political science from the University of Bern. She was born in the village of Ochsenbach and attended *Gymnasium* in Thun before moving to Bern after her first year at the university. Is that correct?"

"Yes." Nisha nodded, and the thick braid of black hair pulled over her right shoulder moved slightly; it was so long it reached almost to her waist. She wore a navy sweater over a white blouse with a pattern of tiny red flowers. "I'm four years younger than she is; we never knew each other at Uni."

"How did you meet?" asked Giuliana, writing "Nisha age 29"in her spiral notebook, although she knew this would be in the case file somewhere already.

"Five years ago, I was doing an internship at the Federal Office for the Environment. That's where I work now. A Civi doing his service there was creating problems, so Andi came from the civilian service office in Thun for a day to try and straighten things out. I was just one of the group she sat down with at lunch." Nisha's quiet voice grew thicker and more halting, and she reached for a tissue from the box on the low glass table in front of them. She clutched it tightly but didn't cry.

"We fell in love during that lunch," she added, "or, at least, that's how I see it now. We talked so long that both of us were late for our meetings afterward." She gave the ghost of a smile at the memory.

"Do you know when she came out as a lesbian?" Giuliana asked.

"When she was twenty-one," Nisha answered promptly. "Her first year at Uni Bern, she commuted from home and kept on seeing her local boyfriend—Beat, his name was. Then she moved into an apartment near campus, sharing with three other people. She went to a meeting about discrimination against women at the university and met a lesbian couple there who invited her to dinner. She said"—Nisha paused, and this time she used the tissue in her hand to wipe her eyes—"she said that being with them was a revelation. All of a sudden, she understood who she was. She knew about women being together, but it hadn't clicked for her. Until then." Talking about her partner filled Nisha's thin face with life.

"I understand you didn't know Andi then," Giuliana said, making a point of using the dead woman's first name, "but can you tell me anything about those seven years—the time after she came out but before you and she met?"

Nisha frowned and bit her lower lip. "Not much. For four of those years, she was studying—quite hard, I think, since she got both her bachelor's and master's degrees in five years. And curling, of course— she took it up soon after she moved to Bern. There were lots of different part-time jobs she did, too, so she could pay her rent: waitressing, temping in offices, working in shops. Stuff like that." She paused, pressing one hand to her cheek.

Giuliana waited quietly, hoping she wouldn't have to push Nisha to talk about Andi's other relationships.

Nisha sighed and went on. "Those years were when Andi became part of the lesbian scene in Bern—lots of political activism and quite a few partners. I don't know the names of most of those women, but one of them is our lawyer, Susanna Käser. You'd probably want to talk to her anyway about Andi's will, but she's also the person who'd know the most about Andi's life before she met me."

Giuliana wrote down the name. "What about enemies? Either recent ones or from her past. For example, what about the ex-boyfriend, Beat?"

"Beat!" Really smiling this time, Nisha shook her head. "I don't think so. He still lives near my parents-in-law, and he and his wife exchange Christmas cards with Andi. My guess is that if he thinks about Andi at all, it's her skating he remembers. She told me they were good buddies who spent more time on the ice than in bed."

After another moment, she added, "As for her other exes, I don't know. She didn't talk about them. Anyone from her past that I'm acquainted with is friends with both of us. I've never . . ." she paused and started again, "I've never felt anything like hatred from them." She shook her head. "God, how weird that sounds. It's horrible, imagining someone we *know* killing Andi."

Giuliana made a sympathetic face, even as she thought about the statistics—most murder victims were killed by someone they knew, usually very well. "What about while she was living with her parents? Is there anything I should know about her childhood that might be helpful?"

Nisha shook her head. "For her, being a child meant school, helping out at home and in her father's appliance store, and ice-skating. Yannick"—she raised her eyebrows inquiringly at Giuliana, who gave a quick nod to say that she knew who Yannick was—"started playing ice hockey when he was five. Andi often walked him to practices, and that's how *she* discovered hockey, which she played until she went off to university. Only with boys, though; she mostly hung out with boys in those days. She . . . well, I think she had a happy childhood."

Okay, Giuliana thought. Time to move on. The baby would be waking up soon, and she needed more information. "You said before that there was a will."

Nisha nodded. "Yes, Andi wrote it after Saritha was born to make sure the baby and I inherited the maximum amount. We made wills together and discussed everything with Susanna. But we didn't expect to need them for . . ." her voice dropped to a whisper, "decades."

"Was anyone upset about you and Sari being Frau Eberhart's main heirs?" Giuliana couldn't afford to get sidetracked by sympathy; she was expecting a wail from Sari's bedroom any minute.

Nisha twisted her hands in her lap, eyes down. Giuliana thought she hadn't heard the question until she said, "Andi's parents were here yesterday, and it turned out they thought they were going to be collecting her things. They didn't understand . . . They knew we were a couple, but somehow . . ." Her voice trailed off.

Giuliana imagined the scene. Had the parents actually started dragging furniture to the door while Nisha tried to stop them? "How painful for you," she said and realized what an understatement that was. "It must have been awful."

Nisha nodded before hurrying to add, "Not that they were desperate to get hold of her stuff. I mean, it's not as if they wanted to inherit anything. They're heartbroken. They just don't . . ." She sighed deeply.

"What is there to inherit?"

"Half this condo, which is mortgaged, of course, and about twenty thousand francs. And half the car, maybe? I don't think Andi had anything else, but you'll have to ask Susanna." Nisha's hands covered her mouth again; her eyes had grown dull. Before Giuliana could ask another question, Nisha said, "Yesterday I told Andi's parents and Yannick about the poison-pen letters and . . . that she might have been murdered. They were shocked. But Andi's mother said she'd like to talk to you."

Giuliana made a note and went on briskly. "Let's move on to your family."

Nisha stared down at her hands again. "My family," she echoed expressionlessly.

"How many people here in Switzerland do you consider family?"

"My parents, my two brothers, older and younger, and my older brother's wife and their two sons—that's it. Some relatives on my mother's side emigrated after we did, but they settled in Schaffhausen. We visited back and forth a few times when I was a child, but I haven't seen them for years, except at my brother's wedding."

Giuliana wondered about the size of Nisha's extended family still living in Sri Lanka but didn't ask. "When you were at the police station, you indicated that your parents wanted you to marry a Tamil man. So . . . how did they and your brothers feel about your living with Frau Eberhart?"

Nisha leaned forward as she looked up, her eyes meeting Giuliana's. "My younger brother Rajan is much more Swiss than Tamil. He's studying engineering, and he's refused an arranged marriage. In fact, he has a Swiss girlfriend—she's called Alina. He had dinner with Andi and me quite a few times, and he liked her."

Giuliana nodded, knowing how well integrated first-generation immigrants could be. Look at Renzo! "And your parents?" she asked.

"My mother acted like Andi and I were just roommates, but she knew the truth, and she and Andi were always kind to each other. My mother mainly visited me when Andi was at work, but that was for practical reasons; she has to come during the day so . . ." Here she flushed a little. "Well, so that my father won't find out." Nisha paused before going on. "He's more complicated. He doesn't let me come home anymore, and he'd be upset to know my mother's visiting me, but he's never said anything bad about Andi because . . . well, as far as he's concerned, it's me who's behaved badly. He has a strong sense of right and wrong, and I . . . I respect him for that." She took Giuliana's wrist for a moment as she said this, as if to make sure she understood. "In Sri Lanka, he was in trouble with the Tamil Tigers as well as the

Singhalese because he didn't approve of the Tigers' methods. Their violence. He's a very good man who lives by his principles."

"And your older brother?"

"Mathan is . . ." She leaned back, her shoulders hunched. "He's the only one of us kids who can remember something about our life from before." Giuliana nodded encouragingly. "It's Mathan, not my parents, who thinks life would be better if we still lived 'at home.' I think he's . . . it's like a fantasy world to him, Sri Lanka. When he was twenty-six, he let my parents arrange his marriage to a nineteen-year-old from our hometown. Before she flew to Bern, she'd never been more than ten miles from home. The poor girl—even after four years here and two sons, she's completely lost. And he's disappointed in her and angry. But what was he expecting?" She stopped talking abruptly, as if reining herself in with an effort, and stared down at the hands folded in her lap.

Giuliana told herself to tread carefully. "What was Mathan's reaction to your and Andi's relationship?" she asked.

"Oh God," Nisha said. "He *hated* it."

"How do you know?" Giuliana prodded gently. "Did he visit you? Tell you on the phone? Send you emails?"

Nisha met her eyes. It seemed as though she was deciding whether to speak. Finally, she said, "Texts, emails, phone calls. I even changed my number, but . . . he wheedled the new one out of my mother, and it started again."

Giuliana leaned forward, keeping her voice calm despite her excitement. "Did he threaten you or Andi with violence?"

The question set the other woman off like a firecracker. "No," she said loudly. Then she lowered her face into her hands. Giuliana waited. "No," she said again into the hands that still covered her face. Finally, she lifted her head, but she still didn't look at Giuliana. "There was a lot of . . . disgust. Anger, too, maybe hatred, but he never said that he'd do anything to either of us. Still, I . . . it worries me."

"Do you think he had something to do with your partner's death?"

"It seems impossible to me, but I just don't know." She shook her head.

"You've read the letters," Giuliana went on. "Do you think your brother wrote them?"

Nisha's eyes opened wide. "No, not that," she answered quickly. "They're very Christian, with lots about God and the devil. Mathan wouldn't write that stuff."

Giuliana watched her intently. "When we talked at the police station, you told me you thought the anonymous letter writer had killed Andi. You don't believe your brother wrote those letters, yet you still suspect—"

Nisha stood up and crossed her arms over her chest. "I don't know what I suspect." It was almost a yell. "I'm trying to be honest, but . . . don't ask me to accuse my own brother."

It was time to change the subject. Giuliana would speak to Mathan and the rest of Nisha's family herself. "Fair enough," she said and waved her hand toward the other end of the sofa. Nisha looked at her wildly for a moment and then, with a shaky breath like a sob, sat back down. Giuliana went on. "An investigator is at Frau Eberhart's office at the civilian service today, looking for anything suspicious. Do you think one of her workmates or clients could have had something to do with her death?"

Nisha grabbed at this new topic greedily. "Well, she's worked with hundreds of young men during her six years there, and quite a few *were* difficult. There's a work colleague she often disagreed with, too, but I can't see why . . ." She looked directly at Giuliana. "Andi talked about her Civis a lot, but she was careful never to use their names, certainly not their last names. She came to like most of them, even the ones that started out by infuriating her. She had so much patience with them. And sympathy." Settling back into the sofa, she went on. "She used to tell me how clever many of them were at managing to seem busy while doing nothing. If they'd put the same energy into working that they do into avoiding work, she used to say, they'd be wildly productive. She thought they just needed someone with a sense of humor to give them a poke now and then."

As she continued to talk about Andi's work at the Civi office, Nisha's hands danced in extravagant gestures, her voice rising and falling. Giuliana jotted things down; it was all useful information about Andi's priorities.

"Did one of her Civis kill her?" Nisha said at last. "I guess it's possible, but she certainly wasn't afraid of any of them. I mean, God, Andi . . . Andi wasn't afraid of anyone." Her voice trembled. "She loved her job. It sometimes frustrated her, but it never bored her."

Giuliana closed the notepad and set it on the coffee table. "That's very useful. Now I want to ask you something more personal." She saw Nisha flinch, but she went on. "I need to know who Saritha's father is."

Nisha shook her head. "Don't you think I'd tell you if I thought there was the slightest chance . . . But he'd never hurt Andi, I know that."

"How do you know?"

"Because he loved her. He's devastated by her death."

Giuliana considered the former boyfriend, Beat, but dismissed him. What man would be devastated by Andi's death? A friend, obviously, but no one had mentioned Andi and Nisha having a close male friend. Then a light flared in her brain. If you couldn't combine your own genetic material with that of your child's mother, you'd choose the next best thing, wouldn't you? "Andi's brother," she said softly.

Nisha bent her head, hiding her face. Giuliana waited. Finally, Nisha raised stricken eyes, and Giuliana knew she'd guessed correctly.

"We've only told our friend Susanna," she whispered. "Even Andi's parents don't know. I'd like to tell them, but Yannick and his wife Sophie . . . well, they think the time isn't right."

"What did the procedure involve? Did you use a Swiss clinic now that it's legal?"

"No, because before the law changed, we'd already visited a clinic in Germany, and I'd had some tests there. It isn't far, less than an hour north of Basel. Yannick donated the sperm, and we did artificial inseminations. We were lucky—it worked after two tries."

Giuliana was starting to imagine the complications. "Does Herr Eberhart have other children?"

"He has a two-year-old son, and he and Sophie want at least one more child."

Giuliana said nothing, trying to think through the legal and emotional issues raised by Saritha's parentage.

Nisha broke into her thoughts. "Are you planning to speak with Andi's parents? Because if you do, please don't tell them that Yannick is Sari's father. Please." She leaned toward Giuliana, twisting her hands.

Privately Giuliana thought that the sooner this secret was revealed, the better, before someone said or did something unforgivable. Unless someone already had. But it wasn't up to her to break the news, not yet, anyway. "I won't tell them unless I think the truth will help me find out who killed your partner. I assume your sister-in-law, at least, isn't in the dark about this sperm donation."

"Of course not," Nisha said hotly. "Andi discussed it first with me and then with Yannick, but we would never have gone ahead if he hadn't told us Sophie supported the idea." As she spoke, she was already up from the sofa, moving restlessly toward the hall.

"But you've never talked with her about it?" Giuliana kept the surprise out of her voice.

Nisha faced her from the doorway. "We . . . Yannick said . . ." She started over. "I should have talked to her about it. I realize that now. But . . ."

A wail filled the apartment, and Nisha, murmuring "Sorry," disappeared.

Giuliana skimmed through her notes, making small additions and contemplating what, if anything, to tell Nisha about her plan to interview the rest of the Pragasam family. When a buzz came from the street door, she stood up and went, undecided, into the hall. Nisha appeared in a doorway. "I'm sure that's my babysitter. Do you mind letting her in?"

Giuliana lifted the speakerphone and said hello.

"Hi, Nisha," a voice crackled through the speaker. "I'm here for Sari."

"Just a minute, please." Giuliana turned to see Nisha coming toward her with her daughter in her arms.

"That's my neighbor, Vivienne," Nisha said as she pushed the button to open the downstairs door. "Do you think I should give her Sari for a half hour? I mean, do you have a lot more questions?"

"Not now, but I'm sure I'll be back in touch. And you? Any questions for me?"

A knock forestalled Nisha's answer. She opened the door, and a tall, thin woman in her mid-fifties bustled into the apartment, dressed with stylish eccentricity in earthy colors, her hennaed hair pixie cut to accentuate large blue eyes.

"Are you all right, Nisha?" the woman said, moving inside to hug Nisha and stroke the baby's cheek. "I'm a bit early, but I was on my way home and thought I'd come by now to see if I could help."

"I think we're almost done," Nisha said, "but why don't you stay for a minute anyway. Giuliana Linder, this is Vivienne Marti. Frau Linder is from homicide."

"Homicide? Why? What have you . . .?" The tall woman turned to stare at Giuliana, a hand darting to her mouth in surprise. "I mean, I knew Nisha was talking to the police, but I thought it was something routine. I had no idea . . . Wasn't Andi killed in a bike accident?"

"We have to consider all the possibilities in a case like this." That was enough for now, she thought, offering Vivienne her hand. Nisha had disappeared with Saritha.

"Well, goodness." Vivienne stood frozen in the hall another moment, then said, "Excuse me, I'm just going to make Nisha some tea," and began to busy herself in the open kitchen, filling the kettle and putting things away in cupboards. She seemed quite at home in the apartment. Perhaps this was someone who should also be interviewed, someone who, unlike Andi's activist friends or curling teammates, knew both women well.

"Could I talk to you, too, Frau Marti? If you'd give me your address and telephone number?" She held out her notebook and pen to Vivienne, who was searching through what looked like jars of teabags.

"Of course, of course. Have you heard about Andi's horrible anonymous letters?" Vivienne asked as she wrote down the information.

Nisha walked into the room; Sari was now holding a small stuffed leopard.

"Nisha, you must tell her. Those ghastly letters. Could that person have . . .?"

Nisha put a hand on her friend's arm. "The police know all about that. They're talking to a lot of people." She turned to Giuliana. "Are we done, Frau Linder? Please phone me if there's anything else."

Heading downstairs, all Giuliana could think about was the baby's paternity. Nisha's brother-in-law was her baby's father. His wife knew about it, and his parents didn't. On the one hand, it was a sensible choice on the part of the lesbian couple, faced with a difficult situation—keeping it all in the family, so to speak. On the other hand, what an emotional can of worms!

And what did Nisha's parents and brothers know? Giuliana wondered how soon she could assemble the Pragasam family and whether it would be better to confront them separately or together. Maybe that very evening would work—it was only noon now, so there was still time to track them down. Renzo could do the interrogating with her; she was sure he'd want to be involved. She spared a thought for Fränzi, who'd have to put up with Renzo's lateness again. Then her mind turned to Ueli: if she scheduled the interview for that evening, Ueli would be left to worry about Irène's upcoming operation alone.

She forced that thought away. An evening interview was practical for witnesses who worked during the day, and that was all there was to it.

As she left the building, she was already dialing her office to assign someone to dig up contact details and background information on Nisha's parents and brothers. And to find out if one of them had a red car with a damaged front.

14

Renzo and his favorite trainer at the gym had come up with a new set of routines. One was chin-ups with a weight strapped around his waist. This morning he'd thought he was finally going to be able to do two sets of six reps each, but he'd barely managed one set. Well, shit! At least the new forward and backward lunges he was working on were getting smoother.

He stepped out of the shower into the changing room and pushed all thoughts of his workout away. As he dressed, he focused on the trip to Andi Eberhart's office in Thun. He and Fränzi had been at a big indoor playground with the kids on Sunday afternoon when Vinz had called to ask him to switch his focus to Eberhart's job, and, with Fränzi glaring at him, he hadn't been able to ask enough questions—well, any questions, really—about what he was supposed to be looking for. After Fränzi had fallen asleep that night, he'd managed to spend half an hour online finding out more about how the civilian service system worked, and he thought it sounded interesting. It had never occurred to him at nineteen *not* to do his Army service; he'd assumed the Civi alternative was only for pacifists and weirdos. Twenty years before that, it had been army or jail.

There was just one problem with switching his focus, he thought as he got into his car, stowed his coffee in the cupholder next to the driver's seat, and put the address into his GPS—he'd have less chance to work with Giuliana.

Most of the traffic on the highway at that hour was heading into Bern, not away from it, so it took only about twenty minutes to drive to Thun, a city about a third the size of Bern with a magnificent medieval castle on a lake, the Thunersee. For the last two-thirds of the journey, the Bernese Alps should have been visible, but today the entire range was buried in fog. With the radio blaring Baby K's "Non mi basta piu," he drove along in the cocoon of his Fiat, singing a line now and then and thinking about Giuliana. "It's not enough for me anymore, and it never goes away," Baby K sang. What a fool he was not to move on from such a useless crush, Renzo thought. "I want more, more." Fuck it, he thought, it really isn't enough for me anymore, and he realized he no longer meant just his feelings for Giuliana but also the mess that was his marriage to Fränzi. "*Non mi basta piu*," he sang to himself and thought that this time he might do something about it.

Renzo's meeting that morning was with Andi's boss, Christoph Luginbühl, and the colleague Andi had worked most closely with, a man named Loïc Amrein. The three of them sat around Luginbühl's desk in his small office, which was saved from being claustrophobic by a glass wall that offered a breathtaking view of the lake. Renzo appreciated the view and Luginbühl's Nespresso machine.

He guessed that Andi's boss was about fifty. He was round without being fat—a balding round head on a soft round body. His kind, round face with its round glasses looked like it probably wore a worried expression most of the time—as it did right now. Amrein, on the other hand, looked like an elf. A slight man of middle height who radiated cheerful, lively energy, he had small, pointy features and short, spiky black hair. Renzo placed him at just under thirty.

"Is anyone looking into those suspended prison guards?" Loïc asked Renzo as Luginbühl put small cups of coffee in front of both men and sat down heavily with his own.

"My colleagues are following up on that," Renzo said, "which is why you're dealing with me today. You've given us a promising lead, but we still need to know more about Andi's work and the people she dealt with here."

"You think one of her Civis could have killed her?" As Loïc asked the question, Luginbühl began to shake his head, his worried frown growing deeper. But he didn't speak.

Or one of her officemates, Renzo said to himself. But all he said aloud was, "At this point, anything's possible. I believe the other investigator, Madeleine Trachsel, has already asked all of you for your alibis. Those are still being checked. What I need today is a list of all the Civis Andi has worked with and their jobs."

"*All*?" echoed Luginbühl. "During the six years Andi was here, she dealt with thousands of men. I'm not sure—"

"It's not so bad, Stöffu," Loïc broke in. "She may have dealt with thousands on paper, but she only had personal contact with hundreds. I'm sure I can find the files."

"Thanks, Loïc," Luginbühl said, but before he could go on, Renzo interrupted.

"I don't want to overwhelm you. Why don't I start by asking for information on the men she got to know during the past year and a half? It makes sense to start with her most recent clients."

Luginbühl looked like he was pulling himself together at last. "Tell you what," he said. "Loïc will get started right now coming up with that list, and I'll give you some background on the civilian service and what Andi did for us. Then I'll show you to her cubicle and get you logged into her computer. The woman who was here on Friday searched her desk, and I understand you already have her home laptop and phone, but to get access to her work files, you'll need our passwords." He raised his eyebrows. "That sound good?"

"Sure," said Renzo. He'd start with this plan of Luginbühl's and see how things went for the first hour or so. It looked like he was going to be here all day, if not longer.

"Great," said Loïc, draining his coffee and heading for the door.

"I'll work on the list and bring it to you in Andi's office," he said over his shoulder to Renzo.

Andi's boss smiled after Loïc; then his face grew grave. "Before I tell you about what we do here, I wanted to say that I . . . well, Andi's death is a personal loss for me. She was absolutely dedicated to making the experience of being a Civi a good one for as many young men as possible, and I don't think I've ever known anyone so thorough. Which means you'll find her records about the youngsters she worked with very complete."

Renzo decided to pursue this. He leaned forward. "I feel like I need a better picture of how Frau Eberhart interacted with people, so tell me: what were the qualities she had that might have made someone want to kill her?"

He expected Andi's boss to be shocked, but his expression remained pensive. "Actually," he said after a moment, "I've already started telling you her faults in a roundabout way because if I'm honest, her dedication to her job and her thoroughness were part of what also made her . . . difficult. She had a very . . . hmm, let's say, a strong personality. Still," he added hastily, "everyone got along with her fine. Almost everyone. But I don't think she had any friends here except Loïc."

"A strong personality," Renzo repeated. "You mean bossy? Overbearing? Critical? Cruel, even?" He'd forgotten his coffee, which had cooled, but he picked it up anyway and finished it as he waited for Luginbühl's answer.

"Never cruel and not deliberately overbearing, either, but certainly intimidating and sometimes critical." Christoph paused, tugging on one ear. "She wasn't one to suffer fools gladly—fools or fakes. I respected her, but I confess to being a bit scared of her." He grinned sheepishly at Renzo and went on. "If she felt something was the right thing to do, she wouldn't stop pushing, and I can picture someone wanting to hurt her at a moment like that. Still, to go from being angry after an infuriating encounter to planning and completing a murder is a step I can't imagine."

After what Karolin Itten had told him at the curling restaurant,

Luginbühl's words didn't surprise Renzo, but they sharpened his picture of the dead woman. "That's very helpful," he said. "Now, tell me what you think I should know about the Civi." He leaned back in his chair, crossed his arms, put on a pleasant expression, and braced himself for a lecture.

"The civilian service lasts one-and-a-half times longer than the standard army service," Luginbühl began, "so a Civi's tour of duty is about thirteen months. He has to complete it sometime between the ages of nineteen and thirty-four, and there are eight fields he can work in."

Renzo, who wanted to make it clear that he'd done his research before coming, counted them out on his fingers. "Health, social service, education, culture, farming, environmental protection, natural catastrophes, and . . . I can't remember the eighth."

"Humanitarian service in developing countries—not too many openings there, although lots of youngers are eager to do it." Smiling, Luginbühl added, "Most of their service days are spent taking care of either Swiss people or Swiss land, however."

"What does that mean exactly?" Renzo asked.

"Civis spend the bulk of their time in senior centers, health facilities, or daycare centers or else working out of doors, improving paths in the forest, pulling up invasive plants, or doing something for the environment," Luginbühl explained. "That's where they're most needed."

"Do young men try to get their full thirteen months done as soon as possible?" Renzo asked. Like most Swiss soldiers, after his basic training, he'd chosen to spread his remaining service out over the maximum number of years.

"Well, I'd say the majority are finished by the age of twenty-five, but we deal with lots of exceptions, too, like boys signing up at nineteen, doing a summer's worth of Civi work, and taking off in the fall to study or travel abroad. Then they have their service waiting for them when they get back—which sometimes surprises them." He gave Renzo a mischievous smile. "Andi's clients' last names started with L through P; that's how we divide up the cases. Most of them will have completed their full thirteen months under her supervision. But some deliberately drag out the process for a decade; a man like that could have begun to serve before Andi got her job here and six years later still not be finished." As Renzo made a few notes, Luginbühl added, "Please remember that all the information you find in her files or that Loïc Amrein gives you about these young men is confidential."

"Right," said Renzo. "If you could get me started now, I'd appreciate it. Then, by the time Herr Amrein is done with his list, I'll know how to track down the names he gives me."

"Let's go then." Luginbühl escorted him out of the office and through a labyrinth of desks to a decent-sized cubicle. Like all the other cubicles, it was furnished with a cabinet, lamp, desk, and chair; a computer, screen, mouse, and keyboard; and a wastebasket and pinboard. On the desk was a large framed photograph of a thin, dark woman with huge brown eyes and a mass of black hair piled casually on her head. She beamed out at the camera, holding a plump baby girl whose arms were outstretched toward the photographer. The baby's eyes were shut, and her mouth was wide open with laughter. Renzo drew in his breath, thinking of Andi, who would never see that beautiful baby grow up.

He pulled his attention back to Luginbühl, who was turning on the computer under the desk and entering a password to call up Andi's desktop page. "Everyone in the office has access to each other's official files," he told Renzo, "because we work with a lot of the same information. Let's say Loïc wants to place one of his Civis in a job that one of Andi's Civis filled a couple of years ago. He can talk to her about it, of course, but first, he'd probably read her notes on what her Civi thought of the job and whether she had to intervene with the employer."

"Do you think Andi had any other files on this computer besides the ones everyone had access to?"

Luginbühl frowned. "I don't know. And why would she want to, anyway?"

Renzo knew the question was meant rhetorically, but he could have answered it easily: for secrecy. Millions of people keep private stuff on their work computers, he wanted to say. But before he could explain, Luginbühl went on: "I sometimes saw Andi coming or going with her private laptop." He frowned as if it was only now occurring to him that bringing your laptop to a job where you already had a computer might be a bit odd. "Well, I'll leave you to it," he said hurriedly. "Loïc should have some names for you soon." With that, he squeezed out of the small space, calling cheerfully to someone in one of the other cubicles as he made his way through the maze of partitions and desks.

Left on his own, Renzo put on latex gloves, sat down in Andi's chair, and went through her desk. He knew Madeleine had already done this and perhaps even removed things—he'd have to ask her—but it was his turn to form impressions now. The drawers were neat, although not obsessively so, and their only revelation was a hoard of lemon-flavored throat lozenges. That done, he glanced through emails and started looking at the names of files and folders, then at her file history. He'd search systematically once he had the names of her most recent clients; for now, he was merely fishing around. A file with photos of Andi's daughter had been opened on the last morning of her life. Renzo wondered if she'd looked at those pictures most days.

He was skimming emails when Loïc arrived and set a USB stick on the desktop. He dropped into the spare chair to the side of the desk and immediately began talking. "Okay. Here's a list of fifty-eight men Andi had a lot of contact with during the last eighteen months. I've given you just their names because you'll find data about them in her files. Plenty of data. You'll see how much she cared about a lot of these guys."

"Thanks," Renzo said, "I'll . . ."

Loïc was on his feet again. "Look, I'll give you two hours to check the information, and then I'll come back, and you can ask me any questions you have about it. Okay?"

"That sounds good," Renzo had time to say, before Loïc clapped him on the back and was gone.

The list on the drive ran alphabetically by last name, from Laabs,

Florian, to Puig, Jorge. Renzo picked a name at random from Loïc's list, Kai Odermatt, and opened Andi's files. Under the heading *Contact with Clients*, he found a series of folders labeled by year. A click on the previous year showed him last names in alphabetical order beginning with "L." He scrolled down to Odermatt and began looking through notes. Andi had typed:

April 28: KO *requested two weeks' vacation after four months at Alpenblick Senior Home in Brig. Told him if he could work it out with employer and finish rest of service immediately upon return, I'd okay it.* NOTE: *Make sure 180-day tour of duty completed by August 15 of this year.* Below that, in blue letters, was *August 15: Assignment completed; boss Rosemarie Habegger satisfied; would hire KO again.*

Renzo saw that along with the *Contact with Clients* folder, there were *Letters*, *Notes on Employers*, and one simply called *Civis*. Its subfolders were *Routine* and *Of Interest*. A glance at the cases Andi had considered routine revealed not much more than a list of names—if not the thousands that Luginbühl had mentioned, then certainly hundreds. Over half the names had a sentence or a few phrases next to them, like *finished October 2019, no problems*, or *still four months; stalling*. Kai Odermatt's name was in the "Of Interest" category. Why, Renzo wondered. What made some more interesting than others?

When Renzo clicked on Odermatt's file, he saw that Andi had written a series of short notes to herself. There were impressions of the young man and his attitude to his different jobs, followed by brief statements about his employers. Skimming the phrases, Renzo chuckled. This was not what you expected to find in a government employee's official files, especially not in files to which her colleagues had such easy access. The notes on Kai Odermatt were written over a period of several years. First came *KO is major pain; had to be coerced into first assignment*, then *KO still complaining—supervisor says lazy but not hopeless.* Most recently: *KO finally got a grip. Enjoying six-month service at Alpenblick; no complaints from either side.* Below that she had written, *KO reports Alpenblick okay (cleanliness, food, activities, general organization); elderly not neglected. Head of home competent. Lots of foreign workers in patient care and kitchen. Check.*

Renzo could understand why someone responsible for matching men and jobs would want insider tips on each workplace. Plus, an honest assessment of each man's strengths and weaknesses would protect the office's best employment sources from getting landed with the unruliest assignees. But this was a lot of information—just what Luginbühl had said he'd find.

Renzo fetched another coffee, making friendly noises to everyone he ran into on his way to and from the office kitchen, and settled down to read what Andi had written about the fifty-eight Civis she'd contacted most often during the previous eighteen months.

In his online research of the night before, Renzo had learned that there were over twenty thousand men serving as Civis each year. About 70 percent of the one million, seven hundred thousand days of work they did annually took place in health and social services, and that was indeed where most of the fifty-eight men had worked or were working, although none at a big-city hospital. He looked at emails that had gone back and forth between Andi and "her" young men, trying to find something on either side of the exchange that could be interpreted as threatening. All of the fifty-eight had contacted her about some problem or other, sometimes in response to an inquiry from her. That seemed normal. The vast majority of youngsters who chose the civilian service as an alternative to the Swiss Army were self-sufficient. They consulted an online list of Civi-approved job opportunities, chose the ones that looked interesting, contacted the employers, went for interviews, got work as quickly as they could, and served their obligatory months. Andi and her colleagues in Thun only came into the picture when something wasn't working.

A little after eleven, Loïc dropped into a chair next to Renzo's. Rubbing a hand back and forth over his spiky black hair, he asked, "How's it going? Any questions?"

"A couple," Renzo told him. "Andi"—he'd decided to drop the "Frau Eberhart" with this guy—"kept notes on the cases she considered in some way nonstandard. All the names on the list of fifty-eight you gave me are in that category of her files, but there are more names, too. Well over a hundred, but they go back several years. After each name, she added some . . . code, I'd call it. Like the man's date of birth, followed by the date he enrolled in the Civi. That's clear. But then there are some emojis I'm not sure about."

Loïc leaned back in his chair, stretching his legs out as far as they'd go. He crossed his arms and said, "Try me."

"Okay. By some names, she puts a carrot. When I compare her writeups on the men with carrots to the ones without, there's more detail about the carrots. They seem to have given her more info, but . . . well, it could be something else."

"Carrots, carrots," Loïc mumbled to himself before starting to laugh. "I think I get that one. Andi had some favorite phrases for describing our more clueless Civis, like 'not all his cups in the cupboard,' 'one slice shy of a loaf,' or 'not rowing with both oars.' One of her favorites was 'a few carrots short of a carrot cake.' So maybe she put a carrot as a sign that a guy was intelligent and . . . well, just generally with it. Someone with all his carrots."

"Ha! That makes sense." Andi'd had a sense of humor, then. "Then there's a smiley, but only sometimes. I'm pretty sure it means she likes the guy—whether he has a carrot or not. After that, many names are followed by a key emoji, and some—only fifteen among your fifty-eight—are marked with a bolt of lightning."

"Key and lightning bolt," Loïc repeated, his narrow face still. Then he shrugged. "Sorry, no clue. But I'll think about it. Anything else?"

"Yeah," said Renzo, turning away from the computer to face Loïc as well as he could in the narrow space. "Tell me, did you and she talk about the Civis you were working with?"

"Yes, constantly. We all talk about our cases. They're . . . hilarious." Loïc's blue eyes glinted. "Think of thousands of men in their twenties going out each year to places they've never been and taking jobs they don't know how to do. You can't imagine the amount of trouble they get into. The ones in forestry fall out of trees, and the ones working on farms fall off tractors. They break their legs while they're pulling up invasive plants in the mountains; they break priceless pots in museums. We assign them to take care of refugees, and they punch some poor Somali's lights out; we send them to look after elderly folks, and they let the old dears fall out of bed."

By the time Loïc finished this list of disasters, Renzo was laughing out loud.

"Don't get me wrong," Loïc went on, clearly enjoying Renzo's amusement. "They do great things, too. There are Civis with no more than a bit of first-aid training who've saved lives, and we've had quite a few letters from parents about how a Civi assigned to an afterschool program has turned their kid's life around."

Still smiling, Renzo said, "I never really think about them out there, you know. But one million, seven hundred thousand days of work a year! They must be everywhere."

"They are," Loïc sat up straighter in his chair. "Every day, they're out there helping tens of thousands of people. Well, not all of them directly, of course, although they do work a lot with oldsters and the handicapped. But also by building drystone walls and clearing hiking trails—improving the country's infrastructure. Or showing kids around museums. But," he grinned again, "those rays of sunshine aren't the entertaining ones! It's much more fun to talk about the ones caught selling weed to school kids or accidentally shredding important documents."

This wasn't what Renzo had been expecting when he'd asked Loïc if he and Andi had discussed their work. But before he could make his question more precise, the younger man went on. "Andi and I didn't just tell each other funny stories—she also gave me advice on difficult cases, and occasionally she shared her problems with me. I appreciated that."

"I've already read about some of those problems," Renzo commented as he glanced at the computer screen in front of him. "So far, I've got two men who apparently dropped off the face of the earth, three being bullied at their jobs and another one doing the bullying, and two who cut work every Friday and most Mondays. Only one of those has a carrot, though, along with a key."

"Sorry I don't have any ideas about the key, but I'll text you if I think of something." He raised his eyebrows at Renzo. "So . . . if there's nothing else, I'll get back to work."

"Sure. Thanks for the help." Renzo smiled and returned to scrolling through the files.

By the time he left the Civi center at four, he'd read everything he could find about the list of men Loïc had given him; he'd also read notes on a few other clients whose names were marked with carrots, keys, or lightning bolts. He was left with the feeling that some of Andi's notes and emails were missing. Follow-up actions that Andi had suggested in emails were never mentioned again, and there were questions from Civis that Andi didn't appear to have answered. He considered asking Luginbühl about these lapses, but they didn't seem important enough. Still, they didn't match up with Andi's reputation for thoroughness. Unless, of course, the exchanges had continued on her mobile or her private laptop. He wondered where those were—Madeleine must have taken both back to the police station. He'd need to track them down. And to check her cell phone records to see if she'd been in touch with any of the men on Loïc's list.

But that was for tomorrow, he thought as he drove back to Bern. At five, he was seeing Giuliana so they could prepare for their talk with the Pragasam family that evening at eight. She'd phoned him twice to update him about that, but her most interesting revelation had been the identity of Saritha's father. Up until that moment, Andi's brother Yannick had just been an incidental character in this tragedy, but now, suddenly, he was center stage. Not that Renzo could imagine why he'd want to kill his sister, but . . . well, someone certainly needed to talk to him. That step seemed more likely to reveal important information than all this fishing around in Andi Eberhart's files. Still, his curiosity had been aroused by her odd recordkeeping. Now he couldn't stop reflecting on keys and lightning bolts.

15

The conference room wasn't crowded, but it still felt claustrophobic. Giuliana thought it was because of all the tension swirling around. Across from her and Renzo, Nisha Pragasam's parents and brothers sat taut with strain. Half-hidden in one corner of the room, even the translator, a Swiss Tamil who'd worked with the police for years, was nervously tapping her pen on the open notebook in her lap.

With basic contact information established, Giuliana began simply. "You're all here because of the death of Andrea Eberhart. I'd like to ask each of you—"

Nisha's younger brother Rajan interrupted her, his mouth twisted and his voice heavy with scorn. "Do you think we're Pakistanis?"

Rajan was twenty-five and almost finished with a master's degree in software engineering. He worked part time in a central IT office at Swisscom headquarters. With the same large dark eyes and attractive features as his sister, he was a handsome man—and well turned out, too, in a collared shirt and leather shoes. His Swiss-German dialect was as Bernese sounding as Giuliana's own, and his records showed he was a Swiss citizen. All in all, he was a poster child for refugee integration.

Except for being furious. His eyes narrowed into slits as he said, "Perhaps it would help if I showed you a map of Asia. Pakistan—north; Sri Lanka—south. Them—Muslim; us—Hindu. Them—light skin; us—dark skin. Them—thousands of honor killings a year; us—none. Not to mention that if this were an honor killing, Nisha would be dead. Not Andi."

"I take your point," said Giuliana calmly. "Still, many Tamils in India, Sri Lanka, and Switzerland oppose marriages that break inter-caste taboos. Your sister was living in a relationship that is not tradi-tionally acceptable, and she has a child outside of marriage, at least in the eyes of the law. I've heard from Nisha herself that she has been excluded from the family, so I *know* there has been opposition to her relationship."

Rajan looked at her steadily, then spoke again, this time without his previous sarcasm. "I was not at all against Andi and Nisha being together. I met them several times for coffee and visited them at home, before and after Saritha was born." He had been speaking to Giuliana, but now he turned his head and looked directly at his father. "My niece is a beautiful, loving little girl. As far as I'm concerned, we—" He broke off and sighed. Something in his father's expression had appar-ently subdued Rajan—for now, at least.

The father, a small square man in his fifties named Siva, sat with folded hands, fighting for dignity even as his face shone with sweat. Giuliana knew how intimidating any encounter with the police could be to a political refugee, no matter how innocent he was. His wife, Devi, thin and birdlike, sat quietly, casting occasional worried glances at her husband.

Mathan, the member of the family who interested Giuliana the most, was the hardest to read. Bigger than his father and brother, he lounged in his chair, trying to project nonchalance.

Before Giuliana could ask anything else about the Pragasams' attitudes toward Andi, Devi spoke in Swiss German. "No one in my family do this kill. Never. Make Nisha very sad."

Giuliana was surprised, and so, she thought, were the men. Siva stared at his wife, Mathan glared, and Rajan gave her a grin. Whether they were responding to her use of Swiss-German, her courage at speaking up, or the content of her comments, Giuliana couldn't be sure.

Giuliana smiled at Devi. "I hope you're right. But we still need to know what each of you was doing last Wednesday night, March twenty-fifth, when Frau Eberhart was hit by a car." The woman in the corner translated her words.

Still sprawled in his chair, Mathan crossed his arms and leaned his head back slightly, thrusting out his chin. "I was at home all evening," he said, also in Swiss German. "My wife knows that."

Rajan laughed. "And she'd say the sky was green if you told her to."

Rajan's father spoke a word to his younger son—Giuliana assumed it meant something along the lines of "Shut up, you fool." The police translator sitting in the corner of the room taking notes said nothing; her job was to translate out loud when asked and otherwise note down what she heard.

So Rajan was an equal opportunity gadfly, Giuliana thought, apparently as ready to antagonize his brother as the police. And Mathan's Bernese dialect was just as fluent as Rajan's. Yet his sister had said that he was the only one of the three children who didn't fit into the life their parents had brought them to twenty-eight years earlier.

There was silence for almost a minute. Eventually, Rajan said in a much calmer voice than he'd used before, "I checked my calendar on the way over here. I went to a play at the Effingerstrasse Theater that night with a friend. Afterward, we had a drink together, and I got home at midnight. I share an apartment with two other students, but they were already in their rooms when I came in. I don't know if they heard me—you can ask them."

Giuliana nodded and turned to Siva, who slipped his trembling hands into his lap before saying, "I worked all day in the kitchen at Engeried Hospital, and my shift finishes at six." His Bernese dialect was strongly accented and ungrammatical but easy to understand. "We live within walking distance of the hospital, and I got home at six twenty, as usual. My wife and I had dinner. After that, we watched a film, and I think we went to bed around eleven, our normal time. Neither of us left the house that night." He paused and asked, "Do you . . . will you have to talk to my boss?" He slipped a handkerchief from his back trouser pocket and wiped the sweat off his forehead.

Giuliana exchanged a look with Renzo, who was sitting quietly at one end of the table, taking notes. "I don't know yet, Herr Pragasam," she said in a voice she hoped was neither reassuring nor menacing.

Devi spoke again, even more urgently than before. "Andi love my girl, love baby. Good woman, work hard, make home. Nisha happy. Not bad. *Nothing* bad." Her jaw clenched as she finished, and she turned to look down the table at her son Mathan.

There was a pause, and then Rajan patted his mother's arm. "Bravo, Amma."

An explosion of Tamil followed, and the translator scribbled furiously. Giuliana let it go on for a minute or two, observing faces and postures as the words flowed past her. Both Mathan and his father leaned forward to speak to Devi. Siva spoke gravely; Giuliana read it as supportive acknowledgment without agreement. But Mathan slammed a palm down on the table and rattled on, his words becoming louder and higher pitched, a spiteful look on his face. His father was clearly trying to calm him down, while Rajan, still resting a hand on his mother's arm, made periodic comments that the other two men seemed to ignore.

Mathan tossed one last shot at Rajan, who started to rise from his chair and then, with an angry retort and shaking his head, sat down. After that, Rajan stared pointedly at the translator, who hadn't looked up from her frantic writing, and spoke one loud sentence that Giuliana's imagination interpreted as, "You do realize that woman in the corner is writing all of this down, don't you?"

At this, Giuliana raised her own voice. "That's enough now." The three men fell silent. Devi, who had not spoken at all since her defense of Andi, was looking at her lap.

"Frau Pragasam," Giuliana said to Nisha's mother, who raised her head and stared nervously across the table, "I am going to speak to you in German since you have spoken to me that way, but please ask for a translation if there is anything you don't understand." At Devi's nod, she continued, speaking slowly and clearly. "Do you agree with your husband about what you both did last Wednesday night: had dinner, watched a film, and went to bed? Devi nodded again. "Have you met your daughter's partner and their little girl?" Nod. "Did you visit their apartment regularly?" Nod. "Were those visits a secret from your husband?" A glance toward her husband was followed by another nod.

Giuliana had hoped that speaking with the whole family would reveal something about the way they interacted, which it had. But now she was beginning to think she had made a bad mistake. Questioning each of them alone would have allowed Nisha's mother to keep her secrets. But it was too late to change now, so she carried on. "Herr Pragasam, would you like to explain to me why your wife has to visit your daughter and your granddaughter in secret?"

Siva gave a long sigh and turned to the translator with a courteous-sounding question, which she answered. He began to speak in Tamil, pausing after each sentence so it could be restated in German.

"I work in a kitchen now, but in my hometown, I was a schoolteacher. I understand cultural differences. I know that when you are forced to raise your children in a foreign country, they grow up with different values, no matter what you do. Nisha always had Swiss friends, and I had no problem with that. Also, I would never have forced her to spend her life with a man she didn't like. When she turned twenty, we began to suggest appropriate Tamil men for her, and her mother told her that if she found someone else, even if we didn't know him or his family, we would gladly meet him and . . . consider him as a son-in-law." He stopped here and glanced at his wife, who nodded in agreement. He listened until the translation was complete and then continued.

"The younger generation—the Tamil children here in Switzerland—don't understand the significance of caste, but it's still important. We older ones represent not just ourselves but our families back in Sri Lanka. We have a responsibility to a great many people to run a proper household, even though we live so far away from our homeland."

Giuliana was nodding, too, as she listened to the translator's voice convey this man's dilemmas. She'd been dismissing Nisha's father as someone who lived by a simplistic code, but now she could imagine him trying for years to reconcile two complex worlds and keep his wife and children balanced between both. She waited to be sure the translator was finished and said, "So a woman living in a partnership with another woman is unacceptable, given the values you represent."

Mathan broke into the translation of her question to say, in Bernese German, "Of course it is. No one—"

His father held up a hand and spoke gently to Mathan, who fell silent. Then he continued speaking to Giuliana and Renzo in Tamil.

"There are homosexuals in Sri Lanka, as I assume there are everywhere in the world. But at home, these people do not live together openly, nor do they raise children together. When Nisha decided to do this, she . . . abandoned us."

Devi muttered something, and Siva stopped. Rajan said to his father, in German, "Amma is right. Nisha didn't leave the family; you asked her to go. She still loves us, and, especially now that Andi's dead, she needs us."

The tension that had held the room in its grip seemed to have faded, to be replaced, Giuliana thought, by sadness. Giuliana imagined that, like most families, this one had avoided openly discussing something all of them felt strongly about. Too bad it took a crisis to get parents and children talking to each other, she thought—and Ueli's family came immediately to mind. The Brand family couldn't even talk *during* a crisis, for God's sake.

Mathan must have been reflecting on his younger brother's words because now he said, "With Andi dead, I bet Nisha does need us. But it's too late. She got what was coming to her." His voice was defiant, and he stared at the wall over Giuliana's shoulder as he spoke. His mother turned in her chair to shake her head at him. Mathan met her eyes briefly before looking back at the wall.

Siva had lost some of his self-consciousness; he had his elbows on the table, chin resting on his knitted fingers. His face sagged with tiredness, and his eyes were full of pain. "You see," he said, speaking through the translator, "we handle things . . . our own way. My wife has been helping our daughter quietly, behind my back." Giuliana was surprised to see him turn and give Devi a small smile. "Now that she has told me in front of our sons that she's doing this, I must forbid it, and she'll have to stop." He shook his head and looked at Giuliana sadly before saying, "I know you can't understand this, but . . ." He shrugged.

Giuliana wished again that she'd seen the family members separately, but the damage was done. "I am sorry this investigation puts you and your family in difficulties, but I have serious grounds for suspicion. Herr Pragasam," she continued, now speaking directly to Nisha's older brother, who wouldn't meet her eyes, "we have examined your sister's phone. We found text messages and calls from you there. They are very . . . nasty. They go back about eight weeks to when you got her new mobile number from your mother, but you were sending them before that, as well, to the old number." Glancing around the table, Giuliana saw that Siva looked surprised, Devi and Rajan angry. "Your texts are why she had to get a new number."

"That's a lie," he muttered, staring at the table in front of him.

"Give my colleague Herr Donatelli your telephone. Right now, please."

Mathan made no move to get out his phone. Renzo got up from where he'd been sitting at the long table and stood behind him.

"You can't just take my phone," Mathan said. There was wonder in his voice, as if he couldn't believe what was happening.

"I can, you know," said Renzo. "I've got paperwork that makes it legal. We'll check the front of your car for traces of Andrea Eberhart's bicycle and search for evidence that you persuaded a friend to kill her or paid someone to do it. But let's start with your mobile."

Mathan took it from his jacket pocket but gripped it in his hand. He stared at it as he muttered, "OK, then. I did text and call Nisha, and I told her . . ." He trailed off. "I said a lot of things to make her feel bad because I wanted her to know I found her life wrong. But I never threatened to hurt her or the baby. Or that . . . woman she lived with."

He gave the phone to Renzo, and Renzo returned to the table. Devi began to speak in Tamil to Giuliana without looking at the translator.

"What my older son did was terrible, but he wasn't responsible for this murder. He is angry and confused, and he talks big, but he wouldn't ruin his sister's life. That's what I believe. But my husband and I will find out. If Mathan or someone from our community killed Nisha's . . . wife"—the translator faltered a little at this last word, clearly surprised, and the three Pragasam men turned to stare at Devi—"we'll find out."

Giuliana nodded to show she'd heard what Devi said. But she also heard what hadn't been said, which was, "We'll find out and deal with it ourselves." Any vigilante action like that would be a disaster. Still, for now, she'd keep quiet and accept Devi's statement without complaint.

From a bag at her feet, Giuliana got out a pad of paper and a handful of ballpoint pens. She tore four sheets off the pad. "We are finished talking for now. I need you to write down the names of anyone who can confirm where you were on Wednesday night, March twenty-fifth. If you spoke on the telephone during that time or ran into a neighbor, write that down. It's very important." She gestured to the translator, who came forward to the table. "You may ask Frau Nadesan to write your words down in German as long as you sign and date the paper. We'll send for a uniformed policeman while you do this, and he will escort you out of the building. Now, is there anything else you would like to say to me at this point? Or ask me?" She paused, but no one spoke. "One more question from me, then—does Mathan own a red Ford Fiesta sedan?"

Mathan nodded, and his father said, "Yes, that is correct."

"What other cars are there in the family?"

"I have a white Hyundai," said Rajan.

"And that's it? Good," Giuliana said. "Please write your license plate numbers on your alibi sheet, so we can follow up." Rajan nodded.

"Thank you, then," Giuliana concluded, and she and Renzo left.

She couldn't help wondering what the family would say to each other once they'd gone.

They walked a few doors down the corridor to a random office. Without flipping the light switch, Renzo walked to the window and leaned against the frame, arms folded, staring across the street. During the day, Nordring was busy with cars, trolley buses, and people, but at nine thirty, everything was quiet.

Giuliana turned on the light. "Sorry," she said as the room blazed, and Renzo winced. "Are you okay?"

He turned from the window and came to sit on one of the two metal desks; she leaned against the other, facing him. "I'm fine," he said. "Just trying to imagine what it was like for my parents to come here in their twenties, both fresh from Umbria without a word of any language but Italian, trying to cope with a weird culture."

Giuliana nodded. Renzo gave her a smile and added, "Hell of a lot easier for them than the Pragasams. At least they were Europeans, using a language lots of Swiss speak."

As he said this, the translator knocked on the half-open door, and Giuliana welcomed her in. "Everything go fine after we left?"

"No problem," she said. She was a plump woman of about forty in a soberly patterned salwar kameez. She exuded quiet confidence; Giuliana didn't think anything could faze her. "I'll write out their statements and send them in tomorrow to be signed. As for their talk among themselves, even when the men were all arguing, they didn't really say anything useful. There was only one thing a bit unexpected."

"What was it?" Giuliana asked her, leaning forward.

"There was a moment when Mathan commented to Rajan, and he looked furious, started to stand up, and then sank back down again and said something sharp to his brother. Remember?" The translator looked first at Giuliana and then at Renzo, who said, "Yeah, I was ready to jump up; I thought we might be about to have a fight on our hands."

"Exactly," the translator said. "Well, Mathan was throwing around a word, *veci*, which I have translated as *whore*. Rajan said, several times, 'Don't call her that'—they were talking about Nisha. But then Mathan made another *veci* comment that I missed because they were all talking at once, and that was when Rajan stood up. As he sat down he said something like, 'Why can't you mind your own business?' I think that was a reference to a different woman. Obviously, someone Rajan cares about, and not his sister."

"Interesting," Giuliana said. She remembered Nisha telling her that Rajan had a girlfriend. "Thanks. As far as the rest goes, if nothing else jumped out at you, we can wait for your report."

Once the translator was gone, Giuliana yawned hugely. Renzo, from his perch on the opposite desk, yawned too, and they smiled at each other.

"You spent today at the Civi office, didn't you?" Giuliana said. "If there's nothing urgent I need to know about that, let's go over it tomorrow. Do you mind?"

"Mind? I'm relieved. There's a lot on Andi's computer, but I feel sure some details are missing, so I need to think about what to do next. Something you could do for me, though—ask the IT guys to get me access to what's on her laptop. Maybe she has some of her work files on her private computer. At the moment, that's my best guess."

"I'll call first thing in the morning," Giuliana said.

"Thanks." He yawned again. "What about Mathan? I'm not sure he'd commit murder himself, but I can see him passing the job on. Asking some lowlife who owes him a favor to crash a car into his sister-in-law on a dark street and drive on."

"Maybe so." Giuliana pictured Nisha's older brother slouched in his chair and thought about how thin his bravado was. "You think he'd know a killer?"

"Their civil war ended in 2009. Most Tamil refugees in Switzerland must know someone who's a killer if you include soldiers; many older people fought themselves. Shall I check his calls?"

"I'll take care of that," Giuliana said, rubbing her eyes. "We'll get all the phone records from his provider—you know that. I just thought we could use some intimidating theater at that point during the interview, so thanks for looming over him and taking his phone. You stick to the Eberhart files. I'll note the calls to his sister and get a check on the other numbers he has called. Any texts in Tamil I'll pass on for translation." Then she sighed. She was desperate to unburden herself—and this was Renzo, after all. "I'm talking to Manfred Kissling tomorrow. The first of my depositions with him. God, I'm dreading it. And while I'm talking to him, my mother-in-law will be having a tumor removed from her colon."

Renzo had frowned at Kissling's name; now he jumped off the desk, came over to her, and put his hands on her arms. "Cancer. That's terrible. How . . . How bad is it?"

"She says it's only stage two, and I hope that's true. We'll know more after the operation. Ueli's at the Insel now, helping her get settled." As she said this, she thought of Ueli in a hospital ward with his parents and brother and hoped they were finally letting him be useful in some way. Or were they just ignoring him?

She tried to smile up at Renzo but couldn't quite manage it; he put his arm around her and pulled her in for a hug. She leaned her head on his shoulder, and they stayed that way while Giuliana let her mind go blank. Finally, she straightened up, and Renzo's arm fell away.

"Come on, let's go home. Actually, I should call Ueli at the hospital. If he's still there, I may need to pick him up. You go ahead. And Renzo." She put a hand on his arm and leaned in to kiss his cheek. "Thanks for the hug. And for . . . everything. I never find the right time to say it, but you do a great job. I'm so glad I get to work with you."

He smiled down at her, and for a moment, she could see what he felt written on his face. But he only said, "You do a great job, too. Good night." He collected his things and left. She listened to his footsteps in the corridor as she got out her mobile and called Ueli.

"Hello, love," he said, and his tone told her all she needed to know about how tired, worried, and discouraged he was. That was twenty years of marriage, she thought—your husband only had to say two words for you to read his state of mind.

"I'm done with my interview," she told him. "Shall I come and pick you up?"

"That would be great," Ueli said, his voice brightening. "We got Mam settled in, and Paps and Mike left twenty minutes ago." Perhaps anticipating her indignation that they hadn't offered Ueli a lift, he said, "I made them go straight home; they have to be back here tomorrow morning before the operation." Then, although she hadn't said anything, he added, "Really. It's okay."

"Where will you be?" she asked. "Main entrance?"

"Yeah, out on the sidewalk."

"Right. Fifteen minutes max," she said. She'd been heading for the parking lot as they spoke.

She drove by the botanical garden, across the Aare, and past Bern's alternative culture center, the *Reitschule*, which was quiet on a Monday night, before looping around the train station. On Freiburgstrasse in front of the hospital, she caught sight of Ueli standing under a streetlight, head bent. In the twenty-six years she'd known him, she'd seen him elated and furious, playful and worried, but she didn't think she'd ever seen him so dejected.

Rolling the car up to the curb, she climbed out and jogged toward him. As he looked up, she threw her arms around his hunched figure, pulled him toward her, and gripped him as if he were drowning.

Her arm around his waist, she walked with him back to the car, where he got into the driver's seat. "After we left Mam for the night, I hoped the three of us could have a quick beer at the cafeteria, but they wanted to get home. Which made sense."

This was no time to say anything critical. She rested a hand on his knee, and they moved through the streets in silence. It started to drizzle, and Ueli turned the wipers on. Giuliana watched them arc back and forth.

"Never wait until it's raining to repair your roof," he said at last.

"Huh?"

"You know—when the sun is shining, or when you're out of town, you put it off, and then, when the flood comes, it's impossible to do the work. You're too busy trying to save your furniture to fix the holes over your head."

Giuliana's tired brain started to whirr. "You're talking about your family," she said.

"Yeah." He drove a while longer before answering. "When I was young, I just wanted to leave it all behind—the farm, Mike, my parents, the way we dealt with each other. Now I'm a forty-eight-year-old with my own family. I see my parents once or twice a month, my brother once or twice a year, and it seems too painful for everyone, too complicated, even too *embarrassing*," he said with scorn, "to sit them down and suggest some family therapy. Or something. Especially since I'm the only one who thinks we need help. That *I* need help. So I keep on letting it go. After all, I have you." He covered her hand where it rested on his knee before gripping the steering wheel. "I tell myself, 'It doesn't matter. Things are fine.'"

"And then comes the rain," Giuliana said.

"More like a hurricane. Something that makes it obvious how messed up we are. But I know that now is not the time to deal with it. At the moment, almost everything's more important than my feelings about the way my parents and my brother treat me."

She couldn't argue with that. Irène was life-threateningly ill, and Erich was terrified of losing her. Mike was here to take care of his parents, not to deal with his little brother's resentments. Yet Giuliana understood Ueli's sense of urgency. If his mother died, there would never be a resolution. Not even the chance to attempt one.

"When this initial crisis is over, and we know more about your mother's . . . future," she said, "there might be time for you to work on fixing things."

"Fixing what? I'm not even sure what I want. But it's good to know you understand how I feel. Though I don't know how you can when I don't know myself."

"Detective work?" she ventured, and he smiled. "Let's go tell Isabelle your mother's ready for tomorrow," she said. "You know how much she wants to be part of things, and she's right—she is old enough for the truth."

"Yeah," Ueli said, "she is." They climbed the stairs side by side to the front door of the building, where he paused and added, "Speaking of truth, I think Lukas *is* upset about something, but he won't talk about it."

"Yeah. 'I'm fine, school's fine, nothing's going on.'" She rattled it out as tonelessly as Lukas had on Friday night, and Ueli snorted and said, "Exactly."

"All we can do is keep an eye on him," she said as he unlocked the door and held it open for her.

They walked into the building's foyer just as another huge yawn overwhelmed her. It was great to be home. Now for a good night's sleep before her dreaded interview with Manfred Kissling in the morning.

If only she'd been able to get something from a consulting psychiatrist on Kissling's wife, Iris. But the interview with Iris had been Saturday morning, and tomorrow was only Tuesday. It was too soon to expect any kind of analysis of her attitude and behavior. Giuliana would just have to see what she could do to get Kissling to reveal something useful without any insight into his wife.

16

G iuliana stood at one of the double casement windows in her bedroom and pushed open the dark blue shutters to let in the sunshine. After thirty days of wind, icy rain, snow, and fog, March was going out in glory. She wasn't fooled by one warm morning; there'd be days of sleet in April and maybe even frosts in early May, but today, at least, it was spring. If only she could ride her bicycle to work. But this morning, she'd be traveling to the Thorberg prison to see Kissling.

Even from her car, the trip to the police station was beautiful. Heading down the hill from her house, she passed the first tulips of the season, radiantly yellow against the grassy hillside. At Waisenhausplatz, the moss on the Meret Oppenheim fountain looked fresher and greener than the day before, and when she crossed the Aare at the Lorraine Bridge, she caught a quick glimpse of the Alps. Thirty miles away, the snowy peaks looked within arm's reach as they glistened in the morning light.

She tried to let these signs of spring ease her mind, but between her mother-in-law's operation and the interview with Manfred Kissling, there was no place for calm. In a couple of hours, the doctors would be poking around in Irène's guts while she tried to poke around Kissling's mind, probably with just as little luck as everyone else who'd interviewed him. She only hoped Irène's operation would produce better results than she expected to have.

Vinz had called a short update meeting at eight forty-five. But first, she'd have to check whether the IT cops had tackled Andi's laptop and make appointments with Susanna Käser, Andi's lawyer and former lover, and with Nisha's neighbor, Vivienne. And with Andi's parents. She'd call them first, she decided, as she was parking the car. On a day like this, an afternoon trip to their home would give her a magnificent drive into the mountains overlooking Lake Thun. Maybe Renzo would come with her to talk to the Eberharts—that added another call to her list since she didn't want to ask him at the meeting in front of everyone.

All the homicide detectives were at their desks for a change, except for Sabine Jost, who was on a walking tour in Iceland; everyone was either on the phone or focused on their screens. She waved a general hand at them all, and Erwin, glancing up from his computer, waved back, which gave her an idea. She walked over to his desk.

"What's up?" he asked, leaning back and looking at her over his reading glasses.

"I've got a quick meeting with Vinz about our hit-and-run murder that I think will be over at nine, and at ten, I'm leaving to see Kissling. You're the one who's spent the most time with him so far. Can we grab a coffee after my meeting? Maybe you've got a few tips for me." She kept her voice light, not wanting to show how unprepared she felt, despite all the transcripts she'd read and videos she'd watched.

"Why not?" he said, matching her lightness. "Come get me when Vinz is done." With that, he pushed his glasses back up his nose and looked down at his keyboard. Giuliana headed for her desk and started on her list of calls and texts.

Vinz hadn't bothered to reserve a special room for his meeting, so Giuliana and Rolf, along with Renzo and Madeleine Trachsel, piled into the little case room and either perched on the desks or leaned against the filing cabinets. Vinz had opened the window, and cool air poured into the room, along with slanting sunlight and noise from the street below, giving Giuliana a shot of energy. She glanced at Madeleine, who had only recently become a *Fahnder*. They hadn't worked together before, and even now, on this case, they barely saw each other. But she liked the look of the woman: tall and thin, with very short hair dyed a dramatic platinum, tiny wire-rimmed glasses, and a large mouth. Early thirties, maybe? She looked like she laughed easily.

Vinz stood in the middle of the office, white shirt pressed, posture perfect, hands clasped at the small of his back. His eyes were tired, though. "Any of you pick up something that has to be shared right away?"

Giuliana thought about Nisha and the rest of the Pragasams and decided that nothing she'd learned was far enough along to deserve mentioning. But Renzo, it seemed, had already taken things a bit further. Mathan's phone records, he told Vinz, were being checked for deleted texts that could be interpreted as threatening to his sister-in-law, and his red car had been brought in and would be examined by forensics for signs of the bike crash. There was nothing visible to the naked eye, however—unfortunately. His wife had also confirmed his alibi, but that had been expected.

"Good." Vinz nodded vaguely. "If there's nothing else, then... um ... I'm disappointed to say that Madeleine and I haven't yet been able to pin anything on the two guards. When Eberhart died, both say they were home alone. One's wife was out, and the other's divorced. We haven't been able to pick up either of them on CCTV at the right time, and there's no trace of the crash on their cars. Phone records proved useless, too."

It sounded to Giuliana like it was time to pursue another lead. Rolf spoke her mind when he said, "Well, negative findings are still findings. Maybe neither of them did it."

Vinz shook his head. "They give off a strong guilty vibe. And you know how bad CCTV coverage is in Bern except in a few key spots downtown. So today, we're going to reinterview them. We'll spread our search wider for the car, too, or maybe even for another driver, a third guard, or a personal friend."

"I thought all the other guards had alibis," Giuliana said.

"Not all of them. A few we barely considered since they weren't part of the racism investigation at the prison—but we'll check them out now. See what their relationship is to the two we're really after."

The two you're getting obsessed with, thought Giuliana. But still, he might be right—many cases got solved through a combination of hunches and stubbornness.

Vinz transferred his hands from the small of his back to his front. His expression didn't change. "The point is, Madeleine and I and a few other *Fahnder* are going to take another day or two to try and dig out the real story on these two. With you following up on the victim's private life, Giuliana, and you checking over her work files"— he looked at Renzo, who nodded—"I think we have enough angles covered. Rolf, any thoughts?"

There was a pause before Rolf said, "I'd say carry on with the guards, but if nothing's broken by Thursday morning, we'll switch to other leads."

When Giuliana has phoned him, Renzo had agreed to come with her to see Andi's parents. As they walked out of Vinz's meeting together, Giuliana said, "I've got to talk to Erwin now before I drive out to the prison. Let's meet in the parking lot this afternoon at two."

Five minutes later, she and Erwin were ordering coffees in the basement cafeteria, and Erwin snagged a large pastry stuffed with hazelnuts and dripping with a sugary glaze.

"My treat," said Giuliana when they got to the cash register.

"I should hope so," he answered caustically, "since I'm going to be so useful to you." Which, in Erwin-speak, was a warning that he didn't have much to say and wished he had more. He was considered one of the best interrogators on the cantonal police force, and in his gruff way, he tried to help anyone who asked him for advice. But Kissling was defeating him.

"That fucker makes my flesh crawl," he told her now, once they'd sat down and he'd swallowed his first bite of pastry. "The whole time I'm trying to get him to spill his guts, I'm also fighting the urge to slam his head against the table till it bursts like a melon." From Erwin, this was probably not an exaggeration.

"You've dealt with enough killers over the years. What makes Kissling worse?" Giuliana pushed her coffee aside and leaned forward, desperate to get everything she could from her colleague.

"Jesus. I wish I knew. In the past, I've managed to break down serial child molesters and rapists who cut women into pieces. But a man who coolly throws his little girls off a cliff and drives home . . . I can't get inside his head at all. They weren't even raped, you know; there was no sign of any sexual interference." Giuliana did know this, as she knew everything in the Kissling files, but that didn't matter.

"But that's good, isn't it?" she said spontaneously.

"It should be, shouldn't it?" Erwin had to pause while he chewed his food and then took a gulp of coffee to wash down his bite. "But somehow, it makes everything worse for me. Well, stranger, at least. Sexual motives we're used to, right? By now, I feel like I've even got a handle on those self-centered fuckers who won't let their families live without them, so they slaughter the whole lot of 'em plus the dog and goldfish before blowing their brains out." He paused, shaking his head, and Giuliana reached for her coffee at last. She hated the way the newspapers always referred to this particular kind of mass murder as a "family tragedy"; the words were much too gentle for such obscene selfishness.

Erwin was using a forefinger to corral the sugary crumbs on his plate. He looked up to say, "Kissling . . . he didn't even try to kill himself afterward. Or go for the ex-wife. Or do anything we'd expect." His heavy shoulders rose to his ears and fell again. "I've had a hell of a time getting him to talk."

Giuliana sipped her coffee. "Any thoughts on what *not* to do with him? Any suggestions at all?"

Another shrug. Erwin was over sixty and overweight; after two divorces, he lived alone and probably existed on junk food and too much beer, but to Giuliana, he was still the toughest cop she knew, and if he was feeling beaten by Kissling, what chance did she have?

"Shit," he said at last. "What can I say? I don't think he's looking for pity or sympathy, but I do think he's looking for some kind of understanding."

"Understanding for his crime, you mean?" Giuliana asked.

"Maybe. I'm not sure. He's also . . . well, I could be wrong, but I think his silence is some kind of game. It's not simply hostile or plain crazy. It's like . . . he couldn't outwit us by getting away with the crime since he was so obviously the killer, so he's created some game that we're playing with him where he *can* outwit us."

"A game," Giuliana echoed, thinking about what that meant. "Like he wins if he's silent, and we win if he talks? Is that what you mean?"

"I don't know what I mean," Erwin said, his voice rising. But Giuliana knew his anger wasn't with her. "If a cop or a lawyer says the right words to him, will he speak? Like Open Sesame. Or is he just going to toy with us nonstop, all the way through the trial, not revealing a word? Or maybe he's planning to pour everything out to the judges? I just don't know."

He stared at her, although she didn't think he was seeing her face. Then he pressed his fists to his eyes and added, "Something tells me there's a key. It won't make sense to us—because he's a fucking loony tune—but it makes sense to him. If we can get onto that wavelength, I think he'll open up."

Erwin picked up his coffee, finished it, and then cradled the cup in both hands. "I don't know why I think he's waiting for something. Maybe it's because when I'm there, talking to him, he isn't spaced out. Instead of praying for me to shut up and leave him alone, he's listening; he's judging. I feel like he's waiting for the right . . . well, as I said, the right words." Erwin set his cup down on his tray. "Sorry this is such bullshit. Just what you need to hear before facing that psycho."

"A psycho," Giuliana repeated. "You think he's a real, honest-to-God psychopath?" She knew what the psychiatrists said, but she wasn't sure she could identify one herself.

"He is in my book," said Erwin and leaned back in his chair. "Now, before we go back to our desks, tell me what's happening with this hit-and-run murder that Vinz is getting his panties in a twist over."

Bringing Erwin up to speed took only a few minutes; even six days after Andi's death, there was shockingly little to tell.

Erwin listened, and when she'd finished, he said, "I like Vinz, and I respect how thorough he is, but I'm glad he has you and Renzo on the case with him. In my opinion, when God was handing out imagination, Vinz was behind a tree taking a leak."

She snorted a laugh, which did her good. "I'd better get ready. You'd be surprised how much what you said has made me think—thanks!"

He stood up when she did and gave her a clap on the shoulder that made her sway. "Good luck with Kissling, and let me know if I can help you with the hit-and-run in some unofficial way. Hey," he added as she started to walk away, "I love the vision of our boy Renzo among the dykes. Five minutes of being interviewed by him, and I bet half will come back to playing for our team." Knowing he was just trying to push her buttons, she gave him the outraged expression he was waiting for. He cackled and wandered over to join a table full of men from vice. She wondered what he needed from them. He'd pick their brains so jovially that they'd never notice he was doing it.

Back at her desk, she phoned the office of Kissling's prosecutor, Konrad Zaugg, and asked if there was a report on Iris Kissling's psych evaluation. Nothing yet.

Five minutes later, she was on her way to talk to Manfred Kissling.

Nisha glanced at the kitchen clock yet again. It was a quarter past nine. So where was her mother? Everything she'd planned for this day depended on Devi babysitting for her. And now she was late.

Nisha sat at one end of the sofa, fretting. Saritha faced her, pulling herself crabwise along the edge of the paisley sofa cushions. Mostly she was silent, frowning with the difficulty of walking, but now and then, she shrieked with glee at her own brilliance, making Nisha smile in spite of her worries.

She'd scheduled a ten o'clock appointment with her boss at the Federal Office for the Environment and a talk with the head of the daycare center in her neighborhood at two. In between, she was having lunch with her friend Rahel, who'd promised to catch her up on work news—and gossip. Nisha represented her department to the press; she needed to know both what was going on officially and what was being whispered.

She looked forward to seeing her colleagues but dreaded the condolences she'd be forced to endure. The right words had to be said—she knew that. Sympathy was a burden people needed to deposit. But the process was miserable for everyone.

If she managed it today, though, things would be easier when she returned to work for real. Just two more weeks, thank God. Nisha remembered how delighted she'd been when she'd managed to increase her maternity leave to over nine months. But without Andi, her leave had become a sentence of solitary confinement.

Her phone rang, and she saw it was Rajan. *He* hadn't been part of the plan. "Things have changed," her brother said breathlessly.

"You're driving Amma over here—that's great. I was—"

Rajan interrupted. "No, I'm supposed to bring Sari back to our parents' place. Put together whatever the baby needs for the day, and I'll explain when I get there."

He disconnected before she could ask questions. It didn't make sense—her mother never had the baby at her place; it was too disrespectful of her father's wishes. What was going on?

She packed diapers, ointment, wipes, and a change of clothes; a bib, a sippy cup, and a bottle, along with a container of formula. When she started adding plastic containers of homemade baby food, she stopped. Her mother had two grandsons—she knew how to prepare something for Sari to eat. She'd just grabbed a few favorite toys to stuff into the bag when the door buzzed. It was 9:23; if Rajan could drop her off first, she'd still be on time.

"Let's go," he said. "I've got a class at ten that I want to make. I'll take you to work, deliver the baby to Amma, and head off. The only problem is going to be parking. Better show me how to deal with Sari's car seat, huh?"

Once the tiny Hyundai was on the move, he began to talk. "Has your policewoman told you she interviewed us last night?"

"What?" Nisha turned and stared at him, although he kept his eyes on the road.

"Yep," Rajan said, "Family meeting at the Nordring police station. And we heard about Mathan's texts and calls. What a shithead! I'm sorry, Nisha. I wish you'd told me. Anyway, Appa found out that Amma has been seeing you and Sari—not that he didn't already know it."

Nisha's hand darted to her mouth. "What do you mean he already knew?"

"Oh, you know how they are—Amma sneaks around doing things Appa isn't supposed to know about, and he pretends not to be aware of it. It's a game they play so that everything appears normal on the surface. Don't tell me you didn't guess that?"

She said nothing, and Rajan glanced at her, eyes raised in surprise. She leaned back in the passenger seat, shaking her head and feeling like a fool—was she the only person in the family who'd fallen for her parents' charade?

Rajan must have read her mind because he gave a wry smile and said, "Well, Mathan hadn't a clue, either. Honestly, I could almost feel sorry for him; he's so out of it. Thinks he's the master of Tamil tradition and doesn't know his ass from a hole in the ground."

She couldn't keep up. "So why does Amma want Sari to come to her?"

"Well, Amma's grounded now." Rajan rolled his eyes.

"You mean she can't go out at all?"

"Who knows?" He sounded exasperated. "Amma called me at midnight last night after I'd taken them home from the interview. She said Appa's asked her to stay home for . . . she doesn't know how long, but she understands that you have to see your boss today. So instead of explaining to Appa—because that would be too simple, right?—she's decided to stay home as he asked but get me to bring Sari to her. I bet she'll call this afternoon and ask me to pick up some groceries, too. Sometimes I don't understand why I bothered to move out," he added, his voice more resigned than bitter. Rajan was a good son. Besides, Nisha knew he played his own games.

Her brother seemed to read her thoughts again. "So now I have to call that detective woman and tell her I *wasn't* actually at home on Wednesday night."

"Because you stayed with Alina?"

"Yeah. I don't mind telling the police, but I'm not saying a word about it in front of the others. Especially now that I know what Mathan's been up to. Imagine if he started in on Alina with his horrible texts." He took one hand off the steering wheel and fished out his phone. "Linder's card is in the glove compartment. Dial her number, will you?"

She made the call for Rajan as he pulled into a delivery-only spot near her work building. "Frau Linder, this is Nisha Pragasam," she said. "I'm with my brother Rajan. He's been telling me about your meeting with my family last night."

She paused to listen as the detective began to apologize for having created a family crisis. Nisha interrupted. "Yes, it *is* going to cause a lot of tension, but if it helps you find out what happened to Andi, then . . . Anyway, look, I'm calling for my brother; he's the one who wants to talk to you."

She handed Rajan his phone and got out of the car. Opening the back door to say goodbye to Sari, she could hear Rajan explaining about Alina, whom he'd been seeing for over a year now. She was an Indian-born Tamil, not a Sri Lankan, who'd been adopted from a Chennai orphanage by a Swiss family. No one had any idea what caste her parents had belonged to, and she was Swiss through and through—except for the way she looked. Nisha liked her a lot, but as far as she knew, their parents had no idea that Alina existed. Or was that also one of the not-really-secret secrets? She was still having trouble digesting what Rajan had told her. What was the point of so much deceit if it wasn't needed? Suddenly, she was caught up in a terrible wave of longing for Andi, who'd hated convoluted behavior like this. She closed her eyes, swallowed, and bent to kiss Sari, who was dozing in her car seat.

"Have fun, sweetheart. I'll see you this afternoon," she whispered.

Rajan got out of the car, and she kissed him, too. "Thank you," she said.

He smiled. "When do you think you'll want Sari home?"

"Three thirty, maybe four."

"Text me half an hour before you're ready, and I'll figure out how to get her back."

"I'd be glad to pick her up myself," Nisha said, as she adjusted her shoulder bag, "but you know I'm not supposed to be in our house. It's all so ridiculous," she said, her exasperation flaring. "How can they live this way? Why do we go along with it?"

Rajan was usually brimming with barbed remarks about cultural straitjackets, Swiss and Tamil. But all he said this time was, "Things will work out somehow—they always do." He waved, then got back into the car and drove away with her precious Saritha.

17

Perched on a steep hill, Thorberg had started life as a twelfth-century castle and still looked like one. It had gone on to house Carthusian monks, hospital patients, and lunatics, among others, before making the switch to criminals in 1893. Since then, it had been expanded and modernized into a high-security men's prison.

Giuliana had been there many times. Standing in the parking lot, she tipped her head back to stare up at the red-tiled roofs of the oldest buildings. In the spring sunshine, even the prison looked brighter than usual. No, she decided, as her eyes fell on the high walls, chain-link fences, and rolls of razor wire; not even the sun could make Thorberg into anything but an awful place.

She went through the routine that got her access to the room where she was meeting Manfred Kissling. It contained a table and two chairs, one of which was attached to the floor. Ten minutes later, two guards brought in a handcuffed Kissling and sat him in the secured chair. Once his ankles were fastened to the chair legs, his cuffs were removed. One of the guards remained in the room, and Giuliana turned her attention to the prisoner.

Kissling was forty-six, one year younger than she was, and handsome in a subdued way. Light brown hair still covered his head, his blue eyes were clear, and his figure was trim. He was the kind of man who was too ordinary to shine at twenty but grew better looking with age, as other men lost hair and muscle and sprouted wrinkles and bellies. Kissling's face was smooth; he appeared unmarked by life. Somehow, this did not contribute anything positive to his looks.

One of Giuliana's preparations for the deposition had been to review the opening lines used by each prosecutor, cop, and psychiatrist who'd interviewed Kissling before. "Why did you do it, you fucking maniac?" was one, with variations on that theme. Then there were expressions of solicitude for his well-being, from "Do you want a cup of coffee?" to "How are you being treated?" There were also abrupt requests for information about his childhood, marriage, and relationship with his daughters. His talks with his defense team were confidential, but through her father, she'd heard that Kissling's own lawyer found him uncommunicative and difficult.

Giuliana's research had shown her that Kissling did sometimes talk during interrogations, especially at the beginning of an interview. Then, as the questioning progressed, he'd fall into silence. She thought about Erwin's theory that Kissling was playing with the prosecution. She imagined a game of chess. Did he start by moving a few pieces, testing the opposition, and then, when he saw how inept the other player was, withdraw in contempt? If that was his strategy, then all she could do was try to be a deserving opponent.

Kissling's elbows rested on the heavy metal table, with his fingers laced. He did not seem unduly tense nor unnaturally calm. He waited.

She introduced herself, leaning forward to shake his hand—although she knew some of the prosecution team had refused to do this. She made sure the recording equipment was on. "I had a long talk with your wife a few days ago, Herr Kissling," she said. Immediately she saw something flare in his eyes. Interest? "She told me you met at the law office where she used to work. What attracted you to her?"

He didn't hesitate. "Her liveliness. She seemed so open and

amusing. And she was very pretty. I was flattered by her interest. Her apparent interest," he added.

"Apparent?"

"She wasn't really interested in me." He said this gravely, with no sign of self-pity.

Giuliana decided to speak the truth. "I found her exceptionally self-centered."

Kissling smiled. "She is. I didn't see that when we were ... courting. I guess you could say I didn't interpret her conversation and behavior correctly."

"According to her," Giuliana went on, "you very much wanted children at the beginning of the marriage when she didn't want them, and then you changed your mind."

"That's right." He nodded, serious again but with a hint of ... was it encouragement? Or was she overinterpreting because of Erwin's theories?

"She said her first pregnancy was an accident and the second solely her decision."

Kissling's mouth turned down. After a pause, he said, "It was her decision, but my fault. With the first one, I thought she was still on the pill, but the second time around, I should have been smart enough to use a condom."

"So you never wanted Mia and Lea to be born."

She'd used the girls' names deliberately. As she said them, his eyes widened; she thought she even saw the glint of moisture there. Was he feeling grief for the two children he'd murdered?

He nodded and said in a low voice. "That is correct."

"Is that why you killed them? Because you hadn't wanted them in the first place?"

At this, Kissling slumped in his chair and leaned his chin on his hand, and, just like that, she'd lost him. But why? What had he wanted from her that she had failed to produce?

The next hour was an exercise in frustration. She never slipped into playing bad cop with Kissling—the earlier interviews had shown he only responded with contempt. So she tried silence, repetition, appeals to his reason. But nothing would induce him to speak again, let alone explain the motives behind his crime. He paid her about as much attention as the dust on the floor.

Eventually, she ended the interview and stopped the camera. Before leaving, she offered him her hand and was surprised when he shook it. On impulse, she said, "After I spoke with your ex-wife, I requested that she receive a psychiatric evaluation. I'm still waiting for the results."

And there it was again: the light in his eyes. He looked at her properly, appraisingly. "I'd like to hear about those findings. Perhaps you could come back and tell me about them."

"I'll do that, Herr Kissling," she said as the second guard returned to join the one who'd stayed in the room, and they recuffed his hands.

Driving to her office, she reviewed every word she could remember saying before Kissling shut down. Later, she'd play back the video and analyze it all—words and facial expressions. So would the prosecutors. She'd already realized that her fatal mistake had been answering her own question about why Kissling had killed his girls—that's when he'd turned off. Still, he'd invited her back. That had to be a sign that she'd done something right.

For now, though, she needed to clear her head and think about her and Renzo's two o'clock appointment with Andi Eberhart's parents in the village of Ochsenbach. Back at her desk, she closed one file and opened the other. There would be no getting away from the parents of dead children today.

After reviewing the Eberhart case, she looked at her watch: it was almost noon. Surely Irène's operation was over? She phoned Ueli, who didn't answer. Of course! The Insel forbade the use of cell phones. She found the main hospital number and got herself transferred to a nursing station somewhere in the enormous complex. Running her fingers compulsively through her hair, she waited until someone finally picked up. Yes, Frau Brand was out of surgery and resting in intensive care. That was all that could be said.

By the time the call was over, her hair was such a mess that she had to take out a comb and redo the bun on the nape of her neck.

Renzo was no nature boy—he had about as much interest in walking up a mountain as in watching paint dry—but he was awed by the immensity of the Bernese Alps as he and Giuliana drove toward them. They'd both skipped lunch, so now she chewed on a thickly buttered whole wheat roll stuffed with slices of Tête de Moine cheese. In her other hand, she held Renzo's ham-and-tomato-on-white so that he could take a bite whenever the traffic let up. A large bottle of fizzy water was wedged into the cup holder between them.

They went through their goals for the interview, and then Renzo asked, "How did things go with Kissling?"

She groaned. "Right at the beginning, I seemed to be getting somewhere, but then it just collapsed. Pure disaster. Tell me about your day at Andi's office instead."

Renzo summed up everything he'd learned from Andi's boss and her friend Loïc and went on to her notes about her clients. "The files are fascinating," he told her. "For years, I've dismissed Civis as too lazy to face military service, but some of them take on a lot of responsibility in these jobs."

"Isabelle thinks it's the lazy, immature boys who go into the army, so all they'll have to do is take orders. The smart ones choose Civi."

He tried not to show how much that annoyed him, but she must have noticed because she added, "Don't get mad. Isa's sixteen—she still sees everything in black and white. Believe it or not, I've been defending the army to her." Renzo caught her smile from the corner of his eye and raised his eyebrows. "Not as an institution," she added, "God, no—but as an experience for young Swiss men. Some of them, anyway."

"The dumb ones?" This came out as more of a growl than he'd intended.

"No. But I do understand why some nineteen-year-olds decide that trying out different occupations will be more useful to them in the long run than learning combat skills."

Renzo could see her point, but he wasn't going to give any more ground. "Army recruits learn skills for civilian life," he said, "once they finish basic training."

"Skills like how to drive a tank or blow up a bridge?" He saw her grin at him and knew he was being teased, so he said nothing. "No, you're right," she added. "Young men learn all kinds of useful stuff during their military service, especially about themselves. That's what I keep telling Isabelle."

The drive had brought them off the highway and onto the winding roads leading to Ochsenbach. In the foothills of the Alps, spring arrived later than at the lower elevations—there was still snow on the shadiest slopes, and masses of snowdrops edged the forests. The ground under the trees was carpeted with winter aconites, their cupped yellow heads peeping out above the mulch of dead leaves and needles.

Most of the village of Ochsenbach straddled its one main road, which traversed a steep, grassy meadow dotted with cows. There were lots of traditional farmhouses with steep roofs and broad eaves shading wooden balconies, but a few modern shops sat further along, next to a white church with a bell tower. Andi's parents lived a block uphill from the main road in a small house designed to look like a chalet. The bushes and hedges were clipped, the front steps swept, and the wooden shutters freshly painted in forest green. Hills, trees, meadows, and mountains in every direction. Renzo would happily agree that the whole place was beautiful—as long as no one expected him to live there.

They rang the Eberharts' doorbell just as the church clock struck two, and their punctuality was rewarded with steaming coffee and a homemade lemon loaf cake, still warm from the oven. Renzo would have preferred to sit in the sunlit kitchen he'd glimpsed from the entrance hall, but their hostess installed them in a formal dining room full of dark, heavy furniture. At least the windows let in plenty of light.

Manuela Eberhart was only fifty-nine, Renzo knew, but she looked seventy that afternoon. In his early sixties, her husband Kurt was not as ravaged by grief as his wife, but his hands shook as he waited in silence at the head of the table, his food untouched.

Renzo praised the cake and got out his notepad as Giuliana began, "Thank you for seeing us. As I think Frau Pragasam told you, the police have concluded that your daughter's death was almost surely not an accident, which means we need to look into every aspect of her life: job, personal relationships, hobbies, and political activities. And her past. We've already talked to Frau Pragasam and other people in Bern who knew her well, and we'll keep doing that. But is there anything in your daughter's early life that you think we should know about as we search for an enemy?"

"How could Andi have enemies?" Kurt Eberhart's question wasn't for them; it was a private cry of pain that Renzo found hard to bear.

"I've talked to her curling friends, political colleagues, workmates, and boss," he told her father, "and I've heard so many good things about her." Some bad things, too, like her abrasiveness, but no need to bring that up. "A lot of people loved her." He received a flicker of a smile from her father, which somehow only made him feel worse.

"Political colleagues?" Her mother was frowning at him. "Andi wasn't political."

This comment was followed by silence. Renzo was too surprised to respond.

"She worked for years to win more rights and more acceptance for gay men and lesbians," Giuliana said. "The issue that most concerned her was families. She was active with a group that lobbied to change the law so people like Andi and Nisha could get married and adopt children or use fertility clinics. And they've been successful—the law changed in 2022."

Manuela looked confused. "Adopt children?"

Giuliana continued patiently. "Yes, your daughter was in the process of adopting Saritha Pragasam."

"But . . . why?"

Renzo tried to hide his shock. Andi had come out to her parents years earlier *and* visited them with Nisha and the baby. Her activism had been written up in the newspaper, for God's sake. How could her mother not know about the adoption? He thought of his own mother, always up to date on what was happening in her four children's lives and straining to help them and their families as much as they would let her. It was one of those moments when he found himself thinking, "*Le Svizzere!*"—the Swiss! How could privacy and independence be so important to them that they pushed away the people they loved?

He forced himself to speak evenly. "Your daughter was Saritha's other mother, and she wanted the law to recognize it. The organization she supported, Rainbow Families, has worked to make that possible."

"But . . ." the older woman said. "But how could she be so cruel to Nisha?"

Giuliana's mouth hung open for a second as she stared at Manuela.

Kurt spoke up gently. "Andi wasn't trying to take Saritha away from Nisha. They wanted to share the baby—to give her two mothers. In other countries, quite a few children grow up with two mothers or two fathers. Not just privately but under the law. It's all part of the . . . the gay movement." Renzo noticed that he said the last two words delicately as if he was afraid that, in his ignorance, he might set off a bomb.

"Oh, Kurt," said his wife, "I know all that. The magazines at the hairdressers are full of these stories. But Andi . . . I didn't know that Andi . . . Why didn't she talk to me about all this? I didn't understand it, and it must have been so important to her."

Dio, le Svizzere, Renzo thought again, but this time there was no irritation in it, just sadness. He'd begun to like Andi. Now he felt angry with her. Why had she shut her parents out like this?

No one at the table said a word. Then Andi's mother blinked back tears. "I need to learn about this Rainbow Families, don't I?" she said to Renzo in a husky voice. "You asked us about enemies. But I can't think of anyone in her past, child or adult, who hurt Andi. You must know what villages are like. No secrets. If Andi had been bullied in primary school or even later, in *Gymnasium* in Thun, we'd have heard about it."

Renzo noticed that Manuela hadn't said, "Andi would have told us." It was an important distinction. He thought of his own children and prayed they'd tell him if they were ever unhappy in school.

Kurt was nodding along, but he said, "You can double-check all this with a girl who was in school with Andi: Bettina Krebs." He passed Giuliana a sheet of paper. "Here's her address and phone number in Thun. Her married name is Sutter. And I wrote down Andi's former boyfriend's number, too."

Manuela crossed her arms and rubbed her hands up and down her upper arms as if she were cold. She licked her lips and said, "Can you show us the letters now, please."

Giuliana handed each of them photocopies of the twenty-three anonymous letters, saying, "The first one arrived just over four years ago, and they worried Frau Pragasam, but she told me your daughter refused to take them seriously. Now we're investigating what they could have to do with her death. They're certainly threatening—very unpleasant reading for you, I'm sorry to say. While you're looking at them," she added, "I'm going outside to make a phone call. Please excuse me. Herr Donatelli will answer any questions." Renzo knew she was desperate to reach Ueli to ask about his mother's operation.

He sat patiently as Andi's parents read the letters, one after another, and saw Manuela set two of them to one side. At last, she looked up, her eyes filled with tears. "My poor girl, having to face this . . . this trash! It hurts me to think of her reading it. Such terrible things about Nisha and her sweet baby. It's ugly." She got up, opened a drawer in the elaborately carved sideboard, and pulled out a box of tissues. She wiped her eyes and blew her nose, then sat down, her expression fierce.

"Disgusting," Kurt agreed, putting down the last letter.

As Giuliana slipped back into the room, Manuela said, "Listen," and read from one of the pages she'd set aside, "*properly christened and confirmed in the Reformed Church*," followed by "*raised within the sound of church bells*" from the other page. "Does that remind you of anything?"

"No," Kurt said. "It makes me wonder, though. These days lots of parents don't bother with christenings, and not that many youngsters get confirmed, either. How would the letter writer know that Andi was christened and confirmed?"

Renzo wanted to point out that folks who wrote stuff like this were usually at least halfway off their rockers and not exactly worried about accuracy. But before he could formulate an answer, Manuela grabbed her husband's arm. "Well, the words remind *me* of something—or someone, in fact. A woman named Agnes Graber."

Kurt looked puzzled, so Manuela turned to Giuliana. "Andi and some other Ochsenbach kids had to take the bus to Dürrenegg for their confirmation lessons because it has about five times more people than our village. The Dürrenegg minister who coached and confirmed them was called Graber; I don't remember his first name, but his wife's name was Agnes. She used to sit in on all the confirmation classes at the church; people whispered that she was afraid to leave her husband alone with anyone in a skirt, even little girls—she was that jealous."

"I remember now," Kurt put in, "because it was so funny. Graber was about the furthest thing from a womanizer you could imagine. Over fifty, a mild, roly-poly fellow."

His wife gave Giuliana a quick eye roll, and Renzo caught Giuliana's answering nod. It was a woman-to-woman exchange that clearly said, *You and I know that what a man looks like has nothing to do with whether he harasses women—or goes after young girls.*

Manuela continued. "Two years after Andi was confirmed, one of the confirmation candidates, a fifteen-year-old from a farm between here and Dürrenegg, started to get terrible letters accusing her of seducing Graber. The girl showed the letters only to her sister, but luckily, the sister went to their parents. It turned out this girl had never been alone with the *Pfarrer*, not once. His wife had made the whole thing up! And the point is, I ended up seeing one of the letters, and it had stuff about living near church bells. Of course, I can't remember the exact words, but this is so similar."

Giuliana met Renzo's eyes before asking, "Who handled the incident then?"

Manuela shook her head. "It didn't go to the police. Not officially. One of the members of the Dürrenegg town council was a policeman in Thun. He talked with the minister and showed him the letters. Everyone who knew the story felt sorry for the man; the scandal was bad enough without his wife having to go to court. Or so people seemed to feel."

Bad idea, thought Renzo. *Now, if it had been my daughter . . .*

Manuela added, "Anyway, I think the girl's parents were persuaded not to prosecute, and it all died down. Now I wish it hadn't. That vicious woman deserves to be locked up for sending Andi this poison."

"Please, Frau Eberhart—don't jump to conclusions," Giuliana warned. "Are you sure this Agnes Graber knew your daughter?"

"Andi told us she was always there, crocheting away, at every session they had with her husband. For three years, he talked to them about Christian values, and Agnes sat there stewing in her evil thoughts. My God. Maybe she killed Andi."

Giuliana and Renzo exchanged another glance, and Giuliana said, "We'll follow up on this immediately and get back to you as soon as we know more. Can you tell us anything about the man on the Dürrenegg council who handled the poison-pen business with the girl all those years ago?"

"His first name is Emil," Kurt said, "and as far as I know, he still lives in Dürrenegg and works for the Thun police. I doubt he's old enough to have retired."

Manuela spoke up again. "Agnes is older, though—must be seventy-five or even eighty. Her husband wasn't too far off from retirement when she sent those letters; that was one of the reasons the parents were talked out of an official complaint."

Privately Renzo thought it unlikely that a woman in her eighties could have been responsible for running Andi down, but he said nothing. After all, you never knew what people were capable of beneath the surface.

"Leave this with us, then, and please don't tell anyone," Giuliana said. "You don't want word to get to the Grabers so that they can destroy evidence. And it could be a false lead. But unless one of you has something else for us, I think we should end our meeting here, so we can pursue this story."

"I'd like to ask a question before you go," Kurt said. "Andi never mentioned Saritha's father, not once, and we assume Nisha would tell us if she wanted us to know his name. But are you looking into the possibility that he killed Andi? I mean, whoever he is, it seems to me he might be jealous or . . . or feel betrayed. I'd like to know if he's one of your suspects."

When Giuliana hesitated a fraction of a second too long, Renzo answered. "Yes, he is a suspect, although, for various reasons, we think he's very unlikely to be involved." As he spoke, he decided that he should meet Yannick Eberhart before deciding if he was truly an unlikely suspect. God, families could be strange—you never knew. Just look at Nisha's brother Mathan.

At the door, as the four of them shook hands, Manuela smiled up at Renzo and said, "I'm going to find out more about your rainbow organization, I promise."

A slight emphasis on the word "your" gave Renzo his clue, even before he heard an odd sound from Giuliana. Careful not to look at her, he beamed at Andi's mother and said, "Rainbow Families, yes. I think Andi would be very happy to know of your interest."

"Has it worked out for *you* to have a family?" Manuela asked brightly.

"Excuse me; I must go. Another phone call," Giuliana interjected and fled to the car, leaving him stranded on the doorstep.

"We have two wonderful children," he answered gravely, "a boy and a girl. They make me happy every day. And now I'd better be off— you can see my boss is eager to leave. Thanks again for the delicious cake."

He found Giuliana slumped forward in the passenger seat, her hands over her face as she shook with laughter. He gave her a mock stern look as he got behind the wheel, but he was chuckling too.

Eventually, Giuliana caught her breath enough to say, "That poor woman meant so well. There she is, convinced you're a gay dad, and this very morning I had Erwin suggesting that exposure to your manly charms will bring Andi's lesbian friends back into the heterosexual fold. Not that he's serious, at least I hope not, but . . . honestly, Renzo, something about you inspires the wildest fantasies."

The only ones I care about are yours, Giule. The thought filled his head before he could stop it, but he cut it off at the roots. That was the sort of thing that could grow into something dangerous. "So what should I do about it?" He kept his voice light. "Tattoo my cheeks? Wear my hair in a Mohawk? Gain twenty pounds?"

Giuliana was still giggling. "Twenty pounds? You'd have to gain a hundred to—" She pulled up short. "Never mind. Oh, it's nice to laugh; life hasn't been very funny lately. At least I got through to Ueli; the doctors are optimistic, whatever that means. Thank God for that. Now let's see if we can find this Emil—I'm glad his first name isn't Hans or Peter. I'll call the cop shop in Thun and see if someone can identify him for us."

Renzo hadn't pulled away from the curb yet. "Don't you want to drive to this bigger village, Dürrenegg, and talk to the Grabers?"

"That was my first thought," Giuliana said, "but I think I'd rather get some background before I approach the old lady. Find out from this local cop about her health, mental and physical. He's more likely to cooperate if we involve him right away. I'll bet he considers Dürrenegg his special responsibility." She'd been looking up a number and dialing as she spoke. "*Ciao* Regina, it's Giuliana." Pause. "I'm near Thun with a colleague, and we're looking for someone you might know—one of your people. Named Emil. Over fifty." Pause. "Right . . . Senn? That sounds like our guy. From Dürrenegg?" Pause. "Yeah, that's him. Tell me . . ."

Listening to her extract information, Renzo drove away from Ochsenbach, reflecting on how much he'd learned from Giuliana about being good at his job. When would he get a chance at a promotion? A wave of despair buffeted him as he imagined Fränzi's response to his taking on more responsibility and more hours. Another thought to push out of his mind—for the moment, at least.

18

Being back at the office wasn't as awkward as Nisha had feared. One semi-stranger flooded her with such syrupy sympathy that she almost choked on a response. But most colleagues greeted her with brief but kind words acknowledging Andi's death and then turned to the happier subject of Saritha. A few of them insisted on being shown photographs, which she had ready on her phone—naturally.

Although she liked her boss, their relationship was professional rather than close, so his wholehearted sympathy for her scheduling problems surprised her. "I don't want to lose you," he told her across his desk, hands clasped on his blotter. "You're an excellent liaison to the media, your press releases are sharp, and you've developed real expertise on several of our most important current issues, especially biodiversity and overconsumption's influence on climate change. What I'd like is to have you here at least thirty hours a week."

Nisha was flattered but also worried. Without Andi to look after Sari, she wasn't sure she'd be able to work even the agreed-upon 50 percent: seven hours a day, three days a week. She'd been counting on at least occasional help from her mother and Sophie, but with her mother grounded—how long was that going to last?—and her sister-in-law avoiding her, her plans were looking very shaky. Why hadn't she made the appointment at the daycare center *before* the one with her boss?

Praying that none of her fears showed on her face, she said, "I really appreciate your saying that, and I hope someday soon I'll be able to work more hours, but right now—"

He broke in, smiling easily. "Right now, I understand that fifty percent is all you can handle. But when your childcare situation improves, let me know. You have a knack for explaining scientific issues clearly, and that's truly valuable to us. Now, let's go over the most urgent things for you to handle when you get back. I know you don't start for two weeks, but you might want to glance at a couple of files. We'll need press releases for . . ."

Listening to him, she smiled. It was going to be great to get back to work. She wanted to read about falling water levels and rising temperatures in Swiss lakes and rivers, worrisome as it was. She couldn't wait to go back to writing about using garbage to generate energy.

At eleven forty, she went to find Rahel, her lawyer friend who specialized in environmental regulations. The two of them had seen each other several times for coffee and once for a quick dinner since she'd started her leave. Rahel had phoned as soon as she'd heard about Andi's death, but this was the first time they'd met since the hit-and-run. As they walked to the restaurant where they were having lunch, Nisha thought, *Six days. Andi has been dead for six days, and I've spent the morning smiling over photos of Sari on my phone and calmly planning my work schedule.* She was caught between pride at her self-control and horror at her callousness. Tears started to run down her cheeks.

Rahel was chatting about the ski weekend she and her husband Leo had just come back from, but she grabbed Nisha and guided her into a doorway, drawing her close. Nisha wept on Rahel's shoulder for several minutes. After two hours of courteous numbness with colleagues, it was a relief to drop the act.

Once they'd ordered lunch, she began telling Rahel about the anonymous letters and the police investigation into Andi's death, although she couldn't quite bring herself to admit how isolated she was from both her own family and Andi's. By the time they ordered coffee, she felt calm enough to ask Rahel what was new at work.

"Don't think about that now," she answered, covering Nisha's hand with hers.

"No, I want to think about it." Nisha paused as the waiter brought their coffees. "It used to annoy me how much of my job involved being put on the spot. You know what I mean—meetings set up with no warning and calls from the press asking about new regulations I'd only just found out about. But now I'm going to be grateful for every distraction. So hit me with the news!"

Rahel laughed and took a sip of coffee. "It's still all about the windmills, I'm afraid. Denmark is full of them, and Germany's doing better every year, but so many Swiss support them in theory but still consider them an eyesore. It's the usual not-in-my-backyard syndrome swollen to become not-in-my-country!"

Nisha had a sudden memory of Andi going alone to see her parents and coming home furious because her mother had been so upset about the possibility of a wind park being built somewhere near Ochsenbach. "She said they ruined the view!" Andi had told Nisha, knocking on the side of her head with her fist as she added. "Hello in there, Mam. Is your brain working? Don't you understand that if we don't reduce carbon dioxide, there won't *be* a lovely green view anymore?" Nisha had defended Manuela. "Look, if all you do is lose your temper, she'll never understand." Andi replied, "You're right, you're right. But sometimes, she drives me nuts."

Now, as she remembered Andi's exasperated expression, she wanted to laugh. Not cry. It was the first time she'd been able to hold Andi in her mind's eye without being overcome by grief.

Rahel spent another twenty minutes telling Nisha about recent progress and setbacks, progressing from wind parks to solar panels to controversies about the use of wood in forests, and Nisha asked questions until it was time for her to leave for her appointment at the daycare center.

"Thank you for having lunch with me, Rahel," she said, with so much feeling that Rahel, who was digging in her handbag for her wallet, looked up. "It's great to have a chance to think about something besides my problems," Nisha continued. "I've been alone too much."

"Well, get out your phone right now, and let's set a date for you and Sari to have dinner with us," Rahel answered. "Don't think this is coming just from me, either—Leo urged me to invite you. He liked Andi so much. He was crushed when he heard about what happened to her."

If only I knew what happened to her, Nisha thought, as they made a dinner plan. But she didn't let her mind go there. It was time to pay for lunch and catch a tram; otherwise, she wouldn't make it to the daycare center in time. Things with her boss had gone so well—hopefully, extending Sari's childcare hours would be equally simple.

But it wasn't.

That night, alone at the table after putting Saritha to bed, all her happiness and hope about getting back to work had been chipped away. She stared, unseeing, at her mug of tea.

The head of the daycare had been as kind and supportive as anyone could be, but she could not change the fact that she only had room for Saritha two days a week. The third day Nisha had been hoping for since Andi's death—had been arrogantly counting on, she now realized—was simply not available. So, working 50 percent was also impossible unless she could conjure up an extra day of childcare. There were other options—a different daycare center, professional babysitting services, childminders. But the thought of having to find excellent care for her daughter in less than two weeks . . . It was overwhelming. Perhaps it felt particularly hard to think about because replacing Andi's day of childcare felt like looking for a way to replace Andi. And when she knocked over her mug of tea, it was too much. All evening she'd been holding back tears; now she gave way to hoarse, shuddering sobs that hurt her throat and stole her breath.

Giuliana heard the automatic door to the restaurant slide open and glanced up to see a tired-looking woman herding two small girls into the restaurant. Her mind flashed to Mia and Lea at the bottom of a cliff. She shook off the image as fast as she could and stared at her fingers gripping the tumbler of water in front of her, her knuckles turning white. Still no sign of Vivienne Marti. God, the woman had a nerve. Twenty minutes late, and she hadn't called or texted any explanation nor answered her phone. And for this, she'd had to leave Renzo to deal with the Thun cop Emil Senn and the poison-pen situation. Not that he couldn't handle it, but she should have been there, too.

Giuliana drank more water, just for something to do, and cursed herself again for giving in to Vivienne's plea that they meet at the main train station. If she'd been a no-show at the police building, Giuliana could have gotten work done during the wait and then come down hard on the woman for missing an official interview. Well, at five thirty, she was leaving. She'd get home early for a change, help Ueli make dinner, and try again to persuade Lukas to talk about whatever was bothering him. This time, she wouldn't give up.

Finally, Vivienne Marti, dressed in a long terracotta-colored coat that matched her hennaed hair, walked through the glass doors. Giuliana stood and called out sharply, then fought to swallow her anger as the woman walked toward her. She wanted information about Andrea Eberhart and Nisha Pragasam's relationship, and raging at this woman for being late wasn't going to coax any confidences out of her.

"My client overstayed. I came as soon as I could after she left," Vivienne said as she sat down at the table without ordering something to drink at the counter. "I keep my phone off during sessions," she added.

"Fine," said Giuliana. "Now that you're here, let me—"

"You want to know about my relationship with Andi," interrupted Vivienne. "The truth is, I wasn't close to her the way I am to Nisha; it's my children who know her, particularly my second son Toby, who's gay. They became friendly through Rainbow Families, and later we all met at one of their demonstrations."

This was not the question Giuliana had planned to ask, but it was as good a start as any. Opening her notebook, she asked, "Who is 'all'?"

"Andi and Nisha had invited Toby to go along with them to a demo, and my husband and I and the other three children went along to show support for Toby." Vivienne had thrown off her coat and was twisting her hands in the patterned scarf looped around her neck.

"When was this?" Giuliana asked.

Vivienne wrinkled her forehead. "A little over two years ago, I think. That's when I got to know Nisha. I'm very interested in yoga and Hindu healing traditions, so I started asking her about those, and she invited me over for tea since we live around the corner from each other. So we became friends. Nisha and I, I mean, not Andi so much."

"I see," Giuliana said, and then, seeing Vivienne open her mouth again, held up her hand like a cop stopping traffic. "What is your impression of Nisha and Andi's relationship?"

She hoped Vivienne would take the question seriously. Neighbors could sometimes spot things that even close friends missed.

"I think they were happy," Vivienne said, frowning. "I mean, I thought Andi was a bit, well, busy—you know, with her job and her politics and her sports—and I felt she didn't spend enough time with Nisha and Sari. Especially when it came to her work, she . . ." Vivienne paused as if planning a revelation. Instead of continuing, though, she shook her head and said, "What I really want to tell you is that during the week before Andi died, I saw a car in the neighborhood that wasn't usually there—and it hasn't been there since."

Giuliana leaned forward. "Yes?"

Vivienne stopped fiddling with her scarf and laid her palms flat on the table. "Well, you know how narrow the streets in our little neighborhood are—there's no parking at all. But twice last week, I noticed someone stopped across the street from the main entrance to Nisha's building. A man, just sitting there."

Giuliana was scribbling notes. "Tell me about the car."

"It was silver gray and . . . well, just a car. Not a van, not a sports car or a mini or an old clunker. Not fancy, not cheap. Just a car—with four doors."

Gray. Not red. Still . . . "And the man? Age, size, coloring?"

Vivienne shrugged. "I'm sorry. He was slouched in the seat and had on a baseball cap—I never really saw him clearly. I'd put him out of my mind until yesterday when I met you at Nisha's. Then I thought about those poison-pen letters Andi got, and I suddenly remembered seeing the car."

It had been worth meeting this woman after all. Giuliana was itching to pick up her phone and call Vinz. They'd need Vivienne to come into the station, where they had specialists who helped witnesses remember what they'd seen using a sketch artist and photographs. They'd get more details about the car and the man, and they'd do it much better than Giuliana could.

"I have to go," Vivienne said, starting to put on her coat, although she'd only been there fifteen minutes. "I have to make dinner for my family."

Giuliana stood, too. "You'll need to schedule several hours at the police station tomorrow."

"Oh, but . . . I mean, I have clients. I have . . ."

Giuliana forced a smile. "I know it's a nuisance, but if there's a possibility you saw Frau Eberhart's killer, that takes precedence over everything else." Another smile. "We need you at the station to give us details about the man and the car. I'm sure you can understand how important that is." Final, teeth-gritting smile.

"But I've honestly told you all I can remember," Vivienne almost wailed.

"That's what you think, but you'd be surprised what our experts can help you recollect. You'll get a call tonight from a police colleague. Please be sure your phone is on. And thank you for sharing this information."

The two women stood, and Giuliana put out her hand, which Vivienne shook. Then, instead of leaving, as she'd been in a hurry to do, she continued to stand across from Giuliana, chewing her lower lip, her brows furrowed. Eventually, she must have reached a decision because she gave Giuliana a quick smile and said, "Well, OK. I hope it helps you find whoever did this." Then she turned and walked away, her scarf fluttering behind her and her boot heels clacking on the tiled floor of the restaurant.

Giuliana wondered what had been on her mind as she'd stood there. Perhaps she'd been about to expand on her criticism of Andi and decided not to. Which was a shame—Giuliana wished she'd encouraged Vivienne to speak up. But right now, it was more important to report her sighting of the gray sedan. Sitting back down, she got out her mobile and called Vinz.

19

Giuliana managed to get home in time to make dinner—her version of spaghetti carbonara. It meant frying cubes of bacon, beating spoonfuls of heavy cream into a bowl of eggs, grating a pile of Parmesan, mixing the resulting sludge into a pot of hot pasta, and dividing the meal onto four plates while her family watched expectantly.

It was a happy meal because Ueli was able to reassure them that his mother's tumor had not yet broken through the wall of her intestine, and there was a good chance her operation had been literally lifesaving. With dinner over, Giuliana left the kids loading the dishwasher and sat on the sofa with Ueli, who laid out the follow-up care his mother would need. He was just explaining the pros and cons of chemotherapy when the landline rang, and Giuliana reluctantly got up to answer.

It was Lukas's teacher, Frau Tanner, whom she knew from parent-teacher conferences. The woman greeted her cordially and then, without more preamble, said, "I've been aware for several weeks that something was going on with Lukas, but I thought I'd wait to see if it got better before I called you. Unfortunately, it's getting worse. Tell me, is something happening at home that could cause him to behave badly at school?"

At this, Giuliana's whole body went on alert. "He found out last week that his grandmother has cancer," she said, working hard to keep her voice calm, "and the operation was today. I'm sure he's been concerned about her, but you say this problem has been around for weeks, and we only learned about the cancer a few days ago." She paused. "Does whatever's going on at school involve Joel and Niko?"

"Yes. I guess you know even better than I do what inseparables Niko and Lukas are."

"Since kindergarten," Giuliana confirmed.

"Ah. Well, today, Lukas ignored Niko and Joel all day, pointedly—he even asked me not to put him on the same team as Niko in gym class. Not that I'd call you about that—friends have tiffs. The problem is that Lukas refused to cooperate with almost anything today. He usually contributes . . . irrepressibly in class"—Giuliana heard amused affection in the teacher's voice and was momentarily relieved—"but today he didn't even answer when I called on him, and he turned in a completely blank math quiz, so I asked him to stay after class. He apologized for behaving badly, but he said he wouldn't talk to me. Then he brought up a book we read in class last fall. It's called *Holes*—about a boy who's sent to prison. Lukas wanted to know if Swiss children who commit crimes go to work camps like Stanley."

"Oh, no." Giuliana drew in a sharp breath. Her fingers were raking through her hair. *What in God's name is going on?*

"That's when I knew I had to call you and Herr Brand. I reassured Lukas about prison, but I couldn't get him to tell me what's upsetting him."

"Joel only joined our class after Christmas," Frau Tanner continued, "and I was glad when Lukas and Niko took him under their wing. But . . . well, even so, Joel's having some trouble fitting in. It worries me to see Niko and Lukas so unhappy. Niko isn't falling apart quite as obviously as Lukas, but there's trouble there as well. I'm about to call the Cléments, Niko's parents. The boys are such good friends that I imagine you know them." She paused.

"We do," Giuliana said, "and we like them very much. You have my permission to tell them about Lukas's behavior and explain that you and I have talked. Would you mind also saying that my husband or I will be in touch with them to see if we can figure out what's going on with the boys?"

The teacher promised her that they'd get to the bottom of the problem and hung up. Ueli, who'd been listening to Giuliana's side of the conversation, said, "Lukas, huh? What's going on?"

As Giuliana summarized the call, he fingered his beard anxiously. "I should have paid more attention to this," he said.

Giuliana put a hand on his shoulder. "You've had Irène to worry about."

"Well, let's go talk to him now."

They found Lukas sprawled on the floor in his room, looking at a book, which he thrust under his chest of drawers when they walked in.

"Frau Tanner phoned to tell us she is worried about you and . . ." Giuliana began. But that was as far as she got.

Without warning, Lukas jumped up and ran at her, yelling, "Get out, get *out*!" and shoved her in the chest.

At eleven, he still looked like a child, but he was strong, and she stumbled backward into Ueli, who steadied her and then threw his arms around his raging son, saying, "Hey, stop that!" But Lukas wriggled out of his grip, flung himself across the hall into the bathroom, and slammed the door.

Isabelle came out of her room. "What's up?"

From inside the bathroom, Lukas yelled, "Just leave me alone!" and burst into sobs. Giuliana, Ueli, and Isabelle stood in the hall gaping at each other.

"Why don't you two disappear for now?" Ueli said. "I'll try to talk to him."

Giuliana shrugged and followed Isabelle into her bedroom, where she explained what Lukas's teacher had said, also mentioning the tensions she'd observed between the three boys on the night Joel had stayed for dinner. "What about you?" she asked Isabelle. "Do you have any idea what's upsetting him?"

Isabelle shook her head. "Prison?" she said. "He's afraid of going to prison? That's . . ." She stopped, gazing at her mother.

"Yeah, it's strange. And very worrying," Giuliana said.

A few minutes later, trying to do paperwork, Giuliana heard the bathroom lock turn. She jumped up and peeked into the hall in time to see Ueli join Lukas in the bathroom. Soon afterward, the two of them came out and went into Lukas's room. Another door closed.

Fifteen minutes later, Ueli sat down next to her on the sofa and slumped into the cushions, dark shadows under his eyes. He'd been at the hospital for most of the day during his mother's operation and had come home to Lukas's outburst. And who knew what deadlines he had for articles he hadn't yet finished? Shifting position to put his head on her shoulder, he said, "I still don't know anything. We went from his saying how much he hated Frau Tanner, Niko, Joel, and us to saying it was all his fault, he was sorry, and he'd handle it. I told him over and over that it was our job as parents to help him cope with anything that worried him; that whatever had happened, we wanted to know because we love him."

Giuliana rested her hand on Ueli's thigh. "Did you say we'd love him no matter what was wrong?"

"Over and over," Ueli repeated, his body slack against hers. "But he says he has to deal with it himself."

Giuliana sat up and stared at her husband with wide eyes. "What can he possibly mean? It sounds like he has some kind of plan, doesn't it? Oh, God. What's he up to?"

Ueli rubbed his eyes. "I thought about keeping him home from school tomorrow, but he says he wants to go, and maybe that's the best place for him. Still, I'm taking him all the way to the classroom door. And I'll send Frau Tanner a text, so she can be on the lookout for whatever this 'deal with it' means. I'll phone Niko's dad tomorrow too. Do we know anything about Joel's parents? I know they're separated, but does his father live in the city somewhere?"

Giuliana frowned. "Wait a minute. You don't have time for all this. I can stay home tomorrow." He shook his head. "I mean it," she insisted. "I can handle it."

He gave her a crooked smile. "Sure you're not just trying to get brownie points for asking?" Before she could be offended, he grinned and kissed her cheek, adding, "Really, it's okay. I don't have any deadlines, thank God. I had one, but my editor was able to pass it on to someone else. As for my other stuff, I've gotten extensions without pissing anyone off too badly."

"But what about your mother?"

"The doctor thinks she should have chemotherapy to be on the safe side, and so far, she's fighting him. But either way, he seems optimistic. In any case, there's nothing I need to do for her tomorrow."

She reached for Ueli's hands. "You must be so relieved."

"Honestly?" He pulled away. "I am, very, but . . . well, I'm not about to open a bottle of champagne. She's got an ordeal ahead of her, whether she'll admit it or not. And I think she should do the chemo." He trailed off, then added, "All it takes is one cancer cell spreading. Still, I'm trying to be happy."

"Good," she said. "Any chance of talking to Mike about the . . . the family stuff?"

"Look, let me deal with that," he said with a snap in his voice. Then he added, more gently, "I'm forty-eight, not eleven. I can manage my problems with Mike."

Well, you haven't managed them during the last four decades, she wanted to point out. Instead, she said, "Can you think of anything criminal the boys might have done?"

Ueli shrugged. "It might be shoplifting. They stole something, and Lukas's 'dealing with it' is probably putting whatever it is back."

"Could Joel be into tagging? Maybe they got hold of some spray paint and graffitied a wall?"

"Could be," Ueli agreed, "or some other kind of vandalism. God, I hope they haven't taken a crowbar to some public statue."

"Maybe the Cléments will get something out of Niko," she said as Ueli dragged himself back to his desk.

She had an interview with Andi's lawyer the next day, but sitting in the kitchen with the case notes in front of her, she could only think about Lukas. Suddenly remembering the book he'd hidden under his chest of drawers, Giuliana slipped into his room, where he was curled up asleep, kneeled, and fished it out. It was a paperback from the school library called *Looking After Your Pet*. That didn't make any sense. Lukas had no pet and hadn't asked for one since the age of five when he'd requested a Saint Bernard puppy and been devastated when his parents had laughed in his face.

Giuliana gave up trying to do any police work and went to bed, but she was still awake when Ueli came in an hour later. "Maybe I should cancel fitness with Renzo tomorrow," she told him. "I can send him a text. I don't want to leave so early when—"

"Don't be silly," Ueli interrupted. "How can an extra hour of you being home make a difference? Do you think Lukas is going to throw himself on you and confess everything just because you're around for once to pass him the Nutella?"

That was below the belt. But true.

She set her alarm for Wednesday's usual five forty in the morning and thought about having breakfast with Renzo.

That Tuesday night, Renzo never made it home to put Angelo and Antonietta to bed nor for a late dinner with Fränzi. Instead, he followed up on the poison-pen story with the Thun cop and the Grabers until almost eight o'clock, phoned in a report to Giuliana and Vinz on his drive back to Bern, and, at eight forty-five, was sitting in Dolce Vita, waiting for his older brother Davide to join him for a drink. The restaurant was walking distance from Davide's apartment in Breitenrain, and Renzo was making up for his sandwich lunch by eating a plate of osso bucco. The juice from the long-cooked veal shanks and vegetables gave an orange tinge to the pale risotto piled next to them, and Renzo ate with slow enjoyment, glancing around. The place, inexpensive and friendly, was packed with people of all ages. Davide and his family were regulars here, and Renzo could see why.

He saw his brother come through the door and waved to him, then watched Davide's slow progress across the restaurant, shaking hands with the manager and half the waiters in the place, not to mention quite a few of the diners. Others, farther away, called out greetings in Swiss-German or Italian. Renzo grinned. Since childhood, he'd always been proud to be related to Davide. "That's my brother," he'd say when Davide kicked a perfect goal or walked by holding hands with a pretty girl. He stood up now to hug Davide. It had been a month since the last family dinner at their mother's house, and even there, they rarely talked one on one.

Renzo poured his brother a glass of red wine from the carafe of Primitivo he'd ordered. "Sandra okay?" he asked.

For five minutes, they chatted about Davide's wife Sandra and their two daughters. Then Renzo fell silent. He didn't know how to begin.

As usual, Davide came to his aid. "You told Bianca you wanted to talk about things with Fränzi, but if you've changed your mind," he shrugged, "no big deal."

Renzo raised his eyes to the ceiling. "You know Bianca," he said and stopped.

"Look, it's great to see you—we don't do this enough," Davide went on. "You can drink your wine and tell me about whatever cases you're working on, and I'll bore you with my latest sales figures." Then Davide reached across the table to clasp Renzo's upper arm, just for a moment. "But if you feel like talking about other things . . ."

"It wasn't my idea," Renzo said. How easy it was to fall back into being the little brother. "I wasn't complaining. But then I heard Fränzi's been talking to all of you about me, so . . ."

"Yeah. Well, she didn't need to; it's been obvious for a while that things aren't good. Besides, why does she gripe to us? Doesn't she grasp that we're on your side? Always."

Renzo wanted to smile, but he was too sad. Ashamed, too. This was his marriage Davide was talking about, his private life. He hadn't planned to say it, but the words burst out: "You and the sisters think I married Fränzi for her looks."

"Well, who could blame you for that? Not me. She's the sexiest woman I've ever seen outside the movies." Davide cocked his head and waited for Renzo to go on.

"It's true that I couldn't keep my hands off her from the moment I met her," Renzo admitted. "But it wasn't just that; those first years, we had so much fun together. Going to parties, dancing, laughing, telling each other stories about what we'd been up to. Remember how funny she used to be?"

"I remember how happy you looked—we all saw it."

"I was happy. And so was she, I think. But now she's . . . angry all the time," Renzo said. He'd thought a lot about Fränzi's resentments—and God knew she'd never been shy about saying what pissed her off—but he'd never talked to anyone about them.

"So what changed?" Davide asked. Then he shook his head. "Stupid question. You've been married six years and have two kids; everything's changed. But . . ."

"I know what you mean. It's . . ." He sighed. "She's always telling me I don't spend enough time with her. But when we *are* together, we don't . . . interact. I mean, why is she nagging me to stay home if she doesn't want to talk to me? What you said before about listening to me tell you about my cases—she never does that."

Davide opened his mouth, closed it, took a sip of wine, and just nodded.

"The other day, Antonietta refused to eat something on her plate, and Fränzi made a big deal." Renzo realized this story was probably lame, but he stumbled on. "Later, I brought it up really calmly. It was just a little thing, but I wanted to talk about other ways of handling it. She got angry. Said since I was never around, I had no right to criticize how she raised the kids. I . . . I just wanted to discuss it. But we never discuss anything."

Davide looked at him over his wine glass. "How many hours a week do you work? No, that's not the right question. How many hours a week are you away from home?"

Renzo almost said, "Aren't you listening to me? Who the fuck's side are you on, anyway?" But he swallowed it. He thought about hitting the gym by six, four mornings a week, leaving Fränzi to deal with getting the kids up and out. He thought about coming home no earlier than seven most evenings, after Angelo and Antonietta had already eaten, and taking an hour to bathe them and put them to sleep, which meant he and Fränzi seldom had supper before eight. Then there were evening staff meetings and the interviews or stakeouts that took place at night or on weekends, not to mention all the times he was on call and had to be ready to leave home at a moment's notice to join an investigation. There were weekend courses in unarmed combat or in new investigation techniques, too. Jesus, how many hours a week *was* he away?

"Too many," he answered. "Way too many. Tonight I haven't been home at all yet. But the problem is I love my job. I don't want to choose between it and my marriage."

Around them, people were paying their bills. Finally, Davide said, "The problem with divorce is—well, it's the children."

Renzo nodded. "I know. And I refuse to be one of those fathers who never sees his kids. I can't do that to Angelo and Antonietta. No, that's not true. I can't do it to me. It would kill me." He refilled his glass. "We went dancing Friday night, Fränzi and I. First, a nice dinner, then a club or two, followed by lots of sex. The kind of evening where Fränzi gets dressed up, and we spend money; we do that at least every six weeks, which I think is pretty good for a couple with two small kids."

"I doubt the 'lots of sex' part is limited to every six weeks."

"That's never been Fränzi's problem," said Renzo with a smirk.

"Nor yours, either, as I remember only too well," Davide retorted. "One minute you were this pudgy kid with ugly glasses who read all the time, and the next minute, wham! The times I used to cover up for you with Mamma." Davide grinned at Renzo, who gave him an elaborate eye roll, thinking all the while how much he loved his brother.

"So," Davide asked, "did you and Fränzi have fun on Friday? Was it like old times?"

"I had fun, but . . . what can I say?" Renzo put his chin in his hands. "I don't know what's wrong, but . . . She enjoys dancing with me and fucking my socks off, but I don't think she enjoys me. As a person. Lately, I think . . . I know it sounds weird, but she doesn't like me."

"Do you like her?" his brother asked.

Without stopping to think, Renzo answered, "No." He pressed a clenched fist to his mouth, but the word was already out. "She's someone else now. So . . . bitter. But if I've made her that way, then . . . well, I can't push her away when it's my fault, can I?"

The two men stared at each other bleakly.

"Jesus, Renzo," Davide said. "It's bad, isn't it? One thing you haven't told me—is there a girlfriend in the picture?"

"No," he said. It was the truth, even if . . .

"Maybe girlfriend's the wrong word. I mean, have you been cheating on her?" Renzo looked up sharply, but Davide wasn't giving him a hard time, just asking.

"Well." Renzo thought about lying but decided to tell the truth. "I'm not going to say that in six years of marriage, I haven't . . . But it's been a quickie with some stranger, and not since . . . I don't know. It hasn't happened in two years, at least. Why? Does Fränzi say I'm cheating on her *now*?"

Davide shrugged. "It's one of the things wives worry about when their husbands are away all the time. I mean . . . duh!"

"Well, I'm not," said Renzo.

Davide nodded and said nothing for a moment or two. Then he smiled at Renzo and reached across the table to give his cheek a couple of soft slaps. "Okay, *bimbo*. Do you want me to keep all this to myself, or can I tell Sandra?"

Of course, he'd want to tell his wife, and she'd want to pass it on, so . . . "I guess you can tell all of them," Renzo said with a sigh. "I'd do it myself, but it seems . . ."

Davide waited before going on. "Okay. But you should be the one to talk to Mamma."

"It'll just make her unhappy." Renzo stared at the tabletop.

"Hell, I think wondering what's going on and hearing only

Fränzi's side of it makes her pretty unhappy, too. Don't you think?" Davide gave him a sharp look and added, "Don't be an idiot."

"Okay, okay. I'll talk to her," Renzo promised. "Once this hit-and-run case is over."

Davide pushed his empty glass toward the middle of the table and said, "We should go—especially if you haven't been home yet."

Renzo paid. On the way out, Davide introduced him to the owner, and then he, too, had to shake hands and call goodbyes as they left the restaurant. Side by side in a drizzle, they walked under the streetlights to Renzo's car.

"Thanks," Renzo said, hugging Davide tightly. His head fit on his big brother's shoulder, just as it always had.

Letting go, he fumbled with his keys as Davide headed off with a wave.

Divorce. Davide had said the word Renzo didn't dare to say. He thought about it all the way home. It made him sad—and exhausted. No matter how dissatisfied he and Fränzi were with each other, surely it was less miserable than being divorced. And being unhappy in a marriage was much less complicated than getting a divorce. Working out the money, finding new living arrangements, deciding who got the children on what days. Christ! It just wasn't worth it. Now, if Giuliana . . . But that was never going to happen. He knew that.

Just for a second, he'd considered telling Davide about Giuliana. Thank God he hadn't. Nothing was more worthy of ridicule than unrequited love. It was unmanly. He knew Giuliana would have laughed at the word, but that was how he felt. And yet, it wasn't unrequited, was it? Not really. She loved him; he knew she did. But . . .

He tried never to let himself imagine a life with Giuliana, but the talk with Davide had shaken some of those thoughts loose. Fuck! It was time to stuff everything back into the big wardrobe in his brain and decide what to tell Fränzi about dinner with his brother. Hmm. He'd have to come up with a good story and then text Davide the details in case he needed his brother to back him up.

20

Bern,
Wednesday morning, April 1

On Wednesday, when Giuliana's alarm went off at 5:40, Ueli was already up, showered, and almost finished getting dressed. "Don't look so amazed," he said as she stared at him blearily. "I texted Bänz Clément last night, and we're going to get to the bottom of this thing with the boys. I'll walk Lukas to school, and Bänz and Tina will drop off Niko, and afterward, we'll do a little brainstorming."

"I'm sorry I'm not going to be there," Giuliana mumbled. They were talking through the half-open bathroom door, and she had a toothbrush in her mouth.

Ueli, fully dressed, came in and stood behind her, his hands on her shoulders, looking at her seriously in the bathroom mirror. "You're a good mother," he said. "I know it, and Lukas knows it. If Tina and Bänz want to think you're a monster because you go to work instead of hovering around Lukas when I'm already on the job, then to hell with them."

Her heart lightened. She spat toothpaste, rinsed her mouth, and kissed him. "Thanks," she said. "I'm off to the gym. And I love you."

Outside, she stood on the sidewalk for a moment. At ten after six, sunrise was about an hour away, and fog swirled around the streetlights.

She checked the day's weather on her phone and shook her head. Snow on the first of April. So much for that taste of spring the day before.

Now she had to find the car. Every night, with her mind on her work or the kids or dinner or anything but what she was doing, she found a different parking place somewhere in the neighborhood, usually, but not always, a legal one. Twelve hours later, she had to remember where the hell she'd left the car. Last night? Hmm. At last, she remembered making her way slowly up the steepest part of the hill and smiling at the lights she could see streaming out of her apartment windows. Okay, then: she'd parked on Alpenstrasse.

Walking there now, her feet almost slid out from under her; the temperature was dropping fast enough to turn the fog into black ice, so she drove to work more slowly than usual, thinking about what Ueli had said: to hell with what Niko's parents thought of her as a mother. Yet she did care. She knew her kids had not suffered at all being raised mainly by their father, but still, she worried that people might think they had. And *that* made her ashamed of caring about something so foolish as others' opinions of her parenting!

She slowed down even more on the Lorraine Bridge and gave the finger to a driver who rode on her bumper, honking at her. That spark of aggression made her feel much better, especially when she imagined how surprised the guy'd be if he knew she was a cop.

By seven thirty, she'd worked out hard for fifty minutes, showered, and joined Renzo for their usual croissants and coffee. "Thanks for the report on Agnes Graber," she told him and took her first sip of coffee. "I read it, but I still want to know—"

Renzo stopped buttering half a croissant to say, "I'm going to talk about Graber at Vinz's meeting, so can you wait until then?"

Giuliana tried not to look taken aback. "Sure I can," she said, "but . . . why?"

"Because I want you to tell me more about the interview with Kissling!" he said, setting down his knife and picking up a spoon to attack the strawberry jam. "Yesterday in the car, you only managed a sentence or two."

"Oh." Now she did raise her eyebrows in surprise. "I just wish there was more to tell. The only thing that seemed to get a response from him was when I told him I'd ordered a psych evaluation for his wife. He wants to know the results. It'll be part of what we have to hand over to the defense team anyway, so . . . Zaugg agrees I can share it with him. It's taking the shrink a long time, but he promised Zaugg his report by tomorrow afternoon. So I'll see Kissling again on Friday." She brushed flakes of croissant off her lapels and wondered why she could never manage to eat pastry without making a mess.

After his workout, Renzo was usually in a great mood—Giuliana often wondered why endorphins seemed to do their job so much better on him than her—but today he seemed . . . subdued. Shadowed, almost. "I've got a question," he said. "Did Kissling try to get custody of his daughters? I mean, at least fifty percent?"

"His wife told me that he tried for full custody, and I know from the files that he only got every other weekend. According to her, he didn't fight the judge's decision, but what she says can't be trusted. Her statements to me, especially about the girls, were contradictory. Why? What are you thinking?"

"Everyone assumes he killed his children to punish his wife. Or because he'd decided the girls couldn't live without him and therefore shouldn't live at all. Both those explanations presume that the girls were just possessions in his eyes. But suppose he loved them very much and, when he couldn't be with them, destroyed them in a fit of grief?"

Giuliana puzzled over this. "Aren't those more or less the same? 'If I can't have you, nobody's going to have you.' Surely it has more to do with machismo than love. I don't mean to sound sexist, but any cop knows men are more likely to reason that way than women. Killing a woman or a child they can't possess. It's dog-in-the-manger behavior, isn't it?"

Renzo was shaking his head, eyes down. The Kissling case got to everyone, and Renzo's son and daughter were almost exactly the ages Mia and Lea would be if they'd lived. But that didn't quite explain his odd theory. When he looked up at her, there was something in his expression that worried her. "I think there's a difference between jealous rage and grief. Find out who handled the divorce and ask about the arrangements for the girls' care. That's my advice."

And then they were dashing across the street to the staff meeting. As they hit the stairs at a run, Giuliana thought about what Renzo had just said—and his face when he'd said it. Something was going on with him. Whether it was any business of hers to pry it out of him was another question.

Rolf, Vinz, Giuliana, Renzo, Madeleine—who was called Mädi—and the prosecutor, Oliver Leuthard, arranged themselves around the case room. Mädi was leaning on a filing cabinet, and Renzo noticed she had a small tattoo on her inner right wrist. He stared at it, trying to figure out what it was. He'd thought he was being subtle, but suddenly she raised her hand and grinned at him. With her open hand and wrist facing him, he could see her tattoo was a bird, black and white, wings spread, flying toward a red sun. He liked it. He smiled back and held up a thumb in approval.

Vinz was already talking. "Here's our problem. We keep digging up new suspects but not eliminating old ones." He paused, but no one said anything, so he went on. "Start with the two prison guards. We still can't be sure where one of them was on the night of March twenty-fifth, although Mädi managed to find someone who'd seen the other one, so we can eliminate him now. Quite honestly, we're stuck. Giuliana, you and Renzo seem to be piling up possibilities, too. Can you give us the latest?"

"Sure," said Giuliana. Renzo thought she looked slightly annoyed, and he agreed that Vinz could sound a little more grateful. Better too many suspects than none at all—even if Vinz did prefer things to be nice and neat.

"Andi was blunt and sometimes got on people's nerves. Renzo and I," said Giuliana, smiling across the room at him, "have decided that's not a sufficient reason to kill her. But we still have four suspects." He nodded, and she went on. "The first is a woman on the curling team,

Barbara Weber. She was seen driving away from the hall on her bike, and her boyfriend says she got home around eleven, which is only a bit later than usual. But she could have biked to a rental car parked nearby, killed Andi, driven home, unloaded her bike from the car, and—"

"Right," interrupted Vinz. "We're working on that one. The main rental companies report no red car out that night showing any signs of having been in an accident. But that doesn't include every little garage in the city that might rent a vehicle now and then. We're checking with them—and looking for her on CCTV."

"Great," Giuliana said. "Next suspect is Mathan Pragasam, the older of the victim's two brothers-in-law." Renzo watched her messing up her hair with her fingers, the way she always did when she was stressed. Why did she bother putting her hair up every morning when it was only going to end up a scramble of curls by midafternoon?

Giuliana was saying, "Pragasam has a red car, and his alibi for Eberhart's death was provided by his wife, who's afraid of him. So," she said, forestalling Vinz, "more digging to do there, too. CCTV has been checked, but there are no cameras near the scene, as you know. All we can say is that there's no evidence of a collision on the car's bodywork."

"Not to mention," put in Renzo, "that this guy strikes me as all lime and no tequila."

"I agree. But this is the kind of hands-off crime that would fit someone like this man," said Giuliana.

Vinz looked surreptitiously at his watch, and Giuliana went hurriedly on. "Okay. Then there's an unknown suspect in a gray sedan who was watching Eberhart's house for a couple of days before she was killed. I only heard about this person—who's probably a man—last night from a neighbor."

Vinz nodded. "I got your report about that last night. We're following up." He couldn't resist his lozenges any longer; Renzo swallowed a smile as Vinz fished the little box out of his shirt pocket and put a mint in his mouth. Vinz was a bit of an oddball, but Renzo was impressed by how fast he worked. He found himself thinking about the promotion he'd been planning for a while now. Was he organized enough to juggle all the details like Vinz did? Maybe that was something to talk to Giuliana about before he got his hopes up.

"Our fourth suspect, Agnes Graber, is almost surely the writer of those anonymous letters Eberhart was getting," Giuliana was saying. "She's a *Pfarrer's* wife in a village above Thun called Dürrenegg. Renzo should talk to you about this; he investigated it yesterday with a local cop."

Renzo was ready. "Right, so Giule and I went first to Emil Senn from the Thun force, who investigated an earlier case of this woman sending nasty accusations to young girls she imagined were sleeping with her husband. In those days, she did a lot of correspondence for the parish, and the poison-pen stuff was written from his office typewriter."

"Typewriter?" asked Madeleine. "When was this, 1980?"

Renzo raised his eyebrows at her with a grin. "No, about fifteen years ago—not every little parish had a computer then. Today, the church office has an old laptop and printer, and we took them away—or, rather, Senn took them to the Thun station for us—to see if what comes out of the printer matches our letters. Which are also full of fingerprints, and I've got Graber's for comparison. I expect to know by tomorrow midday if there's a match there."

"Did you talk to her?" Vinz asked.

"Yes, in her home with Senn present," Renzo answered. "She says she doesn't know anything about the letters or the accident. She's in her mid-seventies and seems fit enough physically; she regularly drives to Bern and back, doing errands. So she *could* have mailed the letters from Bern and driven into Andi. She and her husband sleep in different rooms, and he goes to bed early. He says he's sure she was at home the night Andi was killed, but he didn't actually see or hear her after nine. So, more work to do," he nodded at Vinz as he used the detective's words. "As soon as this meeting's over, I'll get people onto the CCTV footage of cars coming on and off the autobahn and also any footage we have of the back roads—we'll see."

"What's your gut feeling?" Vinz asked him.

Renzo didn't have to think for long. "Despite her denials, everything in the interview made me think Graber wrote the letters. But is she nutty enough—and at the same time sane enough—to find out about Andi's movements, stalk her on the way home from curling practice, and attack her with the car? I should say *a* car because the Grabers' car is dark green and hasn't crashed into anything recently; we've already checked that. So she had to find another car to use. Assuming she left her prints all over the letters, which I'm anticipating she did, would she have the cunning *not* to use her own car for the killing?" He shrugged.

"Okay. Anyone have anything else?" Vinz asked. After a short silence, he said, "Renzo, normally you'd follow through with Graber, I know, but I'd like you to keep going through Eberhart's Civi files to see if there's anything else we need to worry about—even though I know that may give us even *more* suspects." Renzo appreciated Vinz's little joke at his own expense. "So I'm going to push the Graber follow-up over to Mädi."

Renzo nodded—what else could he do? But he was fine with sticking to Andi's Civi work. The Civis were much more interesting than he'd expected.

"Giuliana, you're still on family and friends, right?" Vinz asked.

"That's right," she answered. "I'm seeing someone this morning who should be able to put me on the track of Eberhart's ex-lovers since she's one herself. Then I'll talk to Eberhart's brother and his wife. There's someone the parents mentioned as well—a school friend—that I'll contact, plus a long-ago boyfriend. No theories yet about any of these folks, but I expect to get ideas as I go along."

"What about the partner? After all, she's the one who fed us the poison-pen letters in the first place. Could that have been to put us off track?"

"My gut says no," Renzo put in, and Giuliana nodded, adding, "Another 'I was asleep' alibi there, but nothing we've found makes her seem suspicious. I'll keep asking the couple's mutual friends, though."

"Which reminds me," said Mädi, "I've gone through all of Eberhart's calls and texts during the month before her death, but nothing stands out except that she wasn't good about getting back to people. Which sometimes makes me want to kill *my* friends—but I don't think we need to consider that a serious motive for her murder."

Renzo smiled at Mädi to show he appreciated her attempt to lighten the atmosphere; he didn't notice that anyone else did, though.

"So that's it," said Vinz, his mouth a thin, straight line. "We all have our plans. Let's meet again tomorrow." With that, he turned to the prosecutor, who was asking him a question, and everyone else stood up. Giuliana was first out the door, off to meet Andi's lawyer and ex-lover, Susanna Käser. Rolf headed down the hall toward the homicide office, and Renzo walked along next to Mädi.

"Thanks for taking over the Graber stuff," he said to her, although she hadn't had much choice either. "Anything I can tell you?"

"Nope. The Thun cop's number is in your report. I'll read it for background, phone to tell him I'm on Graber now, and after that, if I have questions, I'll let you know," Mädi said. As they moved down the hall side by side, Renzo saw she was slightly taller than he was, even in flat-heeled shoes. She smiled at him, her face suddenly full of mischief. "So, do *you* have a tattoo somewhere?"

"God, no," blurted Renzo, then, hearing how old-fashioned he sounded, added, "But I like yours."

"It's an albatross." Flashing the black-and-white bird again as she waved to him, she headed for the staircase while he turned in the other direction toward the unused conference room where he planned to spend the day reading Andi's files. First, though, he checked his emails and found one from Andi's colleague Loïc Amrein.

Salut, *Renzo*, he wrote. *I had an idea about that "key" emoji that Andi put next to some of the Civis' names. It wasn't a secret that Andi gathered more info from her guys than the rest of us did. Whenever one of them finished a job, she always asked how it went. Lots of them had nothing to say, but some were willing to "debrief" with her, as she called it. I was thinking maybe she used the "key" to identify the guys who'd opened up to her. If I'm right, there should be more notes about their jobs. Let me know what you find. Loïc.*

Loïc's guess about the key made sense, but he'd already looked for differences between Civis with a key next to their names and those without. On average, the keys did have more complete notes in their files—but barely. A few extra phrases but no in-depth information setting their files apart. So . . . still a mystery.

Sighing in frustration, Renzo opened one of the files Andi's boss had let him copy from her work computer. In a second window, he displayed the list of fifty-eight names Loïc had given him—the clients Andi'd had the most contact with during the past eighteen months. Thirty-two of the fifty-eight had keys by their names in the Excel file. A quick check told him that nineteen of the remaining Civis among the fifty-eight were on their first assignment, and seventeen of those had no keys.

So far, so good, he thought. If Loïc was right that the keys referred to a post-assignment debriefing, it would make sense that youngsters in the middle of their first assignment wouldn't be marked with keys because they wouldn't have had anything to tell Andi yet. They might have aired complaints or problems with their employers to her, but they wouldn't have been in a position to discuss their assignments as a whole.

And the two first-assignment boys *with* keys? Renzo looked them up in another of Andi's files and discovered both had called her after about two months of a six-month assignment. One youngster had found working with dementia patients so depressing that he wasn't sure he could continue; the other loved his assignment at a small zoo but had developed an allergy to the straw bedding he was handling.

There were keys in the Excel file next to the names of several men besides the thirty-two on Loïc's list. If Andi *had* debriefed all of them about their jobs, where was the data she'd collected? He leaned back in his chair and stared at the ceiling, his hands locked around the back of his head. "Key" informers? About what?

Giuliana had promised to call IT for him yesterday morning.

She'd probably done it—but maybe she wasn't high enough up the food chain to get results.

He pulled his phone out of his pocket and dialed Rolf Straub. "It's Renzo," he told the older man, "and I'm calling for a favor. I need to get into Andrea Eberhart's personal laptop *now*. The IT folks have had it since Friday—could you put some pressure on them for me?"

"Sure," said Rolf. "No guarantees, but I'll do my best."

Good, thought Renzo. That was a step in the right direction. Suddenly he was excited. He turned back to Andi's work files to read more about the jobs held by the few men whose names were marked with lightning bolts—all of whom also had keys.

Just then, his landline rang. It was the guard at the front desk. "Hey, Renzo. I've got Giuliana Linder's son here to see you—about ten years old, named Lukas Brand. He and another kid walked in and asked for Erwin, but he's out, so they followed up with you. Know anything about it?"

Well, that was not what he'd been expecting. Renzo frowned. "Giuliana's son is named Lukas Brand, but I didn't get a message about his coming in. Maybe his school's having a visit-your-mother-at-work day. I'll be right down." Could Giuliana have forgotten to mention it? He sighed and hoped the kids weren't planning to spend the whole day at the station. If they were, he owed it to Giuliana to organize some kind of interesting experience for them, but he hated to lose the time. He looked at his watch. It was almost nine thirty, and he'd wanted to spend a full day with the files.

When Renzo reached the bottom of the stairs, he saw the two boys standing in the entrance hall, shoulder to shoulder, glancing around them. No excited grins, no jostling each other: the eyes that met his were serious, unsmiling. Renzo had never seen Giuliana's son, and he was startled by how much Lukas, with his wild dark curls, brown eyes, and full mouth, resembled his mother while still managing to look like a child. The other boy was taller and skinnier but just as childlike. Both were wearing old-fashioned school satchels on their backs. He tried to remember Lukas's age. Older than ten, but not by much.

The desk man was dealing with a phone call, but he waved to acknowledge Renzo assuming custody of the kids.

Renzo held his hand out to Lukas first. "Hello, Lukas. I'm Renzo Donatelli, and I can see you're Giuliana's son. Who's your friend?"

"He's Niko Clément," Lukas answered. Niko shook hands, too, with a shy smile, and Renzo guided them to the stairs. At least he could show them the room where Giuliana worked while they were here.

"What can I do for you?"

Lukas, who seemed to be the duo's spokesman, stopped on the landing. Renzo heard him take a deep breath. "We're here to report a crime."

"You mean . . ." Renzo stared at him. "You mean you saw someone do something illegal? Just now?"

"No," Lukas and Niko said in unison. They stood on the landing a moment, and then Lukas repeated, "No. We want to report *our* crime."

21

Renzo's first response was anger at their silliness. Was this an April Fools' joke? Then he reminded himself how young they were. "Is this some kind of school assignment, or are you trying to be funny?" he asked, biting back his irritation. "Our work here isn't a joke, you know."

"I do know," said Lukas, his voice quavering. "I've been thinking about coming here for two weeks."

Renzo wondered whether he was in over his head. Should he call Giuliana, even though she was conducting an interview? First, he'd find out what was going on. "I see," he said, looking from one boy to the other. "OK. Let's sit down so you can tell me about it."

The boys followed him upstairs and into the room where he'd been working. He pushed his laptop and papers to one end of the table, and the three of them sat at the other.

Faced with having to explain, Lukas began to wriggle around in his chair and rub his nose. When at last he began to talk, it was fast and breathless. "Mam told me a detective called Erwin is the toughest cop she knows, so we asked to talk to him, but he isn't here. Then I remembered your name. You aren't in homicide like she is, I know that, but you're her friend."

Renzo put up a hand, and Lukas fell silent. "Before you tell me what you've done, I need to know a couple of things. First of all, do your parents know about this crime you've committed?" They shook their heads. *Oh shit*, Renzo thought. "Second question: Does anyone know where you are?"

Niko and Lukas looked at each other, and Niko said, "No."

It took five minutes to alert the boys' school to their whereabouts. That done, Renzo showed them where the toilet was and fetched them glasses of water, then got out his notebook and asked for their story.

Lukas pulled a messy stack of paper out of his school bag and set it in front of Renzo. On top was a missing cat flyer, in grainy black and white, for an animal called Tiger that had been missing since mid-March. Lukas had at least ten of these posters, crumpled and torn.

The boy stared down at the pictures. His face was working, and his fingers were scrunched into fists.

"What is it, Lukas?"

"We . . . we killed this cat," he said, finally, his voice squeezed and thin. "Niko and I and . . . and another boy. We killed it on purpose. With a sword." He put his head down on the conference table and began to cry; Niko, sitting next to him, sat huddled in his chair, tears rolling down his cheeks, too.

Renzo half rose from his chair; his instinct was to gather these sad children onto his lap and rock them as he would his own kids. Poor little guys, worrying about this awful thing for two weeks and not even daring to tell their parents. Then he sat back down. They had come to the station so their confession would be taken seriously. Not to be cuddled. He owed it to them not to treat them like babies. Hadn't Lukas asked for the toughest cop at the station? Erwin wouldn't hug them. Still, he didn't have to be quite as gruff as Erwin, did he?

He left them crying and found a box of tissues in the third office he searched. By the time he was back, both boys were calmer. Lukas said, his voice still shaky, "Niko and I . . . we know a lot about swords. For Christmas, we got plastic ones—shields, too—and we used to go to the woods near where we live to fight with them. On

YouTube, you can . . ." He seemed to realize he was digressing because he stopped.

"So you both have plastic swords," Renzo prompted.

With another look at Niko, as if getting permission to continue, Lukas went on. "There's a new boy in our class—he came just after Christmas because his parents got divorced. He started coming with us to the woods, and we'd take turns lending him one of our swords. But he said he had a real sword, a sharp metal one, at his father's."

"I didn't believe him," put in Niko. "A real sword?"

"One weekend, he went to visit his father and came back with it, a heavy metal sword. A sharp one. The next time we went to the woods, he brought it."

"And he fought us and broke our stuff to bits," said Niko.

Renzo nodded. What kind of parent would let a child go around with a sharp sword? Thank God what got hacked up was only plastic and not a child's hand or face. Although . . . He waited for more.

"The next day, Sunday, Jo—the boy," Lukas covered his slip of the tongue, "wanted to meet again. He said we could play with his sword, so . . . we came to the woods. And he brought a cat. In a big plastic bag."

"It was yowling and wiggling around in there," Niko explained. "So he took it out."

"And then it scratched and bit him," Lukas went on, "and he was screaming at us, telling us what to do. I . . . I tied a piece of string to its tail, really tight."

"I tied the string to a tree," Niko whispered.

The story stopped. Renzo waited. When neither boy spoke, he asked quietly, "Who hit the cat first—with the sword?"

"Joel did," Niko answered, and neither he nor Lukas seemed to notice that the name had been revealed. "He said he'd chop its head off in one blow, but he couldn't. I think the sword wasn't sharp enough. He just . . . kind of smashed it a couple of times. The cat, I mean. And then . . . he gave us the sword, and we smashed it, too."

"I went first," Niko said. There was something protective in the way he said it; Renzo realized he was trying to make Lukas feel better.

"But I was the one that killed it," Lukas said. "It was covered with blood and making a horrible noise. Its . . . its insides were coming out. I couldn't . . . I just hit it in the neck with the sword over and over until its head fell off. Then I threw up."

"Joel smeared some of the cat's blood on his face," Niko added. "We wouldn't do that, so he said we were pussies."

They'd left the cat where it was, gone to Joel's apartment—he was "the boy" again now—because no one was there, washed the sword and themselves, and sworn never to tell anyone what they'd done. Then Niko and Lukas went home. The next day the "missing" posters had gone up on lamp posts and fences all over the neighborhood. Lukas had torn down every single one he'd seen. Then he'd taken a garbage bag from the kitchen cupboard and a garden trowel from the cellar, located the remaining parts of the dead cat in the woods, pushed them into the bag with the trowel, added as many rocks as he could find, tied it closed, and thrown it into the Aare.

"I know I destroyed evidence," Lukas said. "But I was so scared. And . . . and I didn't want the people who put up the flyers to find their cat. To have to see Tiger all squashed and in pieces."

Trust a cop's kid to worry about evidence, Renzo thought. But he didn't find anything about the story funny. Joel sounded like the kind of little beast he'd be arresting in a few years. He'd need to make sure social services followed up with the family. But right now, he had to handle Niko and Lukas correctly, and he wasn't sure how. He wished Erwin *was* there instead of himself, someone older and wiser. Should he be kind or stern? What was better for them? Hadn't they suffered enough?

After a long pause, he said, "You did the right thing talking to me about this. Is there any part of the story you've left out?"

Lukas and Niko shook their heads simultaneously. "During the past two weeks, our parents and teachers have been mad at us," Lukas said finally, "because we've been . . . kind of awful, I guess."

"Two days ago, Lukas told me he wasn't going to hang out with us anymore," Niko added. He wouldn't look at Lukas but stared at the table. "So after that, only I stayed friends with . . . the boy. I didn't want to, but I . . . I didn't know how to stop. But yesterday, I told him to leave me alone. Lukas and I, we've been friends since kindergarten. We talked about what to do, and after our first class this morning, we decided to come here."

"That was a good plan," Renzo said. "But I still have a question for you. I'd like you to think a minute and tell me the most important thing you should have done."

"Told our parents," Niko answered right away.

"That's true. But it's not enough. There's something you should have done earlier. Go through the story again step by step in your minds and tell me when you should have acted. What was the bravest and best thing you both could have done?"

There was silence for almost a minute. Then Lukas, his dark eyes looking huge in his paper-white face, whispered, "Saved Tiger."

Not breaking the boy's stricken gaze, Renzo nodded. Then he looked at Niko, who was staring at his hands. "There were two of you. You could have tried to take the cat away from the sword boy. Instead, you went along with his plan. You knew it was a terrible thing to do, but you did it anyway."

Niko was looking down again, but Lukas was still staring at Renzo, his face distorted as he tried to keep from crying.

"Think about that," Renzo said. "About why you didn't tell this boy to fuck off"—he used the bad word deliberately, thinking it would make an impression, and by the look on Lukas's face, it did—"and then grab the cat and run." He paused a minute and then said, "You need to think about that now, so it won't happen again. So that next time you're in a situation like that, whether you're a kid or a grownup, you'll remember not to do the wrong thing just because someone tells you to. And, if possible, you'll either stop the thing from happening or go tell someone who can stop it."

The boys said nothing, but Renzo thought they'd understood. "Will you both try to do that next time? Niko?"

Niko looked up from his hands and said, "I'll try."

"Lukas?"

Giuliana's son had never stopped staring at Renzo. "I promise," he said.

"Good. Now I have a job for you before you leave here. You need to tell me the name of the boy who killed the cat."

"We won't snitch," Niko said immediately. Renzo thought this must be a pact they'd made beforehand.

"We turned ourselves in to you instead," Lukas explained.

"Did your friend—if he is still your friend—do something exceptionally bad?"

"Yes," answered Lukas; Niko nodded.

"Did he do it on purpose?" Decided nods from both boys.

"Do you think he could do something like it again?" After a moment, tentative nods.

"So, is it cowardly to tell me his name, or is it brave?"

"His name is Joel Rentsch," Lukas said immediately.

"Thank you." Renzo was relieved that he could follow up on the story in good conscience now instead of taking advantage of the boys' slips of the tongue. "From what you've told me about Joel, I think he needs . . . special people to talk to."

"Will he go to jail?" Niko asked.

"No. We don't send children to jail."

"He's twelve-and-a-half," Lukas said, his face drawn with worry.

"Not even twelve-year-olds."

With an effort, Renzo kept himself from checking the time. He needed to get back to work, but he also had to make sure the boys were in good hands.

"You got here on your own, I know," he told them, "but I want someone to come and pick you up now. I don't know when your mother will be back here, Lukas, so we need to call one of the other parents—any suggestions?"

"I'll call my father," Lukas said, then looked at Niko, who nodded and produced a phone. "I don't get a phone until I'm thirteen," Lukas told Renzo matter-of-factly.

The conversation with Ueli was short. "My father's already on his way," Lukas said. "He'll be here in a few minutes."

Renzo suddenly realized he felt—God, was he nervous about meeting Ueli after all these years? He'd read the man's articles online and checked out his appearance, but he'd never seen or spoken to him, not even on the phone. Of course, he could just leave the boys with the desk guard, but that would be ridiculous.

Renzo called the front desk to say he was bringing the boys down and that Giuliana's husband was due soon. The children gathered up their stuff. As Lukas stuffed the missing-cat flyers back into his school bag, he looked up at Renzo. "These people don't know what happened to Tiger," he said.

Renzo hated to cause the kids more pain, but he knew he owed it to Giuliana to take the correct stance.

"That's true," he answered, keeping his voice neutral. The three of them started down the stairs.

"Do *we* have to go tell them?" Lukas asked. His voice shook, and tears filled his eyes again. "Do we have to?"

What a great job Giuliana has done with this boy, Renzo thought. Then he caught himself. No, not Giuliana. It was Ueli who'd organized his work life around his kids' schedules. He was the primary child raiser.

He stopped on the stairs and finally did what he'd been longing to do: he put his arm around Lukas's shoulders and squeezed the boy to his side. "It's up to your parents, but I think it's the right thing to do. But I'm sure you wouldn't have to go alone—your father would go with you."

He turned and gave Niko a one-armed hug as well. "You boys have been"—he fished for the right word—"honorable. Like knights." At their age, he'd been crazy about knights. Somewhere in young adulthood, he'd realized that most knights must have been thugs galloping around raping, stealing, and slaughtering on command—or on a whim. But these were boys who loved swords, so they probably glorified knights the way he had. "You blew the whistle on something wrong. That's a very brave and difficult thing to do."

"What does that mean?" Lukas asked. "Blew the whistle?"

Renzo didn't answer because he was suddenly far away.

Whistleblower.

Andi's debriefings. Could it be that Andi was a whistleblower? That she asked some Civis in detail about their jobs because she suspected something shady was going on? And then she'd followed up? The way she'd reported the racist guards in the *Amthaus* prison.

Renzo was so lost in speculation that he scarcely noticed Lukas racing down the stairs, closely followed by Niko, and leaping into the arms of a smiling man with yellowish-brown eyes, pumpkin-colored hair, freckles, and a closely cut beard the same color as his hair but with a streak of white in it. Renzo pushed his thoughts about Andi away, picked up his own pace, and held out a hand to Ueli, who, mouth slightly open, stared at him for a second. Then he asked, "Renzo?"

He nodded, and Ueli stepped forward and took his hand in both of his. "Thank you for taking care of the boys," he said. "We've been . . . very worried."

He hadn't expected to feel this . . . confused by a meeting with Ueli. He'd resented the man for years, almost hated him at times, and now he was faced with someone likable, someone he found himself respecting as a father.

"You're welcome," he said, stammering slightly. "It . . . uh, it turns out it wasn't just some stunt, their coming here. They—"

Lukas interrupted him, to his relief. "We came to confess, Vati."

"Confess to what?" Ueli's smile vanished, and he looked up at Renzo. "What . . . what have they done?"

Before Renzo could answer, Lukas spoke up again. "It's okay now. We'll tell you. We can explain everything now."

"It was Joel Rentsch's fault, really," Niko said.

"But our fault, too," Lukas added. He was holding his father's hand and gazing up at him, his face serious but with no sign of fear. "Renzo says we should have stopped Joel, and I . . . I never thought of that. Now I don't understand why not. We could have—"

Ueli held up a hand to stop his son's flow of talk. Beckoning

Renzo, he moved to the other side of the open area at the foot of the stairs. "What do I need to know?" he asked Renzo in a hoarse under-tone. "Has Lukas broken the law?"

Renzo clasped his upper arm briefly in reassurance. "No, no. Well, not exactly. He and Niko and this third boy, they killed someone's pet cat with a sword, but . . ."

Ueli sucked in his breath, and his eyes filled with horror. "Jesus, no!"

"They're ready to tell you and Giuliana about it now," Renzo reassured him. "I think the fact that they came here wanting to confess to a cop shows how seriously they take their . . ."—he paused, not wanting to say crime—"what they did. I listened to them and tried . . . I hope I handled things appropriately. I mean, both my kids are under six, so . . ." He paused.

"Whatever you did, it worked. Lukas is like a new person. He's been in a terrible state for weeks now." Ueli shook his head.

Renzo couldn't help grinning. "Yep, he told me he's been driving you and Giule nuts. Listen, you have a great son there. He impressed me—a lot."

Ueli's smile was worried, but he said, "Thanks. That's good to hear."

Renzo glanced over at the boys and saw they were being entertained by a young policeman who was identifying each item he wore on his duty belt, so he went on. "Look. One more thing you need to know. The boy with the sword who stole the cat, Joel Rentsch—I'll need to report him to social services. Shall I keep Giuliana informed?"

"Yeah, that's good." Ueli shook his head. "I'll talk to the school and Niko's parents after I hear the boys' story. Then . . . well, we'll see." This time, he held his hand out first. "Thanks again, Renzo. We'll leave you to get on with your day, finally. Boys," he called, "Herr Donatelli needs to go back to work, and we're leaving. Come and say goodbye."

Lukas and Niko walked over and shook hands.

"We'll think about what you said," Lukas told him. "About stopping bad stuff from happening—if we can." Niko nodded, and Renzo left them at the foot of the stairs.

He was back to thinking about whistleblowing. And wondering what Andi had hidden on her laptop.

22

Susanna Käser, a small, plump woman with short gray hair, shifted in the office armchair across from Giuliana and cocked her head, examining Giuliana with open curiosity. "Giuliana Linder," she repeated. "Any relation to Max Linder?"

Giuliana sighed inwardly. She should have expected this middle-aged, lefty lawyer to know her father. "His daughter," she said.

"Didn't your brother take over Max's defense practice recently?"

Giuliana was glad to be able to plug Paolo. "That's right. He's handling some really interesting cases right now."

Susanna ignored this. "And you're a cop! That must give them fits."

Giuliana had heard it all before, but she kept her voice pleasant. "They've had two decades to get over the shock. I think by now they're coping."

Curiosity satisfied, Susanna Käser turned to the reason for their meeting. "I'm glad Max's daughter is investigating Andi's death. Because I'm *not* coping. Not at all. It's still . . . a shock." As she spoke, her eyes filled with tears, which she angrily wiped away. "I want to help any way I can. Shall I give you the legal information first?"

Giuliana nodded. "Go ahead."

Käser settled back in her chair and folded her hands on her desk as if assuming her lawyer pose. Once in position, she said, "I guess you know that the laws about what percentage of your property you have to leave to your parents and children and so on—that changed recently. So now it's no problem for someone in Andi's situation to split all her money and property between her legal partner and her child. But since her adoption of Saritha wasn't complete when she made the will, we agreed she'd leave half her property to Nisha and the other half in trust for Saritha, with Nisha having the right to use it for her own and Saritha's benefit."

"I see. What 'property' are we talking about?" Giuliana asked.

"After splitting the down payment on the apartment with Nisha, Andi had around twenty thousand francs left. The place is worth a little over four hundred thousand now, and the neighborhood's a gem, so its value will increase over the next ten years. That's all, except for her car, which was five years old."

Giuliana ran the fingers of both hands through her hair, stopping only as she felt the strands loosen from the knot at her neck. She sighed. "How long have you known Andi?"

"Since she was twenty-two. More than ten years."

"Would anyone kill her for money? Are there hidden sums lying around somewhere?"

Susanna raised her eyes heavenward in derision, but Giuliana persevered. "No vault of gold in Gringotts? No fabulously wealthy great-aunt torn between Andi and another heir? No secret millionaire lover? No hidden stash of cocaine? No blackmail victims fed up with paying her? You're sure?"

Susanna had smiled at the mention of Gringotts, but by the time Giuliana finished speaking, she was shaking her head. "There's no one, aunt or girlfriend, planning to leave Andi money, and she certainly didn't sell drugs or extort money from anyone." Her eyebrows drew together fiercely. "If you can even think that, then you don't know Andi at all."

"Sorry," Giuliana said, although she wasn't—such questions had to be asked, and Susanna knew it. "I'm not trying to brand her a criminal. I'm trying to imagine why someone would kill her. Not blackmail, maybe, but . . . Could she have slept with a woman who'd be afraid to have that revealed? A conservative politician who's living as a straight woman now but has a lesbian past?"

Susanna was no longer defensive—she laughed. "Wow. You should write trashy novels. I don't think I can give you the name of everyone Andi's been to bed with, but I'm sure she'd have told me if one of them had become famous. Or was seeking revenge."

"But if it was a secret?" Giuliana was not letting go of her idea so fast.

Susanna shook her head. "Look, Andi didn't *have* secrets," she insisted. "She was honest and open to a fault—and I really mean to a fault. If she knew or even suspected anything shady, she'd blurt it out. *That's* what used to get her into trouble sometimes: her directness, not her secrecy. Over the years, she learned to be more discrete. And less judgmental. But . . . believe me, she wouldn't keep something like that secret from me."

"For someone who hated secrets, she doesn't seem to have communicated very openly with her parents." Giuliana heard the tartness in her voice and regretted it.

Face clouding over, Susanna looked at her levelly for a moment, then shrugged. "How well do most of us communicate with our parents? Can you talk to yours? Max is a great lawyer and a charming man, but I doubt he's a piece of cake as a father."

Giuliana nearly snapped at the lawyer to mind her own business. But Susanna was right—she and her father loved and admired each other, but they didn't have easy conversations. The truth was when they had something difficult to say to each other, they sometimes used Aurelia, Giuliana's mother, as a go-between. So who was she to cast stones?

She paused, leaned back in Susanna's comfortable chair, and let her eyes drift around the room, which had several large reproductions of Persian miniatures on the walls, reminding her that Susanna was mainly an immigration lawyer.

"This is turning into a brainstorming session rather than an interview, isn't it?" Giuliana said, at last, looking back into Susanna's eyes. "I appreciate your putting up with me and my inappropriate questions. Tell me, why do *you* think Andi was killed?"

Susanna stared at her, then put her elbows on her knees and hid her face in her hands for a moment. When she looked up, her eyes brimmed with tears.

"Just imagine how much I've thought about it," she said. "I've considered every last one of our mutual acquaintances and every story Andi's told me about her private life and her job, her curling competitions, and her rainbow politics, and I can't think of a single reason for anyone to kill her. Unless it was some kind of random hate crime against lesbians."

"Maybe," Giuliana agreed. Then she waited to see what else Susanna might say.

Chewing on her lip, Susanna seemed to stare into her memories. At last she said, "Andi was never able to sit by and watch people misbehaving without interfering. Years ago, she got punched in the face by a drunk dyke"—Giuliana's eyes widened, and Susanna raised an eyebrow. "You may not be allowed to use that word, but I am. Anyway, she tried to break up a fight between two women she didn't know and was lucky not to get her jaw broken. That's the kind of person she was."

"So," said Giuliana, half to herself, "maybe this time she took on an opponent who didn't back down."

By the time she left Susanna Käser's office, it was ten thirty, which left her with an hour before her drive to Andi's brother's place. The obvious thing to do was go back to the police station and get some work done. But she couldn't stop thinking about Lukas.

As the forecast had warned her, this first day of April was buffeting Bern with gusts of wind and drenching it in sleet. Passersby dodged trams and buses as they dashed across slushy streets with inside-out umbrellas. Susanna's office was on Länggasse, the street that bisected Bern's university campus—if such a hodgepodge of buildings scattered across several square miles in the middle of the city could be called a campus. Giuliana realized she was right next to UniS, a complex of classrooms and lecture halls that hadn't existed when she was at university. Not even risking her umbrella to the wind, she scuttled along the sidewalk until she reached the nearest UniS door, where she was met with warmth and the smell of bacon frying. She didn't have to explore far before finding a kind of student lounge, almost empty. She plopped onto a saggy corner sofa and dialed Ueli.

"Has Renzo told you about Joel?" he asked before she could say a word.

"*What*? Joel from Lukas's class? Why would Renzo—?"

Ueli interrupted. "Ah. I see you haven't talked to him yet. Don't panic. I'll explain everything. But I can't talk right now; it's too public. I'm on a bus with Lukas and Niko, taking them back to school. The meeting with the Cléments has been postponed until noon, and then, after school, we'll meet with the boys' teacher and very possibly with the school head as well. Everyone understands why you can't be there, so don't worry about it."

Giuliana had called to be reassured. Now she felt even more anxious—and left out. Everyone seemed to know more about Lukas's troubles than she did—even Renzo, of all people. "How can I keep from worrying when I don't know what you're talking about?"

"Okay, I'll tell you just a bit. And I promise to explain everything when you get home." With that, Ueli blurted out a few garbled sentences about Lukas and his friends bashing a cat to death with a sword and then going to the police station to tell Renzo—Renzo?—all about it. Then, with a "Sorry, got to go now," Ueli disconnected, leaving Giuliana slumped dizzily on the sofa.

It seemed too much to take in. Lukas had tortured a cat to death? It was so horrible she simply didn't believe it. Yet apparently, Renzo and Ueli did. If Lukas could do such a thing, then . . . What did it mean? What kind of parents were she and Ueli? What kind of child was Lukas?

The more she thought about it, the more confused she felt. That

Lukas could be filled with genuine remorse for something he'd done wrong, yet also turn his confession and penance into a dramatic adventure—yes, that was her boy. He was brave about taking punishment, too, with a strong sense of justice. But surely he would have confessed about the cat right away? And how could it have happened in the first place?

Right now, the only person who could give her the full story was Renzo. In a moment, her phone was out, ready to speed-dial him. Then she stopped herself. Ueli had promised to explain everything to her as soon as she got home, and instead, she was turning to Renzo. For what seemed a long time, she sat, phone in hand, staring into space. Then she looked at her watch. There was still half an hour before she had to leave for Yannick and Sophie Eberhart's apartment. Time for a bowl of soup from the cafeteria she'd passed on her way to the lounge—and for phone calls to the people whose numbers Andi's parents had given her: Andi's school friend Bettina Sutter and her high school boyfriend Beat Tschanz.

Twenty minutes later, empty bowl on the table in front of her, she was staring down at a notebook page filled with nothing but doodles. She'd talked to two people who hadn't seen or spoken with Andi in over five years. Their relationships with her had dwindled to an exchange of Christmas cards, birthday texts, and birth announcements. She sensed a real affection for Andi in both of them—which said a lot for Beat in particular—but neither could offer a single idea about who might have wanted to hurt her.

She hauled herself to her feet with an effort, feeling as if she'd aged over the past hour. It was time to see what Andi's brother—Saritha's father, she reminded herself—had to say about Andi's death.

Renzo forced thoughts about Giuliana's husband and son out of his mind and tried to look for patterns in Andi's files. After about half an hour, there was a perfunctory knock on the open door, and he looked up. In the doorway stood a plump young man he vaguely recognized.

"Renzo, right? I'm Beni Hug from IT. Can I talk to you for a minute?"

"Sure." He stood and gestured to the seat across from him. Hug looked momentarily surprised, then sat down. "What's up?" Renzo asked him.

"Look, we . . . um . . . we owe you an apology. We were supposed to crack open a laptop for you, and, well, it just sat on the shelf. Then Rolf Straub called my boss, and it became a priority. Turns out the work was no big deal. So you're getting, like, a special delivery from me to . . . um . . . atone for our screwup." He gave a tentative smile, clearly unsure how Renzo would react.

Renzo couldn't get over a guy from IT actually being here in person, not to mention apologizing; he smiled right back. "Look, shit happens—thanks for coming. What'd you find?"

The younger man pulled a USB stick out of his pocket. "This is everything I've got so far—all easily accessible. We'll hang onto the laptop itself, and I'll do some more digging to see if the owner has hidden something on it or deleted anything significant. But I thought I should bring you the stuff I've found."

Renzo beamed at the techie as he plugged in the drive. "Great—I really hope these are the files I need."

Hug had barely left the room when Renzo found what he was looking for: a folder labeled Civilian Service. Inside were two more folders: Debriefings and Follow-Up. *Yes, yes, yes.* He started with the Follow-Up folder, which contained fifteen files going back four years. The newest ones might have more relevance to Andi's death, but he decided to read chronologically. First, a quick glance at the young men mentioned in each file showed that each name was one of the ones marked with a lightning bolt in the original folders he'd examined in Andi's office. Renzo pumped his fist a few times before settling down to read.

The oldest file was full of details about how a Civi assigned to a large nursing home had become convinced that the home's doctor was prescribing excessively strong tranquilizers for elderly patients without the knowledge of the patients or their next of kin. This was against the home's regulations, not to mention the law. The Civi was a medical student, the son of a doctor and a social worker, and had decided to speak out, supported by his parents. Andi's description of the case ended as follows:

> Action: *Registered letter to president of nursing home's board of directors from Civi, with copy to Swiss Medical Association*
>
> Result: *Nursing home ended practice of giving tranquilizers over the long term without permission (only for the time being?). No disciplinary action taken against doctor. Civi assigned to another job, received* no *praise from any organization involved.*

The notes revealed how the young man had come to Andi with his concerns, which she'd discussed with Luginbühl, her boss.

The same was true of the next case, in which a forester had made no secret of the fact that, as far as he was concerned, appropriating wood for his own use was one of the perks of his job. The Civi assigned to him, an ardent environmentalist, liked both the job and the forester but talked to Andi about it at the end of his three-month tour of duty. Together, they'd come up with a plan: the young man would contact Pro Natura, Switzerland's oldest and most important nature conservation organization, about the problem. Andi had followed the story to its conclusion, since the file ended.

> Result: *No action is to be taken against forester, who retires in two years. Successors will* not *be given such liberal use-of-wood privileges.*

Moving back and forth between background on the different cases, the appropriate debriefing file for each one, and the more cryptic notes and to-do lists Andi kept on her work computer, Renzo saw her pattern of action change. Gradually, her involvement had grown from responding to the concerns of her Civis to actively searching for ethical transgressions. It wasn't that she'd sent her young men out deliberately as spies—she didn't have enough initial contact with most of them for that—but the notes showed her checking in every few weeks with those on longer assignments. In addition to asking conscientiously about their well-being and job satisfaction, she'd apparently thrown in other questions: Had they noticed anything troubling at their work-place? Was there anything going on among their new colleagues and bosses that worried them? Then, at the end of certain assignments, she'd suggest to some of the Civis that they meet for a debriefing. And so her career as a vigilante had begun.

Renzo read through all fifteen whistleblowing files, then read them again. The "Action" in the latest one was dated ten days before Andi's death; it, too, involved a home for the elderly. This time it was Andi herself who had made the phone call to a Canton of Bern ombud-sperson handling eldercare grievances. Based on the observations of a Civi, Andi reported a caregiver who was severely neglecting patients with dementia, and she'd followed the call with a written report. There were no notes under "Result"; Andi must have died before she could follow up. Based on what he'd read, Renzo hoped the caretaker had, at the very least, lost her job. Even if she was angry enough to take revenge, though, it was hard to see how she'd have been able to trace the complaint back to Andi. Nevertheless, he made a note to ask if anyone at the ombud office had mentioned Andrea Eberhart.

He decided to speak to all fifteen of the lightning bolt Civis, just in case one of them had been shooting his mouth off. He'd also phone at least one other person mentioned in each file to confirm the out-comes. But three files stood out, and those were the ones he needed to take most seriously. All three had resulted in serious consequences for the culprits. One was a professor cheating on medical research, the second a male secondary school teacher sleeping with a ninth-grade girl, and the third the director of a nonprofit slipping donations into her own pocket. According to Andi's "Result" notes, all three of these people were under investigation at the time of her death. By the police, Renzo wondered, or just by their employers? It would be easy to find out.

Andi's files displayed the extent to which her Civis had been underestimated by those around them. The head of the nonprofit organization, for example, had proved as stupid as she was greedy. Her Civi was a twenty-two-year-old with four years as a bookkeeping apprentice, followed by a job keeping track of invoices at a small building firm. During a six-month tour of duty, he was asked to "straighten out" the firm's computer files; the embezzler herself gave him access to all the records. The vagueness of his assignment, combined with, as he'd told Andi, its towering boredom, had led the Civi to expand his mandate until he was reviewing all the donations the organization had ever received. It hadn't taken him long to realize that a lot of money that should have been going to support primary schools in Gabon was never leaving the office.

Renzo found his prejudice against young men who chose the Civi over the Army evaporating. In these three cases, at least, the Civis had been diligent, smart, and—this was key—very, very curious. He was looking forward to contacting them.

23

"Did you ever hear Andi mention anyone she was afraid of?"

Giuliana was pretty sure neither of the adults heard her question. Sophie Eberhart was chasing two-and-a-half-year-old Hugo across the living room while Yannick distractedly picked up blocks and threw them into a toy chest. Hugo was singing two lines from an Ariana Grande song over and over, at the top of his lungs. Impressive. She didn't think either of her children had been able to belt out a recognizable tune at his age. Her mind darted straight to Lukas. Oh, Lukas. How *could* he? And why hadn't Ueli called back?

She needed to focus. It was difficult with Hugo around, but she tried to push down her frustration. After all, she was the fool who'd imagined she could talk seriously with the parents of a two-year-old while he vied for their attention. She crouched down next to Yannick Eberhart on the scuffed parquet floor. "Is there anywhere else we can talk? I need to interview you and your wife separately."

Yannick looked up from his block gathering, frowning. "We'd like to do this together. Um . . . we didn't realize Hugo would act up this badly. How about if you wait while we try to get a babysitter over here? We could . . ."

She smiled to soften her answer. "No. Definitely not. If there's not a quiet room we can use here, we'll do this at the station."

A few minutes later, she and Yannick were squeezed into a small home office with the door closed, while Sophie kept Hugo at bay. Giuliana repeated her question.

"Never. Andi wasn't afraid of anyone. And she was happy. At work, with Nisha and Sari, just . . . happy. That's part of what makes me—" Yannick broke off, dug a tissue out of his pocket, and wiped his eyes. "I can't get a grip on myself," he said. "I'll be fine for a while, but then some picture of Andi comes into my mind, and I start crying."

God, her job could be unpleasant sometimes. "Don't beat yourself up—that's natural," Giuliana told him. But she had no time to tread gently. "Is there anyone from her childhood or adolescence who could have held a grudge? Or someone more recent?"

Yannick shook his head. "I just . . . there's no one."

"An officemate? A Civi? Someone from one of the companies employing Civis? A fellow gay rights activist?"

Yannick kept shaking his head, and Giuliana sighed. She had hoped for more, and Yannick was just repeating what she'd heard from Nisha and Andi's friend Susanna. Maybe it was time to stop digging and focus on the suspects she already had. Especially Agnes Graber.

"Let's move on then." Watching Yannick closely, she said, "I thought you should know—Nisha told me that you're Saritha's father." His eyes widened, and he drew in a breath. Good; he was surprised—she'd push on. "Who else knows?"

"I . . . I have no idea. It was their secret. That was the way we set it up." He shot a quick glance at the door to the office.

"Was it difficult for you, deciding to be their donor?"

"No. Not at all." His gaunt face suddenly looked happy. "I already knew Andi and Nisha wanted a baby. Over two years ago, Andi mentioned that they'd started exploring possibilities and that they'd decided to use a German fertility clinic. By the time she asked me about being a donor, I said yes then and there. I mean, it was so obvious I was the right choice for them that I didn't even think about it. It was like being asked to be a baby's godfather: an honor and a responsibility, but somehow perfectly normal, under the circumstances."

Yes, she thought. Why not keep the process as private and familial as possible? But something jarred with her. "You didn't talk to your wife about it first?" she asked.

Yannick looked away. "No, but . . . Andi wouldn't accept my answer until I'd talked to Sophie. But I felt very sure it was the right thing to do."

"And Sophie—what did she say when you consulted her?" Giuliana was alert to every change of expression now.

Yannick stood quickly and turned to a shelf behind him to grab a box of tissues, clearing his throat. "She agreed with me. Of course." His face was turned away as he spoke, his voice a little too loud.

So. Perhaps Sophie had not shared Yannick's conviction that he had an obligation to help his sister. She tried to imagine an infertile Ueli asking Mike to father a child for them and didn't like the feeling of revulsion she experienced. One thing she could be sure of was that, for most people, this wouldn't be a simple decision. Certainly not as clear-cut as Yannick seemed to be suggesting.

"Thank you, Herr Eberhart. Could you send your wife in, please?"

He didn't budge. "May I . . . may I stay here while you talk to her?" he asked.

"Definitely not," she said. She got up and opened the door to the little room, called for Sophie, and watched the couple make their switch. Yannick was clearly trying to catch his wife's eye, but she stared resolutely at the floor.

Sophie's pale, sweetly pretty face was blotchy, and she wrung her hands in her lap. She didn't answer Giuliana's first simple question: how long had she known Andi? Instead, she took a deep breath. "Look," she said. "I know Yannick has told you that I agreed to his being Saritha's father. We talked last night about what he was going to say. But the truth is . . ." She looked up, and when she met Giuliana's gaze, her eyes were full of tears. "He never asked me . . . He never even *told* me! I only found out a month ago, and Sari's nine months old."

Giuliana's professional persona failed her. She could only stare at Sophie, aghast, as the younger woman rushed on.

"I've known Andi since I was nineteen. She was like a big sister—Nisha, too. Maybe you think it's . . . To be so close to women who are gay, but I loved them. They were part of my family. They helped us a lot, looking after Hugo. And then, to find out . . . I'm so mad at them. And for Sari to be Yannick's . . . Yannick's daughter. It's not her fault, but . . ." Her voice rose. "Keeping secrets. Leaving me out of . . . everything!"

As Sophie sat there crying, her words grew more and more incomprehensible. Giuliana thought she heard "kill." Or was it "killed?" Before she could press Sophie, Yannick burst into the room, crouching to take his wife in his arms. She gradually began to calm down. Then he said, "Shush now," and she wrenched herself out of his embrace.

"No, I won't be quiet. *I'm* not a liar."

Yannick gave Giuliana a scared glance before he told his wife, "Don't you understand that you're . . .?"

"Herr Eberhart." Giuliana stood, and the young man looked up at her again, one hand still around his wife's shoulders, the other falling to his side.

Sophie drew a shaky breath, and, in that moment of silence, they could hear Hugo crying. "Get out of here now," Giuliana told Yannick. "Go to your son. I'll speak to you again after your wife and I are finished talking. Do not come into this room unless I call you."

Yannick let go of Sophie, but as he backed out, he kept speaking. "Sophie, it was wrong not to ask your permission. I've told you over and over how sorry I am. If you won't forgive me, then, well . . . but don't talk anymore. Don't you see what she"—he waved his hand at Giuliana—"is going to think?"

Giuliana gripped Yannick's upper arms and propelled him out the door; he was still speaking as she closed it in his face.

Sophie was breathing hard. Giuliana sat down again, and before she could open her mouth, Sophie started talking.

"A while back, Andi and Nisha wanted an afternoon to themselves, so they dropped Sari off here." She counted on her fingers, lips moving. "The last Sunday in February. We took Sari sledding with Hugo. When the girls picked her up, we chatted, but they didn't stay for coffee. Then Yannick went out to their car to have a few extra minutes alone with them."

There was something both resigned and resentful in the last sentence. Giuliana wondered if Sophie, despite her love for Andi, had been a bit jealous of her husband's close relationship with his sister. Or had she worried he was too fond of Nisha?

Sophie went on. "I don't know what Andi and Nisha said to him, but that night, Yannick told me the truth at last. At least, I think it was the truth, but how can I know anymore? That Andi suggested the idea of his donating the sperm for Saritha months before he did it, that he promised her he'd talk to me about it but kept putting it off and, when the time came for him to go to the clinic, he just went. On her second visit, Nisha got pregnant, and he kept planning to tell me. But now he didn't because now he *knew* I'd be angry."

Sophie broke off and sat very still, her mouth a thin line. She *was* angry, and Giuliana didn't blame her. What a coward Yannick was! She compared his behavior to Lukas's, confessing at the police station. But then she remembered Ueli's words in the car on Monday night, driving home from the hospital. "Don't wait till it's raining to fix your roof." It wasn't easy to tell the truth to the people you loved.

Sophie's face was red, and her hands lay in fists on her thighs, but she kept talking, her voice low. "I asked Yannick why Andi and Nisha hadn't come to me—I think that hurt me almost as much as Yannick's lies. And he took all the blame. He said they kept wanting to talk to me—to thank me for agreeing, to tell me about their plans for bringing Yannick and me into the baby's life. But he told them I was embarrassed to discuss it. How could they believe something so stupid? Andi's always thought I was a bit ... prudish. Which maybe I am compared to her. But all those months of not knowing that Nisha was carrying my ... my stepdaughter. And then, after she was born, not a word. How could they?"

Because they were waiting for *you* to speak up, thought Giuliana. What a mess!

"I was furious that night after Yannick finally told me," Sophie went on, her voice sinking almost to a whisper. "First surprised, then hurt at being left out. But eventually, all I could feel was rage. Yannick kept saying, 'I told them you knew, and you were happy about it. They thought everything was fine because I told them it was.' It made me even madder that he didn't defend himself, just the girls."

"What was his explanation for why he hadn't consulted you?"

"He said, 'I thought you'd say no, and I had to do this for Andi, to make it *her* baby. I couldn't risk your saying no.'"

"Would you have said no?" Giuliana asked this as a wife, not a cop, and Sophie flashed her an angry look. Her voice rose again. "How do I know? How will I ever know? No one gave me a chance." She paused and added more calmly. "My first reaction would probably have been no because it feels ... wrong to me. Like sharing my husband. I feel like they took something away from me." She banged her fist on her thigh. "They gave Hugo a sister, but she's not mine."

"What did you do after you found out?"

"I told Yannick I'd never trust him again and that I was never going to see Andi or Nisha or Sari again. On Monday morning, I got up and went to work, like always, but on Tuesday, I took some leave and went home to my parents with Hugo for a few days. I didn't tell them why, but they clearly thought Yannick had been cheating on me." With a bitter snort of laughter, she added, "And maybe that's how I feel about it, too."

Giuliana's sympathy was beginning to dissolve in this sea of melodrama. Maybe Sophie needed a dose of real-life drama, the kind the police dealt with, to bring her marital problems into perspective. With deliberate woodenness, she asked, "Are you suggesting your husband and his older sister had a sexual relationship at any point in their lives?"

"Of course not." Sophie's mouth fell open. "How can you even ...?"

Giuliana went on relentlessly. "Do you suspect your husband of sleeping with Frau Pragasam?"

"No! Why are you . . .? He wouldn't do that. Nisha was Andi's *wife!*" Sophie had raised her voice again, only this time it was in defense of her husband.

Giuliana shifted forward in her chair, ready to jump up if necessary. "Did you make any plans to harm Frau Pragasam or her baby?" she asked.

Sophie stared at her. Then she slumped, shrinking back until she was practically huddled against the back of her chair. "Harm them?" she whispered. "Never. I love . . ." She stopped.

"Did you drive a car into Andrea Eberhart on the night of Wednesday, March twenty-fifth?"

Despite Yannick's warnings, Sophie appeared flattened by the question. Her voice shook. "Me? Kill Andi?"

Giuliana kept pushing. "You've just told me how angry you were with both your sisters-in-law. You blame Andi for what you call your husband's betrayal." Personally, Giuliana would have called Yannick's lies a betrayal, too, but this wasn't the time to say so. "Maybe you've been jealous of her influence over your husband for years, of his love for her, and the business with Saritha was the last straw. You said you never wanted to see Andi again. Did you decide to kill her?"

"No. No." Sophie shook her head, her eyes never leaving Giuliana's.

Staring right back, Giuliana asked, "So, where were you that night?"

Sophie looked down into her lap and said nothing.

Giuliana's voice sharpened. "Frau Eberhart?"

She looked up, eyes glazed. "I . . . I was here, at home, by myself. Yannick and Hugo spent that night in Ochsenbach with my parents-in-law. He was with them when the news came about Andi, thank God."

"Do you have any proof you were at home?"

"Proof? How can I prove I was here alone?"

This was not the moment to discuss methods of checking her alibi. Sophie's entire interview had been so naively self-incriminating that it was difficult to imagine her as the hit-and-run driver. But something was worrying Yannick; he seemed afraid.

Giuliana decided to leave Sophie rattled. She crossed her legs and began flicking through her notebook. "Thank you for your openness, Frau Eberhart. That's all for now. Would you please send your husband back in here?"

Sophie didn't move. "I didn't hurt Andi—I would never do that. I swear it."

Giuliana glanced up with a tight smile and spoke what she knew to be one of the great lies of police work: "As long as you've told me the complete truth, everything will be fine."

And she caught it: the flash of fear and doubt. It played across Sophie's face before she turned away. Somewhere in her story was a lie—and Yannick must know that.

Renzo found phone numbers and addresses for the names in Andi's lightning bolt files and began making one call after another. This time he worked from the most recent files backward, speaking first with the Civis and then with officials who had received complaints from Andi.

He decided not to contact the people against whom complaints had been made since they were obvious suspects. He'd discuss how to approach them with Giuliana and Vinz. If the men and women who were now in trouble had no idea Andi had been responsible for the actions taken against them, telling them about her involvement might cause repercussions for the civilian service, perhaps even for Nisha and Saritha. And if they did already know something about Andi's role, why alert them to the police's suspicions? No, Renzo wanted to get more information about who knew what before he focused on possible suspects.

If Andi's killer was someone she'd blown the whistle on, Renzo expected that person to deny any knowledge of her. It was perfectly plausible to claim never to have heard of her; the local newspapers had covered the hit-and-run without naming her. Yet whoever had killed her had planned the crime in advance: the stolen bike helmet was a clear sign of premeditation. No one had suddenly recognized Andi on her bike in the dark, sped up, and spontaneously crashed into her.

Shortly before two, Renzo phoned the twenty-three-year-old Civi who'd told Andi about a teacher sleeping with a pupil. "Every kid in secondary school seemed to know," the young man told him. "A couple of ninth-grade guys even joked with me about which girl I'd start having sex with now that I was their teacher. I thought for a long time it was just because I was so young. I didn't realize they were talking about JoJo. That's what they called the teacher because his name was Jonathan Joos."

Renzo typed notes into his laptop as he talked. "So what did you do?"

"It wasn't until about four months in that I figured out what all the jokes were about. I watched Joos with the girl—her name was Anouk—and they acted . . . strange. So I thought maybe I should tell someone, and I got up the courage to talk to one of her classmates. I'm not an idiot; I knew I shouldn't be talking to a pupil about sex. But I told her I was concerned about the idea of a fifteen-year-old sleeping with a man who was over thirty, and was it true? She said it had to be, because Anouk had a picture of JoJo in bed, naked. She'd taken it to prove to her girlfriends that they were together. I was amazed the photo hadn't hit the internet." His voice grew angry. "She was too nice to that fucker."

Well, it wasn't conclusive proof. But it sounded like evidence that the teacher was sexting with the girl, at the very least. "How did you decide who to tell?" he asked the former Civi.

"That was bizarre. At first, I figured if I was clued into what was going on, lots of teachers must be, so it wasn't *my* business to act. Plus, Anouk was leaving the school at the end of ninth grade anyway, which was in a few months. Then I saw her in an empty classroom, crying. So I decided I had to do something."

Ah, thought Renzo, *you'd be surprised how much people can manage not to see if they don't want to.* This youngster had a conscience.

"Did you go to the school rector?" he asked.

"I didn't feel I should. So I went to the teacher who was officially supervising me and told him what I'd heard. He said it was a hoax the kids had made up, and I shouldn't say a word about it to anyone. But I'd already mentioned the story to Frau Eberhart in a phone call, and when my six months were over, she and I talked again. She said even with Anouk leaving school in June, we had to act if only to keep him from doing the same thing again."

Everything he heard about Andi made him like her. "So what happened?"

"I don't know. I left it up to her. Do you know?

Renzo thought for a moment and decided to tell him. "She met with a member of the school board and told her your story."

The young man whistled softly. "Well, that's good. Did it all turn out to be true? Is Joos going to get fired?"

"That seems very likely."

Losing his job would be the least of the man's worries, Renzo thought. According to Andi's notes, the school board member she'd talked to had four kids, one of them a fourteen-year-old girl. The woman had not shrugged off the accusations; within a week, the teacher had been suspended pending an investigation. Two weeks later, criminal proceedings against him had begun.

Renzo had decided not to mention Andi's death to anyone he phoned about the whistleblowing files. He claimed to be investigating an open case, and so far, no one had followed up with any inquiries he couldn't deflect with officialese. This young man, too, happily answered questions about Andi without asking any of his own. Before he hung up, he told Renzo that he hoped Frau Eberhart wasn't in trouble for anything because she was "okay." Behind the understatement, Renzo could hear the kid's genuine affection for the dead woman. Silently, Renzo mourned her.

He was about to follow up with a phone call to the schoolboard mother to find out if she'd told anyone about Andi's involvement in the teacher's suspension when his mobile rang. It was Giuliana.

"Sorry to interrupt you," she said, "but I'm on my way to the case room to tell Vinz about Andi's sister-in-law, Sophie—I just interviewed her. Why don't you come along to hear my report, and then, if you have a few minutes . . . well, would you mind telling me what happened with Lukas today?"

She sounded tentative—almost nervous. That wasn't like her. Was she worried about what he'd thought of her son?

He hastened to reassure her. "Of course. The only reason I didn't call you about it before was so as not to interrupt your interview. I'll head for the case room right now." It was two o'clock—thanks to Andi's files, he'd forgotten to eat lunch.

A few minutes later, Giuliana was trying to explain the Eberharts' family drama.

"Yannick, Andi's brother, fathered Nisha's baby without telling his wife, Sophie, who only found out shortly before the hit-and-run. She is furious with all of them, and she has no alibi for last Wednesday night. She says she spent the evening at home alone, but I think she's lying, and I think her husband knows she is."

Renzo saw Vinz gaping at Giuliana. "What is it?" Giuliana asked him in surprise, and Renzo laughed as Vinz rolled his eyes extravagantly.

"It's like one of those Brazilian telenovelas my mother-in-law watches," Vinz said. "The brother is sleeping with the lesbian partner of his sister, who has his baby, and when the brother's wife finds out, she murders the sister. And that isn't even getting into the different skin colors of everyone involved."

Giuliana grinned at last. "Nothing so dramatic as sex, just sperm donation at a German clinic. According to the internet, it's not uncommon for a brother to provide sperm for a lesbian sister. Or a sister to donate an egg for a gay brother's partner to fertilize."

"It's all too much for me," said Vinz, his eyes wide. "Please don't tell me what happens to the sister's egg; I really don't want to know."

Renzo couldn't help barking out another laugh. The Rainbow Families message had not yet reached Vinz. Not that Renzo was Mr. Gender Sensitivity—he knew that. But . . . well, he did try. Didn't he?

He wondered what Andi, with her bluntness, would have had to say about that.

Giuliana wasn't going to let Vinz remain in ignorance. "The egg is fertilized in vitro with the brother's partner's sperm and implanted in a surrogate mother," she told him. "But never mind that. What's important is to find out where Sophie Eberhart really was last Wednesday night."

"Need help with that?" Vinz asked, reverting to his usual seriousness.

"I'll let you know," Giuliana said. "But one thing you can do is tell me if anyone else reported seeing that silver-gray car in Andi's neighborhood. The Marti woman sounded very sure."

Vinz shrugged. "She came in this morning and met with the ID experts. Nothing useful on the driver, but she picked out a few possible makes of car, so I sent two investigators out to ring doorbells. No one has reported anything, and that's a neighborhood where cars on the street are rare since no one parks there—or even drives through. Rolf and I decided it wasn't worth any more time and money until we've eliminated a few of our more obvious suspects. If only the woman had described a person to go with the car."

Shaking his head, Vinz turned to Renzo. "Anything from Eberhart's files yet?"

Renzo was so deep in his whistleblowing research that it gave him a shock to realize he hadn't told anyone about Andi's Civi-related ... activities. Should he call it her hobby, perhaps? But his work hadn't generated a suspect. He decided, on the spur of the moment, that he'd keep quiet about what he was up to. He wanted to run it by Giuliana first, which he'd do after he told her about Lukas.

"I'll have more soon, I'm sure," he promised and left it at that.

24

Giuliana didn't want to ask about Lukas in the police station cafeteria, so she and Renzo dashed—half slid, really—across the street to the bakery tearoom. The snow was still half sleet, and the gutters were full of icy slush. Giuliana hadn't bothered to put on her jacket or even grab an umbrella, and neither had Renzo. By the time they burst into the bakery, they were damp and frozen; even the effortlessly elegant Renzo looked bedraggled. With the lunch crowd gone, however, there were few customers to see them.

At the counter, they exchanged friendly words with one of the women who always served them their post-workout breakfasts. Renzo ordered a large wedge of apple-and-custard pie, and Giuliana, who'd had lunch at the Uni café, asked for black tea with lemon. The middle-aged woman pointed toward their usual table in the corner of the backroom and said, "Go ahead and have a seat. I'll bring this over to you when it's ready." Thank goodness the table was next to a radiator, Giuliana thought, as she selfishly took the chair closest to it and spread her hands on top of the grill.

She hadn't wanted to discuss Lukas with anyone but Ueli. But she'd decided she couldn't wait anymore—she was too upset by the whole thing. Now, with Renzo occasionally pausing to devour his pie, he told her what had happened. She knew it could have been worse, but she was still horrified.

Renzo was in the middle of praising Lukas when she interrupted. "You're just trying to make me feel better, so stop! There's no getting around the fact that he did something unforgivably cruel and . . . and *evil* just because another boy told him to. I can't fathom it."

Renzo stopped talking. There was an odd look on his face: appraising, judgmental even. Did he blame her for what had happened?

Lips tight, he stared at her. "And I can't fathom how you can call anything your son did 'unforgivable,'" he said. "Even if he wasn't desperately sorry, which he is, he's eleven years old. He made a mistake, and he's ready to accept punishment and try to make up for it. What else do you want from him?"

Her mouth fell open. "I didn't mean . . ." she began and then stopped. What *had* she meant? She tore her eyes away from Renzo's; she couldn't bear the chill in them. Why had she thought she could talk to him about her family life? Judging her and finding her wanting. She should have waited to speak to Ueli.

As if he could read her thoughts, Renzo said, "I'm not going to say another word about this because it's between you, Ueli, and Lukas. Except . . ." She looked up, angry and knowing that whatever came next would make her even angrier. "Expect too much of yourself if you have to, Giule," he told her. "But not of your kids."

She glanced at her watch—it was a quarter to three. In a moment, she'd made up her mind. Standing up, she said, "I'm going back to the office to get my stuff, and then I'm going home. I need to be with Ueli and Lukas. You're right—about that."

"Glad I'm right about something," Renzo said. She was relieved, despite her anger, to see the ghost of a smile on his face.

On Tuesday evening, Nisha cried for several hours straight. Unable even to make herself dinner, she went to bed drained and exhausted, and Saritha didn't wake her all night, so she slept better than she had in weeks. Wednesday morning found her filled with unaccustomed energy, determined to deal with her childcare problem.

She printed out a list of every daycare center in Bern and pinpointed each on a map of the city, so she could identify the ones closest to either her home or her office. Then, with Sari settled into her first nap of the day, Nisha started phoning. Not quite everyone turned her down immediately; some offered to call her back. But the outlook was bleak.

Next, she made an appointment at the city's Office for Daycare Mothers, which was responsible for training and licensing women to care for children in their homes. "But to tell you the truth," the woman on the phone confided, "I don't see any places becoming free for at least another six months unless a family moves away unexpectedly. And, by the way, we're called the Daycare *Parents* office now."

"Do you have many men who sign up to provide care?" asked Nisha.

"Very few, actually. Which is just as well, since people looking for childcare don't want to place their kids with a man. It's sad for our daycare fathers, but I understand the parents' uneasiness. Anyway, I've got you down for an appointment next Friday morning. After we talk, you'll be on our waiting list, and we'll be able to let you know when a place becomes available."

Nisha thought about how Andi would have chortled at this new example of political correctness. Would Andi have scoffed at the newly renamed Daycare Parents Office, whose childminders were still all mothers, or would she have approved? Probably both. Andi's take on life's contradictions had been quirky, but it'd always made Nisha laugh. Suddenly, she missed Andi so fiercely that she couldn't breathe. But she clenched her fists. She had done enough crying for now.

Between searching for childcare and looking after Sari, it got to be four o'clock, and she'd run out of options. She'd even phoned three Sri Lankan friends, girls she'd known through family parties and traditional dance classes who'd married appropriate men and now had young children. Ostensibly she was phoning to ask if they had advice about daycare; her real hope was that one of them, hearing how desperate she was, would offer to take Sari one day a week until Nisha could find a place for her. All three were polite, but none offered help. Even Iyla, the one who sounded truly glad to hear from her and chatted with real warmth, merely suggested they get together for tea sometime with their babies.

Nisha wondered why she hadn't called Iyla during the long and sometimes lonely months since Sari's birth. This break with her past hadn't been Andi's fault. Once she'd decided to live with Andi and been cut off from home because of that decision, it was she who'd severed ties to the Tamil community. That way, she'd told herself, she wouldn't risk putting anyone she cared about in a difficult position. But now she realized how cowardly she'd been, how fearful of rejection. And how unfair! Perhaps one of those friends would have liked to see her again—but she hadn't given any of them a chance to choose.

As for the Swiss girls she'd hung out with at school or university, she'd sacrificed those friendships for her relationship with Andi, too. Had Andi expected her to do that? No. It was just that Andi and their friends as a couple had seemed like enough to fill Nisha's life—and then Saritha had come along and filled it even more. Without Andi, though . . . The future looked pretty lonely.

Sari was entertaining herself with a set of colorful stacking cups. Nisha watched her concentrate on dropping the smallest cup into the largest and then, grasping the big cup in both hands, turn it upside down so that the little cup tumbled out onto the floor. Her small face was intent as she repeated this process over and over. Observing her child, Nisha felt a flood of wonder at the presence of this little person in her living room and in her life. Sari looked up from her cups, caught her mother's eyes, and beamed, showing her two-and-a-half upper teeth. Nisha was shaken by the force of her love for her baby.

As she reached for Saritha, her phone rang. Praying that it would be one of the daycare workers calling back with good news, she picked up, said her name, and heard Sophie's voice on the other end.

Nisha rushed into speech. "Oh, Sophie, I'm so glad you called. I've wanted to see you all this time, but Yannick said you didn't want any contact for now, so . . ." Nisha stopped, playing her words back in her head. Why had she just accepted Yannick's statement without questioning it? Just because Andi had always gone along with whatever her brother said didn't mean that she had to.

"Are you all right, Sophie?" Nisha asked now. "Why haven't you been in touch?"

"Don't you know?" Sophie asked, her tone icy.

"Um . . . no, I don't." Nisha was confused. She tried to imagine what she could have done.

"Remember that Sunday you dropped Saritha off with us, and we took her sledding? Don't you know that was the day Yannick told me that he was Sari's father? Until that moment, I had no idea."

"Oh, Sophie. My God. I . . . We thought he asked you before we went to the clinic. We would never . . ." Nisha found no more words to say to Sophie. It was too awful.

"Didn't you wonder why I never once talked about Yannick being Sari's father? No, I guess not. Not after you got what you wanted." Nisha started to answer, but Sophie went on. "You asked me if I'm all right. No, I'm a wreck. Especially since we had a policewoman here at lunchtime trying to find out if either of us killed Andi."

"What?" Nisha went cold. The possibility that Mathan could have caused Andi's accident was bad enough. But Andi's brother? Or Sophie? Never. "I can't—"

But Sophie didn't let her speak. "So I'm calling you," she broke in, her voice quavering, "to tell you that no matter how mad I've been at you and Andi for keeping secrets from me and . . . and ignoring me"—her voice was thick with tears now—"I didn't crash a fucking car into her!"

The line went dead. Nisha stared at the phone in her hand for a moment. Then, before she could pause to consider what she was doing, she phoned back.

"Listen to me!" she yelled into Sophie's ear before lowering her voice. Speaking deliberately, she went on before Sophie could speak. "Andi and I were wrong not to involve you in the whole pregnancy project from the start. It was selfish of us, and you have a right to be upset. But you are the one who is wrong now. Andi has been dead seven days, and I thought you'd finally called to offer me help or at least sympathy, and instead you want me to feel sorry for you. And then you hang up on me! So now I'm going to hang up on you. But first, I want to tell you—get over yourself, Sophie!"

Nisha cut the call and put a hand over her mouth, breathing hard. She wondered what Andi would have thought if she'd heard her words. Suddenly she grinned, and a laugh bubbled up inside her. Andi would have approved; she might even have cheered—she was always encouraging Nisha to stand up for herself.

Saritha had stopped playing with her cups and was staring at her mother from her spread-legged position on the floor, her little face confused. *What were you yelling about?* she seemed to be asking.

Nisha scooped her up and swung Sari over her head while the baby chortled with delight.

25

R enzo watched Giuliana walk away from their table in the bakery. He wasn't sorry he'd told her off, but he was already pretty sure that ten minutes with the real Lukas—as opposed to the cat-slaughtering changeling she was terrifying herself with—would calm her down.

No, he didn't regret what he'd said to her, but he did wish the whole Lukas business hadn't distracted them because he'd wanted her advice on his whistleblowing ideas. So often, Giuliana's questions helped him untangle snarled data. In fact, just organizing his thoughts enough to explain to her what was going on in his mind usually gave him insights. Perhaps tomorrow. In the meantime, he had a museum director to contact about an employee suspected of stealing some semi-precious stones he and a Civi had been responsible for sorting. And he needed to find out more about the woman who'd been stealing donations for Gabonese children.

An hour later, he'd eliminated the museum employee since the man had been in Germany for the past year, under investigation for more serious thefts there. The African charity's scammer had managed to vanish with most of her stolen money, so she remained a suspect. First, though, he'd have to figure out if she could have traced her downfall back to Andi. Thinking that the Civi who'd originally blown the whistle on her might be in some danger, he called the young man, who still lived with his parents. Like the names of all the other men on Andi's lists, he was an L through P, in this case, Milo Petković.

When Renzo explained that he was calling to check on Milo's safety because the woman he'd fingered had disappeared, Milo laughed. "Thanks, man, but if you could see *me* standing next to *her*, you'd know why I'm not worried. She's . . . well, the wind could blow her away."

Renzo wondered if he should ask to talk to Milo's parents instead. They'd take him seriously—at least, his mother would. But the kid was twenty-two; he deserved to be spoken to like an adult.

"I wasn't suggesting she'd come at you with her fists, you know," he told the kid. "She could come to your workplace and make a scene—or run you over with her car. I don't want to worry you, but I do think you should keep her in the back of your mind."

"Okay, then. I'll keep an eye out for her, but if you want to know what I think, I bet she's gone off somewhere and is doing this all over again. She speaks a lot of languages."

Milo was smart. Most career swindlers didn't waste time on revenge; they went off and found a new bunch of people to cheat. "You're probably right, but I want to warn people anyway. What about Andrea Eberhart, your Civi advisor? She's the one who got in touch with the charity certification board, isn't she?"

"Yeah, but she told them not to use her name, and . . . well, I can't be sure, but I doubt they did. And I never told anyone she was involved, I can promise you that."

He still wanted to check with the folks who certified Swiss charities, despite Milo's reassurances, but first, he congratulated the youngster on uncovering the fraud and wished him good luck in the future—and good hunting. "We can use people like you in the police," he told him, "as forensic accountants. Think about it."

Another hour and several phone calls later, Renzo still couldn't be certain that Andi's name had been kept from the con woman. His talk with the schoolboard mother was the same. Everyone said that Andi had asked for anonymity, and they'd provided it—but would they tell him if they hadn't? Would they even realize what they'd done if they slipped up and let a clue drop? Lukas and Niko had revealed Joel's name without meaning to; adults might be more sophisticated, but they made the same mistakes.

It was almost five when Renzo phoned Fabian Oppliger, who'd uncovered a University of Bern professor named Eduard Schmid cheating on his research. Oppliger was one of the most recent of Andi's lightning bolt files. Because he'd studied biochemistry in Berlin for five years, he hadn't been able to complete his last six months of civilian service until he was back in Switzerland at the age of twenty-eight. He'd had the good luck to find a Civi job in his field—assisting in a biochemistry lab at Uni Bern, where he was currently doing the last month of his tour of duty.

Renzo decided it was time to step up the seriousness of his questioning, so he introduced himself to Oppliger by telling him he was looking into a homicide.

"Really? Wow. I don't know anyone who's been killed," Oppliger said. "At least, I hope not."

"I'd like to explain things to you in person. Could you meet me this evening?" As Renzo said these words, he thought of the phone call he'd have to make to Fränzi if Oppliger said yes. Still, the momentum of the case pushed him forward. Plus, he knew he wanted to show Rolf and the other homicide detectives that he could follow a lead on his own.

"I'll be finished here in the lab soon," said Oppliger. "So . . . um . . . I guess it works for me to get a beer and a pizza before I go home. I usually eat at Warteck—on Hohgantweg. You want to meet me there in about forty-five minutes?"

After promising a frosty-voiced Fränzi he'd be home at eight for a late dinner, Renzo hurried to the pizzeria. Oppliger had described himself as a science nerd with a ponytail, and Renzo recognized him immediately. Medium sized and wiry, with dark-framed glasses and a scraggly hank of brown hair hanging halfway down his back, he was drinking a tall glass of beer at a window table.

Once Oppliger had ordered a ham and pineapple pizza and Renzo's own glass of beer had arrived, they turned to business.

"What homicide?" the biochemist asked again as if their telephone conversation had been interrupted just a few seconds earlier. Renzo explained about Andi's death and the possibility that it could be connected with the uncovering of Professor Schmid's fraud. As he spoke, he watched shock and sadness replace the good humor on Oppliger's thin face.

"My God. I can't take it in. I only spoke to her two or three times on the phone and once in person, but she impressed me. A lot. She mentioned a couple of other situations where Civis had uncovered a—what did she call it?—an 'irregularity,' and how she'd helped them take appropriate action. It really made my Civi job seem a lot more interesting. But I never . . . it never occurred to me what she was doing could be dangerous."

Renzo took a drink of his beer and said evenly, "The police are looking into lots of reasons Frau Eberhart might have been killed. I'm following up on this particular idea."

"Revenge, you mean?" Oppliger's eyes gleamed, and Renzo sighed inwardly. Science nerd or not, Oppliger clearly had a love of drama. Probably played superhero video games. And he was right—the possibility of someone taking revenge on Andi for blowing the whistle was exactly what Renzo was pursuing. But he didn't want Oppliger getting overexcited. He set his beer down and said, "Before I ask you about Professor Schmid's work and what you uncovered about it, tell me more about what Frau Eberhart said to you. About 'irregularities.'" He made air quotes.

Oppliger nodded. "See, that word shows you how low-key she was. I said something about her 'crusade,' and she insisted witch hunting was the last thing she wanted. She said she'd more or less fallen into this business because of the stories Civis were bringing to her, but once she knew, she couldn't *not* act."

Andrea Eberhart should have been a cop, Renzo thought. "Interesting," he said and drank more beer.

Oppliger nodded vigorously. "Yeah, she was great. She told me she grew up in a village where the residents spent their lives trying not to stir up trouble, even when it meant looking away from things like . . . like public funds going missing or men beating their wives. Stuff like that. She said she didn't want her Civis to experience that kind of pathetic response to wrongdoing."

He rubbed flat palms over his eyes. When he lowered his hands, it was clear that a lot of his excitement had drained away. "I remember exactly what she said about people looking the other way. Laziness, cowardice, and cynicism. Man, that is so true. I'm still thinking about it."

A young waitress in a tight dress brought Oppliger an enormous pizza. Renzo found her very cute, and so, clearly, did Oppliger, who stopped talking to stare at her and make a few lame comments about the music playing in the background. She smiled at him politely and then turned to Renzo, her smile much more than just polite. "Can I get you another beer?" she asked, leaning close to him. "No, thanks," he said neutrally and glanced away from her out the window. No way was he going to piss off his interviewee by drawing the girl's attention to himself.

The waitress sauntered away, and Oppliger said nothing until he'd finished about a quarter of his pizza. Renzo watched him take large bites of tasty-looking food desecrated by chunks of canned pineapple. Pizza Hawaii, the Swiss called it. As far as Renzo was concerned, it was the equivalent of mustard on chocolate ice cream. He sipped some beer and finally asked him about the professor who'd gotten in trouble. "Tell me what Eduard Schmid was up to. Is he the person you work for as a Civi?"

Oppliger swallowed his bite. "No, my job is with another professor, a Dane called Madsen; he researches a blood cancer called multiple myeloma. I was lucky to get a job with him because it's in my general field, but the actual work's not . . . well, it's not really at my level. I spend a lot of time doing stuff a good undergraduate could do, like preparing slides and culturing cells. It's totally okay, though; I wouldn't want you to think I'm complaining. For a Civi job, it's great. Everyone in Madsen's group treats me like I belong, and the professor's a good guy."

Renzo wished he'd get to the point. His impatience must have shown because Oppliger stopped eating and started talking faster. "The point is, I was getting bored with my Civi work, so I started setting up some little experiments of my own, with Madsen's okay. Plus asking other people about their work and kind of . . . watching what they're up to."

"So you were snooping around Schmid's research project," Renzo summarized. "What's it about?"

"Schmid is associated with IKIM," Oppliger said, and, seeing Renzo's raised eyebrows, quickly added, "That's Bern's Institute for Complementary and Integrative Medicine. It has one professor's chair that's jointly held by three medical doctors who practice standard and nontraditional medicine."

"Which means . . .?"

"Nontraditional medicine can mean anything from . . . let's see, sweat baths to birchbark teas. At IKIM, though, it means what's practiced by these three doctors, which are homeopathy, anthroposophic treatments, and traditional Chinese medicine. That last one boils down to acupuncture and herbs, I think. All three . . . um . . . disciplines are recognized by the Swiss government and covered by Swiss health insurance. Not by some expensive extra-care policy, but by the cheapest, basic model that everyone has to have."

"Really?" Renzo said. He didn't even know what anthroposophy was, but wasn't homeopathy . . .? "Are you saying our basic health insurance policy pays for people to take those super-diluted poisons transformed into tiny balls?" he asked.

"Yep, that's homeopathy, and Uni Bern has a professor for it. The German who invented it in the early eighteen hundreds preached that to cure a symptom like, say, nausea, you have to give people stuff that makes them nauseated. But first, you dilute it about a million times, and then you shake it in a predetermined way. The shaking gives it . . . a special force." Oppliger was smirking as he explained this.

"Something tells me you aren't a believer," Renzo said, grinning at the expression on the young man's face.

Oppliger shrugged. "I'm dubious about all types of alternative medicine, but homeopathy is the craziest of them all. And it's the one that rakes in the most money."

Renzo realized *he* was getting Oppliger off track now. "So . . . was Schmid testing homeopathic treatments?"

"No, no. He's the anthroposophic one. He was testing PSK, a protein complex taken from a mushroom called *Trametes versicolor*. It's used in Asia for treating cancer. There's nothing crazy about it, as far as I know, but it's unproven by the standards of Western science. That's because most people who support alternative therapies don't believe in using normal scientific testing on their pet remedies."

"So, were you surprised Schmid was doing these experiments?"

The younger man nodded but didn't speak while he ate a few bites of pizza. Renzo drank more beer and glanced around the room, where tables were filling up.

"Yeah, I was," Oppliger said at last. "Surprised and pleased. Turns out Schmid got funding from the Federal Office of Public Health for his research. See," he waved his fork around before stabbing another bite of pizza, "right now most alternative treatments, not just PSK for cancer, but way weirder stuff, like . . . like applying leeches or taking Bach flower solutions, they're only covered by a special supplemental insurance policy, which costs extra. But the public health office is funding experiments to determine whether it should recommend that our *basic* insurance policy cover more remedies, the way it already covers homeopathy and acupuncture."

Renzo brought the Civi back to the point. "So Schmid was testing this extract of mushrooms on patients?"

"No, no. He grew colon cancer cells in two sets of lab dishes. He added PSK to one group of cells and saline solution to the other—that was his control—and took regular measurements to see where the cancer cells grew more slowly. Hoping, of course, that the PSK would be retarding cancer cell growth."

Renzo had no trouble following this. "So he must have been in the lab a lot."

"The cultures were usually looked after by his postdoc, who told me he was worried because the measurements were jumping around wildly."

Renzo pushed his beer glass aside, got out his notebook and pen, and took notes. "So what happened?"

"I was working late on one of my own projects and thought the place was empty except for me and the cleaners. I heard a noise in the lab, so I poked my head around the door and saw Professor Schmid adding something to his cell cultures. He didn't see me."

"Surely there are times when scientists work on experiments at night," said Renzo.

Oppliger grinned. "Yes, but I confess—my prejudices went into overdrive. Schmid is a big-deal advocate of alternative medicine, so I got suspicious that he was 'helping' the PSK to kill tumor cells by adding a conventional anticancer drug to them. I figured he wanted to make damn sure the PSK worked so it would get included in the cheap insurance reimbursement package. Besides," Oppliger added, his mouth full of pizza, "What was he doing there at all? I mean, why him and not his postdoc? It was . . . out of character."

Renzo leaned forward, caught up in the youngster's story. "So what did you do?"

"Nothing. I just wondered. But a week before, Andi'd called to ask if anything on the job was worrying me. I'd said no then, but now I thought, 'Well, this is worrying me.' So I told her what I'd seen Schmid do. We talked about different ways I could respond, and she made me see that I had to be very cautious. For Schmid's sake, in case he wasn't doing anything wrong, and also for the sake of my own career." His eyes were serious as they met Renzo's. "In the end, I decided the only person I could safely talk to about what I'd seen was Madsen, my boss. But first, I thought I'd get a better sense of what was going on."

"So you staked out the lab," Renzo said with a smile. He'd been right about Oppliger picturing himself as a superhero—or a secret agent.

"Exactly." The younger man rolled his eyes at his own expense. "I found out just how boring police stakeouts must be because I sat at my desk in the dark for hours. I didn't even play chess on my phone in case Schmid saw the light. Luckily, I only had to wait two nights for Schmid to come back, and this time I was able to watch which dishes he was adding stuff to and where he stored whatever he was adding. After he left, I checked it out. And then came the big surprise."

He paused to heighten the drama of his story, and Renzo obliged him by saying, "Which was?"

"He *was* adding a conventional anticancer preparation, but only to his control dishes."

"Wait." Renzo looked up from his notes and stared at his companion without really seeing him, trying to make sense of the Civi's words. "Are you saying he was making the mushroom stuff, the PSK, look useless by killing cancer in his controls? Even though he's an advocate of alternative medicine? Why would he do that?"

Oppliger raised his eyebrows and asked, "Why do you think?" before turning back to his last few bites of pizza.

Cocky, aren't you, you little smartass? That was Renzo's first thought, but the challenge amused him. He thought out loud while Oppliger finished his pizza.

"You're asking me to figure out who would benefit if an alternative remedy was shown not to work. Hmm. Not Schmid himself, since he's a professor at this IKIM Institute. But he'd benefit from a payoff. So who'd give him money to screw up his own research project and make PSK look like a flop?"

Oppliger couldn't keep out of the conversation after all. He swallowed hastily and said, "Exactly. Who benefits financially if various alternative remedies don't live up to scientific testing and don't get covered by the basic insurance policy? The *cheapest* policy?"

Oppliger made dramatic motions with his arms, gesturing toward Renzo and saying, in a game show host voice, "And the answer is?"

Renzo rolled his eyes but played along. "The answer is the insurance companies, who want to keep selling expensive extra coverage for alternative medicine."

Oppliger beamed at him. "Exactly! The story going around the department, now that the whistle has been blown, is that Schmid got a nice chunk of change from one of the big health insurance firms—nobody seems to know which one. In return, he was supposed to make sure that all the alternative remedies he tested for the Department of Public Health failed!"

"Okay," said Renzo. "But you still haven't told me what actually happened—after you figured out what Schmid was adding to his cancer control cells."

"I did what I said I was going to do—I told everything to Madsen, and he took it from there. I'm lucky Madsen is more powerful than Schmid, or I might have gotten fired."

"What date did you talk to your professor?" asked Renzo, and Oppliger got his mobile out of his back pocket and started checking his calendar.

"Let's see. I saw Schmid doctoring his culture for the second time on Saturday night, March fourteenth, and called Madsen for an appointment on Sunday evening, so I told him on Monday. That was the sixteenth."

"Since then, Schmid's been fired?" Renzo looked up from his notebook and saw that it was now Oppliger's turn to roll his eyes.

"You must be joking—that would make the university look bad. No, disgrace in academia is more subtle than that. Word spreads around, everyone gossips, and you don't get invited to present papers at conferences, no one cites your work anymore, and eventually, you're a has-been."

Renzo thought he'd rather be fired than be destroyed by slow drops of poison like that. He sighed and said, "Okay, here comes my most important question. Could Schmid have heard Andrea Eberhart's name in connection with any of this?"

"How? I talked to Andi and to Madsen, and Madsen also talked to

Andi before he confronted Schmid. But Andi never talked to Schmid. There's no connection between them."

Renzo met the young man's eyes. "Herr Oppliger," he said gently, "the connection between them is you. Have you told this story that you're telling me with such enthusiasm to anyone else . . . and mentioned Andi's name?"

Oppliger sat staring at him. Renzo waited.

The young man raised his hands to his face. Eventually, he answered. "Yes," he said dully. "The day after I talked to Madsen about Schmid, I had coffee with a postdoc friend from my Berlin days. I told her everything, including how my Civi advisor was the one who helped me figure out what to do about Schmid. I don't know if I mentioned Andi's name or not, but . . ."

Well, thought Renzo, not at all surprised, at least Oppliger hadn't actually told Schmid about Andi to his face. "Where did you meet your friend?"

"In a coffee place at the biochemistry institute. Anyone could have overheard me. Or my friend could have spread the story. God, do you think—?" He stopped and pressed his hands to his cheeks again, eyes wide.

Renzo decided to reassure him. "I told you this business is only one of a whole list of leads we're following up on. It could be nothing." Despite these words, however, he was excited. Here was clear-cut evidence of a whistleblowing incident where Andi's identity could have come out. Assuming the dates worked, of course.

"When did Andi get knocked off her bike?" Oppliger asked Renzo grimly.

"The night of March twenty-fifth."

Clasping his hands on the edge of the table, Oppliger was quiet for a moment. He stared across the room before saying, "And I was shooting off my mouth about her on the seventeenth. Oh God, I'm so sorry she's dead. I hope—" He broke off.

Renzo stopped scribbling dates long enough to reach out and touch Oppliger's hand, which made him lift his head. Renzo caught the man's eyes and said, "The reason she's dead is not because of what you or anyone else said. It's because someone crashed into her."

It was time to go home, he thought. He needed to write this up. And think about it. "Herr Oppliger, that's all I need from you for now. Thanks for talking to me."

On his way out of the pizzeria, he caught the waitress and paid for the Civi's beer as well as his own. Poor guy—Renzo hoped his dramatic tendencies wouldn't lead him to wallow in guilt.

It was almost seven thirty. He'd promised Fränzi to be home by eight. If he hurried, he'd make it. All the way home, his thoughts were on Eduard Schmid and whether he had an alibi for the night Andi had died. When he pulled into the garage under his apartment building, it was only ten to eight. Suddenly, it seemed very important to tell Giuliana where he was going with all this. He reached for his phone and stopped, remembering that Giuliana needed time with Lukas. Then he punched her number in anyway.

She took a while to answer, and only when he heard something odd in her voice did he remember that they hadn't parted on the best of terms; he'd been so wrapped up in the investigation that it hadn't seemed important. Now he realized she might be angry with him for what he'd said to her about forgiving Lukas.

"Giule, I called to talk about work," he said immediately, "because I think I might have a new lead, but first I want to apologize for . . ."

"It's okay. Really," she said, and he was relieved to hear the usual warmth in her tone. "But let's talk about Lukas another time. Tell me what you've got."

He spoke fast, cutting details, until he'd explained his whistle-blowing theories and outlined Oppliger and Andi's roles in the downfall of Professor Schmid.

"What were you planning to do next?" Giuliana asked when he'd finished. No praise, but also no criticism. How should he take that?

"I want to talk to Madsen, the professor who confronted Schmid, before I approach Schmid himself. I'd like to understand what the consequences of his fraud are for him. Get Madsen's sense of him as a person, too. I mean, avenging yourself by killing someone is . . . well, Bern isn't rural Albania. And a professor? Could he really have done it?"

"Like you, I think this whistleblowing could turn out to be central. Excellent work," Giuliana said after a pause. Renzo grinned into his phone before guilt made him look at his watch. He was now officially late for dinner with Fränzi.

"I'll tell you what, though," Giuliana went on. "You should talk to Nisha Pragasam, too. Andi *must* have told her about some of these crimes. I'm going to call her right now, and I think you and I should see her tomorrow morning. I want to talk to her again anyway about her brother and her sister-in-law. Okay? We'll leave from work."

Renzo wasn't happy to be diverted from Schmid, but he could see Giuliana's point. "Sure. I'll talk to her with you. And . . . thanks."

He got out of the car at last and started up the stairs to his flat, thinking how fond he'd grown of Andi Eberhart during this investigation. It was time he met her partner. *No,* he told himself. *Don't say partner; say wife. That's what Andi would want you to say.*

Giuliana and Ueli sat on either side of Lukas, who was already bathed and in his pajamas. All serious talk with the boy was over, at least for that day, and he was snuggled up on the sofa under Ueli's arm, listening to his father read him *The Martian,* about an astronaut who's abandoned on Mars and what he does to survive. Giuliana had been surprised when Ueli suggested the book, but it turned out that Lukas, who loved to ask questions, was enchanted with its detailed explanations about how the hero manages to generate water and oxygen and grow food to survive.

"Hey, love," Giuliana said. "Why don't you and Vati get to a good stopping place, and I'll put you to bed?"

He didn't argue. Giuliana figured that within a week, Lukas would be his loud and sometimes disobedient self, but right now, he was still on his best behavior.

Twenty minutes later, she returned to the sofa. She'd thought Ueli might be at his desk but was glad he wasn't. Since she'd arrived home midafternoon to be a part of whatever was happening with Lukas, they'd barely had a moment alone. Now, she sat down next to her husband and reached for his hand, which she held for a moment and then kissed. "Thanks for being such a good father," she said. "Do you think . . .?" She paused. After what Renzo had said about her overly demanding standards, she felt unsure of herself. Still, she had to say it. "I think we need to talk about a punishment."

"Absolutely," Ueli agreed. "Today was about . . . well, reassuring him that he wasn't a bad person because he did a bad thing. But he has to be punished."

Giuliana, filled with sudden relief, nodded. "Yeah, I think that's why he went to the police station, don't you? Of course, he was milking the situation for drama, but behind it was . . . a need to pay the price."

"I've been thinking about it," Ueli said. "Tomorrow, I'm going to call the folks who owned the cat and tell them what happened. I'm not going to make Lucas break the news to them. That would be too much. But after I tell them, he and I will go over there so he can apologize, and we're going to talk to them about how he can make amends in some way."

"That's an excellent idea," Giuliana said. "Still, there isn't much an eleven-year-old can do to help people, is there? Maybe he could clean something for them or do some gardening, or . . ." She trailed off.

"I know." Ueli grinned. "It's a tough one. We don't want him ruining their parquet floors or destroying their roses bushes while he's trying to show contrition, do we?"

Giuliana snorted out a laugh and shook her head. Then she said, "But besides that, we have to punish him."

"Yep," Ueli said. "And banning computer games doesn't seem like enough. This isn't a good time to forbid him to see Niko, though, is it? They need to work on their friendship. Honestly, I don't know what we should do with him. Let's think about it for a while."

"Okay," Giuliana agreed. They leaned toward each other and kissed lightly.

As Ueli pulled away, he gave her a look she couldn't interpret. "For at least a year now, you've been working closely with Renzo, and you never told me that he . . . looked like that."

Giuliana felt her insides lurch, and one answer after another raced through her mind: *I don't know what you mean.* Or *Why* would *I tell you?* Or *He's not my type.* All of them were idiotic.

Finally, she just shrugged. "I know. Maybe I should have, but it felt strange to come home and say, 'Oh, by the way, I'm spending a lot of time with a gorgeous younger guy these days.' Now it seems strange that I didn't. But . . . well, it doesn't mean . . ." Her throat tightened as she lamely added, "anything. You know that, don't you?"

What Ueli didn't know was that Renzo had made it clear months ago that he wanted to sleep with her. And that she'd been tempted and still was. But Ueli didn't need to know that. The important thing was that she and Renzo hadn't had sex. The rest was her business.

Ueli moved closer and put both arms around her. "Don't look so worried. I didn't think you were having an affair. I was just surprised. I'll bet when you first saw him, you were convinced he was a prize asshole."

Giuliana laughed into Ueli's shoulder. "You know me so well. That's exactly what I thought. I had to work with him to find out that he was okay. A bit vain, maybe, but mostly a really good guy. Clever, funny, hardworking—everything a homicide detective hopes for in a colleague. I'm going to encourage him to apply for a job in homicide."

"When I saw him on the stairs with the boys," Ueli said, "I . . . well, I was also prepared to dislike him, but I warmed to him immediately. And when Lukas and Niko told me how he'd handled their confession, I was impressed."

Giuliana nodded; she'd heard all about that now from Lukas.

"Yeah," she said. "I think he's great with his own kids, too. As for what kind of husband he is, well . . . That reminds me, you should see his wife. She's the female version of him. If I knew she was working with you regularly, I'd certainly worry."

"Nah," Ueli said, standing up and stretching. "You wouldn't. But thanks for the compliment. Oh God," he added, "I'm so behind with my work because of this business with Lukas. Sorry, but I'm off to the computer for a while."

"And I've got calls to make," she told him, getting up to head for the kitchen.

"Forgot to tell you," added Ueli. "Mike's flying back to St. Louis on Friday, so I've invited him for dinner tomorrow. I'll cook. You just have to show up. Okay?"

Mike? Oh, dear. Well, she was glad for Ueli. "Sure," she said. "I'll be there." *Let's just hope I can keep my mouth shut*, she said to herself.

26

Renzo used the time between his morning workout and the meeting with Nisha Pragasam to make phone calls connected to Andi's cases. One of them was to Oppliger's Danish professor, Valdemar Madsen, who agreed to talk to Renzo that afternoon about Eduard Schmid. Right now, Schmid was Renzo's favorite suspect, but he hadn't forgotten the secondary school teacher. A teacher who'd slept with a fifteen-year-old had probably wrecked his life just as thoroughly as a professor who'd falsified his research—and the teacher was younger, which made him more likely to sneak around in the dark stealing Andi's bike helmet.

He met Giuliana in the police station parking lot, and she gave him a subdued hello before getting into his car. Then silence. As they drove toward the apartment in Holligen, Renzo cast sideways glances at her, trying to figure out if she was still upset by what he'd said the day before about her and Lukas. Silence between them was rare, he realized—usually, he started talking as soon as he saw her, which now made him determined to keep his mouth shut. Eventually, though, he couldn't stand it anymore. "I'm still curious about the boy with the sword, Joel," he said. "Did you—?"

As if she'd only been waiting for him to speak first, Giuliana interrupted. "Ueli and the other parents met with the school head and the boys' teachers. Joel's mother went into complete denial-and-defense mode. She accused Lukas and Niko of corrupting Joel while he sat there smirking. As far as she's concerned, everyone else is to blame. She can't deny that Joel owns a real sword, but, hey, that's not her responsibility—it's all his father's fault."

"What a good life lesson for the kid!" said Renzo. "Think he'll graduate from torturing animals to people?"

He heard Giuliana sigh. "God knows," she said. "But at least we've let social services know. And the police can keep an unofficial eye on him, too."

"And Lukas?" Renzo asked, taking his eyes from the road to smile at her. "He okay?"

He was glad to see her smile back. "Seemed like his normal self at breakfast. With Joel still in his class, things may be complicated for a while, but I think he and Niko will look after each other better from now on."

He was gathering his courage to say something about meeting Ueli when Giuliana said, "The psychiatric report on Iris Kissling is finally in, so the second interview with Kissling is tomorrow."

Renzo honestly wasn't sure he could have handled speaking with Manfred Kissling. If he wanted to be a homicide detective, he was going to have to toughen up. "I hope it goes better this time," he said as he backed into a parking place that was as close as he could get to the small, contained neighborhood where Andi had lived—and Nisha still did.

Together, they walked along one of the alley-like streets toward Nisha's. On their left were the decorative front doors of each apartment house; on their right, belonging to the buildings on the parallel street, there were fenced-in back gardens that had been put to bed for the winter but still showed a wealth of lovingly tended trees and shrubs. In front of Nisha's place, someone had planted a matching set of small evergreens and some ivy-like groundcover in two large blue pots on either side of the outdoor steps leading to the front door. A rainbow flag with "PEACE" on it in large letters hung from one window. Giuliana rang the Eberhart/Pragasam bell, and they were buzzed in. Renzo started upstairs to the second-floor apartment and then stopped on the landing and turned around when he heard Giuliana give an enormous sigh. She still had her foot on the first stair.

"God, do you have to do that? Bound up every stairway we encounter like a *Steinbock*?"

Renzo laughed at being compared to a mountain goat. He considered the men and women who did climb mountains—and Switzerland was full of these hardy souls—completely out of their minds. "Come on, come on," he urged, making circles in the air with both hands. "I can't believe you're whining about two flights of stairs." When Giuliana got to Nisha's door in his wake, she wasn't at all out of breath.

Renzo hadn't seen Nisha Pragasam before, but he'd seen her family, and he recognized the beautiful eyes that matched her younger brother's. She was small and almost too thin, with dark-brown skin that seemed to have a reddish gleam to it and very long, shining black hair in a single braid. Her throat rose gracefully from the loose cowl neck of her burgundy-colored jumper, and her expression radiated intelligence. As he shook hands with her, she gave him a sweet smile. Andi had been intelligent, too, but he was quite sure she had not been sweet. It made him happy to think she'd come home to this lovely woman.

Nisha moved them toward a dining room table that held a teapot with three cups and saucers. "I've made some holy basil tea, but it's no trouble to make either of you something else."

"I'd be glad to try it," said Giuliana, glancing at him with a quick smile. "Sure," he felt compelled to say. Holy basil? He hoped he wouldn't have to drink something that tasted like pesto alla genovese without the garlic. Once they were all seated, he looked around the open plan living/dining/kitchen area and saw islands of baby paraphernalia everywhere: blocks and colorful stacking rings, a padded plastic mat, a big box of wet wipes, and a great deal more stuff that he knew only too well.

Giuliana asked, "Is Saritha asleep?"

Nisha gave a relieved smile as she looked up from pouring the tea. He understood the feeling. "No, Vivienne—you met her last time you were here—she's babysitting again."

Aha, thought Renzo. The woman who saw the gray car. He'd have to find out what kind of car Schmid drove. He picked up his cup and said, "Thanks," to Nisha before taking a sip of the tea. Hmm. Not like any basil he'd ever had. The liquid was bitter but drinkable.

"My colleague," began Giuliana, with a nod at Renzo, "has been looking through Andi's work files. We've discovered that quite a few of her Civis reported to her about serious problems they observed on the job, like a teacher sleeping with an underage pupil and a caregiver neglecting patients in a nursing home. Did she talk to you about those cases?"

"About the teacher, definitely," Nisha said, "and lots of Civis serve in homes for old people, so there've been several reports of neglect or overuse of sedatives or bad food. But I don't know if she told me everything."

Renzo waited for any shift in Nisha's face when she would surely guess why they were asking about these Civis and their function as spies. But her pleasant expression didn't change. Tales of Andi's work must have been so much a part of their daily chat that their significance remained hidden from Nisha, even now.

Giuliana went on. "Over the years, there have been some serious consequences to the people Andi's Civis told her about. Quite a few have lost their jobs. We don't know yet if anyone has gone to jail, but some certainly deserve to."

Nisha had her elbows on the table, both hands wrapped around her teacup. She nodded enthusiastically. "I know. Andi was always so pleased when . . ."

Then it hit her, and she sat back in her chair, eyes wide. "Are you saying . . .? You think one of those people . . .? But Andi never confronted anybody directly." She spoke with a fierce intensity, evidently determined to push the idea away. "She was extremely careful handling what her Civis told her because of the civilian service's reputation. I remember her saying that no one would hire the boys if they got a reputation for stirring up trouble and ratting on their employers." Eager to defend Andi's values and commonsense, Nisha stared at first Giuliana and then Renzo, shaking her head.

Renzo felt his heart sink a little, even as he recognized "his" Andi in Nisha's words—the woman who'd gotten upset when Oppliger called her a crusader. If she'd really been that careful . . . Then he thought of Oppliger shooting off his mouth to his friends over coffee. Andi might have been careful, but not everyone whose help she enlisted was.

Catching a glance from Giuliana, Renzo spoke gently to Nisha. "You see, we've kept asking ourselves, 'Why would someone kill Andi?' Your poison-pen letters are a very good lead, but we've considered other parts of her life, too. I've focused on her work for the Civi, where it's clear she was . . . well, dedicated wouldn't be too strong a word—yes, dedicated to finding villains. And that's the point. Exposing thieves and rapists and cheaters can be dangerous."

Nisha was still shaking her head, but as he spoke, she seemed to crumple in on herself. Turning to Giuliana, she said, "When you were here on Monday, you asked me about Andi's enemies. I'm sorry this didn't come up, but all the stories she told me seemed so distant from our shared life. Now I can see how . . ." She turned to Renzo. "What do you need me to do?"

Lifting his laptop out of his leather bag, he opened it to Andi's files. That morning he'd chosen thirty to discuss with Nisha. All of them had involved a debriefing over the past five years, although they weren't all labeled with lightning bolts. "I've brought these to go over with you—to see what you remember. Maybe you'll think of something that could have allowed Andi's name to leak."

Renzo started with the oldest files first because he thought they'd get through them fast, but to his surprise, Nisha remembered them quite well and had a lot to say. They went through one situation after another, in homes for the handicapped, afterschool programs, research facilities, parks, hospitals, and all the other places where Civis had worked and, for all kinds of reasons, had contacted Andi with not just tales of personal woe but stories of their suspicions. Some of these stories Nisha knew nothing about; others she recalled in detail. But Andi had talked to her about them in such a low-key and relaxed way, she explained, that she'd never thought of what was going on as whistleblowing.

"At dinner, she'd repeat what a Civi had told her about a problem somewhere and end it by saying, 'Sounds like that needs follow-up, don't you think?' And that was it. If I asked her a few weeks later if there'd been consequences, she'd say, 'Oh, that. I passed that business on to the appropriate apparatchik; we'll see if anything comes of it.' I can see now that she was downplaying something important, but while it was happening, I just saw it as . . . as part of Andi's job. Not as a big deal."

Renzo stopped moving through pages on his screen while he considered what Nisha had just said. From what he knew about Andi, that wasn't her style at all. Relaxed about rulebreakers? He thought of what her teammate Karolin had called Andi's one big problem with curling: that, in a game with an honor code instead of a referee, players could get away with cheating. Maybe Nisha's alarm bells should have gone off at Andi's casual attitude. But he didn't want to make her feel worse than she already did, so he kept this thought to himself.

They'd been going through cases for almost an hour, with Giuliana taking notes this time instead of Renzo, when Nisha's buzzer rang— someone at street level. "Must be Viv," Nisha said as she leaped up and hurried to the door. A moment later, she was back. "It's Sophie, my sister-in-law," she said. "We're . . . um . . . upset with each other right now, so I can't imagine what she's doing here. Do you—?"

Giuliana stopped her. "I was planning to see her today anyway— she's still a suspect in Andi's death. Would you mind buzzing her up? I don't want to interrupt what you and Renzo are working on, but it would be very practical for me to talk to her."

Nisha didn't move. "Sophie is not a suspect. There is no way . . . *no way* she could have killed Andi."

"All right," said Giuliana calmly, despite Nisha's ferocious frown. "I'll keep that in mind. But would you still let her in, please?"

Renzo, watching both of them, thought Nisha would refuse. After a moment's hesitation, however, she turned back to the door phone and pressed the button for Sophie.

Nisha had not forgiven Sophie for her long neglect or her hurtful words, but no matter what the police said, she knew Sophie couldn't be responsible for Andi's death. And she didn't like the idea of luring her sister-in-law into a trap. So she stood at the open front door, and when she heard Sophie at the top of the stairs, she stepped into the hall and closed the door behind her.

Sophie certainly didn't look murderous. Chunks of her fine blond hair had escaped from her ponytail and hung in scraggly wisps around her face, which was blotched and puffy. From the top of the stairs, she stared at Nisha. "I guess you're not going to let me in," she said. "I . . . I know why, but can I just . . .?"

"No, I am going to let you in," Nisha said, "but you may not want me to. Giuliana Linder, that policewoman who interviewed you yesterday, is here. And a guy she works with. They'd like to talk to you again, but I think that's up to you."

At the word "policewoman," Sophie raised a hand to her mouth. Then she took a deep breath and shrugged. "I'll have to talk to her anyway, and I think it will be easier with you there. That is, if . . ." She paused and bit her lip.

Nisha almost helped her find the right words, but something stopped her. Instead, she waited. So did Sophie.

In the end, it was Sophie who spoke first. "God, Nisha, I'm so sorry for not calling as soon as I heard about Andi and for not being around to help you deal with something so awful. It was . . . there's no excuse. I want to give you support now, but . . . Will you still take it?"

Nisha couldn't have stayed stern even if she'd wanted to—she needed Sophie too badly right now. "Of course I will." She'd thought a lot about what to say next; now that the moment was here, it all came naturally. "That's the thing about Andi asking Yannick to be Sari's father. She did it to make sure Sari was part of her family as well as mine. It was important to her that Sari be an Eberhart. Now that Andi's dead, I want that connection all the more—for Andi and Sari, but also for me. I want you to be my family."

Sophie took a step forward, and Nisha reached for her; between staircase and door, they hugged each other clumsily.

"Are you and Yannick . . . okay?" Nisha asked as she drew back.

"We spent all yesterday evening talking." Sophie looked exasperated. "He's truly sorry, but . . . well, let's just say that his decisions have made me see him in a new way. But you know what? I still love him. We're not going to break up over this, that's for sure."

"Thank God. Look, you'd better come in." Nisha opened her apartment door to find the policeman standing right inside.

"There you are," he said, smiling first at her and then at Sophie. "We were hoping you hadn't both run away. Hello, Frau Eberhart," he added, holding out his hand to Sophie. "I'm Renzo Donatelli."

As Nisha had expected, one look at the handsome cop sent Sophie scurrying into the guest bathroom. By the time she emerged, hair tidied, face washed, and wearing lipstick, Nisha had made a fresh pot of tea and put out a plate of her mother's semolina balls, the last of the batch. Once they were all at the table, they managed a little small talk before getting down to business. Given the way Sophie kept smiling at Renzo, Nisha wasn't surprised when Giuliana let him do the talking.

"It's clear to me that Frau Pragasam doesn't believe you crashed your car into your sister-in-law, or she wouldn't have let you in here. But the problem is, you see, you have no alibi for the time that Andi died." Nisha could see Sophie basking in Renzo's attention, which made her want to giggle. "What's worse, it's clear that even your husband doesn't believe you were at home then. So you can see why we're worried. If you could explain . . ."

Sophie shifted in her chair and rubbed her forehead. "Okay. I'll tell you where I was. It was bad enough telling my husband last night, and this is even worse, but . . . I have to do it. On that evening, while

Yannick and Hugo were staying over with my parents-in-law in Ochsenbach, I was . . . having a drink with my ex-boyfriend. His name is Jens."

Sophie stopped talking, and Nisha turned to stare at her sister-in-law, probably with an expression that looked as shocked as she felt. She immediately glanced down at her hands, but of course, the cops had seen her face. Damn. Everyone was silent, maybe waiting to see if Sophie had more to add, before the handsome cop said, "Well, as long as you were with him when Andi's bike was hit, you have an alibi. What time did you get home?"

Sophie's face was pink, and her hands were in fists as she spoke. "I . . . I didn't pay much attention, but Yannick told me he phoned first my mobile and then our landline at eleven fifteen, and I didn't answer. So . . . um . . . I guess I got home after that. Not after midnight, though, I'm pretty sure."

Nisha was still trying not to look surprised—goody-goody Sophie out late with a man who wasn't Yannick? Giuliana didn't change her expression at all. Nor did Renzo, who asked, "Were you with your ex right up until you got home?"

"Yes," Sophie said. She squirmed in her seat and asked, "Are you . . . are you going to check this with him?"

Renzo nodded. "We'll have to."

"Well, then," said Sophie. She took a huge breath and said, speaking fast, "He might tell you the truth, so I'd better do that, too, because we drank a lot, especially me, and then we had sex in . . . in his car, so . . . um . . . that's why I didn't answer my mobile and why I got home so late and don't know what time I got in, because I was feeling drunk and sick and guilty but still mad at Yannick and . . . generally awful."

Nisha couldn't stop herself this time. "Oh, Sophie," she gasped. "Not in his car. That's so—"

She wasn't sure what she meant to say next, but Sophie seemed to know because she finished the sentence. "Yeah, trashy. And really complicated, too. He has this little Kia, and we did it in the front seat.

I banged my head, and he kept getting. . . um . . . the gearshift kept getting in his way."

Sophie was looking down at the table as she said this, but Nisha caught Renzo's lips twitching. Giuliana had her hand over her mouth, so Nisha grinned at her before saying, "It's okay, Sophie." She rested her hand on Sophie's arm. "Look, we all do stupid things when we're angry." She actually found herself itching to ask her sister-in-law for more details, but not in front of the cops. "Do you think you've shown me enough files now?" she asked Renzo. "I have to pick up my daughter in about fifteen minutes, and so far, I don't think I've come up with a single idea about how someone Andi was investigating could have learned her identity. Are there a lot of cases to go? Do you want to mail some summaries to me?"

He closed his laptop. "We were more or less finished going over what I'd planned to show you. If I need help again, I can phone." He turned to Giuliana. "What do you think?"

She nodded at Nisha and said, "We're done for now. All we need is the full name, address, and phone number of your ex-boyfriend, Frau Eberhart." Sophie nodded.

Once the cops were gone, Nisha and Sophie looked at each other. Nisha couldn't hold back any longer—she started laughing and gasping out words between giggles. "Oh, Sophie, I can't believe you, of all people, would . . . and in a teeny car. Is he . . . is he married?"

Sophie was laughing, too, harder than Nisha. "No," she managed. "But a long-term girlfriend. Know what I couldn't tell the police?"

"Oh God," Nisha said. "It gets worse?"

"I threw up! I was so drunk that after I hit my head on the door handle the second time, I . . . I kind of pushed Jens off me and puked in the car. At least I managed to turn my head and hit the floor mat. Not the seat."

Now Nisha was laughing so hard she was afraid tea would come out of her nose. "And you . . . you . . . missed Jens, I hope."

"Yep. But the way he reared back from me when I started to chuck . . . he . . ." Sophie snorted and gasped, "You should have seen the look on his face. And the way his—no, no, never mind. Oh, God, just imagine his having to clean it all up before his girlfriend could see it. And the smell. He'll never speak to me again. Which is great because I'm too embarrassed ever to see him again anyway." Sophie was still laughing, but she was quieting down, so Nisha made an effort to get a grip on herself, too. She felt light with all the laughter—and with relief that Sophie was back in her life.

"Do you really have to fetch Sari?" Sophie asked, wiping her eyes on a napkin.

Nisha nodded. "Yes, that wasn't just an excuse to get rid of the cops. In fact . . ." she said, standing up.

"Can I come with you?" A shadow crossed Sophie's face. Perhaps her sister-in-law had been as worried about their friendship as Nisha had. But there was no need for that now—they were going to be there for each other.

"Of course you can," said Nisha, putting a hand on Sophie's shoulder. "Sari would love to see you."

27

Bern and Bremgarten,
Thursday afternoon, April 2

As a light-brown-haired, hazel-eyed Italian, Renzo knew better than to expect Danes to fit a Scandinavian stereotype. Professor Valdemar Madsen was a bit taller than average, but otherwise, there was nothing about him to suggest he was Danish. With his air of comfortable competence, he reminded Renzo more of a friendly plumber than either a Viking or a chemistry professor. Renzo had already talked to him on the phone about Oppliger's revelations, so Madsen knew exactly what their meeting was about.

"Why don't we discuss this business in private," the professor suggested, in only slightly accented High German. "The sun's out for at least a few minutes; let's go outside." He led Renzo to a picnic table in a clearing between two large science buildings, and the men sat down across from each other. Renzo, facing out toward the path between the buildings, could see that no one was nearby.

"Please tell me about Eduard Schmid," Renzo said. "What will happen to him?"

"The mills of justice at a university grind very slowly." Madsen looked down at his hands and sighed. "That is if they grind at all. It's very bad for a university's reputation when it gets around that one of their professors has made a mess of his research—and even worse if it turns out he's a crook."

"So it's certain he took money to come up with fake results on his experiments?" Renzo asked.

"Oh yes. First, money from the Federal Office of Public Health to conduct the work and then money from . . . well, an insurance firm to falsify it. The FOPH could prosecute. Of course, they don't want bad publicity, either. But here at the university, I think it's all going to proceed very, very quietly. His current experiments will be killed, and he'll find the money for future research scarce to nonexistent. He'll also have trouble getting anyone to publish his work. As for graduate students and postdocs, who'll want to work with him? Within a year, he'll be an academic pariah."

But it sounds like he won't go to jail, Renzo thought. So perhaps not as bad for him as it could have been. He nodded at Madsen, who continued. "At least no one else is involved. Schmid has insisted all along that his postdoctoral student didn't know about the fraud, even though he was the one tending the cell cultures. From what I hear, most people seem prepared to give him the benefit of the doubt. Marti, I mean—the postdoc."

Renzo wasn't interested in the postdoc right now, but he knew he'd need to be checked out, so he got the name and phone number before asking, "Can you take me through what you did after Oppliger came to you with his observations?" He took notes as Madsen summarized his meeting with Schmid and how the man's initial denials had turned into a confession. "And then," concluded the Dane, "I talked to the department chair and the university rector about the business. None of it was much fun. But it had to be done."

That statement could have come out sounding pompous and self-righteous, Renzo thought. But Madsen said it matter-of-factly, the way someone would talk about doing any unpleasant part of his job. The plumber again. "I see," said Renzo. "What about Andrea Eberhart? Did you meet her?"

"No, but we had a long phone call, and she asked me to keep her name and her role in the process as quiet as possible. The civilian service office has worked hard to get Uni Bern to open up a number of jobs for Civis in different departments, and she didn't want to jeopardize those. It made sense to me."

"Did you refer to her at any point, not just in your talk with Schmid but speaking to anyone else?"

"No, I'm quite sure I didn't. I had to tell the chair about Oppliger, of course, but he's not looking for anonymity!" Madsen cocked his head and raised his eyebrows.

Renzo gave a crooked grin and said, "No, I'm sure he isn't. He likes being in the thick of things, doesn't he? I take it he's doing a good job for you?"

"Oh, yes," Madsen said. "Oppliger's a hard worker and a good biochemist. I'm hoping someone in our department will have the funding to take him on as a postdoc."

There was silence between the two men, and Renzo felt a wind starting up. Above the university buildings, the sky was now a flinty gray.

"If you have more questions, I think we should move inside," the professor said.

"Just the obvious one. Apart from whatever Oppliger may have said to friends, can you think of any way Schmid might have heard Eberhart's name?"

"No, I can't," Madsen said. "Sorry not to be more helpful. I suggest you speak with Schmid, though. I'm not a psychologist, but, honestly, I don't think he's the type to seek revenge." With that, he stood up and clambered over the bench he'd been sitting on. They shook hands, and Madsen wished Renzo good luck and walked briskly toward his building. Renzo started to jog toward his car and made it just before the first raindrops hit.

It was time to find Professor Eduard Schmid.

Giuliana had caught a ride with Renzo from Nisha's flat to the main train station. She also had an appointment, but it had nothing to do with the Eberhart case. She wanted to talk to Kissling's divorce lawyer

Roger Urech. Renzo's suggestion that she look into Kissling's attempt to get custody of his children had intrigued her, and she hoped the lawyer might give her some insight into the killer's relationship with his little girls.

On her short walk to Spitalgasse, she let herself give way to frustration. She hadn't phoned Sophie's ex-boyfriend yet, but she was certain he'd confirm Sophie's alibi. That meant another suspect gone, and there were several others on which she and Vinz were making no progress: the curling teammate, the remaining police guard, and the poison-pen woman. Since alibis couldn't be established for them, it was time to bring each of them in for a grilling. And then there were Renzo's . . . what should she call them? Whistleblowees? Renzo was excited about this fraudster professor, but she couldn't see it. It had been helpful to take notes as he went over potential suspects with Nisha—now she had an overview of the cases he was dealing with. If she had to put her money on any of them, she'd choose the young teacher. A thirty-one-year-old man who slept with his fifteen-year-old pupil had big problems with impulse control. Would he drive his car into someone he blamed for wrecking his life? She thought he just might.

She crossed the gray cobblestones of Spitalgasse to its arcaded sidewalk and found the door she was looking for next to a small lingerie shop. This wasn't a bad address for a law practice, but nothing about Urech's fourth-floor office was impressive—and Urech himself looked as cramped, gray, and dusty as the room he sat in. An earlier call to her father, whose forty-year defense practice had brought him into contact with most of the lawyers in Bern, had not enlightened her on the subject of Herr Urech. What had brought Kissling to this man? Quite possibly, it was nothing more than his location near the train station.

Seated in one of the lawyer's two client chairs, she took a long look at him. He gave her a limp handshake, then sank back behind his desk. His face was clammy with sweat, his eyes wide, and he was rubbing his hands together.

"Herr Urech," she said, "you look upset. Tell me why."

"Kissling," he said on a shaky breath. "You must realize I barely saw him. He hired me to represent him during his divorce. That was well over a year ago—how could I know what he would do? He was strange then, his conversation a bit off, but who could imagine . . . ?"

Now she understood. He thought he was in trouble for not having somehow predicted that Kissling was a killer. She opened her mouth to reassure him, but he kept talking.

"He wanted me to get him full custody of those girls, but even then, I knew better. It was obvious he wasn't fit to . . . My colleague and I, we thought one weekend a month would be enough. It was the judge who allowed him a second one. And no one could have known . . . A maniac like that. Surely the police don't blame . . ."

Giuliana tried to pick through these broken sentences. "Are you saying Herr Kissling hired you to get him as much time with his daughters as possible—ideally full custody? But you and 'your colleague,' by which I'm guessing you mean his wife's lawyer, decided that wasn't a good idea, and, between the two of you, you did your best to make sure he got as little time with his girls as possible."

"That's right." Urech sat back in his seat, smiling with relief. "He seemed pretty desperate to get those girls, but I did everything I could to keep them out of his hands."

"And you made Herr Kissling pay you for it, too. What reasons did he give for wanting his daughters with him?"

"He told me his wife was unable to take care of them properly. A lot of stuff about neglect, tantrums, unfitness. When I met her, I found her attractive and pleasant. Imagine," he added with a frown, "a man like that calling his wife incapable when he . . . What is it the psychiatrists call it? Projection? Not that I saw anything insane about him then, I assure you," he added, panic starting in his eyes again. "If I had, well . . . He was just a bit awkward and silent. Eccentric, but not . . . Still, no one to entrust with small children." Urech nodded as he said this, looking pleased with his sagacity.

"You were Herr Kissling's lawyer, Herr Urech. He told you his wife was unfit to care for his children. Did it occur to you to do some research and find out if that accusation was true? Did you ever observe

Frau Kissling in the company of her daughters? Did you talk to a teacher at their daycare center? Did you consider a psychiatric evaluation of the mother? If you thought Herr Kissling wasn't fit to care for his children because he was 'strange,' as you put it, and he thought his wife was neglecting them, why didn't you talk to the child protection authorities and get their advice?"

Urech was no longer smiling. "It is common practice for young children to be placed in their mother's care in cases like this," he spluttered. "I'm not responsible . . ."

"You are not responsible," Giuliana repeated and felt fury course through her as though a second, hidden heart had pumped fire into her veins. She clasped her hands so they wouldn't tremble. So she wouldn't slap this gray man's face. She took a deep breath. "Hmm. Let's see. I'd say a good case could be made for your having lied to your client and falsely represented him, particularly since you colluded against him with the opposing counsel. But that's not your biggest problem."

"How dare you . . .?" he began.

"Shut up and listen to me," she said, her voice shaking. "On my desk right now is a psychiatric report indicating that Frau Kissling is severely mentally ill; she was without a doubt unfit to care for her daughters when Herr Kissling walked into your office sixteen months ago. If you had listened when that man told you about his wife's mistreatment of their children and gone to Child Protection Services, they would almost surely be alive."

As she spoke, the gray man turned even grayer and clapped both hands over his mouth. Then he lowered his hands to the desk and started to shuffle papers on his blotter. He didn't meet her eyes as he said, "You're not making any sense. It was their father who killed them, not their mother."

Giuliana stood; Urech still hadn't raised his eyes from his desktop. She knew her anger was irrational. It felt so good to berate Urech mainly because she couldn't confront the other people who'd had far more reason to take action: the children's relatives, teachers, neighbors, and all the others who must have known Iris Kissling was unstable and closed their eyes to it because they didn't want to interfere. Too lazy? Embarrassed? Afraid?

She thought of Andi. Maybe if one of Andi's Civis had worked at the girls' daycare center . . . She knew better than to get into these tortuous "what ifs," but sometimes it was impossible not to when so much horror and suffering could have been prevented.

She left Urech's office without another word to him and walked down the four flights of stairs to the street, hoping some of her anger would dissipate with the exercise. Instead, it turned inward, and she began to reproach herself. Urech was right about one thing. It *was* Mia and Lea's father who'd killed them, not their mother. And tomorrow, that father would sit across from her, listening to her questions and providing no explanations. Again. And the deposition would be useless. Again. No one, not even the prosecutor, would criticize her since Kissling had treated all his interrogators to the same cold silence. But she'd wanted to succeed where others had failed. How presumptuous of her.

She heard the hard rain falling before she walked out of Urech's building and saw it soaking the cobblestones. Luckily, the Spitalgasse sidewalks on both sides of the street were under arcades, so she remained dry. Walking toward Bollwerk, she stopped beside an outdoor flower stand where buckets of water sat filled with flowers. She stared at a large bunch of white tulips mixed with delicate greenery, breathed deeply a few times, and felt her pulse slow. Finally, she opened her umbrella, stepped into the rain, and turned her steps toward the police station across the Aare.

Eduard Michael Schmid, University of Bern Professor of Complementary and Integrative Medicine—Renzo had scribbled down the man's full name and title next to his mobile number—agreed that Renzo could drive to his house and speak with him. Expecting to hear outrage at this intrusion by the police, Renzo detected nothing but defeat in the man's voice. Schmid, he reminded himself, was not yet fifty—and he'd just shattered his life. Full university professors were very well paid in Switzerland, but maybe when you were one of three sharing a chair, you only got a third of the money. Still, how could he have thought the payoff was worth the risk?

Cold April rain was hurtling down as Renzo pulled up to the man's attractive house in Bremgarten, a small town north of the university that lay across yet another loop of the Aare. An extension at the side of the house had its own sign and mailbox. Renzo waited a moment for the rain to ease up. When it didn't, he sighed, opened the car door, put up his umbrella, and walked over to read Schmid's sign, which told him the man wasn't just a professor of alternative healing but a practitioner as well. "Anthroposophic Medicine," said the sign, under Schmid's name and list of degrees, "An integrative approach to healing the whole person." As he walked back to the sidewalk and up to Schmid's other door, Renzo thought that anyone who tried to heal "the whole person" must be as much psychotherapist as physician. And maybe part priest, too.

Schmid opened the door before Renzo was even on the front porch and greeted him with the single word "*Grüessech.*" That said, Schmid shook Renzo's hand, took his jacket, waited while he deposited his umbrella and thoroughly wiped his feet on the indoor mat, and then, still unspeaking and unsmiling, led him into a beige room. Schmid sat behind his pale brown desk, and Renzo lowered himself into an oatmeal-colored chair across from Schmid.

"What would you like to ask me?" he asked in the same affectless voice he'd used on the phone. If he'd been enraged enough to drive his car into Andi the previous Wednesday night, that state of mind certainly seemed to have spent itself. Or else he was very good at hiding it. "Herr Donatelli?" said the man, and then paused a bit too long, as if he'd momentarily forgotten what he'd meant to say. "On the phone, you said I could help you with a case you're investigating."

Renzo had already considered asking Schmid if he'd heard the name Andrea Eberhart—and discarded the idea. That might come later, but first, there was only one truly important question. "I would like to know what you were doing a little over a week ago, on the night of Wednesday, March twenty-fifth, between, say, seven and midnight."

Perhaps there was the smallest spark of curiosity in the dull eyes; Renzo wasn't sure.

"Are you going to tell me why you're asking?"

Renzo shook his head, making sure he looked sufficiently regretful. "Not right now. But eventually, if I can."

"Well," said the man, "I guess I'll have to be content with that." Schmid reached for a big leather-covered datebook lying on his desk, the kind that trailed silky ribbons to use as bookmarks. Like the Bible, Renzo thought. Schmid pulled the tome toward him, opened it, and turned the pages slowly. "I was . . . at home all that day," he said, "either in this part of the house or over at my medical office. I had dinner with my wife, probably around seven because that's when we always eat, and then she left for a bridge tournament. She didn't get home until . . . Well, I know it was after eleven because she complained about it. She likes to get home earlier."

The bridge tournament could be verified. As Renzo wrote down times, he thought, *So far, so good*, and asked, "And between eight o'clock and when your wife got home?"

"I was alone," Schmid said calmly. "I'm pretty sure I wrote up notes on the patients I'd seen that day, but how long that took me . . ." He shrugged. "After that, I have no idea what I did. My wife almost always plays bridge on Wednesday nights, so I can't keep them straight. If I'm at home while she's away, I sometimes read a medical article or the newspaper, or a novel. Or I write an email to our daughter, who's doing a *Gymnasium* year abroad in Australia. Or I just . . . waste time." He gave a bitter laugh. "I'm getting good at that now."

Nodding, Renzo waited while Schmid stared down at his datebook, brows knotted in concentration. If it was a performance, Renzo found it realistic. Then Schmid brightened. "At least I know what I did between nine fifty and ten fifteen. My wife and I always watch the *Ten-to-Ten* news program, and if she's out, I watch it alone. And then . . ." He smiled. "Of course. Our compost is picked up every

Thursday morning, so after the news on Wednesdays, I always wheel the bin full of green garbage out to the street. And I usually see my next-door neighbor through the hedge doing the same thing, and we have a three-minute chat about what we've just heard on the news. That's about the only time I talk to him, both of us standing there on the sidewalk in our slippers." Schmid was smiling faintly as he said this, but Renzo was not. He felt like throwing his notebook at the professor's head.

"Last night was Wednesday night," he pointed out. "Did you see your neighbor last night?"

"No, I didn't," said the professor immediately. "My wife had her bridge, and I went through the same kind of evening that I've just told you about, but . . . when I got the compost to the front of the house, my neighbor's bin was already there. But I'm sure I saw him the week before. Yes," he said, nodding at Renzo. "I remember. A week ago, there was something on the news about vandalism increasing in Bern and Zürich, and we talked about that."

Renzo needed to check the content of the *Ten-to-Ten* news on March twenty-fifth and talk to the man next door. He sighed quietly. Mathan Pragasam had an intimidated wife to vouch for him and Agnes Graber, a sleeping husband, neither of whom were exactly reliable witnesses. But Schmid's neighbor sounded like the real thing—a surefire supplier of an alibi.

"Do you have a car?" he asked Schmid.

"What? Yes, although my wife uses it most of the time to get to her job."

"What color is it?"

Schmid's bleak expression lightened with relief. "Oh, this is all about a car accident. Thank God. I know I haven't been in any car accidents. I . . ."

"The color?" Renzo repeated.

"Oh, right. It's white. My wife has it now, so you can't see it unless . . ."

Renzo hadn't been able to imagine Schmid having a red car—it didn't fit his personality. At least not his current one. Still, the white car was another blow.

"I don't need to see your car right now, thanks," he said. "But I do need to talk to your neighbor."

"I'm not sure I have a phone number for him . . ." began Schmid, adding, "I guess you could just walk next door and see if he's there."

Renzo looked past the professor to his front garden and the street beyond, where sheets of rain soaked the grass and filled the gutters. It was not yet five o'clock on a spring afternoon, but the sky looked as dark as on a November evening.

Eduard Schmid's neighbor was about to blow up his theory.

28

t took Giuliana less than ten minutes to walk from the lawyer's office on Spitalgasse to the police station on Nordring. Peering through the rain from the Lorraine Bridge, she could see only dark clouds where the Alps often filled the horizon. At the station, she rode the elevator up to the homicide office, glad Renzo wasn't there to see her do it, and sat down at her desk to phone Sophie's ex-boyfriend. Once he'd overcome his embarrassment, he gave her the same tale as Sophie had, from his perspective, which was crowned by his utter exasperation at her vomiting in his car. Giuliana couldn't wait to share this detail with Renzo.

That was her last bright moment—the rest of the afternoon, she concentrated on the reports coming in from the *Fahnder* who'd been checking CCTV footage and interviewing neighbors to confirm or disprove Barbara Weber, Mathan Pragasam, and Agnes Graber's stories of what they were doing on March 25 at ten thirty in the evening. At least she knew for certain that Graber was the poison pen—her fingerprints were all over the letters and their envelopes. But that didn't make her a murderer, as she'd reminded Andi's mother more than once when she'd called to give her the news and thank her for her insight.

Meeting at the coffee machine to vent their frustration, she and Vinz agreed that it was time to put serious pressure on their main suspects.

It was not yet six when she decided to give up and go home, although she packed what she needed for a last careful review of her Kissling notes after dinner. She was just beginning to look forward to a meal with Ueli and the kids when she remembered Mike was coming to dinner. Which meant that if she wanted time alone with her family first, she had to hurry. Her key was in the ignition when Ueli phoned her.

"Hey, love," she said. "I'm just heading home. Need me to pick up something for dinner?"

"There is no dinner. My day went to hell. The last interview took so long that I missed the train from Luzern. Mike's due at seven. Just give him a drink, and when I get home, we'll go out to eat. You'll have to throw something together for the kids, though. I'm sorry."

Sitting in the parking lot, she banged a silent fist against the steering wheel. "Wouldn't it be better to cancel Mike?"

"I told you, this is his last evening before he flies back to St. Louis."

Ueli needed to spend time with Mike—it was important. "Okay, don't worry. As long as we still have Mike's bottle of bourbon . . ."

She parked illegally on the sidewalk in front of the neighborhood grocery store a few blocks from their apartment, ran inside, and bought bread, butter, milk, eggs, a block of Gruyère cheese, thin Italian breadsticks, and a couple of sad-looking tomatoes. Cheese omelets, bread, and tomato slices for the kids; *grissini* for Mike. She dashed out in time to receive the glare of a grandmother maneuvering an immense baby carriage past her car. With a loud "*Exgüsee*," she tossed the groceries into the passenger seat and sped home.

By the time the kids were finishing their omelets, she'd changed into jeans and found Mike's whiskey in the back of the liquor cupboard. He buzzed at two minutes after seven, which made her smile. Mike might drink like an American, but when it came to punctuality, he was very Swiss.

For half an hour, he chatted with Lukas and Isabelle while she watched and listened, trying to analyze why she couldn't warm to him. The kids loved him, and although he was childless, he didn't talk down to them. He was pleasant looking, too, with his mother's straight brown hair, light brown eyes, and strong chin, and he kept himself in shape. He wasn't really arrogant, either, just a little bit too pleased with himself sometimes.

But he lacked something, something she couldn't quite name. Perhaps, she thought, it was the ability to see and hear himself from someone else's point of view and imagine his impact on them. Like now, with Isabelle, who'd just finished proudly telling him about a letter-writing campaign she'd helped to set up for Bern's Amnesty International chapter. There was no need to shower her with praise, but here he was mocking her for believing that any dictator took the organization's work seriously. Okay, she *was* a bit earnest about it all, but had he forgotten she was sixteen? What kind of person made fun of a teenager's commitment to human rights? He didn't seem to realize he was hurting her feelings.

As the kids drifted back into their rooms, he and Giuliana settled down on the sofa to munch breadsticks, nurse their drinks, and find topics of conversation. The good news about Irène's successful operation and probable recovery lasted about fifteen minutes. Then Giuliana explained briefly how the hit-and-run had become a murder investigation, and Mike described some new pest-resistant seeds his firm, Monsanto, was developing. He asked about the children, and Giuliana stuck to funny stories, avoiding any mention of Lukas and the sword. When a longish silence descended on them, Giuliana offered to refill Mike's drink, and he followed her into the kitchen.

"Do you ever cook?" he asked. He hadn't commented when she'd explained that, with Ueli running late, they'd have to eat out instead of at home, but now he seemed curious.

"We've tried lots of different arrangements over the years—they change depending on our schedules and the kids'. Right now, I try to make dinner twice during the workweek and once on weekends, but sometimes Ueli steps in and does my meal shift if I have to stay late. I can't tell you how grateful I am that he's so flexible."

Mike smiled—a warm, genuine smile. "Everyone needs a housewife, don't they? I just wish I had one. I have a cleaning lady, but it's not the same."

As Giuliana handed Mike his Wild Turkey on the rocks, she examined what he'd just said. There had been nothing sarcastic in his tone, but . . . "Did you just compare Ueli to your cleaning lady?"

"Of course not," he countered, laughing easily. "My brother may be a carrottop, but he's much better looking than my cleaner."

"I'm intrigued. How do you picture Ueli's average week?" She kept a smile plastered to her face as she poured a little more white wine into her own glass.

They stayed standing in the kitchen instead of returning to the sofa, and Mike paused to sip his bourbon before he answered. "A little childcare, a little shopping, a little cleaning, a little writing. Nothing that pins him down." He leaned back against the kitchen counter; when he spoke again, his voice was full of good humor. "I've known Ueli all his life, don't forget, and he isn't big on accountability. As you said, flexibility is his thing. He's not going to get up every morning and go to an office and work all day like I do. And he ran like hell from the farm, which I can understand, because I did, too. Instead, Ueli found you, which means he can have the kind of life he wants." Mike laughed again indulgently. "It's great for him. And you seem happy too, so—all is well."

Did Mike know how contemptuous he sounded? Probably not. He was just falling back on the usual Brand family clichés. Didn't any of them have a clue what Ueli did all day?

Giuliana kept her voice light. "It sounds like you don't think Ueli's capable of . . . well, taking on responsibility."

"I know he's good at a lot of things, but he'll never be a captain of industry, will he? Not that it matters. He's a great guy; we all love him."

Standing across from Mike in the kitchen, Giuliana put her wine glass down very gently. She breathed as if she'd been running, but she kept her voice level. "Every month, Monsanto deposits a check in the bank for you, right? In return, you do what your boss tells you." Mike made a noise of protest, but she continued. "Sure, sure: you manage a lot of employees, you make difficult decisions, but unless you get fired, the money keeps coming in."

Mike took a slug of his drink. "Okay, I'll go along with that."

Giuliana stared into his eyes. "And how many deadlines do you have to meet? I'm sure you have meetings to prepare for and reports to write—so do I—but I'm talking about career-breaking deadlines, ones that can't be missed. One or two a year, I imagine? Now let's take Ueli," she went on, not giving Mike time to speak. "You think he isn't accountable, but he has two or three deadlines *a week* that can't be missed, and his writing has to be perfect since editors don't seem to edit much these days. Plus, he doesn't have a boss. He has to come up with his own assignments all the time, with topics that are interesting enough to pitch. Someone may commission a piece on a particular topic, and he has his regular columns, but most of the time, everything he works on starts in his own head. About half his work is freelance, which means, unlike you, he doesn't know from month to month where his next paycheck is coming from. Since he earns close to half the income we live on, he's under constant pressure."

Mike set his drink down on the kitchen counter. "I didn't realize he contributed that much to your finances. That's . . ."

Giuliana raised her voice. She knew she was going too far, but she'd held all this in for so long that she couldn't stop. "You probably also didn't realize that while you go to an office every day, where you can concentrate, Ueli fits all his work around taking care of the kids and making sure the four of us eat decent meals and have clean clothes. You've just told me you think Lukas and Isabelle have grown up to be good kids, which makes me happy. But I'm not the one who's here when they get home from school, and I wasn't here very much when they were toddlers and preschoolers, either. It's all Ueli! You think he's lucky he found me, but I'm the one who's lucky. My whole life depends on Ueli, how hard he works for this family, and how well organized he is. Yet you see him as irresponsible. I just don't get it."

She stopped. Oh, God. What had she done? She hadn't said a word that wasn't true, and she thought Mike needed to hear it all. But what would Ueli think? He'd be furious.

Mike dropped into a kitchen chair, staring into his empty tumbler. When Giuliana stopped to draw breath, he looked up and met her gaze. His eyes were full of anger, but she thought there might be some shame there, too. "What the hell gives you the right to . . .?"

"Only one thing," she said. Faced with his anger, hers had turned into guilt. "Which is that I love Ueli, and I know he wants your respect. I think he's accepted that his mother's never going to take him seriously, but . . . it's different with you."

This time, as she spoke, Mike held her gaze, but she couldn't read his deep frown. She braced herself for an outburst, but there was none. As an excuse to turn away from him, she began putting away the dishes in the drainboard.

As if on cue, Ueli's key turned in the lock. Lukas ran out of his room to throw his arms around his father. Mike stood up, and Ueli, smiling, walked into the kitchen with one arm around his son. The brothers shook hands. If Ueli noticed anything odd about the atmosphere in the room, he didn't comment.

"Hey, Mike. Sorry for the screwup with dinner. I just couldn't get away from this interview. The guy was an elderly beekeeper, and you'll be interested in what we talked about because it had to do with pesticides. I'll tell you later. Just give me a minute or two to get ready. The restaurant is a couple of blocks away."

He leaned in to kiss Giuliana hello, and she resisted the impulse to throw her arms around him the way Lukas had. "I hope you don't mind, Ueli, but I'm going to let you and Mike go out on your own," she said. "Sorry, Mike, but I've got to prepare for a deposition tomorrow, and, in any case, I feel like we've had a good catchup already."

"Don't worry about it," Mike said, giving her one of his easy smiles, which she tried to return. "I've enjoyed our chat." They kissed cheeks, their bodies rigid, and then she slipped into Isabelle's room, closing the door behind her. "Mike is about to go to dinner with Vati, and I don't think you'll see him again on this visit, so you might want to go say goodbye."

"Sure." Isabelle walked to the door, then stood with her back to it. "What were you fussing at him about?"

"Oh, dear, was I that loud?"

Isabelle shrugged. "Was it to do with Mémé's cancer?"

"No, no. Not at all. Sorry, sweetie. I shouldn't have lost my temper. It's just that sometimes I get upset at the way Vati's family treats him. Like . . ." She stopped. No, it wasn't appropriate to draw Isabelle into this.

To her surprise, however, Isabelle nodded. "I know what you mean. Mémé acts like Vati is Lukas's age, and Päpu and Mike go along with it. It makes me laugh, but it's insulting, too. Especially when they make fun of him. It's meant as a joke but, sometimes . . . well, it's not so funny."

Not for the first time, she was brought up short by Isabelle's sensitivity. Her daughter could be so perceptive, and of course, she'd been watching Ueli and his family interact all her life. It shouldn't be such a surprise that she'd come to the same conclusions Giuliana had.

She nodded at her daughter. "That's exactly what I was talking to him about. Now, go say goodbye."

After the men had left for dinner, Lukas got ready for bed.

"How are you feeling?" Giuliana asked him, watching him wriggle into his pajamas, totally unselfconscious about his skinny eleven-year-old nakedness. That wouldn't last much longer, she knew, which made her all the more grateful for being part of his bedtime routine.

His face, when it reappeared out of his top, was serious. "Vati called the cat people today and told them Tiger was dead. But he decided not to tell them on the phone how . . . how he died. So he's going over tomorrow afternoon alone and then after that . . . I'll talk to them. But . . . I'm scared. Even with Vati there, I'm afraid of what they'll say to me."

Giuliana was convinced that Lukas had to apologize in person, just as Ueli was, but that didn't mean she wanted him frightened.

"Would you like me to come, too?" she said before she could really decide if this was a good idea. To her surprise, Lukas came to sit next to her on the edge of his bed and gave her a tight hug.

"I love you, Mam," he said. "But . . ." He leaned back from her and looked into her eyes, shaking his head solemnly, and she realized he was trying not to hurt her feelings. "It looks silly, you know . . . like, like I'm a baby. I think it's better if I go just with Vati. But only because it's more grownup, not because . . ." He gave a little hop, which brought him into her lap, put his arms around her neck, kissed her cheek, and then, from her lap, launched himself around her into bed. "Sorry," he mumbled, as he accidentally kicked her while battling himself under the covers.

"Can you read to me?" he said, handing her *Harry Potter and the Order of the Phoenix*, which he'd been reading to himself for weeks already. "See my bookmark?"

She was very touched by this consolation prize.

Afterward, she sat at her laptop until late, rereading reports on the Kissling case, fast-forwarding yet again through videos of previous interviews with him, and taking more notes. Eventually, she got into bed, trying not to fall asleep over the newspaper. Finally, she heard Ueli come in a little after midnight. He tiptoed into the bedroom and looked surprised to see her sitting there with the light on.

"You okay?" they asked each other in unison. And laughed.

"I'm better than okay," Ueli answered. "I'll tell you once I'm in bed."

Giuliana watched him go into their bathroom. Relief buoyed her up. Mike must not have told him about her outburst. Now she had to decide if she would tell him.

The bedroom was chilly. Bare-chested and in boxers, Ueli emerged from the bathroom, made a running dive under his duvet, and slid over to snuggle up to her. It was like being grabbed by a snowman. She yelped but let herself be enveloped by him. Even the tip of his nose against her neck was cold.

"What did you and Mike do after dinner, take a dip in the river?"

The Aare was barely 50 feet from their apartment house. Fifty feet down a steep wooded hill, though. And it was April!

"No, but when the restaurant threw us out, we walked along the Aare for another hour. I wasn't dressed for that."

"Did you and Mike have a good talk?" she ventured.

He nuzzled her neck and put his cold hand under her pajama top. She shivered.

"He told me more about his work and his girlfriends and talked about how strange it is sometimes, being a Swiss in the US Midwest. But he also asked me about the articles I'm working on and truly listened; I don't think he's ever done that before. And he asked me if I was happy. You know Mike, he's almost never serious, so at first, I just said, 'Sure,' but he said he really wanted to know. So I told him I thought I was amazingly lucky to have had so much variety in my work—and in my life, too—and so much time with my kids."

He raised his head onto his elbow so that he could meet her eyes and added, "I also said that sometimes I get mad at the way I'm always having to fit my research and interviews and writing around your schedule."

"I know," she murmured. She clasped the hand on her stomach, which was getting warmer, and moved it up to cover one breast. "I'm sorry."

"But I told him that's not a big deal—because it isn't; you know that—and that we have a really good marriage." He leaned over and kissed her, then flopped away onto his back and went on. "Mike said he's sometimes sorry he doesn't have kids. And then . . . he told me maybe that's why he still sometimes treats me like a kid."

"He said that?" Now it was Giuliana's turn to prop herself up so she could look into his face.

"He did! It gave me the perfect chance to talk about being left out of the loop with Mam's cancer. I didn't go on about it, but at least I told him how I felt."

"I'm so glad." She moved over even closer to Ueli and laid her head in the hollow of his shoulder. He put his arms around her.

Mike hadn't betrayed her, and she wasn't going to ruin the moment by confessing. Sure, families didn't fix themselves from one hour to the next, but maybe this was a start.

Pulling off her top, she lay down on Ueli and pressed her body and mouth against his. They made love with such joy that it took them both by surprise. Afterward, panting, laughing, and still trembling, they curled up spoon fashion.

"Mike said he thinks maybe he and Mam are overprotective of me because I'm the baby," Ueli said into her ear. "Sounds nuts to me, but then, parents' ideas of how to protect their kids are pretty deluded. I mean, look at Joel's mother. She thinks she's taking care of her son by closing her eyes to what he's done—and to the kind of child he is. So I suppose it's possible my mother thinks she's helping me by not letting me help her."

Giuliana wasn't sure she agreed but was too sleepy to answer. "Mm," she said. And fell asleep.

29

Giuliana got up very early, leaving Ueli and the children still asleep. After the evening rain, there'd been an overnight frost, and she cursed as she scraped ice off her car windows before setting off for Thorberg. Her interview with Kissling wasn't until eight thirty, but she planned to stop for a pastry and a second cup of coffee once she got close. At seven thirty, Renzo called; from the timing, she knew he'd finished his workout and was eating breakfast. Instead of fumbling her headset out of the glove compartment, she pulled over onto the side of the country road to talk to him.

"Schmid has an alibi," he said without a greeting. "When the *Ten-to-Ten* news finished, he took out his compost bin, and his next-door neighbor did, too, and they chatted about some bullshit they'd just seen on the news. I want to believe it's a setup, but unfortunately, I'm convinced it's legit. The neighbor is so . . . well, it seems very unlikely he's lying."

Andi Eberhart was far from Giuliana's mind, but she tried to boost Renzo's spirits. "That's a setback—but it doesn't mean you're on the wrong track with the whistleblowing. Confront some of the other people, like the teacher."

"You want to have lunch?" he asked. "I'd like to go through my notes with you and think about next steps."

"Sure. Assuming I get done at the prison in time. Let's say one instead of noon."

"Thanks. And . . . good luck with Kissling."

"Yeah." That was all she managed to answer.

She parked next to a bakery café in the village of Krauchtal, got out of the car, and stretched. The sun had risen shortly after seven, but forty minutes later, the world still looked new. Beyond the small parking lot, the Emmental, with its rounded hills and cow-filled meadows, stretched out all around her. In fact, a large brown-and-white cow with a great brass bell stood stock-still in the field just behind the parking lot, gazing at Giuliana and chewing her cud. Giuliana's mind felt wiped clean by the sun on her face and the soft beauty of the morning. She, too, stood unmoving, dimly aware only of the chomping of the cow's teeth, the twittering of unseen birds, and the faint scent of baking bread.

In that moment, she decided what she wanted to say to Kissling. So she left the cow behind and went inside the café to drink coffee and eat a brioche.

At Thorberg, everything was the same as it had been three days before: Kissling's shackled ankles and free hands, his expressionless face, his cooperation with her preparations for recording and filming. When Giuliana started the interview, she once again noted the date and time and their names for the record. Then she asked, "Is there anything you'd like to bring up right away before I begin talking?"

"Yes." She was surprised he had answered. "I hope you've brought the psychiatrist's report on Iris."

She already had a stack of notes in front of her; the report was at the top of the pile. "It's here," she told him. "Although the doctor who spoke with your ex-wife considers his findings preliminary, he has diagnosed her with both narcissistic and borderline personality disorders," she said, watching Kissling closely as she spoke. At the word "borderline," he thumped one of his fists on the table.

Giuliana continued, glancing down at the report. "That means, among other things, that she's likely to be selfish, impulsive, and inclined to risky behavior and to get bored easily, lack empathy, and require constant admiration from those around her." She looked up to see Kissling nodding vigorously.

"In terms of her mothering," she added, "the doctor wrote that she'd likely vacillate unpredictably between affection and rejection, which would be very difficult for her children."

"Yes," Kissling agreed, as calmly as if they were discussing the weather. "I went on the internet to find a name for the way she was treating the girls and me, and borderline was what fit best. I did tell people," he added.

Giuliana paused before speaking. Her job was prosecution, not defense. But however the trial went, there was no chance this man was going to walk free at the end of it. Right now, nothing seemed more important than getting at the truth.

"Who did you tell? And when did you start telling them?" she asked.

Instead of responding, he began to talk more generally, his blank expression replaced by one that she thought looked—apologetic. "I should have figured it out sooner," he told her, "but I'm not very good at understanding people. Even my own wife."

This was it, she thought. He was starting to explain what had happened. She waited, not daring to interrupt.

"I got suspicious because I could see how mixed up the girls were—they didn't know if their mother was going to hug them or smack them. My mother-in-law would never accept the idea of an illness. She said Iris had always been temperamental." Kissling spoke calmly, but his eyes searched hers for comprehension.

"But, to answer your question precisely," he continued, "when Mia was about six months old, which would be thirty-three months before her death, and Lia was over two, I told Iris's mother and sister that I believed Iris had a serious mental condition, and I asked them what they thought we should do. Because of the girls, I mean. I'd already been living with her for a long time by then. I wasn't happy, but I . . . well, I managed."

His face was no longer blank; something else was there now, something questioning. He wasn't judging her anymore, Giuliana realized; he was worried about her judging him. He needed her to understand. "So you told your in-laws," she repeated, and he seemed reassured.

"Yes, but they wouldn't help. Then I called up . . . an ombudswoman, I think it was, at Insel Hospital and asked if it was possible to *make* someone go to a psychiatrist when she didn't want to. I thought maybe we could put her in the hospital for a while and see if she got better. I think the woman didn't take me seriously. I know I should have tried talking to someone else after that, but I . . . well, I get discouraged too easily. That's a fault. But I find people often don't . . ." He trailed off, which surprised her. This wasn't his usual careful speech.

She had no trouble sounding sympathetic as she asked, "Did you tell anyone else?"

"I went to the girls' daycare center and talked to the head there. I knew she found me difficult to deal with, so I wasn't very hopeful, but I asked her what she thought I should do. She . . . brushed me off. Iris can be charming when she wants to be. Like the psychiatrist said, she needs admiration, and she knows how to behave to get it, at least when it comes to casual encounters. Our neighbors felt more comfortable with her than with me. I guess everyone we knew did—and we really only knew most people casually."

There was a long pause, which Giuliana didn't interrupt. Then Kissling added, "The girls loved me, though. I think they really did."

He spoke matter-of-factly. Giuliana felt it like a blow in the gut.

"Yesterday, I talked with the lawyer who handled your divorce," she told him. "He said you wanted full custody of the girls because, according to you, your wife was crazy."

"I'm sure I never said she was crazy," Kissling corrected stiffly. "But that's correct. By then, I'd decided the only way to protect the girls from Iris was to divorce her and take them myself. I explained everything to my lawyer several times, and still, the judge only gave me two weekends a month with them. I don't understand what went wrong."

Giuliana swore to herself that she would talk to her father about what needed to be done to make sure Roger Urech never practiced law again.

"Things were much worse for the girls once Iris had full custody," Kissling continued. "Lea started to stutter and wet herself, even though she was five, and Mia insisted on talking baby talk all the time. They seemed scared of everything, and they cried whenever I had to bring them back to Iris."

Giuliana was grateful for Kissling's calm voice as he carefully unfolded this drama before her—a tragedy whose ending she already knew. His restraint kept her from leaping out of her chair, leaning across the table, and screaming into his face, "Why do you think we have Child Protective Services, you fucking idiot?" But he wasn't an idiot, and it was too late for protection. Besides, maybe even someone from that office would have rejected his claims.

He was still taking her, step by step, through his decision process. "After the divorce . . . well, after it made things worse for the girls instead of better, I thought about going abroad with them. I decided we'd have to run away to Germany or Austria because, otherwise, I wouldn't know the language. I began planning our escape, but I kept worrying. How would I enroll the girls in school if they had no papers? How would I be able to find a job and support them? And all the time, the police would be after us. I wanted to take them away, but I kept putting it off because I couldn't seem to work out how to do it properly."

She shouldn't interrupt, but the question burst out of her. "What about the police? It's against the law to mistreat children. Didn't you think of calling them?"

"The police?" Kissling said. Finally, he raised his voice. "The police are useless. They've never listened to me about anything else, so why would they have listened to me about Iris and the girls?" His mouth puckered, and his nose wrinkled like he'd put something revolting in his mouth. "I hate the police."

Why? Did he have a police record? How could they have missed that?

"I don't know anything about your earlier history with the police, Herr Kissling. Can you tell me about it?"

"I had a stepbrother. He was five years older and . . . he helped me. When I was fifteen, he got arrested after a fight. I went to the police station. I had the sense to ask who was in charge. Two men came along and took me into an office. I explained all the reasons why the fight wasn't my brother's fault." He grimaced. "I was so sure everything would be all right after that. I mean, it was all so clear—to me."

Giuliana pressed her lips together. She was already wincing inside.

"But they thought I was a joke. First, they laughed at me, and then they got mad and threw me out of the station—and one of them kicked me when I fell. My stepbrother went to prison. He became an addict. Heroin." She stayed silent. "About every five years, I deal with them, the fucking police." As far as she knew, this was the first time Kissling had ever sworn in an interview. "A problem with my car, with one of the neighbors, always something—and whenever I try to talk with the police, they . . . they simply will not take a word I say seriously. Call the police about Mia and Lea. Pfeuh!" He'd turned his head and literally spat on the floor, this silent man who was always in control. Giuliana wouldn't have been surprised if he'd spat in her face.

She sat without moving, picturing a fifteen-year-old Manfred Kissling in the days before anyone had heard of the autism spectrum, lecturing a couple of village cops on how wrong they were to arrest his stepbrother. The disaster would have been predictable. Just like the man's attempts to talk to the daycare teacher and everyone else he'd turned to for understanding and advice about how to help his daughters.

Seeking to find the right way to continue the interview, Giuliana began slowly. "Let me sum up what you've told me so far. You say the people you explain things to often fail to understand you, so I want to be sure *I'm* following you. All right?"

He nodded.

Please let me get this right, she thought and went on. "You were very worried about your daughters remaining in your wife's care, and you didn't know how to get them away from her. Her family didn't help you, the girls' teachers didn't help you, and your own lawyer didn't help you." She drew in a deep breath and went on. "You didn't feel comfortable discussing your fears with any officials, especially the police, and you decided against taking the girls away in secret and trying to hide them in another country because it was so complicated and probably wouldn't work anyway."

"Exactly," Kissling said. He gazed at her like a village teacher with a prize pupil reciting a poem in front of the school board: hopeful but nervous. "I thought a lot about killing Iris, too," he said evenly. "Of course, that was by far the best way to protect Mia and Lea from her. I would have gone to jail afterward, but at least they would have been free of their mother. But they would have ended up in an orphanage. Or else with Iris's mother. I despise Iris's mother. I think she played a large part in making Iris . . . the way she is. I don't know how she did it, but suppose she did the same thing to my girls?"

The small space where they sat seemed to vibrate with tension. Giuliana could feel it in her chest, a tightness that blocked her breath. She imagined that Kissling, too, must be fighting for air, but he sat motionless, expressionless.

For almost a minute, neither of them said anything.

Finally, Giuliana risked a question. "Will you tell me why Mia and Lea had to die, Herr Kissling? I don't want to put words in your mouth."

Kissling shook his head. His lips quivered faintly; his features had started to lose their firmness. It was as if his face were melting. The interview would go to pieces very soon—because the prisoner was disintegrating before her eyes. Still, she mustn't hurry things.

"I'll tell you what I think happened, then, since it's . . . difficult for you to speak right now," she said in a low, gentle voice. "I think you saw your daughters growing more and more frightened and unhappy, and you decided that death was the only refuge you could give them."

He nodded twice and then froze. "I didn't know what else to do," he whispered. His eyes stared somewhere over her shoulder. "I knew it wasn't the right decision. I *knew* that. But I couldn't keep watching them suffer, and I didn't know ... I didn't know ..." Suddenly, Manfred Kissling threw back his head and howled.

Giuliana jumped up and darted around the table as guards rushed into the room. For a moment, no one moved. After all, the man was fastened to a chair that was bolted to the floor. He wasn't threatening anyone. He began to beat his head with his fists, still howling—an awful, animal sound. Two of the guards grabbed his wrists, one on each side, as his cries continued. Before they could stop him, he slammed his whole face down against the metal table. When he raised his head, his nose and lips were bleeding. Before he could do it again, Giuliana and a third guard pulled him upright. With blood from his nose trickling down his windpipe, his next scream turned into a choking gurgle. Someone ran in to say the doctor was coming with a sedative and a straitjacket.

Giuliana felt herself choking, too. Her face was wet with tears. Camera forgotten, she rested her hands on Kissling's shoulders as she stood behind him. She put her mouth close to his ear and said, "Hush now, hush now" over and over. The man's rigid torso shuddered under her hands, and she felt his shoulders slump. By the time the breathless doctor arrived, Kissling was sobbing quietly, blood and tears dripping onto the steel table.

Only after the prisoner had been escorted away did Giuliana remember to turn off the camera. She should have felt triumphant. Instead, she concentrated on feeling nothing at all.

Walking to the car, she thought suddenly of Joel's mother. What had Ueli said? That her ideas about how to protect Joel were delusional.

Now she knew just how twisted parental love could be.

The cafeteria was almost empty when Renzo set his lunch tray down on a corner table and watched Giuliana walk across the room to join him. She looked so utterly drained that he jumped up and took her tray from her as if she were an old lady.

"Are you all right?" he asked her as he put her lunch on the table and hovered next to her, restraining himself from guiding her into her seat. Once she'd taken her chair, he went back to his. "What happened?"

"Kissling finally talked, and it was . . . hard to hear," she said.

"You got him to talk!" He was stunned, yet it was obvious from her face and tone of voice that congratulations were not appropriate. "Do you feel like telling me about it?"

She took her lentil salad off her tray, looked at him, and finally smiled. "I will, just not right now. But you should know that you were the key to figuring out what happened."

Renzo's fork with its tortellini paused on its way to his mouth. "I was?"

She nodded. "You suggested I find out what kind of custody agreement Kissling had hoped for, and my talk with his divorce lawyer was crucial. But it was more than that. I kept remembering something else you said—that I should assume the girls' deaths had to do with Kissling's love for them."

"I'm glad I helped." He thought about explaining to her that it was his own feelings of desperation at the thought of losing his kids if he divorced Fränzi that had given him the idea. But he didn't want to talk about that, even with Giuliana. Instead, he gobbled up the rest of his pasta, pushed his plate to one side, and spread out his papers. For the past hour, he'd been writing a list of his steps on the Eberhart case so far and his suggestions for further action, officially for Rolf and Vinz but mainly for himself.

"Shall I talk you through it?" he asked her. "I want to know what you think I've missed. Just interrupt me."

He was almost finished summarizing everything he'd done up to that point when his phone rang. He checked the name on the screen. It was Schmid's postdoctoral student, whom he'd been trying to reach since the evening before.

"Sorry, but I have to set up an appointment with this guy," he said to Giuliana and made a hurried arrangement for Marti to come into the station later that afternoon.

"Who are you seeing now?" Giuliana asked when he'd hung up.

"Just a minor lead. Even with Schmid in the clear, I'm not quite willing to give up on the cancer cell fraud. This guy is Schmid's postdoc, Marti. He's the one who gave Oppliger all the background information. He appears to have come out of the whole fiasco smelling of roses, but I still want to tie up loose ends."

Giuliana had frozen in her seat as he was speaking; now, she was frantically flipping through the little spiral notebook she always carried in her purse.

"What is it?" he asked, frowning at her.

"Schmid's assistant—what's his full name? How old is he?"

"Marti with i. First name Flurin. Age twenty-nine."

She read out from her notebook, *"Alain Marti, wine dealer; Vivienne Marti, alternative therapist; children Flurin, Tobias, Selina, and Maya Marti, ages 29, 24, and 16 (twins)."* They're Andi and Nisha's friends and neighbors, and Vivienne babysits Saritha. There must be a thousand Martis in Bern but not many Flurin Martis. Is this the same man?" Her brows furrowed, she said, "Can you call Flurin back and see if his parents . . . no, actually, we don't want to say anything to him about his parents yet. Just ask him if he ever lived on Krippenstrasse."

Flurin Marti answered Renzo's call right away. Sounding puzzled and scared, he confirmed that he'd lived on that street with his parents when he was younger.

"It can't be a coincidence," said Renzo. "This is the closest connection to Andi we've found yet—at least in these Civi cases."

"I agree," Giuliana said. "Listen, do you mind if we interrogate Marti together?"

"Of course not. But . . ." At that moment, Renzo was feeling about as puzzled as Marti had sounded on the phone. What reason could the postdoc student have to kill Andi? Nothing bad had happened to *him* as a result of her inquiries.

Giuliana grinned at him, and he saw that her previous weariness had fallen away. "You wanted to brainstorm—I suggest we brainstorm about this. You've got Marti coming at two thirty, so that gives us an hour. We'll need our laptops. Let's grab coffees, go find an empty room, and figure out what we need to ask this man."

30

Giuliana thought that Flurin Marti's receding hairline made him look older than twenty-nine, but his plaintive voice made him sound younger. Over and over, he asked, "Why am I here? What do you want to know?"

She and Renzo sat him in a room with a two-way mirror, behind which Vinz would follow the interview. While a guard brought Marti a milky coffee, a caramel biscuit, and some mineral water, Renzo and Giuliana exchanged a thumbs-up with the uniformed woman in the back of the interview room who was going to take notes. Then they focused their attention on Professor Eduard Schmid's former postdoc.

Renzo and Giuliana's notebooks were open in front of them, and Renzo began by asking, "Are you familiar with a woman named Andrea Eberhart, Herr Marti?"

Marti, who was already pale, turned paler. "She's dead. I know that. Are you . . .? Do you think . . .?" His mouth was opening and shutting like a carp's.

"Just answer the question, please."

"Of course I know her. Knew her. I mean, I know who she is, and I've met her a few times. She's . . . I mean, she was my parents' neighbor and sort-of friend. She knew my brother and my sisters better than she knew me. In fact, I barely—"

Giuliana interrupted. "I'm aware that she knows your younger brother through her involvement in Rainbow Families. Why does she know your sisters?"

"They figure skate, and Andi's a very good skater. When they were younger, she took them to the rink a few times and gave them pointers." He bit at the edge of his thumbnail and then lowered his hands to the table, squeezing them together.

Giuliana looked at Renzo, who asked, "We're interested in Professor Eduard Schmid's PSK experiments at the university, which you were running for him."

Marti froze, eyes wide and mouth working. "But . . . but this is . . . you are homicide. Why would you . . . ?" He stopped, narrowing his eyes, put a fist to his mouth, and tore at the nail on the ring finger of his right hand.

"How did you find out that Schmid had been accused of doctoring his experiments?" Renzo asked. Marti stared at him. "And when exactly did you hear it?"

Marti reached into the back pocket of his jeans, then said, "You have my phone."

Renzo withdrew Marti's phone from the breast pocket of his shirt and handed it over.

The younger man studied it for a minute. "On March eighteenth— that was a Wednesday morning—Schmid and I were supposed to meet to discuss an article I was writing with him, but the department secretary told me he wasn't in. I sent him a text telling him I'd be at my desk, and then I worked on the article for a while. At about ten thirty, I went into the lab—"

Renzo interrupted. "Schmid's lab?"

Marti shook his head. "The one he used for the PSK experiments, yes, but it isn't exactly his; other biochemists run experiments there, too. I went in to see if anyone I knew was working there and wanted to join me for coffee. Two guys, grad students I know, stared at me as if I had two heads. Finally, they asked if I'd known what Schmid was up to."

Marti stopped to bite at one of his fingernails again, and Giuliana watched him, trying to decide if he was pausing to construct his answer. To her, he mainly seemed panicked and afraid, not as though he was hiding something. Taking his hand out of his mouth, Marti continued. "I said I had no idea what they were talking about. At first, they acted mysterious, but then one of them told me about a Civi who'd been spying on Schmid and had found out he was messing up his experiments for money. They said this guy worked for a woman at the civilian service who tracked down criminals—they made her sound like someone from a comic book."

"Did they tell you who the woman was? Or did you guess?"

Marti shook his head again, this time emphatically. "No. I wasn't curious about her, only about who the Civi was. They told me it was Fabian Oppliger, so I went looking for him to ask what was going on, but I couldn't find him, and I didn't have his number." His brows drew together, and his hands on the table closed into fists. "That bastard Oppliger! I wanted to know what he'd done—to ask him why he'd fucked up my life. He knew my career was tied to Schmid's. I was the one that had been looking after the experiments. I'd even explained them to him. I couldn't know he'd go and . . ."

Giuliana wondered if Marti had noticed anything odd about the experiments. As if he'd read her mind, Renzo said, "But you were the one who told Oppliger that the measurements weren't consistent."

"That's what pisses me off the most," Marti burst out. "I said that because, at first, the PSK dishes were doing better than the controls, and then the cancer cells in the control dishes started dying, too. Oppliger knew I was worried about it. He should have warned me."

"Did you tell Professor Schmid about the inconsistencies?"

Marti nodded vigorously. "Naturally I did, and he told me to carry on. Now I know why he didn't react! Schmid screwed me. Who was going to believe I wasn't in on the plot he was brewing?"

"Let's get back to you trying to reach Oppliger," said Renzo, who'd been writing in his notebook. "What happened next?"

"I knew he was a Civi, and I realized I had the main number for the Thun office in my phone, left over from when I was a Civi, so I phoned, and eventually I got through to someone who told me that I'd need to talk to Oppliger's advisor if I wanted his number. They connected me to her phone, and there was the recording—Andi Eberhart asking me to leave a message."

"Wait a minute," said Renzo. "They connected you just like that?"

"I said I was from the university," Marti said defiantly. "I guess they thought I was someone official."

Giuliana caught Renzo's eye, and he raised one eyebrow. *You mean you encouraged them to believe you were official*, she knew they were both thinking. But now wasn't the time to deal with that. She turned back to the young man, who'd watched this silent exchange with a frown, and said, "So at that point, on Wednesday morning, March eighteenth, you believed Andrea Eberhart had asked Fabian Oppliger to spy on you and Professor Schmid, and that you were both in big trouble. Did you ever call Oppliger?"

"No. I still didn't have his number, and by then I was . . . well, I was so upset I went home."

"To your parents?" Giuliana asked.

"No, I haven't lived with them since I started to earn money as a PhD student. I live with three graduate students in an apartment on Malerweg. Once I was there, I called Schmid, but he didn't answer, and I . . . I didn't leave a message. I just . . . It was like I was paralyzed."

Not once during the interview had Marti expressed any concern over Schmid falsifying his results, Giuliana reflected. Did he not believe it, or did he just not care? She couldn't blame a young man just starting his academic career for being very upset about his mentor being caught committing fraud. But wasn't he at all concerned about the fraud itself? To her, he seemed depressingly self-involved.

Renzo leaned toward the young man. "Did you ever find anyone to tell you the whole story?"

"Christ! Who knows what the whole story is?" Marti's voice rose in exasperation. "Not me. Even now, it's all still rumors. Even if Schmid's PSK experiments have been stopped, he hasn't been fired, so—what does that mean? I don't know."

"Did you talk to Oppliger or Eberhart to find out what they knew?"

"No. I decided to just . . . lie low for a while. I was afraid to talk to anyone about anything in case it backfired on me. Well, actually," he added with an embarrassed smile, "I talked to my mother, but you don't care about that."

His mother.

The words echoed in Giuliana's head for a moment before she stiffened. His mother, Vivienne Marti. She touched Renzo's arm, and he turned to look at her, eyebrows raised.

She said slowly, "We're interested in any way the information about Frau Eberhart could have spread. So why don't you tell us what you said to your mother."

Marti's embarrassment increased—he looked ready to curl in on himself like a hedgehog. "But . . . but surely it's not important."

Renzo said, "I'm Italian. I have a wife and two kids, and I still talk to my mother about everything. *I'd* have told her about something like this." He won a grateful glance from Marti, whose face was still red. Once again, Giuliana admired Renzo's skill with people.

"Okay, well, if you really want to know. The thing is, first you have to understand that my mother was ridiculously excited when I started working for Professor Schmid because she's a big believer in complementary medicine. My brother and sisters and I grew up swallowing one kind of remedy after another and being taken to healers for every sort of manipulation and laying on of hands that you can imagine. We were never seriously ill anyway, before or after the treatments, so it would be hard to say which ones made a difference. Some helped, though. I'm sure of that."

He said this defiantly. Hmm. It must not be easy, Giuliana realized, pursuing a career in biochemistry when you'd grown up in the world of homeopathy, reiki, biofeedback, and God knows what else. She nodded at Marti, so he would see she was taking him seriously, and he went on.

"So I had respect for Schmid. And after I heard about this . . . business with his experiments, I didn't know what to think—or do. Schmid hadn't called me back, and I got worried that calling Oppliger might somehow make me look guilty, so I just sat around at home for days, worrying. Like I said, I didn't even want to show my face at the biochemistry department. Then, on Sunday afternoon, my mother called and asked if I wanted to come over for dinner. My father was doing inventory at his wine store, and my sisters were out for some reason—anyway, she was by herself, and she thought I might like a homecooked meal." Marti stopped, his face reddening again. "You sure this is what you want to hear?"

"This is exactly what we want to hear," said Renzo. "All the details."

Marti shook his head but continued. "So I went home and . . . well, I unloaded everything on my mother. I said Andi, her so-called friend, was probably going to cost me my job and my career, and I'd never get decent work again because her—my mother's—precious Schmid had turned out to be a crook, and Andi would make sure it all came out, even though she knew me."

"You said 'your mother's precious Schmid,'" said Renzo. "Are you saying she had something to do with your going to work for him?"

"No, no." Marti cringed—probably at the idea of his mother getting him a postdoctoral position, Giuliana decided. "She'd heard him speak a few times, met him at some alternative healing gatherings, and fawned over him a bit. And, as I said, she just loved the fact that I'd gotten a job with him." He paused, and, for the first time, Giuliana saw something in his face that she thought might be shame.

"Look," he said to Renzo, "I guess I just wanted someone to rage at, and my mother was there, so I . . . dumped everything I was feeling on her. I told her I didn't dare go to the lab because I was just waiting for the axe to fall."

The three of them sat in silence after that. Giuliana's mind worked furiously as she considered the timing of Flurin Marti's rant at his mother in relation to what had been going on at the university and what was about to happen to Andi. Slowly, she asked, "Did your mother understand that the damage had already been done, do you think?"

Flurin frowned. "What do you mean?"

"I mean," said Giuliana, "when you think back to what you said to your mother, did you tell her Schmid was already in trouble? That Oppliger had already blown the whistle, and Madsen had spoken to Schmid that Monday? That your fate, whatever it would be, was more or less sealed? Or did you make it sound like it was still possible nothing would come out?"

"I don't know." Marti frowned in concentration. "I didn't mention Madsen or Oppliger by name. Just Andi. The least she could have done was warn me before the shit hit the fan."

Giuliana was having trouble believing what she thought she was hearing, so she had to make sure. "Herr Marti," she said, and he met her eyes. "Do you have any evidence at all that Frau Eberhart knew you were involved? Do you know for a fact that Oppliger identified you to her by name? Even if he did mention you, Marti is a very common surname."

He stared at her for a minute, confused. "Well, I'm Schmid's postdoc, and I'm the one who told Oppliger about the experiment. I mean, he must have . . ." Marti stopped, and Giuliana saw true puzzlement on his face as if it had never occurred to him that he wasn't somewhere in the center of the narrative. She held his gaze, and eventually, he looked away.

There was a moment of silence before she pressed on. "You're telling us that with no proof that Frau Eberhart even knew you worked for Schmid, you told her mother that your career was in danger and it was all her neighbor's fault?"

Marti didn't answer.

Renzo's voice was gentle, but Giuliana knew him well enough to know that he was working to keep it that way. "We've already asked you this, but I'm coming back to it because it's so important. When you spoke with your mother Sunday night, March twenty-second, could she have believed that Andi was about to reveal that you'd been working with Schmid and were part of his scam?"

"I don't know," Marti burst out. "I don't remember exactly what I told her, but, more to the point, God only knows what she *heard*. She hears what she wants to hear half the time." Marti rolled his eyes like a teenager. "And then she twists it into some kind of story that fits an idea of her own." He put his hands on either side of his head and shook it, eyes closed. "Look," he spoke with exasperation, "part of why I can't tell you exactly what happened was because . . . well, she got very upset. In the middle of my telling her about Schmid's experiments and the fraud, she started to cry, and I couldn't calm her down. She kept saying it wasn't fair, that there had to be something we could do about it, and I started to worry that she was going to contact Schmid, so I got mad, too. I told her not to go near my professor or call him about anything. Then I left." He shook his head, staring down at his hands.

At the words "something we could do," Giuliana turned to Renzo at the same moment as he turned to her. They stared at each other, and Renzo raised one eyebrow. Giuliana could imagine Vinz behind the window, holding his breath.

Renzo continued to keep his voice calm. "So when you left her on Sunday night, it sounds like your mother believed it was still possible to save your career, perhaps by calling your professor or . . . by stopping Frau Eberhart from revealing that you'd been part of Schmid's fraud."

"That makes no sense," said Marti angrily. "I mean, I never knew about the fraud while it was happening, did I? Besides, what was there left to reveal? Madsen knew it all."

"But did your *mother* know that?" Renzo asked, his voice finally raised. Giuliana could hardly believe the young man hadn't guessed what they were driving at.

Marti opened his mouth and closed it. "Her phone calls . . ." he whispered.

Suddenly, Giuliana realized she didn't want Marti to catch on—what if he clammed up to protect his mother? But for now, he still seemed more like someone puzzling over a problem, so she risked repeating, "Her phone calls?"

"Last Monday and Tuesday, she phoned me, like, ten times. 'Are you in trouble at the university yet?' she kept asking me. I told her no every time. Then I stopped answering her calls, but she kept it up on Wednesday, too."

"What about Thursday and Friday? Did she call then, too?" Renzo asked.

Marti shook his head. He was starting to look scared again.

"Have you talked to your mother since that Tuesday when she was phoning you over and over? That was Tuesday, March twenty-fourth." Renzo was careful not to remind Marti that Andi had been killed the following night, on Wednesday the twenty-fifth.

Marti nodded slowly. "I called her this past Monday and told her I was sorry I'd been so out of control and made her cry. I said I was looking for other jobs and didn't think I'd have trouble finding one." His frown cleared, and for a moment, he looked almost happy again. "Since then, I've talked to a professor at the Biozentrum in Basel. I still have to go through the application process, but I think my chances of working there are very good."

"What did your mother say when you told her you were job hunting?" asked Renzo.

"That she was very glad I was—" Marti broke off. He slumped in his chair and pressed his hands against his cheeks. Giuliana remembered his mother doing something similar at Nisha's.

"We'd like to know what she said," Giuliana prompted.

Marti was chewing on a nail again. "She was . . . She said she was glad I was out of danger," he muttered.

"She said she was glad you were out of danger," Giuliana repeated.

There was a long silence in the room. Marti stared at the floor. "It's not possible," he said. He didn't say what he meant. He didn't need to.

Giuliana heard Renzo take a deep breath as if moving on to

another topic. Then he said, "Herr Marti, where were you on the night of Wednesday, March twenty-fifth?"

"Me? My God, I never . . ."

"Please answer the question."

Once again, Marti put his fingertip on his phone, called his screen to life, and checked his calendar. His face filled with such obvious relief that Giuliana thought it was almost certainly genuine. "I was eating sausages in front of the TV and watching soccer that night. With all three of the guys I live with."

He looked at Renzo and rushed on to say, "See, one of them, the astrophysicist, is from London, and he follows Spurs. They had a game with Man U that night, and we'd promised to watch with him. In return, he treated us all to beer and what he calls bangers. We don't usually spend much time together in the evening, but this was . . . well, it was a big deal. Anyway, the game didn't start until nine, but we got together at about eight to have a few beers."

"Good," said Renzo. "We'll check on that."

Giuliana gave the mirrored wall to her right a long look. She hoped Vinz would get someone busy confirming that Tottenham Hotspur had played Manchester United that night and that Marti's flatmates had been at home watching them do it.

Renzo was ready with his next question. "Do you have a car?"

Marti didn't look worried about this one, although he should have. "Yes. It's in a garage in Holligen near where my parents live."

"When was the last time you drove it?"

Marti leaned his head back and stared at the ceiling. Finally, he said, "On the first Saturday in March, I drove to Ikea and bought two new bookcases for my room. Then I visited some friends who live in Uztenstorf and came back to Bern. That was it."

"Do your parents have cars?" Renzo persisted.

"No. Neither of them drives much. The wine store has a van for deliveries, but an employee drives that."

"Does your mother know how to drive?"

"My mother?" Marti's voice cracked, and there was a silence that threatened to go on forever. "My mother," he finally repeated in a whisper and, again, "It's not possible." Before Renzo could prod him to answer, he added, "If she needs to drive, she uses my car."

"What color is it?"

"Red," he mumbled. Some spark of satisfaction must have shown on Renzo's face because Marti said, "Oh, God," and closed his eyes.

"That's all for now, Herr Marti," Giuliana said, and then intoned, "According to the federal regulations for criminal procedure, you can be held for forty-eight hours without charge if there is a clear and present danger of your interfering with an ongoing criminal investigation." She lapsed back into everyday speech. "We don't want you talking to your mother about this interview, so we're locking you up. We'll try to let you out as soon as possible; I don't think we'll need the full forty-eight hours."

"You're . . . going to arrest her?" His shaky voice made his words hard to understand.

Giuliana didn't answer. Marti looked at Renzo as though expecting him to be more sympathetic somehow. "It's not possible," he said for a third time.

Renzo had no comfort for him. Instead, he handed Marti a pen and turned to a fresh page in his notebook. "I need the phone numbers of the men you live with and the addresses of your apartment and your garage. Plus, I'd like you to give me the keys to the apartment, car, and garage." Without even raising his head, Marti checked his phone's address list, wrote a few lines, and then awkwardly passed the cell to Renzo, along with a bundle of keys. Renzo called in the guard, who asked Marti to stand and cuffed his hands in front of him. Tears had begun trickling down his cheeks, but he said nothing as the cop led him away.

Fifteen minutes later, Giuliana and Vinz were in the case room, waiting to hear from Renzo, who'd gone with a woman from forensics to examine Marti's car, and from Madeleine, who was one of the people tracking down and questioning Marti's flatmates. Vinz was on the phone with the case's prosecutor, and Giuliana had perched herself on the edge of the second desk. Staring blankly at Vinz's back, she was trying to piece together what Vivienne Marti might have done between Sunday night, when she'd convinced herself that her son Flurin needed saving, and Wednesday night, when she'd almost surely driven Flurin's red car into Andi's bike.

Giuliana had been around Vivienne enough to know that she was a talker. So, the first thing she'd have wanted to do after Flurin left was confront Andi—which meant Giuliana needed to take another look at the calls Andi'd received in the last three days before her death. Giuliana opened her laptop and found the appropriate email with its attached file. She'd read it already but had had no reason to note calls from Vivienne in particular. Now she saw that between Monday morning, March twenty-third, the day after Flurin had dinner with his mother, and Wednesday night, March twenty-fifth, shortly before Andi died, Vivienne had called Andi's cell six times. The only message each time was some variation of "Call me back." Which Andi apparently hadn't done, at least not from her cell: there were no calls to Vivienne listed.

So Vivienne had tried to reach out to Andi to talk about Flurin and had been ignored. Which had probably made her feel even more desperately worried and angry. By Wednesday, she may have convinced herself that Andi was deliberately avoiding her and actively trying to destroy her son. Whatever reasons she'd concocted, Giuliana thought, they had been enough to cause her to stage the hit-and-run. And Andi—who probably hadn't even known that Flurin Marti was Professor Eduard Schmid's postdoctoral student—had died, her head smashed in and her neck broken.

Giuliana sank her face into her hands, allowing herself a moment of intense sadness.

Madeleine called in to report that two of Marti's three roommates had separately told the same story of Wednesday night's English soccer and sausages; they couldn't find the third. Shortly afterward, Renzo rang too: the car showed clear signs of having hit something—and, while refusing to commit herself, the forensics woman would at least admit that the marks on the red car appeared to be the same blue as Andi's bike. They were bringing the car in for further examination.

It was time to arrest Vivienne Marti.

31

They had probable cause to arrest Vivienne, but Vinz wanted a warrant, and although she was eager to find the woman, Giuliana respected his caution. While they waited for the legal documentation to arrive, he leaned against the other desk to talk to her.

"I'd like to have you and Renzo make this arrest."

She was taken aback. "But . . . it's your case," she said.

His eyebrows rose, and he gave her a twisted smile. "Yeah, but I backed the wrong horse, didn't I? I was too determined to get those prison guards."

This self-analysis was so unlike him that it was a moment before she said, "When I think of the number of times I've followed the wrong lead! It should still be your arrest, Vinz."

He shook his head. "Renzo started looking at Civi jobs and spotted the whistleblowing angle, and you made the connection with the Marti woman. Plus, you've spoken with her twice, and I've never even seen her. I'm not being gracious—it *should* be your job."

Giuliana rested a hand on his arm. "Okay, then. Thank you. Shall I call Renzo?"

"Please," he said. "And keep me posted."

"Any thoughts about how we should handle the arrest?" she asked.

"She's in her fifties. I don't think you and Renzo will need any backup, do you?

"No, we should be fine," she agreed and speed-dialed Renzo.

Giuliana couldn't think of anyone she'd rather make an arrest with than Renzo. But for some reason, she was twitchy. Maybe it was the possibility of having to do it in front of the suspect's kids. At three thirty in the afternoon, the twins might very well be home—even the husband and the second son could be around. On the drive over, they agreed that Renzo would handle the family, so Giuliana could concentrate on getting Vivienne into handcuffs, out the door, and down to the waiting car with minimal fuss.

Because the street was so narrow, Renzo pulled the car up onto the sidewalk in front of the Martis' building. They got out, did a quick equipment check, and headed for a dark-green door under a glass roof. Spring seemed to be making another surprise appearance, and Giuliana took a second to feel the warm sun on her back before she pushed the buzzer. A girl's voice said, "Forget your keys, Mam?" and let them in.

Giuliana sighed. "First complication—she isn't here."

Renzo shrugged. "Might be better this way. We can wait outside in the car, nab her when she walks up to the door, and not put the family in an uproar."

Not if one of her kids phones to tell her that we're on her doorstep, thought Giuliana. For a moment, she debated not even talking to the family. But suppose the woman had gone out of town for a few days? They needed to know where she was.

The Martis lived on the second floor; the apartment door was slightly open, and the rhythmic croon of K-pop—Giuliana thought it might be BTS—leaked out into the hall. Giuliana rang the bell. They waited a full minute, then rang again.

A slight teenage girl opened the door wider and stared at them. "Oh. I thought you were my mother."

"Hi," Giuliana said. "Are you Maya or Selina?"

"Maya," the girl said, with a toss of her long hair that meant, *not this again*.

"Hello, Maya. I'm Giuliana Linder, and I spoke with your mother on Tuesday about Andrea Eberhart's bike accident. I'm here with my colleague because we wanted to follow up with her. I guess she isn't here, huh?"

"No, she's out. Seli!" She turned and yelled over her shoulder, and a head poked out from a doorway off the hall. Unlike many identical twins who seemed to take a perverse pleasure in making themselves indistinguishable and then being annoyed when people confused them, these two were very different: Selina's hair was cropped close to her skull, and she looked like she weighed twenty pounds more than Maya, although that only made her look normal instead of skinny.

"What?" Selina snapped.

"Do you remember . . . Is Mam with one of her patients, or did she go shopping or what? These guys are looking for her."

"She's at Nisha's," Selina said, disappearing back into the room where the music was coming from. Meanwhile, Maya had switched her attention to Renzo. Head to one side, she was staring at him like a deer pinned by headlights.

Giuliana had no patience this time for the silliness Renzo's looks provoked. "Thanks," she said curtly and turned away, Renzo at her heels. It wasn't really rational to be worried since Vivienne had visited Nisha a number of times since Andi's death. But it scared her nonetheless. And it would make the arrest more complicated. Nisha didn't know about Vivienne yet.

"How should we handle this?" Renzo asked her.

"Let's talk about it in the car," she said as they took the stairs down to street level.

Wriggling into the passenger seat, Giuliana felt her SIG Sauer P228 shift slightly in its belt holster, and she settled the handgun more comfortably at her waist. Renzo had tried a few times to get her to wear a shoulder holster, as he did, but she preferred having the gun on her hip. He watched her maneuver her pistol but didn't comment.

"Okay," she said, "I guess we'll go around the corner and try it all again. I don't like it, though. It's going to be hard on Nisha. Finding out her friend . . . someone she trusts to look after her baby . . . killed Andi—it's . . ." She shook her head. "Plus, with Saritha there—there's more risk."

"It's a bad situation," agreed Renzo, leaning back in the driver's seat. "But what else can we do? Do you want to wait until tomorrow or try to lure Vivienne away?"

Giuliana stared out of the window, considering her choices. "Our best option would be to get Nisha and Sari out of there before we do anything. I could call Nisha's cell; she could tell Viv that Andi's mother is outside in the car, and she needs to take Sari downstairs for a minute to say hello."

"Do you think Nisha could manage that without getting upset and making Vivienne suspicious?" Renzo looked worried; Giuliana knew that he, too, was afraid of provoking a hostage-taking situation. Not that Vivienne had a weapon, as far as they knew, but kitchens are always full of knives, and the woman knew Nisha's kitchen well; Giuliana had seen how she'd moved around in it, making tea.

"If we go in with a lot of armed backup, the chance of one of the women or the baby getting hurt increases," she mused. "I think the first thing to do is phone Nisha and find out what the situation is."

Renzo drove to the end of the block and turned onto Eggimannstrasse, where Nisha and Andi's apartment was, but this time they parked two houses down from Nisha's building. Giuliana phoned Nisha's cell, but there was no answer. There was still no answer after two more calls. Giuliana could see Renzo frowning.

They walked from the car to the building and pressed the buzzer, a long ring. Nothing. Renzo raised his eyebrows at Giuliana and then pressed all four buzzers at once. They immediately heard a noise to their right and looked over to see a casement window swing open. A fiftyish man in a T-shirt stuck his head out and called, "What do you want?"

His words were in Bernese dialect, but his accent was clearly Italian. Giuliana gave Renzo a nod, and he jogged off the front porch toward the man, calling out a friendly "*Ciao.*" Renzo held his police ID up toward the window, and they exchanged a few words. The man disappeared from view, and a few seconds later, the door buzzed.

Renzo rejoined Giuliana at the now-open door. "He looks after the building," he said as they began walking quietly up to Nisha's floor. Giuliana nodded but said nothing. Why hadn't Nisha answered the door? Given how sunny and pleasant the weather was, perhaps she and Vivienne had taken the baby out for a walk. But she'd be glad when she knew for sure.

They rang the apartment bell twice, then Giuliana called Nisha's cell again. There was no answer, so she left a message asking Nisha to phone back, then called again right away. Just as she was expecting to hear the voicemail kick in again, there was a hoarse, "Yes?"

Renzo, standing close, heard it, too, and their eyes met in relief.

"Frau Pragasam, it's Giuliana Linder from the police. Are you with Vivienne Marti?"

"No," Nisha said. "I've been taking a nap in the bedroom, and I'm still half asleep. Vivienne's babysitting for me."

"So she's there? In your apartment?"

"No, no, I'm here by myself. She's taken Sari for a walk to give me a break. We—"

Giuliana interrupted her. "We're standing outside your apartment door, and we need to talk to you. I mean, take the time you need to get dressed, but it's important."

"Be right there," Nisha mumbled and disconnected. Three minutes later, she opened the door wearing a red T-shirt, a cardigan, jeans, and socks, her hair braided in her usual single plait. The dark shadows under her eyes showed she could have used more sleep. As she let them in, Giuliana could smell toothpaste on her breath. "What's wrong?" Nisha said, ushering them into the entrance hall. "Have you found out something about Mathan?"

Of course. Giuliana hadn't thought about Nisha's older brother all day, but the possibility that he'd killed Andi must be haunting his sister.

"No. In fact, we're almost sure he's in the clear," Giuliana said immediately, and Nisha's thin frame relaxed a little.

"Come and sit down," she said, leading them to the sofa and then turning to go into the kitchen. "I'll just—"

"Nisha." Somehow it felt right to use her first name now. The woman was about to have her world knocked out from under her for a second time.

Sitting down on the paisley sofa, Giuliana pointed to the other end of it. "Please."

Frowning, Nisha perched on a patterned cushion as Giuliana asked, "When is Frau Marti due back from her walk?"

"Between five and five thirty."

Renzo, who was still standing, looked at his watch. "I'll move the car so we don't alert her."

Nisha was sitting hunched forward on the sofa. Her eyes followed Renzo out of the room before she gave Giuliana a frightened glance. "What is it?" she whispered. "What's happened?"

"I'd like you to try and think back to last week," Giuliana began.

Nisha bit her lip, her eyes enormous, and nodded.

"A day or two before Andi was killed, did you get a number of calls or emails—maybe even visits—from Vivienne Marti?"

Nisha stared at her. "I think . . . I mean, yeah, I did." She reached into a pocket of her long cardigan and got out her phone. Giuliana breathed slowly and tried to relax her shoulders, dreading the pain she was about to inflict. But Nisha would have to know sooner or later—and Giuliana needed confirmation.

Nisha pressed on an icon and looked up. Her voice sounded more puzzled than upset as she said, "Yeah. Starting late Sunday night, she sent me some weird texts about her son. Not Tobias, whom Andi knows, but the oldest one, Flurin. She wanted to talk to Andi about him. It was urgent, she said. I figured it was something about his civilian service, which he finished a couple of years ago. Some kind of confirmation of his tour of duty, maybe."

"What did you do?"

Nisha glanced down at her phone again before saying, "On Monday, I texted her back once to say that Andi would contact her soon, but that right then, she had a lot on her mind about another client—which was true. I told her it might be the end of the week. Viv sent me a couple more messages after that, but I . . . I'm afraid I ignored them." Nisha's mouth twisted. "She always thinks anything to do with her kids is urgent." Frowning, she added. "Sorry, that doesn't sound very nice. She's a dear, but she can be bossy. I would have made sure Andi called her by the end of the week, but then . . . Andi died." She stared at the floor before raising her eyes to Giuliana. "Why are you asking me this? What's happened?"

Giuliana was saved from answering by Renzo coming back into the room slightly out of breath, turning one of the straight chairs at the table to face the sofa, and sitting down. "Car's as close as I could get it without calling attention to it," he said. Giuliana nodded.

Nisha looked back and forth between them. "Tell me what's going on," she said, and now her voice sounded angry rather than scared.

Renzo gave Giuliana a quick glance, and she nodded. Then he turned to Nisha, leaning toward her as if prepared to catch her. "I'm sorry to have to tell you this. But we are convinced that Vivienne Marti killed Andi," he said.

Giuliana waited for denials or questions; she steeled herself for shrieks and sobs. Instead, Nisha leaped up and dashed for the door.

Giuliana sprang out of her seat, shouting, "Wait!" But Renzo was there already. Standing in the hall, she watched him take Nisha's arm gently to keep her from flinging open the apartment door. She fought him so hard that he had to put his hands on her shoulders; when that didn't stop her struggling, he pinned her arms to her sides from behind and wrapped himself around her. As he half-guided, half-frog-marched her back to the sofa, she kicked and wriggled, yelling, "She's got Sari. You have to let me find her. Let me *go*!"

Finally, she stopped struggling and stared at Giuliana with tears on her cheeks. She was breathing hard. "Aren't you going to let me look for Sari?" she said, her voice cracking. Renzo let go of her arms but kept his hands lightly on her shoulders, and Giuliana took one of her hands. She understood the woman's terror. But it had to be kept under control.

"We came here to arrest Frau Marti," she said in her gentlest voice, "but keeping Sari safe is much more important. That's our priority now, and we need your help to figure out how to do it. Can we sit down and talk about the best way to get the baby back to you? Because we have to do it without scaring the woman."

Nisha nodded, and Renzo released his grip on her shoulders, although he waited behind her until both she and Giuliana were seated at the table. Then he picked up the chair he'd just been sitting in and moved it so that it faced the table but also blocked the path between Nisha and the front hall.

"Are you all right?" he asked Nisha. "I hope I didn't hurt you."

"I'm fine," she said, her voice shaking. Giuliana watched her press her lips together and clasp her hands as she made a conscious effort to calm herself. "Tell me why . . . why you suspect Vivienne. It seems impossible. Insane."

Over Nisha's shoulder, Giuliana saw Renzo point to his watch. He was right. Nisha had said Viv would be back between five and five thirty, and it was already ten to five. They didn't have much time. Still, Nisha needed some kind of explanation.

"I promise to explain it all to you in detail as soon as we have Saritha safe and Frau Marti in custody," said Giuliana, watching Nisha as she talked. "But, essentially, Frau Marti became convinced by some things her son Flurin said that Andi was going to destroy his career at the university. She tried to talk to Andi about it, and when Andi didn't get back to her, she decided she had to kill Andi to protect Flurin."

By the time Giuliana finished, Nisha was holding her head in her hands. "But . . . that truly *is* crazy. Oh God, why didn't I answer her texts?" she whimpered. "Why didn't I make Andi call her?" She moaned with the pain of it, rocking back and forth.

"Nisha, it's a terrible thing to hear—I know that," Giuliana said. "But right now, we have to think about Saritha. Frau Marti could be here in five minutes. Does she have a key?"

Nisha stopped rocking and took her hands from her mouth. "Yes," she breathed.

"Does the door to your bedroom lock?" Renzo asked. "If so, where's the key?"

"The key's in the righthand corner of my top dresser drawer." Nisha was alert again, successfully controlling her grief. Giuliana was impressed.

"I'll check the lock," Renzo said and left the room.

Giuliana went on. "Has Vivienne acted at all hostile to you since Andi's death? Has she said stuff that scared you, handled Sari differently—anything like that?"

"No, not really. She . . . talks a lot, and I don't always pay attention to every word, but I haven't felt threatened, and I don't think she's been anything but sweet to Saritha. Everything seems . . . the same." Nisha shook her head. "It's horrible. I can't believe it. She's my friend! Or I thought she was. You . . . you should have heard her saying how sorry she was for me because of Andi's death. Is she . . . *is* she insane?"

"No," Giuliana reassured her. "I think she does feel sorry she killed Andi and truly sad for you. She just has . . . irrational priorities."

Before Nisha could reply, Renzo was back. "Nothing flimsy about either the door or the lock," he told Nisha as he sat back down. "I've never seen this woman, but I don't think she could break into that bedroom without a sledgehammer. And even then, she'd have to get through Giuliana and me first."

"Okay." Chin resting in her hand, Giuliana continued to talk. "Do you know where Viv went with Sari?"

"Well, one of her usual routes is to walk straight down Bahnstrasse to the cemetery and up and down the paths there. But . . . there's no guarantee that's where she went. Sometimes she has a coffee at the Rösterei or walks in the other direction toward the Weyermannshaus

pool because there's a nice meadow there. God, I . . . I just don't know."
Nisha's voice broke again.

Renzo reached out to cover her clasped hands for a moment. "Of course you don't. Until a few minutes ago, you had no reason to worry. I think you still don't need to worry, but we have to cover all the possibilities."

Giuliana looked at her watch again. "She could walk in the door *now*. Nisha, we are not going to go near her while she has the baby in her arms. Here's what I suggest: Renzo and I will wait in here, in this room, standing so Viv can't see us from the foyer. When you hear the front door open, go to her and take the baby, or if Sari's still in the stroller, just wheel her down the hall and into your bedroom and lock the door. Key's in the lock on the inside, Renzo?"

"Yep."

"That's your only job, Nisha—get the baby away from Viv and lock her and yourself in the bedroom. We'll take it from there. Just don't come out until one of us tells you it's okay."

Nisha got up and then didn't seem to know what to do—she was breathing in and out too quickly. Giuliana put an arm around her and said, "Let's make sure you have everything you need for Sari—diapers and wipes and snacks—in your bedroom." Together, they went to check the room, picking up Nisha's always-ready diaper bag from the floor and bringing it with them.

When they came out of the bedroom, Renzo was at the front door, peering from different angles into the living-dining area to see where he and Giuliana should stand. They were all still in the corridor when there was a knock at the door, and before they could go to their stations, a man's voice said, "Signore," and began talking in Italian. Growling something unintelligible, Renzo opened the door and dragged the startled man inside. The ground-floor resident was upset and talking fast, and Renzo clutched his head in dismay before grabbing his jacket from the hook beside the door where he'd hung it up. Before Giuliana could ask what was going on, he said, "This guy told Viv we were here, and she ran off—with the baby. You try her house; I'm going to the garage where they kept Flurin's car."

Giuliana heard Nisha strangling a shriek. Renzo was already moving; Giuliana followed him to the head of the stairs and called, "She's tall and thin with hennaed hair.'

Nisha appeared at her side and leaned over the banister to yell down the stairwell, "Dark-green wool jacket, red stroller." Giuliana grabbed her hand and squeezed it. When they heard the front door slam, Giuliana's cell phone was already at her ear.

Now that they had a kidnapping on their hands, it was time for backup.

32

Holligen in Bern,
Friday afternoon, April 3

Renzo ran. He was better at fighting—or kicking a soccer ball, for that matter—than running, but at least he'd be faster than a woman of fifty-something pushing a stroller. The Italian neighbor said she'd turned left, so he did, too, and then turned left again onto the paved footpath that connected the neighborhood's narrow streets. In no time, he was at Krippenweg, which was Vivienne's street as well as the location of the neighborhood daycare. Might Vivienne have deposited the child there? He ran past the Marti house and the daycare, seeing no red stroller, either abandoned or with a baby in it. Now he had to decide—would she head for the garage, where she believed she would find Flurin's car, or for the railway station at Europaplatz? In a flash, he picked the station, which was also a central tram and bus stop. But what was the fastest way to get there?

It was after five, he remembered. Rush hour.

He stopped searching for a head of red hair crowning a green jacket. Standing at the edge of the garden-filled neighborhood of narrow streets and alleys where Nisha lived, he stopped running altogether. He turned in the direction of the train station so that he faced a circle of large, modern apartment buildings, and he made himself wait. And watch.

There. Coming down what he'd assumed was a driveway, three teenagers emerged into the street, then a man on a bike and a woman with a briefcase, followed by a little knot of people, some with grocery bags. *That* was the shortcut to the station. Now he ran full-out, past a big federal office building, through a tunnel under a road.

He came out at a skateboarding ramp and ran on to stand among the squat white pillars that crisscrossed the barren space next to the House of Religions. There he slowed down to look around. Above him was a wide slab of highway, which made this bit of Europaplatz a place of shadows, even during the day. A grocery store sat at one end of the expanse; could Vivienne have gone in there? He ran on toward the walkway that passed under the railway tracks—and then he saw her.

She was climbing the stairs that led to the train platform. She had a neat cap of orange hair and wore an elegant green wool blazer with skinny jeans. Over one shoulder, she had an incongruously colorful diaper bag, and in her arms, a baby—not an infant, but a sturdy little person whose head rose over the woman's shoulder, black eyes watching everything in sight, mouth open in a fascinated "o." The baby's skin was caramel; the woman's was white.

He'd found them.

So Vivienne had dumped the stroller. Hmm. It gave her ease of movement, but it made her much more conspicuous because of the contrast between her and Saritha. A strange decision, thought Renzo, as he started up the stairs behind her. Then again, none of her recent decisions were going to win her prizes for rational thinking. Thank Christ she didn't know what he looked like, so he could stick close to her until a good moment came to grab her. It frightened him that she was holding the baby. If he had to choose, he'd focus on getting Sari away from her, even if it meant letting her escape. He experienced a sharp longing to arrest Andi's killer—it felt like a craving—but the little girl was more important.

They were on the platform now with maybe fifty people spread out along the tracks. Vivienne moved forward, not looking back. What train was next? Renzo checked the nearest display. In four minutes, the

S1 would arrive and then head to Bern's main station and eventually on to Thun. Even as he read the sign, he heard the metal rails below him start to hum. It was early for the Thun train, but he moved closer to Vivienne until he was hovering three feet behind her and to her right. She was standing about four feet from the edge of the platform. Not close enough to be really risky, but not at a safe distance either.

Renzo heard first one and then another siren whine; the two sounds blended for a moment. He wasn't sure they were even police sirens, but he saw Vivienne's head whip back and forth as she glanced around fearfully. His quick glimpse of her expression disturbed him; she looked hunted. Saritha, balanced on Viv's right hip, began to whimper and wriggle. Viv's grip on her tightened, and Sari gave a kind of squawk and then started to wail. The heavy-looking diaper bag slid off Viv's left shoulder to rest in the crook of her elbow. She was wrestling with the weight of it and shushing Saritha frantically.

For a moment, Renzo risked taking his eyes off the woman and baby to check the train entering the station. He saw at once from its speed that it wasn't the S1 but an express speeding through to Bern's main station. Vivienne looked at the train, too, and tottered a bit closer to the edge of the platform.

That one movement was enough to make up his mind.

He leaped forward, threw his arms around her from behind, and yanked her to his chest. He clamped one arm around her left side, passing his hand through the strap on the diaper bag so that it was caught in his grip. His right arm scooped up Sari, and he wrenched her away from Vivienne and pressed her to his chest, her hot face buried in the crook of his neck. Freed of the baby, Viv's right arm flailed, but her left was locked to her side as Renzo hauled her, heels dragging on the pavement, away from the tracks and backward across the platform until he felt the wire fence behind him. Vivienne was screaming, but with the express train still roaring through the station, he doubted anyone could hear her—yet.

People on either side of them had turned to stare. Two burly young men were moving toward him, puzzled frowns on their faces. Shit! He needed to find his ID before these two good Samaritans jumped him. But, hands full, he couldn't get the card out of his pocket. He whirled around, dragging Viv upright and pushing her face forward against the fence. Then, one hand pressed against Viv's back to hold her in place, he passed a thrashing, screaming Sari to the nearest of the two menacing young men. The stranger took her automatically and cradled her to him with both hands, his eyes opening wide in surprise. His friend paused in shock, and, with the train finally past, Renzo pulled out his ID as he yelled, "Police. This woman was kidnapping the baby!" Then he reached into his jacket for handcuffs and fastened Vivienne's right wrist to the fence. Only then did he realize how hard he was breathing, his pulse racing.

People were gathering, and Renzo expected Vivienne to start making a huge fuss, trying to get the crowd on her side. But she stayed clinging to the fence as though for support, her left hand covering her face as she sobbed.

"What'd she do again?" a man yelled, and Renzo saw he was filming the scene with his cell phone—and he wasn't the only one.

Turning his back on the cameras, Renzo reached out for Sari. Apparently, being cuddled by the unknown young man had calmed her down; she came to Renzo without a fuss, and he immediately positioned her against his chest so her face was shielded from the cameras.

Just then, the S1 chugged into the station, and Renzo's audience began turning away to get on the train. "Thanks," he said to the two would-be rescuers. "Not just for taking the baby, but for coming to help the woman. Normally, that would have been exactly the right thing to do!" He clapped one guy on the shoulder, shook hands with the other, and received two uncertain smiles before both of them jogged toward the open doors of the nearest train carriage. He imagined them telling the story to their friends later over a beer.

Now, at last, he could call Giuliana. Then he'd get the nearest set of uniformed cops to come and pick them up. Jiggling Sari up and down on his right arm as her curious fingers poked his neck and explored his ear, he used his left hand to maneuver his phone out. As he lifted it, Vivienne whispered from under her fingers, "I never meant to kill Andi."

It felt like a lifetime since he'd raced down Nisha's stairs to find this woman, and he'd kept his cool that entire time. As he was supposed to. But at her words, his rage boiled up and threatened to drown him.

"Shut up, you—" he hissed and swallowed a nasty Italian obscenity. "Of course you meant to kill her—you stole her bike helmet! And it was all for nothing."

Vivienne moaned, "No. She wanted to destroy Flurin, and I—"

"No," Renzo yelled, so loud that now a new set of passengers waiting on the platform turned to stare. Vivienne stopped talking. He'd already said too much; for the sake of the case they would build against her, he didn't dare open his mouth again.

But, in his mind, he raged at her. *Andi didn't have anything against Flurin; she didn't even know the self-obsessed little prick worked for Schmid. You didn't like Andi, so you were willing to believe the worst about her. But none of it was true. You killed her out of sheer hysteria— hysteria and idiocy.*

As his silent rant descended into curses, he turned his back on Vivienne, nestled Saritha closer to his chest, and fought to calm his anger. Then he walked a few steps farther down the platform and phoned Giuliana.

33

A noise woke Giuliana. She reached for her alarm and realized it hadn't gone off. It was Sunday morning, a little after eight, and the noise had come from the kitchen, where muffled voices and rattling pans told her Ueli and Lukas were trying to make breakfast quietly—and failing.

She didn't mind; she'd seen so little of them during the previous two days that she was eager to join them for breakfast. But there was no rush. Curling up again under the duvet, she luxuriated in not having to go to work. Friday night after Vivienne Marti's arrest, she'd slept four hours, returning to the office Saturday morning at seven. Finally, at almost midnight, Rolf had sent her, Renzo, Madeleine, and Vinz home and insisted they take Sunday off. "I'll see you Monday morning at eight—until then, do something with your families."

Later, with her second mug of coffee at her elbow, Giuliana sat at the kitchen table chopping onions for the chickpea soup Ueli was making; it would serve as supper on at least two of the upcoming weeknights. Next to the cutting board, a jumble of carrots and a large knob of celery root waited to be peeled and diced. Ueli stood at the stove frying cubes of bacon. "Could a woman really murder her neighbor without anyone in her family knowing?"

Giuliana sniffed—the onions were making her cry—and said, "We spent Friday and a good part of yesterday interviewing the husband and all four kids, and we still aren't done. They all admit Viv's been more on edge recently, but I believe them when they insist they didn't know why. One of the daughters said, 'We're used to Mam being stressed,' and that probably sums it up." She passed her onions to Ueli and blew her nose.

He scraped them from the cutting board into the sizzling bacon at the bottom of the soup pot and added a generous slug of olive oil. "How did she do it? Vivienne, I mean."

Giuliana started peeling carrots onto the pile of onion skins. She could hear Lukas across the hall in the living room, crowing over the game he was playing on Ueli's laptop—a Sunday treat. "She told us that when Andi and Nisha still hadn't talked to her by Wednesday afternoon, she decided to act. She fetched Flurin's car and followed Andi that evening to the curling hall. She kept her in sight using her bright-blue bike helmet and decided only then that the helmet had to disappear. So she stole it and threw it in a dumpster. She rammed Andi by the park because no one was around. The whole crime was unplanned, but, sadly, it worked."

Ueli shook his head. "And all because she got it into her head that Andi was about to accuse her son of something illegal."

"It was a mishmash of her weird interpretations and fantasies!" agreed Giuliana. "I've questioned Flurin again and again about what he said to his mother, but he claims not to remember. Still, it's clear he incited Vivienne to act without knowing it. He was convinced Andi knew he worked in Schmid's lab and that she would blame him for the fraud along with Schmid, when, in fact, he wasn't even on Andi's radar. It's just as Renzo and I thought. Neither the whistleblowing Civi, Fabian Oppliger, nor Oppliger's professor ever mentioned Flurin Marti's name to Andi. But that didn't matter. As Flurin whined on and on about how unfair it was that Andi hadn't protected him, Vivienne began to spin her own story."

The smell of sautéing bacon and onions filled the kitchen. She took a deep breath and added, "I think it's ironic that the person who kept Flurin out of trouble wasn't his mother but his boss Schmid, the actual bad guy, who assured Madsen that he'd never told his postdoc anything about the scam or let him do anything shady."

Ueli turned to look at her. "Do you think that's true?"

"Yes." Giuliana passed him a plate of carrot slices. "Not because I'm convinced of Flurin's integrity or Schmid's good heart, but because Schmid would have been nuts to involve someone else in what he was doing. It would have opened him up to blackmail. Or to Flurin exposing him the way Oppliger did."

Turning back to stir the contents of the soup pot and speaking loudly over the stovetop fan, Ueli kept asking questions. "I still don't understand why Vivienne didn't make a bigger effort to confront Andi or Nisha. She can't have tried very hard. She had all of Monday and Tuesday and most of Wednesday. Even after the curling practice was over, she could have stopped Andi before she got on her bike and insisted on defending Flurin. And Andi would have told the woman that she had no idea what she was talking about, that she didn't even know who Flurin was working for."

Giuliana looked up from the celery root she was peeling. "Renzo asked Vivienne that question yesterday. She admitted that she never really expected Andi to change her mind and 'spare' Flurin."

"Why, for God's sake?" Ueli turned away from the stove again, frowning.

"Ten days before Vivienne killed Andi," said Giuliana, "she and her husband went to a dinner party at Andi and Nisha's. That evening, Vivienne learned that, during a curling match, if players break the rules, they have to turn *themselves* in. She remembers Nisha saying to Andi, 'I think a curling competition is the only time you ever let anyone get away with anything.' She was teasing Andi, but Vivienne must have heard another message, because she told Renzo she was convinced Andi would never give Flurin the benefit of the doubt."

"And all that time, her son hadn't done anything wrong," Ueli said as he took the celery from her. "At least, he claims he hadn't, and you believe him. I wonder if his mother didn't believe him." He reached into the pantry for a can of chopped tomatoes and then, precariously balancing them on each other, three cans of chickpeas. "Do you think Vivienne intended Andi to die?"

"I'm not sure Vivienne herself knows. Given that she stole Andi's helmet and then crashed into the bike, going at least forty miles an hour, which was twice the speed limit, she couldn't have been too worried about that possibility. But it's true that if Andi hadn't been pitched into a tree headfirst, she might have survived."

"Andi's partner must be devastated." Ueli turned around, can opener in one hand, and stood there shaking his head. "First, losing the person you love and then discovering your friend killed her." He emptied the cans of chickpeas and chopped tomatoes into the pot. "Can you get me some rosemary?"

Giuliana fetched the kitchen scissors and opened the glass doors to the small, raised porch off the kitchen. Over the years, it had become the family's substitute for a garden shed, with stacks of terracotta planters, shelves full of pantry items, a jumble of cleaning equipment, and, amid it all, several pots full of herbs. Giuliana snipped a long twig of rosemary off a plant that was threatening to outgrow its pot and said, over her shoulder, "I think I told you that Nisha's father forbade her to contact her family, which must make things especially hard for her. Before I went back to the station on Friday night, I called her lawyer, who's also a good friend, and she said she'd go right over to Nisha's. I hope it was the right thing to do. At least it made me feel better about leaving her."

Giuliana stood, rosemary in hand, and gazed out across her neighbors' back gardens to the trees at the top of the steep wooded hill plunging down to the Aare. The morning was still foggy, but the sun was beginning to break through.

She came inside and closed the doors against the chilly air.

Ueli took the rosemary twig from her and began to strip off the spiky needles. "It sounds like some people are going to feel devastated and blame themselves," he told her. "But surely no one could have predicted Vivienne's deciding to kill Andi."

"No, it was such an irrational thing to do," Giuliana agreed, leaning back in her kitchen chair to get closer to the radiator along the wall. "Even Flurin couldn't have imagined the violence that his self-important little temper tantrum would unleash."

Ueli stirred the soup for a while, then said, "What about that silver-gray car whose driver was watching Andi's building? I take it Vivienne made that up."

"Yeah. She wanted to throw us off the track, and that was what she came up with."

Silence fell between them as Ueli added the rosemary and a couple of dried bay leaves to the pot and turned up the burner.

Giuliana took a gulp of cold coffee, grimaced, and got up to empty the rest of her mug into the sink. "You're taking Lukas to talk to the cat owners at two, aren't you? They're not going to scream at him, are they?"

Ueli was bent over the granite-top counter, breaking up bits of chicken with his fingers, picking out slivers of meat, and transferring them to a plastic container. His face was set. "They're still very upset, which is understandable, but I think they've grasped that Lukas was not the ringleader. We'll just have to see what happens. I'll tell you all about it tonight."

"Depending on when you and Lukas get back from seeing them and how he feels afterward, I'd like to take the kids over to my parents' for an apéro at around five. They've invited Paolo and his family for dinner. Us, too. I said no, but I'd like to say hello to everyone, and the kids can see their cousins. I'll be back by seven at the latest, and we can have some of your soup."

"Here"—he handed her a long metal spoon—"keep an eye on the veggies, will you? You might have to add a little water. I'm going to call my mother before I pour in the chicken broth. I want to ask her and Paps to have lunch here the next time they're in Bern for one of her checkups." He washed chicken fat off his hands and went into the bedroom.

"Good idea," she called after him, but what she thought was, "Good luck!" Irène usually found an excuse not to eat at their house, preferring to have everyone under *her* roof—which meant under her control.

Giuliana started washing dishes, but then curiosity got the better of her. Turning the heat under the soup way down, she went to hover outside the bedroom door.

Ueli's voice was low and even, but it had an edge to it. "I'm not inviting you to lunch because I'm worried about you or think you can't take care of yourself anymore. I'd simply enjoy seeing you and Paps, and lunch is a good time for you because it doesn't interfere with milking, and it's a good time for me because I'm at home feeding Lukas anyway."

He paused to listen and then said, "No, it's not too much trouble—not for me and not for you and Paps, either. Just let me know when you want to come by."

He paused while his mother spoke, but not for long. "No, Mam. I'm not sulking, and I'm not being childish. I haven't been childish for over thirty years. I'm very glad you're feeling so well after the operation. Please get Paps to give me a call when he comes in. Bye now. Take care of yourself."

Before Ueli could come out of their bedroom, she snuck back into the kitchen, grinning. She'd never heard Ueli talk to his mother with such calm but stern conviction before. She swallowed her smile as he came back to poke his simmering vegetables with a fork. Then he set the kitchen timer. "That's to remind me to call Paps if he hasn't called by one," he commented. "If he's worried about Mam, I think he'll tell me."

"But she sounds okay?" Giuliana asked, more concerned than amused now.

Ueli shrugged. "She says she's feeling great. If she's lying to keep me from worrying . . . well, I can't keep agonizing about that. Trying to second-guess her is . . . it's exhausting. And not very productive." He glanced at her. "Do you think I'm doing the right thing?"

She moved to put her arms around him, and they stood in an embrace. "Absolutely," she told him.

Her head was still on his shoulder with his beard against her ear when Lukas ran in. "Yay! I made it to the next level. I've got new magic powers. Come and see all the stuff I can do now." He tried to propel them out of the kitchen with milling arms.

"We're coming," she said, letting Ueli go. He turned off the burner under the pot, and they allowed Lukas to herd them into the living room.

That same Sunday morning, Renzo woke up much earlier than Giuliana when Antonietta squeezed into bed between him and Fränzi at six thirty. Twenty minutes later, Fränzi was up and bustling around the room. She was meeting three friends at the train station for a trip to Gstaad, where the four women had day passes to a spa in one of the resort's fanciest hotels. She'd been looking forward to the outing for weeks and had organized backup babysitting with her sister in case Renzo wasn't home. But now he was.

"I don't plan to be back before midnight," she warned him as she finished dressing. "That means you're going to see what *my* days are like when you work late."

Renzo didn't dare tell her that a day alone with the children was a rare treat for him—rare, he knew, being the word that made all the difference. He'd start by staying in bed, snuggling with the kids, and reading to them as long as they liked. Then they'd go out and eat jelly donuts for breakfast. After that, he'd take them to the natural history museum, which Angelo cheerfully referred to as the dead animal zoo. When their attention spans ran down there, it wasn't a long walk to the petting zoo, with its very-much-alive goats and alpacas, and that was next door to a playground and an outdoor restaurant. Afterward, he'd have to see how tired they were. And how exhausted he was, as well.

Almost eight hours later, Renzo sat at one of the clusters of tables on the terrace outside the zoo's self-service restaurant. The sun had gone behind the clouds, and he zipped his jacket up to his chin. The kids had finished their hot dogs and chocolate milk and were having a third ride on the small merry-go-round near the table, on which he'd used up the last of his coins.

He picked at the cold French fries left on the children's plates. He wanted a coffee, more for the warmth than the taste, but he couldn't go back into the restaurant to buy one because that would mean taking his eyes off his children. Fränzi was right, he thought. This was the kind of day she had when he worked weekends, and it *was* different from spending a couple of hours on a Sunday morning or afternoon alone with the kids the way he often did, giving them treats and then delivering them, tired and cranky, back to her. So far, there had been a minimum of bickering and whining and only one short tantrum from Antonietta, which he'd been able to short-circuit. But he knew he was pushing his luck. It was time to go home. And maybe even time for some help. Not to mention adult conversation.

He dialed his mother's number.

When he opened the door to Emilia Donatelli later that afternoon, he chuckled. She was clutching a grocery bag full of supplies.

"Don't laugh," she said in mock anger. "How can I make supper without knowing what's in your kitchen? I haven't a clue whether Fränzi has garlic, peppers, or good-quality olive oil."

"The truth is, neither do I," he confessed as he took the bag from her and led her in. "I didn't even think about what I'd feed the kids tonight. I guess I just assumed I'd open the fridge and figure it out. I didn't invite you over to cook for us, though, Mammina—just to keep us company."

"I like cooking for the people I love," his mother said. "You know that. Where are my babies?"

"Fast asleep. I wore them out. I don't think either of them takes a nap anymore, but I put them into bed about half an hour ago to give myself some peace and quiet, and they both drifted off. I'll wake them at five."

"Good," said his mother. "That gives us time to talk about whether you are going to get divorced and how we'll work it out if you do."

Renzo gaped at her.

"You told Davide you'd talk to me about what was going on with you and Fränzi. Now's your chance. And, before you say anything, you should know that we'll support you if you decide to split up. To get custody half the time, you'll need lots of help with the kids, and we'll make it happen. I can do the most childcare, but your sisters will help, and so will Sandra and Davide. You'll *have* to work fewer hours; there's no getting around that. But that won't be enough. We'll fill in the gaps."

Renzo set the shopping bag on the kitchen counter and put his arms around his mother. "I can't tell you how much I . . ."

"Good." She patted his back, gave him a brisk kiss on the cheek, and then reached for the kettle and filled it at the sink. "I can't drink coffee this late in the day anymore. Put the espresso pot on for yourself while I make some tea, and we'll talk till the kids wake up. There's a lot to figure out."

34

Nisha had never been to a Swiss funeral. When she confessed this to Sophie on the way to Ochsenbach, her sister-in-law gave her a rundown of what to expect. Thank goodness for that. Otherwise, Nisha didn't think she could have endured the agonizing hour before the service, when she, Sophie, and Yannick stood beside Manuela and Kurt in the forecourt of the village church, receiving condolences from what seemed like the entire village and from a parade of relatives Nisha had never met. Standing under a dismal gray sky, she shook hand after hand, nodding along to murmured words she didn't catch. She couldn't help but be self-conscious about her dark face, and she caught the sideways glances of some of the mourners. Twice, she and Sophie took a quick break, dashing across the street to see how Saritha and her cousin Hugo were doing with Sophie's youngest sister, who was keeping the children entertained at the restaurant where the funeral lunch would be held.

Eventually, the first of Andi's friends arrived. Soon, men and women from Andi's days at university, the Civi office, the curling hall, and Bern's gay and lesbian communities filled the space in front of the church. They all embraced Nisha; many cried on her shoulder. They, too, shook hands with Andi's parents and murmured condolences, but then they returned to Nisha. Rahel and Leo arrived, breathless but still on time, and Rahel took Nisha in her arms and held her wordlessly. A few more of Nisha's work colleagues arrived as well. By the time the undertakers began herding the mourners indoors for the service, Nisha was surrounded by her people. Armored by their warmth, she entered the church, where the coffin waited on a dais, and walked away from her friends down the aisle to take her place in the front pew.

Kurt sat on one side of her and Yannick on the other. As first the organ music and then the minister's voice rolled over them, Andi's parents sobbed softly, fighting for control, and tears ran down Yannick's face. Nisha took Yannick's hand when she realized he was weeping, but she herself couldn't cry. Instead, she found herself thinking about what would happen when they told Manuela and Kurt about Saritha.

Now that Yannick and Sophie were ready for the truth to come out, it was she who'd suggested waiting another month or so. The first weeks after the funeral were not the right time. But that wasn't the only reason for her hesitation. Sitting here among all these Swiss, Nisha had to confront her fear that she would lose Saritha to this still semi-alien culture, into which she herself had been thrust as a small child. Or, worse, that Sari, innocently stepping forward to take her place in the only world she'd ever known, would be rejected, leaving her with no place to feel at home.

Forcing herself to pay attention to the service, she realized the minister had stopped talking about God and was reviewing Andi's life and accomplishments. Nisha heard her own name mentioned, followed by Saritha's. Kurt squeezed her hand, and she was touched. Still, the minister hadn't known Andi; his words about her didn't seem real. The stark white interior of the church, with its dark beams and pews, didn't have anything to do with her. The coffin in front of her, heaped with flowers, was just a box.

There was a large photograph of Andi mounted on an easel beside the coffin—Andi in curling clothes, grinning at the camera. Nisha focused her eyes on that beloved face and longed for the tears that wouldn't come.

Her gaze was drawn away from Andi's picture by a movement in the aisle. The minister had taken a seat to the side of the lectern, and Susanna Käser, in blue trousers and a long white jacket covered with blue embroidery, was striding toward the front of the church, a piece of paper in one hand and a large white handkerchief in the other. Surprised, Nisha turned to Yannick, who whispered, "She asked me if anyone was going to speak at the funeral besides the minister. I told her to phone my parents."

"Susanna's a courtroom lawyer," Nisha whispered back. "Your parents wouldn't have stood a chance against her if she was trying to talk them into something."

Instead of going behind the podium, Susanna stood next to the picture of Andi. She took a moment to look out at the congregation, and as she did so, Nisha herself turned around and glanced behind her. Mourners were squeezed into the pews, and looking up into the gallery, she could see more people, some of them standing. In the front row of the gallery were two faces as dark as her own; full of wonder, she recognized her brother Rajan and his girlfriend Alina. She smiled at them and turned back as she heard Susanna's voice.

"Andi's accomplishments are impressive. Few of us here were familiar with all the different parts of her life, and hearing just now how active she was made me proud of her. But it wasn't Andi's accomplishments that made me love and respect her so much. What made Andi special to me—and, I believe, to most of us here—was her attitude toward the truth. She was the most truthful person I've ever known. Of course, maybe that's because I'm a lawyer . . ." Susanna's pause was perfectly timed—the whole congregation laughed, even Andi's father, and the wave of relief that accompanied that outburst of humor passed through the church. "Perhaps Andi's love of the truth grew out of the process of telling herself and everyone around her that she was a lesbian, but I don't think so because, according to her parents, she was alarmingly truthful even as a young child."

Nisha saw Andi's parents smiling and nodding. What a gift Susanna is giving them, she thought, providing Andi with the eulogy she deserved. All the love in the world couldn't have given Nisha the strength to speak here. But Susanna . . .

The older woman gathered the crowd with her eyes; she held them in her palm. "To Andi, truth meant action. She couldn't look away from something wrong and tell herself it wasn't happening, as so many of us do. Doing nothing about a problem, as far as Andi was concerned, was not detachment. It was lying to yourself. Lots of facts are inconvenient because they force us out of our comfortable lives. Andi didn't just face inconvenient facts—she collected them and put them on display.

"Everything I've just said makes Andi sound like the kind of person who runs around telling us what to think and making us feel guilty. That she wasn't like that at all was perhaps the most extraordinary thing about her. Yes, she could be assertive. Even a bit bossy, right?" A number of people laughed again, and one person called out, "Not as bossy as you, Susanna," eliciting more chuckles. The lawyer paused to smile at the speaker and continued. "Yes, she was bossy sometimes, but she didn't put pressure on others to do what she thought was right. It was herself she put pressure on, which you'd think would have made her stern. But that wasn't our Andi, either—she was funny and relaxed and a good listener.

"Andi's . . . virtues, all that was best about her, led to her death. We would give anything to have her back among us. But I don't think we'd wish her to have been different. We loved her the way she was, and we love her still. And to keep that thought in our minds, I asked the Eberharts if a friend of Andi's and mine could sing today."

Nisha vaguely recognized the small middle-aged woman who came to the front of the church. The singer put her hand onto the frame of Andi's photograph in a sort of caress and began to sing.

The first word, *"Amor,"* came out of her throat like a spear of light. High and unwavering, her voice carried them away. *Ne mai sí dolci baci a quella bocca avrai* . . . The Italian words were a mystery to Nisha, but the song was pure love and utter sorrow. With enormous relief, she felt her tears start to fall at last.

Hours later, after the strange ritual of throwing a trowel full of dirt onto Andi's lowered coffin; after another interminable hour of standing in the graveyard with Andi's family, as mourner after mourner passed by the open grave; after the awkward milling around in the restaurant, making small talk while drinks were poured; after the three-course luncheon proudly offered to the funeral community by Andi's parents; after the last of the wine was drunk, coffee cups drained, and final cognacs refused; after Sophie and Yannick and Hugo had walked Kurt and Manuela, gaunt with grief and exhaustion, back home, Nisha returned to the churchyard with Rajan and Alina. Jackets clutched around themselves, they huddled together on a bench. The gray sky of the morning was now blue, and the weak spring sun did its best to warm them.

Nisha felt wrung out, scoured of feelings, and so tired that every word was an effort. Yet she was happy to be on a hard green bench with Alina on one side, Rajan on the other, and Sari sleeping heavily in her lap. She was so grateful for their presence. She'd met her brother's girlfriend only a few times but had decided almost immediately that they made a good couple. With all her heart, she hoped they'd stay together.

Alina broke the gentle silence by murmuring, "I'm going for a walk. Back in a bit." With that, she got up and strolled away, heading back to the graveyard behind the church, where the leaves of a few birch trees were beginning to bud.

"I like her so much," Nisha said to her brother. "I was thinking today how nice it is for Sari to have Hugo for a cousin and hoping maybe she'd have your and Alina's kids, too. Someday, I mean," she added hastily.

She expected one of Rajan's barbed comments, but all he said was, "Give us time. We're working on it."

She stared at him, and he smiled almost shyly. "Working on a baby, you mean?" she asked, amazed.

"No, no, not that. Not yet. But we're talking about moving in together and eventually getting married. And we both want children. So, be patient with us."

She hugged him. "I'm so glad. But—" she stopped herself.

"But poor Amma and Appa, you were going to say."

"Well, I was thinking more about what you and Alina will have to go through. Even if Alina is Tamil by blood, she isn't the Sri Lankan daughter-in-law they have in mind."

Her brother shrugged. "That's their problem. And speaking of that, I have a message from Appa. I ate dinner at home last night and told them I was coming to Andi's funeral, and he recorded a message for you on my phone. I haven't listened to it—I showed him what buttons to push, and he went off alone. Do you want me to leave while you play it?"

"Absolutely not. I want you right here to help me cope with whatever he's going to say. I don't know if I have the strength to listen to this now."

"Well, I don't think it's going to be bad. Amma seemed to know something about it, and she didn't give me any cryptic warnings before I left."

Rajan got the phone out of his jacket pocket and held it up between them. Nisha snuggled her sleeping child closer to her and nodded to him. He tapped the screen, and they heard their father's voice, speaking Tamil.

Daughter. I am thinking of you spending this day at the funeral of the person you loved, and I am sad for you. However wrong I may think your decision was, I never wanted you to suffer this loss. Now you are alone, and you have a daughter, and this will be very hard for you. I have thought again about my decision not to allow you to return home, and I have decided that this decision must stand for the present—for my sake and the sake of the family. I know you understand this, even if it makes you and your mother unhappy. But I do not think it is right that Saritha, too, should be shut out of our family and our way of life. I would like to meet her, and I know your mother already loves her. So you and Amma have my permission to organize a way for Saritha to spend time at our house with no limits. To make that possible, you may bring her here and pick her up. I've also given your mother permission to return to the temple at the House of Religions; we'll see what you and she make of that." Here, a hint of laughter entered the measured tone of his words; she glanced at Rajan in surprise. "*I'm very happy to have this chance to speak with you. Who knows? Maybe I'll do it again. Goodbye, Nisha, and good luck. We promise to take good care of Saritha if you let her come to us.*"

Rajan put his arm around his sister as she turned her face into his shoulder and cried again. But this time, it was not for sorrow.

Acknowledgments

The most important thing I want to do with my fiction is entertain people—that's why I write mysteries! But I enjoy using my books to convey information about Switzerland and, in particular, the city and canton of Bern. So I used the first mystery in the Polizei Bern series, *Pesticide*, to give readers a picture of organic farming in the canton. *Sons and Brothers*, the second book in the series, reviews the plight of Switzerland's contract children, who were taken from their parents and forced to work for strangers until well into the 1960s. In this third book, *A Fondness for Truth*, I introduce readers to Switzerland's Sri Lankan Tamils and describe the country's system of civilian service for young men, which provides them with an alternative to the army.

As I point out in this book's dedication, I'm familiar with the civilian service (*Zivildienst*), both from my husband, who has consulted with them about software that allows Civis to find their own jobs online, and from my son, who served his 368 days of alternative service doing everything from helping to mount experimental solar panels on top of a snow-covered mountain to building a drystone wall. For this story, I've drawn on what they've told me and what I learned from my son's friends who were Civis. I'm grateful to all of them for helping me get my facts straight, but any mistakes are mine alone.

Other people helped me make sure that what I wrote was not only correct but appropriate and emotionally on target. I wanted Nisha Pragasam and Andrea Eberhart's life together to ring true and the Pragasam family's reactions to the couple's partnership and child to feel authentic. Many readers gave me feedback about these concerns, but several people deserve special thanks: Liz Davis, Martin della Valle, Heather Koch, Arunasalam Naguleswaran, Sheila Raboy, and Balawijitha Waeber.

Lots of friends and family members in Switzerland and the US read *A Fondness for Truth* in its various drafts and gave me input. Among them are Giuliana Berset-Brignoli, Betsy Draine, Karen Fifer Ferry, Donna Goepfert, Alex Griswold, Bob Hays, Darlene Hays, Natasha Hays, Melina Hiralal, Min Ku, Joanne Manthe, George Morrison, Catherine Puglisi, Dan Reid, Julia Reid, Isabel Roditi, Ruth Smith, Lyn Spillman, Michelle Stucker, Peter Stucker, and Deborah Valenze. Thank you, dear readers! Also, warm thanks to my fellow writers Tara Giroud, Clare O'Dea, and Christina Warren for their comments; Clare, in particular, is an important emotional support for me as well as a terrific critic. My policewoman neighbor, Gabriele Berger, continues to advise me and patiently answer whole lists of questions, and Kathryn Jane Price Robinson, my wonderful editor, is also a superb mentor. I'm so thankful to have these people at my back.

Also supporting me are the folks at Seventh Street Books and Start Publishing. Editorial director Dan Mayer deserves extra gratitude for his encouragement; so does Wiley Saichek for all he has done to promote my books and for the patience and good cheer with which he promptly answers all my emails. Warm thanks, too, to Ashley Calvano for always being on top of things, Jennifer Do for her magnificent book covers, and Marianna Vertullo for getting me through the production process.

Last, thank you to everyone who reads my books. I write them for you.

About the Author

Kim Hays is an American who moved to Bern thirty-five years ago when she married a Swiss; by then, she'd already lived in the United States, San Juan, Vancouver, and Stockholm. She studied at Harvard and Berkeley, and before beginning the *Polizei Bern* series, she worked in a number of jobs, including executive director of a small nonprofit and lecturer in sociology. *A Fondness for Truth* is her third police procedural featuring Swiss detectives Linder and Donatelli. The first, *Pesticide* (2022), was shortlisted for a CWA Debut Dagger Award and a 2023 Silver Falchion Award for Best Mystery. Kirkus called the second mystery, *Sons and Brothers* (2023), "a smart Swiss procedural that keeps its mystery ticking." For more information about Kim or her books, see www.kimhaysbern.com.